FLATMATES

by

Elaine Hankin

Published in 2009 by YouWriteOn.com

Copyright © Elaine Hankin 2009

First Edition

The author asserts the moral right under the Copyright, Designs and Patents Act 1988 to be identified as the author of this work.

All Rights reserved. No part of this publication may be reproduced, stored in a retrieval system or transmitted, in any form or by any means without the prior consent of the author, nor be otherwise circulated in any form of binding or cover other than that which it is published and without a similar condition being imposed on the subsequent purchaser.

Published by YouWriteOn.com

Elaine Hankin grew up in Stanmore, Middlesex. Over the years, she has worked in Italy and Switzerland, and frequently visits Spain and Italy, where she has family. She currently lives in West Sussex.

With thanks to all my writing friends for their encouragement.

"We are all in the gutter, but some of us are looking at the stars."

Oscar Wilde

CHAPTER ONE

His eyes stung, his stomach churned. He rolled over and retched, grasping for something to hang onto, finding only the slippery pavement.

Nausea passed. He wiped a cuff across his mouth, saw blood on his sleeve and spat onto the sidewalk. Fingering his throbbing jaw he summoned up the dregs of his befuddled brain and looked up. A pair of jeans-clad legs straddled him, solid legs, like goal posts. The feet attached to the legs flexed in their Reeboks. Was his assailant about to let rip again? Reece Cassidy held up a placating hand and was relieved to be offered a pale palm instead of a black balled fist.

"Get up, you crazy son-of-a-bitch." The insolent voice was tinged with amusement.

Reece took the proffered hand, flinching as he recalled the damage it had inflicted. Once on his feet, his gaze settled on the face of his opponent. It wore a smile of dazzling brilliance and when he swayed, the smile widened while the grip on his hand tightened.

"Ben, cut it out, you imbecile! You promised no more fighting," called a voice. Reece turned his head and saw a figure resembling a flamingo in full flight. With a puce-coloured overfull duffle bag bouncing on her back and legs encased in skin-tight leggings, a girl jogged towards them on feet clamped in white lace-up boots. The hooting of an irate car horn did little to deter her arm-flapping jog across the road.

"Can't you keep your bloody fists to yourself?" she shouted, skipping over a puddle onto the pavement.

An expression of feigned contrition replaced the grin on the ebony face. "Asked for it. Came in tanked up demanding Big Mac and Fries. Changed his mind three times, hassled Luisa, knocked over a Coke. Looking for trouble, he was," growled the young man, who Reece now saw, was half a head shorter than the girl.

"There was no need to beat him senseless," she retorted, drawing closer to inspect Reece's injuries. He swayed again. It wasn't from faintness this time, but from the shock of her musky perfume, which lingered in his nostrils even after she had moved away.

"You'll live," she announced, turning her attention back to the black man.

The rawness of his cuts and bruises didn't stop Reece from taking a close look at his rescuer. He saw that she was of mixed blood and could almost be described as a beauty with her high cheek bones and large expressive eyes. She was tall and slim and theatrical in manner, but by far the most startling thing about her was her Afro hair-cut, which was tinted purple.

Ben shrugged, pivoted on his heel and drawled, "I'm off, Connie. Just done a ten-hour shift. Got to get some kip."

"Hang on, you can't leave him here like this," protested the girl. "He's a tourist; you'll have to help him get back to his hotel." She turned to Reece. "American?"

"Canadian," he corrected her, wincing as the split in his lip widened.

Concern sprang to her eyes. "Are you all right?"

He nodded. "No bones broken."

"Where are you staying?"

"No-where. Don't worry, I'll be fine."

With more bravado than confidence, he took a couple of paces, then staggered, squinting against the beam from the orange street-lamp, which colour-washed the pavement, polishing surfaces, sending globules of liquid trickling down parked cars like beads rolling off oilcloth.

The girl put out a steadying hand. "You need a strong coffee before trying to join the land of the living."

"There's nothing open except McDonalds," called back Ben, who by now was some fifty yards down the road. "And they won't let him back in there. Let him kip in a doorway." With that, he strode off, hands in pockets, broad shoulders swinging to the tune he was whistling.

"Bastard!" yelled Connie furiously.

Reece took a gulp of fresh air. "I'll be all right now," he muttered. "Thanks for your help."

"I can't leave you like this," she protested, tucking her arm through his. "You'd better come up to my place for a coffee. You can use my mobile to ring the B&B down the road. They keep late hours, someone will still be up." She wagged a reprimanding finger at him. "You shouldn't have meddled with Ben. You were lucky; things could have got nasty."

"Nasty!" muttered Reece. "How much nastier could they have got?"

Ignoring his interruption, she went on, "He's a karate black belt and he's won loads of trophies for boxing." Pride superimposed her earlier anger. "That one really knows how to take care of himself."

By the time they reached the girl's digs Reece's ribs ached and his head throbbed. She led him inside, pausing to place a warning finger to her lips. "Quiet now, I don't want trouble with the landlord."

He nodded and followed her up two flights of carpeted stairs. At the top, yet another flight, steep and uncarpeted this time, wound round to a small landing in the attic. Two narrow doors faced them.

"This is mine," said the girl, pointing to the one on the right.

They entered the room and she pushed him into a thread-bare armchair with sagging cushions before disappearing behind a beaded curtain at one end of the room. Seconds later, she returned with a cold face flannel, which she placed over his blackening eye.

He smiled ruefully.

She went back behind the curtain and he heard a boom as she lit the gas, followed by the rattle of cups. Heavy with fatigue, his head lolled onto the back of the chair, but his eyes jerked open when he saw a huge poster pasted onto the ceiling. It could only be described as soft porn. The discovery sparked his interest and he glanced around the room. It gave every indication of student occupancy with its piles of books and theatrical magazines. A life-size cardboard cut-out of Johnny Depp challenged him from the corner. On the wall opposite, there was a poster of Darcy Bussell and beside it, a picture of Coldplay in concert.

The girl poked her head out of the curtain and asked, "How many sugars?"

He jolted guiltily as if caught snooping and replied, "Two please; make it black."

"Have to, there's no milk," she retorted and disappeared again.

She returned carrying two mugs of steaming coffee. Nudging his foot, she leant across him to set the mugs down on a wobbly Formica-topped table. Again, he was knocked back by her heady perfume and her animal grace. He watched her sink onto the bed, unlace her boots and kick them across the room. Curling her slim legs under her, she enquired, "Feeling any better?"

He nodded, took a sip of coffee, and then asked, "Are you a student?"

She nodded, "Drama. At twenty-six, I'm what they call a mature student." She flung out an arm and pulled a face. "Would you believe it, this place is the best I can afford; yet I still have to flog myself to death to make ends meet." Reece flinched. Her perfect diction seemed at odds with her choice of words. She went on, "I should have achieved something by now and, I will. One day you'll see my name in lights."

Reece was startled by the determination in her voice. "Don't you get a grant?" he asked.

"It doesn't go far, what with all the extras." She put down her mug and listed them on long fingers, tipped with black nail varnish. "Singing tuition, dancing lessons, drama workshops, jazz gear, tap shoes. The expenses are endless."

"How do you manage?"

"I work evening shifts at McDonalds. Ben's the Shift Manager there. He's a great guy once you get to know him."

Reece felt a surge of emotion. Was it envy or disappointment? "Are you two…?"

She threw back her head and let out a peal of laughter. It was as fruity and compelling as the aroma of her perfume. "Sorry," she said at last, wiping a hand across her eyes and trying to keep a straight face. "Course we're not, but we work together and we're mates. Ben won't stand for trouble on his shift. He's got a reputation for being a hard man." She focused her attention on Reece. "What about you?"

"Me? I'm from Montreal." He extended a hand for her to shake. "Reece Cassidy."

"Conchita Dixon. Call me Connie."

He tried to smile, then winced as he fingered his auburn beard where his jaw was beginning to swell.

"It'll hurt even more tomorrow." She couldn't keep amusement from her voice.

"Conchita? I wouldn't have taken you for Spanish."

"I'm not, but my adopted parents have a penchant for things Latin American."

Abruptly, she changed the subject. "So, what brought you over here?"

"It was supposed to be the holiday of a lifetime, but I ran out of the readies. Have to find a job or, like Ben said, I'll end up kipping in a doorway."

"Have you still got your ticket home?"

"Cashed it in."

"That was a stupid thing to do. Spent the cash, eh?"

He nodded.

"Blew it all on booze and pot? What's the matter, girl trouble?"

He was astonished at her perception. How did she know he was nursing a broken heart, that he'd followed his girlfriend half way across the world in the hope of reconciliation?

"Everything's gone wrong for me," he muttered gloomily.

With a toss of the head, she retorted, "*We are all in the gutter, but some of us are looking at the stars,*" adding as an afterthought, 'Oscar Wilde.'

"Oh," he said, nonplussed.

All at once, she seemed to tire of the conversation. Swinging her legs down to the floor, she gathered up the empty mugs and said. "Look here, Stacey - the student from the room next door - well, she's away, and frankly, I don't think she's coming back." She wrinkled her nose. "Dropped out, no stamina, know what I mean? You could sleep in there for tonight. But for God's sake, don't make a noise. We're not supposed to have overnight visitors."

Reece's expression brightened. "Gee, thanks a lot."

She frowned warningly. "Don't let that moron on the ground floor see you leave in the morning. I don't want to get kicked out. Most days, he takes off for work around nine. The other students won't grass on us." With that, she flicked a hand. "Well, go on, if you're going, I've got a heavy day ahead of me tomorrow: college all morning, jazz lesson at three and work from five till midnight."

Reece woke to brilliant daylight. The curtains were drawn but they offered little resistance to strong sunshine. The strains of Will Young's latest hit drifted up from somewhere below.

He ached all over. Lifting his head from the pillow, he realised that he was fully dressed except for his shoes. The room was extremely narrow, barely wide enough to accommodate a bed, a chest of drawers and an upright chair. Flopping back on the pillow, he let out a sigh of despair. What back street boarding house had he stumbled into? A drum thumped at his temples.

Gradually, memory trickled back and he began puzzling about the unusual girl who'd taken him in. Was she so naive that she couldn't see the stupidity of opening her door to a complete stranger, or was she the type who liked to thumb her nose at danger? He smiled grimly. Whatever her motives, she wasn't after money. He'd made it perfectly plain that he hadn't got any. It was apparent that she liked the limelight; she certainly had all the trappings of a stage artist. He could imagine her partying all night with other aspiring Thespians, exaggerating her achievements, embroidering her CV, always on the lookout for the main chance. Yet she did seem to have a soft side. After all, she had intuitively guessed that he was getting over a relationship. Was he wearing his heart on his sleeve?

He forced himself out of bed and went to look at himself in the cracked mirror hanging on the wall. One bleary eye stared back at him, the other was partly closed, the surrounding area black and blue. There was a cut on his lip and his jaw was swollen. His wiry hair stood up on end. He drew a comb out of his pocket and tried to flatten it.

As the minutes ticked by, he began to feel better. No point in hanging around. Connie would be at college by now. Besides, he had to find a job and digs without delay. He had no idea what time it was and glanced at his watch. Shit, the damned thing must have been smashed during the fight!

The strains of music reached him yet again. Clearly, there was still someone left in the house. It could be the landlord and, after her kindness, the last thing he wanted was to get Connie kicked out. He couldn't leave until the coast was clear. A cup of coffee would help to bring him back to life. Then he would sneak out.

"What the hell are you doing here?" For a moment, Reece was taken aback. He'd guessed Connie would be surprised to see him at the college gate, but after her concern the evening before, he hadn't expected her to be annoyed. She went on. "Look, I'm in a hurry. I told you I had a busy schedule. Can't stop, I'm on my way to my jazz lesson."

"Mind if I walk with you?"

"It's a free country."

"Aren't you going to ask me how I am?" he said, falling into step beside her, easily matching her stride and feeling miffed by her lack of concern for his welfare.

"How are you?" she asked disinterestedly.

"Better."

She jerked her head round. "Yes, you do look more presentable today." Several paces further on, she stopped and said, "We're here. You can sod off now."

As she turned to go, he pulled her back. "Just a second, Connie. Look, about getting a job..."

She frowned. "I gave you a bed for the night, what more do you want? It's not up to me to find you work. Have you always been molly-coddled?"

Her attitude riled him, but he pressed on. "Is there any chance of a job at McDonalds?"

Connie burst out laughing. "You've got a nerve! What about that fight last night?" Her brow puckered. 'By the way, what was it all about?"

Reece adopted a sheepish expression and said with a shrug, "I'd had a jar too many, lost my temper with the girl serving me. Ben moved in and one thing led to another."

Connie's eyes widened. "And now you actually expect McDonalds to take you on!"

"I called in on the way here and apologised to the waitress."

"Luisa?"

Reece nodded. "She's forgiven me."

His companion's mouth twitched into a smile. "Turned on the charm, did you?"

Reece grinned back. "I meant it; I know I was out of order." He paused. "Well, is there a chance for a poor redeemed character like me?"

"No way. You can't walk in off the street and expect to serve up French fries and burgers, just like that. You have to be trained and you have to be nifty on your feet."

"I know that," protested Reece. "But you're my only chance. I've got to do something quickly. My luggage is still at my last digs. I can't go back and collect it until I pay the bill." His brows furrowed above the half-closed eye. "Give me a break."

"You've got a black eye," she stated. "They won't accept you at McDonalds with a black eye."

"You could help me. You're a drama student, you must know about make-up. Isn't it part of the course?" His good eye twinkled mischievously as he delivered his trump card. "I know the ropes. I did a stint at McDonalds in Canada."

Having opened her mouth to protest, Connie shut it again. "That changes things," she admitted. "But you'll have to clean yourself up a bit and that means collecting your luggage. If you can't pay the bill you can smuggle it out of the guest house. Meet me at my place at four. I'll be back to change for work. If I take you along with me, you'll have to be prepared to grovel. Ben's on duty tonight."

Reece's first two weeks at McDonalds were hard work. As the newest recruit, he was given the most unsociable shifts. He soon showed himself to be a competent worker, gaining approval from the formidable Ben. When Connie heard that Stacey wasn't coming back, she suggested to the landlord that

Reece should move in. As this saved him the trouble of finding another tenant, he readily agreed.

"Thanks Connie," said Reece. "Once I've earned a bob or two, I'll find something bigger."

"Don't thank me. If Ben hadn't given you the job, I wouldn't have suggested it. And just because you'll be next door, don't get any ideas. I don't want you under my feet. I must have my space. Got that?"

Reece gave a wry grin. "Yes Connie."

She frowned at him. "I'm not joking."

The arrangement at Tennyson Avenue suited him very well, although he did find the small room claustrophobic. Most of the time, Connie's shifts at McDonald's didn't coincide with his. While he was at home sleeping, she was at college. Consequently, despite the fact that they had adjoining rooms, their paths seldom crossed. After a month, he knew no more about the girl than he had to start with.

Despite their inauspicious introduction, Reece found himself warming to Ben and when the West Indian invited him along to Deceptions, the nightclub where he sometimes worked as a bouncer, he went along.

It was mid-June and there had been an unexpected heatwave. Inside Deceptions it was unbearably hot and with the strobe lights and deafening music, it didn't take much for tempers to erupt. Ben's intervention was soon sought. When he moved in to put an end to a dance floor brawl, Reece impulsively offered assistance.

"Bog off, I can handle this," countered Ben and, with the disturbance sorted out in less than two minutes, Reece realised how lucky he had been on their original encounter. Ben could easily have landed him in hospital.

Earlier in the evening, he had wondered whether, he too, could get a job there - after all, the pay would be far better than McDonalds - but after seeing Ben in action, he decided being a bouncer was not the job for him. One aspect of his own character had become clear to him in recent months: he was governed by impulse and emotion. Ben was different. He wouldn't let feelings get in the way of what he had to do. Faced with a situation, he summed up his chances and acted coolly, only bringing his boxing and karate training to bear when the need arose.

On the way home, he asked Ben, "Where d'you train? Can I join?"

Ben threw back his head and gave his arrogant laugh. Punching him playfully in the belly, he replied, "Why? Do you want to lose a pound or two?" With that, he flagged down a taxi and dived into it without a backward glance, leaving Reece to continue to his digs on foot.

The heatwave brought an influx of tourists to the riverside area. In consequence, Reece's working hours increased, which meant that dipping into his pocket for another round of drinks with his buddies from McDonalds was no longer a problem.

One day, he was taken by surprise when Ben failed to turn up for work. The Area Manager was called in to rearrange shifts amid a great deal of complaining. When Reece brought the subject up with Connie, she shrugged and said, "Ben's done it before. He'll turn up when he's ready."

"What about his job?"

She grinned. "They always take him back."

Reece and Connie found themselves at home that Sunday. It was a dull, showery day, the heatwave having come to an abrupt end. With Ben away, time weighed heavily on Reece's hands. He had smoked his last joint hours earlier and now a cloud of discontent descended on him. As always, at times like this, his thoughts returned to Chantal, prompting a flicker of conscience. Hadn't he promised her that he'd cut back on booze and drugs.

Through the wall he could hear the roar of motor racing from Connie's TV. It was a sport he enjoyed watching and, when Connie knocked at his door and invited him to join her, he was only too pleased to leave the loneliness of his own room.

"You don't have to mope around on your own, you know," she said amiably. "You can come and watch TV with me at any time."

This invitation took him by surprise although he was learning that Connie was an unpredictable girl, welcoming company one minute, wanting to be left alone the next.

He flopped into the shabby armchair while Connie lounged on her bed, propped up on an assortment of colourful cushions, a bottle of red wine on the floor beside her.

"I fancy a puff; you got any?" she asked.

He shook his head and she slipped into silence. Lost in the motor racing, it was some time before he realised she was gently snoring into her pillow. Reaching for the remote, he meant to lower the volume but increased it by mistake.

Connie woke up with a start. "What d'you do that for?" she shrieked.

"Sorry, I pressed the wrong button. You're tired; do you want me to go?"

"Course not." She gave a sniff. "Except..."

"Except what?"

"I'm hungry. Be a dear, go out and get something to eat." Picking up a dog-eared Chinese Takeaway menu from the bedside cabinet, she ran a finger down the list and reeled off her favourite numbers.

"I haven't any money and besides, it's pissing down." He pointed at the rain-lashed window.

"I've got some dough. Take my umbrella. It's over there in the corner." She smiled mischievously. "I'll make it worth your while."

Reluctantly he agreed and, on his return half an hour later, he found Connie curled up on the bed fast asleep again. He nudged her gently and she rolled over, looked up at him from under lowered lids and asked, "Did you get everything I asked for?"

"You bet," he replied with enthusiasm.

"Stick it in the kitchen for now."

"Why?"

She gave a stretch and said, "Because I'm going to give you your reward first."

"Stop taking the piss?" he snapped. "The food's getting cold."

"We can mike it." She beckoned to him. "Come here."

"You've got a weird sense of humour," he said.

Puzzled by her ambivalent behaviour, he pushed back the beaded curtain and put the food down in the kitchen. Turning back, he saw that she had lifted up the duvet revealing that she was naked. He had never seen such a beautiful body.

She burst out laughing. "What's keeping you? Hurry up, I'm getting cold."

"Are you sure it's what you want?" he mumbled, although he had already begun to fumble with the metal buttons of his 501's.

"I never do anything I don't want to," she replied with a haughty toss of the head. "Haven't you learnt that yet?"

A rush of excitement coursed through him. Yanking off the rest of his clothing, he climbed into bed beside her. There was no question as to who would take the initiative. Completely uninhibited, she led him on with practised ease, surprising him with innovative teasing. Her extraordinary antics brought him to a delirious climax. He'd never experienced sex like this before.

Afterwards they lay side by side on the bed, flesh touching at shoulder, hip and thigh as if melded together. As the cooling process began, his thoughts turned to Chantal. It hadn't been *that* exciting with her. A chuckle escaped him. Was he getting over her?

"What's the matter?" asked Connie.

"Nothing."

"Well," she said, sitting up suddenly. "It's takeaway time. I'm ravenous."

She leapt cat-like across him to the floor and sweeping up an all-in-one silky leisure suit from the back of a chair, slipped into it and padded into the kitchen.

"Coffee, tea or wine?" she called.

"Wine," he called back.

As they tucked into the meal, Connie lost no time in making her position clear. "I hope you realise that was a one-off," she said, scooping up a strand of noodle from her chin with her index finger.

Later, back in his own room, he pondered on the afternoon's events, feeling mystified by Connie. Why didn't she have a boyfriend? Once, he'd questioned her about it and she'd snapped back, "It's really none of your business, but since you asked, I can do without baggage, thank you very much."

He arrived at work the next day to find that Ben was still missing. A character called Jake had been drafted in to cover for him. Resentful of the move to Twickenham, he made sure the staff suffered for it and, later in the morning, after the breakfast rush, when Reece made the mistake of enquiring after Ben, he snarled, "How the fuck would I know?"

When Connie called in at lunchtime for a hurried Cheeseburger and Fries, Reece asked her if she'd heard anything.

"He's been called home on family business," she replied.

"Trouble?" asked Reece.

"Big trouble."

CHAPTER TWO

Megan Hughes crept downstairs, her baby son in her arms. "Shhh!" she whispered, pressing her finger to his lips as he started to give a hungry grizzle. The grizzle changed to a dimpled smile, displaying three milk teeth at the bottom and two at the top.

Calum was an angelic-looking baby. Everybody said so. Strangers stopped Megan in the street to admire his clear skin, his enormous dark blue eyes and his golden curls. Old ladies oohed and ahhed over him. Obligingly, Calum cooed back at them. Most people took Megan for his big sister.

Sitting the child in his highchair beside the kitchen table, she carefully picked up the draft of her father's Sunday sermon and put it out of harm's way. Then, she took Calum's prepared bottle of milk out of the fridge and warmed it in the microwave.

She made herself a Nescafé and turned her thoughts to the future. Leaving Swansea for London was a big step. Apart from the occasional school trip, she had never been outside the area. She fingered the envelope in her dressing-gown pocket. In the letter, Mrs Goddard sounded friendly and she hadn't minded that her new nanny would be bringing her own baby with her. She seemed genuinely concerned that her seven-month-old daughter should be cared for properly when she resumed her career in the world of advertising. *Your Calum and my little Jessica will be company for one another ...*she had written.

Megan sighed. Yes, she was certain things were going to work out. The appointment had been arranged through an agency so she hadn't yet met the Goddards. She gave a little shudder of guilt, remembering that she'd added a couple of years to her age when filling in the agency's application form.

A glance at the kitchen clock prompted her to her feet. Hurriedly she dressed the baby, scrambled into a jeans and sweater, grabbed her belongings and slipped out of the house.

Michael Goddard was waiting at Victoria Coach Station. One glance at his shiny silver BMW sent Megan into a panic. With fumbling fingers, she fastened Calum into one of a pair of expensive car seats and hoped that the baby wouldn't be sick over the leather upholstery, not something she had needed to worry about in her father's old Mondeo.

"I'm certain you'll like Twickenham," said her new employer as he manoeuvred his vehicle into the traffic. "You'll find it much busier than your part of the world. There's a lot going on in Richmond and you'll get plenty of evenings off; you'll be able to go to the theatre, meet up with your friends."

What friends, thought Megan dismally, I don't know anybody in London. Already, she was beginning to doubt the wisdom of her impulsive decision.

Michael Goddard went on. "My wife likes to put Jessica to bed herself most evenings. She believes in quality time with our daughter. Of course, with her busy lifestyle, this isn't always possible and..." He cast her quick glance. "Did the agency mention this? Lorraine and I do a lot of entertaining. We'll expect your cooperation on these occasions."

Megan nodded politely.

Driving across river, he said, "Nearly there. My wife is looking forward to meeting you. The agency gave you a terrific reference."

Not too terrific, I hope, thought Megan, beginning to feel even more agitated. Suppose they had exaggerated her background! Mrs Goddard might be expecting an experienced nanny. Moistening her lips, she prepared herself to meet the mother of her new charge.

The Goddards were a handsome couple. Everything about them spoke of good taste and affluence. They lived in a three-storied turn-of-the-century house in Strawberry Vale with a large enough drive to accommodate four cars. It was a far grander house than she had been used to.

Mrs Goddard welcomed her warmly, fussing over Calum, insisting he share all the facilities laid on for their daughter. Megan accepted their hospitality shyly, but when she discovered that her son's cot was in the nursery with Jessica, an unexpected surge of protectiveness coerced her into asking for it to be moved into her bedroom.

Lorraine Goddard shrugged. "Certainly, if that's what you want but I wouldn't have thought it mattered since the nursery is right next door to your room and, in any case, there's a baby alarm."

Until now Megan had never felt possessive of Calum, but being away from home, seemed to have brought out her maternal instincts. The realisation tweaked her conscience, reminding her of her mother's ever-watchful eye. Perhaps after that suicide attempt Mum's concern was understandable, although she had emphatically declared that now she had Calum there was no way she'd contemplate taking her own life.

On the day of her arrival, while the babies were asleep, she spent a couple of hours composing a letter to her parents. On leaving home, she had left a brief note on the kitchen table promising to phone them. Now, Swansea and the Reverend Hughes's ordered lifestyle seemed worlds away and she couldn't find the explanatory yet less than hurtful words. At the fourth attempt, she folded the sheet of paper and put it into an envelope. It was a terse letter, which gave no return address or contact number, yet to write more would involve her in lies and deceit since she knew that the slightest hint of her whereabouts would bring her father hot-footing his way up to London.

The next dilemma was where to post it. A Twickenham postmark would give the game away. Fate played into her hands. On picking up a pile of correspondence of her own as she left the house the next day, Lorraine Goddard said, "I'll drop that letter in the post-box for you if you like. It will have to go from Gatwick."

Megan admired her new employer as she checked her appearance in the hall mirror. The woman had a good figure, wore expensive clothes, discreet make-up and subtle perfume. She moved and spoke decisively. Megan caught a glimpse of herself behind her, and felt inadequate in her faded jeans and T-shirt, her fair hair falling limply to her shoulders.

Turning away from the mirror, Lorraine Goddard said, "I hate leaving you in charge so soon after your arrival, Megan, but this Rome Conference is terribly important. I daren't miss it." She flashed a smile. "You have to watch every move those Italian publicists make. I can't tell you how many tedious dinners I have to sit through." She went to the front door, stopping abruptly and speaking rapidly, "I'll be back on Thursday. Will you be all right, Megan?"

"I'll be fine."

"Michael will be home each evening, of course." She frowned earnestly. "Are you certain you know where everything is? Do you want me to go over Jessica's routine again?"

"Please don't worry, Mrs Goddard," Megan assured her. "I can manage."

"My dear, please call me Lorraine. Mrs Goddard makes me feel middle-aged. By the way, in case anyone calls, I use my maiden name for business: Chisholm-Baillie. Oh, there's my taxi. See you in a couple of days."

She addressed her daughter, crooning in a high voice, "Bye, my little pumpkin." And, laden with briefcase, handbag and letters, she tottered back across the hall in her high heels to plant the imprint of her red lips on Jessica's cheek. The baby let out an ear-splitting yell.

"Oh dear, she's missing me already," cried her mother, disappearing out of the door.

The next few days were lonely for Megan. She spent a lot of time reflecting on her reasons for leaving home. To escape from her father's eagle eye and her mother's smothering protection had been a pressing enough motive, but accepting a position in Twickenham had been more than a lucky chance. There had been other placements, even further away from Swansea than London, but she had chosen this one because it was close to Thames Ditton, and Christopher.

She tried to conjure up his features, but couldn't. From her duffle bag, she took out a dog-eared photograph. It showed two teenagers making faces at the camera. Shot in a Woolworth photo booth, it was unflattering, but it brought back the moment, nearly two years earlier, when they'd skipped school to hang around in the town centre, hoping they wouldn't be recognised and questioned about their absence from the classroom by interfering adults.

With a sigh, Megan settled the babies on the floor in the nursery and sat down cross-legged between them. As they chortled happily, she regressed into the past...

How wonderful that summer had been! She had spent the entire six-week school vacation with Christopher: swimming, roller skating, horse-riding, tennis; even going for a drink, although they had to make sure the pub was well away from her neighbourhood.

Calum's arrival had turned her world upside down. She had been genuinely shocked to find herself pregnant. She hadn't believed you could get pregnant the very first time. When she hadn't had a period for three months, she knew she would have to tell her mother.

"I expect you're run down. You've probably been working too hard with all your mocks. Don't worry about it, dear."

"Mum, I...I could be pregnant," she stuttered, shamefaced.

"Don't talk nonsense. You don't get pregnant all on your own ..." The words petered out as the truth dawned on her mother. "Megan, you haven't? Why you're barely sixteen!"

"I'm so sorry, Mum."

The colour drained from Brenda Hughes's face. "What on earth are we going to do?" she cried, her voice rising with hysteria.

"It was a mistake, we didn't mean to..."

"A mistake! Who's the father?" She gripped Megan's arm. "Did he... did he force himself on you?"

"Of course he didn't," protested Megan, shaking her arm free.

"Don't tell me you were willing?" Brenda bunched her fists and shrieked, "Megan, you've got a mind of your own, haven't you? Why didn't you stop him?"

"I got carried away, Mum," replied Megan tearfully.

"He'll have to take responsibility, you know."

"He'll want to."

Telling her father was even worse and when her parents learnt that Christopher was a couple of months younger than her and had been under age at the time of the baby's conception, they were outraged.

"Megan, you've committed a terrible sin," stormed the Reverend Hughes. "This will cause a dreadful scandal." His face was bright red and the veins stood out on his forehead. Megan panicked. Suppose her news brought on a heart attack!

"May God forgive you, may God forgive you," he kept repeating. "My own daughter! Oh Megan, how could you do this to us?"

Megan frowned through her reminiscences as she pictured her father. Approaching retirement age, Charles Hughes was a thin, erect figure with stern features. He had always looked the same: half spectacles balanced at the end of his nose, iron-grey hair with a hint of sideburns. Even his clothes didn't change: new sombre grey replacing old sombre grey year in, year out. The family photo album confirmed his enduring appearance; only the neatly scripted dates beneath each snapshot recorded the passage of time. Megan sometimes wondered whether he had by-passed youth to be born a mature adult. He wasn't an unkind man, nor was he unreasonably strict, but he couldn't understand the way children's minds worked, couldn't understand the casual attitude of modern teenagers and found it impossible to relate to anybody born later than the 1950's.

No wonder he had taken her news so badly. She recalled her mother's attempts to pacify him. "Charles, perhaps, we ought to meet with the boy's parents and discuss it with them."

"Will Christopher get into trouble?" ventured Megan.

"Trouble? Of course he'll be in trouble. He deserves to be," shouted her father.

"But he's ever so clever and he wants to go to university."

"There's little chance of that. He'll have to leave school and get a job if he's going to help towards the child's upbringing."

"Let's arrange to meet his parents," suggested Brenda again. "Do you know his address, Megan?"

"Mum, he doesn't live in Swansea," whispered Megan.

"Where does he live?" demanded her father.

"I don't know. He came to Swansea to stay with his aunt while his mother was in hospital."

"You must have some idea."

"Somewhere in the London area, I think."

Charles frowned as he gave thought to this new information. "Umm, that changes things. Let's not be hasty. The boy lives a long way away, maybe we had better sort this out ourselves, leave him and his family out of it. The less scandal the better."

"Is that wise, Charles?" asked Brenda. "After all, they ought to give Megan some financial support. We're not terribly well off and this is going to put quite a strain on our finances."

"We'll manage. I think it's better to keep the whole thing as quiet as possible. It might even be possible for Megan to go away until after the baby's born. We could always say we've adopted a child."

"At our age?" Brenda gave a harsh laugh. "Really, Charles, that's not very practical."

Suddenly, Megan came to life. Here they were, discussing her future as if she weren't present. "Mum, Dad," she shrieked. "This is my baby. Don't I have a say in the matter?"

"My child, I think you've had enough of a say," retorted her father.

"I won't let you send me away. I'm going to have my baby here in Swansea and you'll just have to put up with it." Turning on her heel, Megan fled from the room.

Her outburst resolved the matter because she never heard another word about being sent away, and her parents decided not to approach Christopher's parents. This decision left her with mixed feelings. On the one hand, she wanted Christopher to know about their baby, but on the other, she didn't want to get him into trouble. She decided to let the matter drop for the moment. Once her baby was born, she would contact Christopher. After all, he had the right to know his child.

Even now, with the evidence in front of her, she couldn't believe it had happened. She looked at Calum and wondered how such a beautiful human being had sprung from such an unremarkable beginning. She recalled the day of his conception:

They walked home hand-in-hand, stopping now and again, to steal a kiss. They'd been drinking cider and she felt a bit light-headed. They turned into her drive and crept to the rear of the house. It was a wonderful, unreal game they were playing. Her father's garden seemed like a secret place; evening shadows lengthened across its lawn, end-of-summer bees dive-bombed late blooms, a few brave butterflies flitted in and out of the buddleia.

"Are your parents in?" asked Christopher.

"Shhh!" she giggled. "You'll wake Mum, she's gone to bed with a migraine. Dad's out at a parish meeting."

"So we've got a little time."

Playfully, Christopher grabbed her from behind, sliding his hands under her sweatshirt as she went ahead of him up the short flight of steps to the veranda leading to the open French window. His touch made her flesh tingle.

"No Chris, don't," she cried, but she knew her protest was feeble. She gave a little gasp as he swivelled her round to face him.

"It's all right," he murmured, as his fingers moved from fondling her breasts to slide down inside the waistband of her joggers.

She took a step backwards up the wooden stairs. Although he was standing on a lower step, he was still taller than her: tall for his age - not yet sixteen. He nudged her into a sitting position and, before she could stop him, pulled her joggers free, pants and slip-on pumps with them.

"No Chris, no......!"

Her mother's words of warning spun in her head ... Save yourself for marriage, Megan dear. Think of your father; remember his standing in the community.

"Oh Christopher!" she breathed, mentally flicking her mother's counselling away. For a moment, he hesitated, confused by the mixed messages: refusal on her lips, invitation in her eyes.

She edged backwards up onto the decking and he followed her, stumbling on the top step. He yanked his jeans undone, pushing them down as far as they'd go. His trainers forbade complete removal. His eyes were half-closed, his lips parted.

She snatched at this last opportunity to withdraw. "Stop! We shouldn't!"

"Yes we should," he gulped as he fell on top of her.

The weight of his body stole her breath away; her head bumped against one of the veranda's supporting posts. Over his shoulder, she saw a froth of clouds scudding across the sky. She concentrated on breathing, fought the smart of tears, smothered a shriek of pain. Was it supposed to hurt?

"No, Chris, no!"

He took no notice as he rocked back and forth, panting rapidly -- faster and faster -- until an upsurge of rhythm forced a strangled grunt from his throat. Don't let Mum hear! prayed Megan. The wooden decking pressed into the small of her back. With a final unbridled thrust he collapsed on top of her.

Minutes passed. Then her mother's voice reached them from inside the house: "Is that you, Megan?"

"Yes, Mum," she called back in a choked voice.

Abruptly, he levered himself upright and pulled up his jeans. He averted his gaze. So did she. She fumbled for her joggers; they were inside out. With trembling fingers, she righted them and tugged them on.

"Megan!" Mum's voice again.

Looking alarmed, he mumbled, "I must be off, see you around."

No kiss, no romantic words; it was as if they'd just shared a Coke and a packet of crisps. He loped away, leaving her gently sobbing.

Mum again. "What's the matter? Where are you, Megan?"

"In the garden. It's all right. I'm coming in to take a shower."

Shoving her panties into the pocket of her joggers, she hurried indoors, brushing past her mother in the hall.

"Leave enough hot water for your father, dear, you know he likes a shower before dinner."

"Yes, Mum."

She took her joggers into the shower with her, scrubbing at them frantically. Would the stains never wash out? Stepping out of the shower cubicle into the steamy bathroom, she wiped the mirror with a towel and looked at herself. A pair of startled eyes stared back as she realised in dismay that she had no other clothes to put on. She heard the front door slam shut and drew in her breath. God! It wouldn't do to bump into Dad on the landing in the nude. She waited until she was certain the coast was clear before scurrying back to her bedroom.

How elated she'd felt the next day! She was grown up. She'd lost her virginity. She'd longed to tell her friend, Isobel, but hadn't dared. All day long, she'd expected Christopher to speak to her, but after a brief nod, he'd elected to mingle with the boys. Covertly, she'd watched him, noticing how he laughed a touch too heartily. Was he deliberately shunning her? Worse! Was he bragging to his friends? Whenever she did manage to catch his eye, he would blush and turn away. By the time school had finished, she was desperate. Why had he avoided her? At four o'clock, she'd run all the way home, locked herself in her bedroom and howled.

By the end of the week, he'd gone; called home to Surrey, his temporary sojourn in Swansea with his aunt and uncle ended now that his mother had come out of hospital.

Calum waddled across the room and flung himself at her. Pushing aside her reflections, Megan decided it was time for action. She'd been in Twickenham almost two weeks now and was beginning to get to know the area.

With Calum perched on her hip, she went in search of the local telephone directory. None of the numbers listed under Mills corresponded with the address Christopher had given her. Never mind, she thought to herself, she would write to him. He hadn't replied to her other letters, but that was because she hadn't told him about the baby.

The slamming of the front door reminded Megan of her duties. She hurried to the nursery door to greet Michael, speaking too rapidly, telling him in detail about Jessica's activities throughout the day. He appeared not to notice her agitation.

"Good, I'm glad you're settling in well. Jessica loves you."

He played with his daughter for five minutes before relinquishing her back into Megan's care.

It was Megan's day off, but to put off phoning home, she wasted time fussing over Calum. After sending the letter, she had geared herself up to make the promised telephone call, but had never found the courage to face the tears and the recriminations which were bound to greet her from the other end of the line.

But now the call had to be made because today was Calum's first birthday and she knew she could never bring herself to cut him off from his grandparents on this special day. She bought a phonecard, found a quiet telephone booth and dialled the number. Her father answered.

"Where in heaven's name are you, Megan? Don't you know how worried your mother and I have been? How could you be so thoughtless, so selfish ..."

"Dad ..." Her father raged on. Megan butted in again. "Listen to me, Dad ..."

She heard her mother's voice distantly. "Let me speak to her." And more emphatically, "Charles, hand me the phone."

"Megan, are you all right?"

"I'm fine, Mum."

"And Calum?"

"He's fine too. It's his birthday today."

"I know ..." She heard the break in her mother's voice. "Give him a kiss from me. We've bought him some lovely presents. Will you be coming home soon?"

"Not yet. I had to leave Swansea, you know."

"Why?"

"You know why." Megan stifled a sob. "I was being smothered. I have to get a life of my own."

"It's because we love you so much."

"It's not you, Mum. It's Dad. I have to show him that I'm not his little girl any more."

"He's terribly upset; has hardly set foot outside the door since you left."

Megan gave a snort. "Ashamed to show his face, worried about what his parishioners will think."

"That's unfair."

No, it's not, thought Megan.

"Where are you staying? How are you off for money?"

"It's all right, Mum, I've got a job."

Briefly, she explained about her new position, careful not to give the name or the address. "These people are really kind and their baby daughter is company for Calum. Don't worry; it's working out well. I must go. No time left on the card," she fibbed.

"Give us the number, we'll ring you back."

"I can't. Goodbye."

"Wait! Your father wants another word."

Gulping back a surge of tears, Megan replaced the receiver and bent down to pick up her son, who was crouching at her feet, making patterns on the dirt-streaked kiosk window with his finger.

She gave him a kiss and whispered, "That's from Grandma."

Making the call released Megan from a sense of obligation. By not giving details of her whereabouts, she had effectively severed the apron strings. Now, she was truly in charge of her own destiny, and Calum's.

Having discovered that the Mills' telephone number was ex-directory, the only way to reach Christopher was by post, or in person. While the children were having their afternoon nap, Megan sat on the bed with a sheet of note-paper balanced on a book on her knee and composed a letter, giving her address and telephone number and saying that she had some important news.

Christopher's reply came three days later: half a page of stilted non-committal language, no suggestion that they should meet. Reduced to tears, she read it three times before tossing it into the waste paper bin. To take her mind off her disappointment, she took the children for a walk, stopping off at McDonalds for a milkshake on the way home. It was four thirty and the place was crowded with foreign students.

Megan fought her way to a vacant table and squeezed into the corner seat, manoeuvring the double buggy in beside her. Both children were sleeping peacefully, oblivious to the confusion around them.

"Mind if I sit here?" asked a tall, slim, dark-skinned young woman, sinking down into the seat opposite without waiting for a reply. Pointing at the babies, she said cheerfully, "I wish I could change places with them."

It was Megan's first encounter with Connie Dixon. She responded to the girl's friendliness by saying, "I feel like that sometimes. Have you been working hard?"

"Yeah, I'm shattered," admitted Connie. Stealing another glance at the children, she turned back to Megan and asked, "They're not yours, are they?"

Megan laughed. "Not both of them; that would be impossible, there's barely five months between them."

Connie laughed too and admitted ruefully, "I don't know much about babies. I think I'd find motherhood awfully boring. Oh..." She paused apologetically. "I'm sure it isn't really. It's just that I'm not into all that stuff."

The remark needled Megan, making her feel dull and put-down. Her initial feeling of warmth changed to distrust. Taking a sip of her milkshake, she pretended to be absorbed in her copy of 'Marie Claire'. But Connie wasn't put off.

"*Do not go gentle into that good night ...*" she quoted.

Looking up with a start, Megan took up the poem: "*Old age should burn and rave at close of day ...*" She broke off. "You know Dylan Thomas!"

Connie nodded. "One of my favourites. He came from Swansea, didn't he?"

"Yes. That's where I come from."

"I guessed as much. I love your accent. Could you spare me some time to talk? I'm studying a variety of accents as part of my drama course. It would be ever so helpful if you could." She flashed Megan a smile. "I'd repay you by doing a spot of babysitting; that is, if you'd trust me with the kids. Are they always as good as this?"

Megan grinned back, her animosity vanishing in response to Connie's enthusiasm. "I'm afraid not. Actually, Jessica screams her head off most of the time."

"Which one is Jessica?"

Megan pointed. "Calum is mine," she said proudly.

"You don't look old enough to have a child ..."

Megan chanted the end of the sentence in unison with Connie, who took the mimicry in good spirit. She said, "I guess you've heard that before."

More students poured into the restaurant, jabbering excitedly in a mixture of languages.

Connie frowned. "Let's get out of here. Where do you live? I'll walk back with you if you like."

During the twenty minutes it took to walk from Twickenham High Street to Strawberry Vale, Megan found herself confiding in Connie.

"What did you say your boyfriend's name was?" Connie asked.

"Christopher Mills."

The girl looked thoughtful. "I think I know his brother, Daniel. He's a second-year student at my college. Would you like me to set up a meeting?"

Megan's eyes lit up. "Yes please," she said.

Connie was as good as her word. Three days later, she invited Megan to meet her at the college gates. She had a teenage boy with her. When she saw Megan, she waved and ran towards her. Taking the buggy, she nudging her forward.

"That's him, that's Christopher's brother."

The young man scowled and asked, "What's this all about?"

"It's rather a long story," Megan started to explain.

"Not too long, I hope. I'm in a hurry."

She gave a swallow and began. "I know your brother."

"So?"

"We met when he was staying in Swansea, the summer before last. We went out together." Megan reddened. "We were close."

Daniel snorted. "He was only fifteen."

From a few yards behind her, Calum's mumbled Mummy reached them. Megan ignored him, but the child started to cry. She glanced back and he instinctively held out his arms for her. Comprehension dawned in Daniel's eyes. Pointing at the baby, he gasped, "You're not trying to lay that at Chris's door!" Shaking his head vehemently, he went on, "Chris isn't like that. He's quiet and serious."

"I know that," said Megan indignantly.

"He'd never touch a girl ..." The boy shook his head again. " ... not Christopher, not good old respectable Christopher." He started to back away, his expression aghast.

"Wait," cried Megan. "Let me explain."

The boy's amazement changed to anger. "Clear off," he shouted. "I don't know what all this is about but I'm warning you, don't try anything. Chris is in enough trouble as it is."

Megan looked over her shoulder and saw that Connie was crouching down beside the buggy comforting Calum. Turning back, she broke into a run, catching up with Daniel as he went through the college gates. "Wait, please wait! What did you mean about Chris being in trouble?"

He brushed her off. "It's none of your business."

Megan's heart began to race as she experienced a surge of overwhelming fondness for the boy whose company had made her so happy two summers ago. Drawn together by a common interest in poetry, each had been shy about it, intent on hiding this romantic leaning from their peers for fear of ridicule. She looked into Daniel's eyes and saw that, although similar in appearance, the brothers were cast in different moulds: this young man wouldn't give a hoot for Wordsworth or Tennyson. His defensiveness angered her. Surely, as the mother of Christopher's child, she had the right to know!

She plucked at his sleeve. "Tell me what's wrong."

"He's ill. Now leave me alone."

Spinning around, he raced towards the playing fields, leaving Megan staring after him. Connie pushed the double buggy up to her.

"What did he say?"

"He says Chris is in trouble, that he's ill," she whispered.

Connie put her arm round the younger girl's shoulders. "He's probably just saying that to put you off. You can't blame him for trying to protect his kid brother."

Megan shook her head in puzzlement. "I must find out. You will help me, won't you?"

A frown of impatience crossed her companion's face. Drawing away, Connie said, "I've done what I can for you. I've got to run now."

"I know, thank you."

Connie's resolve melted. Heaving a resigned sigh, she said, "Meet me here tomorrow at the same time. We'll go over to Thames Ditton together and look Christopher up. That way, you can call at his house while I keep Calum out of sight. It will give the boy time to get over the initial shock."

Hope gleamed in Megan's eyes. "Thank you, Connie," she gasped.

"Suppose his brother's told him about my meeting him!" said Megan as she and Connie made their way along the road the next day.

They were an ill-assorted pair. Megan was in jeans and T-shirt, her fine straight hair pulled back into a ponytail, her pale face devoid of make-up. Connie wore an ankle-length voile skirt of Indian cotton and a brief top, which showed her midriff. The front section of her frizzy hair was dyed purple, her flawless skin, bronzed even more by the recent heatwave, glowed with health. She was a head and shoulders taller than Megan and was forced to shorten her stride to match that of the girl she'd taken under her wing.

"It won't matter," Connie assured her. She didn't say as much, but it had occurred to her that Christopher's mother was more likely to be a stumbling block. She went on, "How old is your friend?"

"Seventeen."

"So young!" gasped Connie.

"He's very mature for his age," replied Megan.

Connie suppressed her dismay. "What will you do if he's not in?" she asked.

"If he's ill, he'll be at home ..." retorted Megan.

Connie kept her counsel. "There's the house," she said, pointing across the road. Taking the pushchair from Megan, she went on, "I'll walk on a bit with Calum."

Megan didn't move. "I can't," she mumbled.

"Go on; don't lose your bottle now. You'll never solve the mystery if you don't meet him face to face," replied Connie, giving her a nudge.

CHAPTER THREE

Ben scowled as he kicked an empty Pepsi can into the gutter. The torrential rain soaked through his white T-shirt, sticking the thin material to his breast bone so that the stark letters of its emblazoned motif seemed etched into his chest. The highly developed muscles of his arms glistened as the headlamps from a passing car momentarily cast their glare on him.

This was a dangerous area of Birmingham. Hot-wiring, petty theft, muggings were commonplace here. Ben didn't give a toss, he was too angry to care. Ma was in Intensive Care fighting for her life because that son-of-a-bitch had laid into her. A conversation he'd had with his mother some time ago came back to him ...

"Pack up and come down to London, Ma. Stay with me," he says persuasively.

A smile splits her broad face in two as she reaches for his hand and croons, "No, sweetness, you not want me in yer life. You good boy, Ben. You not need me nagging."

He stifles shame -- good boy! If she only knew! He recalls how, as a youngster, he had been unable to hide anything from her. She squeezes his hand, looking at him with her large trusting eyes and he forces himself not to lower his gaze. "You'd like London, Ma, there's lots going on: films, shows ..."

Throwing up her hands, Imelda cries, "Oh my, oh my, church on Sunday and bingo on Friday, dat's enough for me. Very sweet! What about your sisters? How can I leave Hannah and Naomi when they still only babbies?"

This last objection had closed the argument with both mother and son expelling a sigh, neither realising how much alike they were, both in appearance and in personality: easy-going on the surface, but rigid as steel on the inside. The only difference was a streak of malevolence the young man carried within him, a characteristic he resolutely refused to acknowledge, a characteristic inherited from his father.

Abe Jenson had been sent down many times, but good behaviour and the required degree of remorse had always earned him early parole. The old bugger's gone too far this time, thought his son. He was drawn back to loiter outside the hospital, knowing that he would have to control his anger before going in. Finally, instead of going into the hospital, he made his way to the sixth-floor tenement flat where his mother, Imelda, and his four sisters lived.

His sister, Thea, greeted him. "Where the hell have you been? I've just come back from the hospital. Ma was asking for you."

"How is she?"

"The same."

"I suppose you were down the Red Lion. Can't you keep away from that place for five minutes?" Her tone grew sharper as she went on, "Even when you do manage a visit, you spend more time in that dive than you do with us."

"Shut yer face!" he snapped.

Undeterred, Thea retorted, "You just listen to me, Ben. This time it's serious. It's no good you packing off back to London leaving me and Clelia to pick up the pieces. You've got to take on your share of the responsibility."

"Forget it, Thea," butted in her sister. "You're talking to a brick wall."

Ben and Thea ignored her.

"I turn up when I'm needed," he growled.

"Only after the damage has been done."

He shrugged his heavy shoulders. "There's nothing to stop you all moving down ..."

"You must be joking," scoffed Thea. "I'm half way through my computer course, the kids are coming up to their GCSE's and ..." She threw out an arm. "Clelia wouldn't leave Nathan."

Ben glowered and turned away. Stripping off his wet T-shirt, he tossed it onto a chair.

"Pick that up, you lazy slob?" shrieked Thea. "You might live like a pig down South but up here, we won't put up with it."

"Shut up for Christ's sake!"

"No, I won't," retorted his sister, her eyes blazing.

"Stop it, stop it, both of you!" Clelia cried out. "Go somewhere else if you want to have a slanging match. Have you forgotten that Ma's lying in hospital?" Spinning on her heel, she ran from the room, tears streaming down her cheeks.

Turning back to Ben, Thea shouted, "Now look what you've done."

"Pa's done it this time," said Thea an hour later, as she and Ben made their way to the hospital the following Saturday afternoon, their differences temporarily forgotten. "Ma's not going to get over this lot."

"'Course she is," scoffed Ben. "She always bounces back."

"Ben, why do you only believe what you want to believe? This time you'll have to face up to the truth."

Entering the hospital put paid to further bickering as brother and sister steeled themselves to face their mother. Both stopped short in the doorway leading to Intensive Care. The curtain was drawn around their mother's cubicle. Sounds of activity reached them; whispered voices and worst of all, laboured wheezing.

"Oh my God!" gulped Thea, clutching her brother's arm. "Ma's dying."

Ben's heart raced. This couldn't happen. Ma always got better. Shaking off his sister's hand, he raced across the ward.

The Desk Duty Nurse hurried after to him. "Stop!" she cried. "It's all right. Your mother's been moved out of ITU. They've taken her downstairs to a general ward. She's very much better."

Arm-in-arm, and smiling now, Thea and Ben followed the nurse's directions. They found Imelda Jenson standing beside her bed busily arranging some flowers. They stood in the doorway for several seconds, looking at her before she saw them.

"Jest look at des," she said when she noticed them. "Des nurses don't know how to make flowers look pretty."

"Ma, I expect they've got more important things to do than flower arranging," laughed Thea. She ran across to her mother and planted a kiss on her cheek. "My, you look much better."

Thea stood aside as Imelda opened her arms to hug Ben. Over his shoulder, she addressed the other patients in the ward. "Dis my boy. He come all der way from London to see his ole ma." Her shiny black face shone with pride. "How long you stay, boy?" she asked, clutching her son's hand as if she were afraid he might disappear.

"Not long, Ma," he said and, on seeing the disappointment on her face, added, "I'll stay until you get out of hospital."

"I can't believe how quickly Ma's recovered," said Thea as they left the hospital later. "Just wait until I tell Clelia and the little ones."

Ben grinned. "I told you she'd be all right, didn't I?"

As soon as they entered the flat, he made for the bedroom, leaving his sister to break the good news to the younger girls.

Snatching up his hold-all, he dumped it on the bed and hurriedly rammed jeans and T-shirts into it. Zipping it up, he went back to the living room.

Thea's eyes widened at the sight of the holdall. "You're not leaving already?"

"Why not? Ma's on the mend, Pa's banged up," he retorted.

"But you promised to stay until she gets home."

"Tell her I'll phone," he said. Delving into his pocket, he slapped a couple of twenty-pound notes down onto the table. "Buy her something nice when she comes home: chocolates or flowers."

Thea's temper flared. "You disgust me," she shouted. "You can't even spare a little time for your own mother. Suppose she has a relapse!"

"Don't be daft."

"She might," murmured Clelia in support of her sister.

"Then I'll catch the first train back," he replied and, spinning on his heel, left the apartment.

Getting back to work after a break made Ben feel good, mainly due to the apparent mixture of fear and esteem the staff afforded him. Despite the criticism and scathing "put-downs' he directed at them, he was popular with the college students who worked for him. They weren't to know that his scorn hid a grudging admiration for their quest for learning.

Connie was on duty. "Hi, Ben, everything okay?"

His white teeth flashed briefly. "Sure, why not?"

It was a busy day, yet Ben found time to joke with the boys and tease the girls. In the evening he invited Reece to go with him to Deceptions where, feeling in an expansive mood, he bought more than his share of rounds. Like his mother, people were drawn to Ben. He would amuse them with his witty banter then, without warning he would withdraw to become reclusive. This contradictory trait in his character puzzled his friends, but his charisma dispelled any affront they might have felt.

All at once, the barman gestured to him. "Call for you."

"Who is it?"

"Your sister."

Leaping to his feet, he sent a glass of lager spinning across the littered table. Reece followed him. Ben snatched up the receiver and, above the din, heard Thea say, "Ma's home, Pa's out. Come quickly."

"I don't know why you had to tag along," said Ben. "Me and my mates will sort this out."

"I thought you could use some help," replied Reece, feeling a touch irritated by his companion's lack of gratitude and regretting that it was too late to get off the train.

"This is family business." He cast Reece a meaningful glance. "Know what I mean?"

"Yes, but suppose your mates aren't around."

"They will be."

Reece shrugged. "Fair enough, I'll get off at the next stop and go back to London."

"Please yourself."

Both men retreated to a window seat, staring out at the passing landscape, ignoring the other's existence. The encroaching darkness gave them the opportunity to guardedly scrutinise one another via the window's reflection. As the train drew to a halt outside Reading, Reece started to get up. Ben stopped him.

"It's all right," he said. "It could be useful having you in tow."

It had gone ten by the time they reached Imelda's flat. Thea rushed to the door, releasing the safety chain when she saw her brother.

"Hi Thea, this is my mate, Reece Cassidy," he said, casually waving a hand in Reece's direction.

Thea eyed the young Canadian up and down and, having satisfied herself that he looked tough enough to take care of himself, turned back to Ben and said, "Pa's sworn to get even. He thinks Ma rang the Police last time. It wasn't her, it was Clelia."

Imelda's voice reached them from across the room. "Better he think it was me." She paused, then said, "You come real quick, son, tank you sweetness."

"Ma, shouldn't you be in bed?" said Thea.

Imelda was leaning for support on the door frame and, on seeing Reece, she pulled her dressing gown tightly round her, tying the belt. Its colourful pattern emphasised the width of her hips, which waggled from side to side as she sat down heavily in the armchair Clelia offered her.

"And who is dis?" she enquired, giving Reece the once over.

He held out his hand. "Reece Cassidy. Glad to meet you, Mrs Jenson."

His friendliness must have dispelled any misgivings she might have had since she took his hand and shook it warmly. Addressing her son, she said, "Well, sweetness, what you stand there for? Where's dose manners? Go get yer friend a drink."

At his mother's bidding, Ben went into the kitchen, closely followed by his sister. Reece could hear them whispering and guessed that Thea was asking her brother about him.

Imelda, too, picked up on this and started talking in her soft West Indian drawl. "It's nice I get to know Ben's London friends. He secretive 'bout der life down there. Only der good lord know what he get up to, how many hearts he break." A mother's love lit up her good-natured face.

"We've not known one another for long," explained Reece, realising that he knew absolutely nothing about Ben's life outside of McDonalds and Deceptions.

Thea and Ben reappeared with a pot of tea and a plate of sandwiches.

"Help yerself," said Imelda, gesturing towards the table.

The conversation was awkward and Reece sensed that his unscheduled appearance had presented the Jenson family with an additional problem. Without him being there they would, by now, have been discussing what to do about Abe Jenson. But the subject could not be avoided forever.

"Thea, how come he got bail?" Ben asked at last.

"God knows, unless Uncle Mel coughed up the necessary dough."

They didn't expound on why Uncle Mel would put up bail. Feeling more and more uncomfortable, Reece ate another couple of sandwiches. Then he said, "I'll push off and find some digs for the night."

"What!" Imelda threw up her hands in dismay. "'Course you don't." Flicking a wrist at her daughter, she said, "Clelia, you go sleep wid your sister tonight. Ben and Reece take your room."

"Ben, what's happening?"

"Nothing, go back to sleep."

"Where are you going?"

In the dim light, Reece could see his companion squatting on the bedroll that had been temporarily laid out on the floor. He was lacing up his trainers.

"I'm going out there to look for him."

"Is that a good idea?"

"Got to do something. Can't go back to London with that bugger loose on the streets. Can't stay up here forever."

"I'm coming with you."

"No! Stay put. If he shows up, keep him out." Ben got up and moved to the door with his customary fleetness of foot. Turning, he flashed Reece a grin and said, "You might as well make yourself useful now you're here."

This begrudging hint of gratitude pleased Reece. He had only just fallen asleep again when the crashing started. He sat up abruptly as Thea appeared in the doorway in her dressing gown. "Where's Ben?" she asked.

"Gone out."

"What?" Her voice rose in panic and she clasped a hand to her mouth. "Do something, he'll kick the door down."

Reece leapt to his feet. "Phone the Police," he called as he rushed through the living room.

A long splintering crack had already appeared in the lower panel. He could hear the intruder shouting and swearing. Thea had picked up the phone; Clelia stood beside her, clutching her sister's arm. She was trembling uncontrollably. Behind them, Imelda's immense frame shielded her two youngest daughters, whose hysterical weeping added to the mayhem.

"It's all right," Reece called to them over his shoulder, hoping that his voice carried reassurance. "The chain will keep him at bay."

The words were barely out of his mouth before the panel split completely and the weakened security chain gave way. Reece gasped in alarm as Abe Jenson burst into the flat. The huge Jamaican stopped in astonishment. An auburn-bearded foreigner was not what he had expected to find.

Reece gulped and took a step back, spreading his arms wide to stop the man getting to the living room. He felt foolish, facing his opponent bare-footed and wearing only a pair of blue and white striped boxer shorts. The hairs on the nape of his neck tingled and the palms of his hands felt sweaty.

"Close the door," he called out to the women behind him.

The door slammed shut, reverberating in its frame, leaving him feeling trapped. The man blocked his only means of escape from the cramped hall. Surprise had given Reece the initial advantage, but the other man had quickly recovered his composure. The Canadian was shocked by his opponent's appearance. Abe Jenson was enormous, far taller than his son, and solidly built. However, he was clearly out of condition and, Reece reflected, more than likely a heavy drinker. Under the circumstances the best Reece could hope for was the benefit of youth and a reasonable degree of fitness. Thank God for those sessions in the gym!

"You'd better get going before Ben finds you," he said trying to soothe the situation, praying that the quantity of lagers the man must have consumed would not make him too belligerent.

"So you're a mate of 'is, are yer?" snarled Abe.

Reeling forward onto the balls of his feet, he swung out his arms in the same loose-limbed way that Ben did. "Out of my way."

Reece flattened himself against the living-room door. "Ben's out to get you so I'd advise you to leave before he gets back."

"You advise me," mimicked the intruder. "Tell me man, what gives you der right to advise me?"

Reece couldn't decide whether the slurred words were due to drunkenness or his West Indian drawl. Again, he tried to appease the man. "Surely you're in enough trouble; don't make matters worse."

Abe gave a hoarse laugh. "Shit, man! Things can't get no worse." He waved an arm. "Out of my fucking way. I want ter see dat she-devil wife of mine."

When Reece refused to budge, he staggered towards him, making a grab for his shoulder, but he was so unsteady on his feet that the Canadian easily thrust him away. Abe fell against the wall, recovered his balance and launched forward in a head-butt. Again Reece was able to ward him off. The smell of alcohol filled the hall, laboured breathing drowned out the quiet shuffles and sobs coming from behind the closed door. Fleetingly, Reece wondered why the neighbours hadn't come out to investigate, then reminded himself that, prudently, they may have decided to mind their own business.

Half leaning against the wall, Abe paused to regain his breath. Reece took a step forward, intending to shove him out of the broken front door, confident the police would turn up at any minute.

As he put out his hand to spin the inebriated man round, Abe lifted his leg and brought his huge boot down on Reece's bare foot. Reece shrieked and hopped back, tears of pain spilling from his eyes. The Jamaican let out a whoop. Shaking off drunkenness, he brought his leg up again to stamp on Reece's other foot. Just in time, Reece hopped aside, but the enraged man was not easily put off. He swung out at the Canadian and, although Reece was able to dodge away, the huge knuckled fist caught his jaw with some force. Stars danced in front of his eyes and, when the next jab came, he slumped to the floor, instinctively cushioning his head from a further barrage of blows.

From afar, the screech of a police siren penetrated his semi-consciousness. The onslaught of punches ceased. He opened his eyes. Abe was standing astride him, although his attention was elsewhere. Suddenly, the West Indian spun around and crashed out of the shattered door.

Through his pain, Reece could hear the gently sobbing little girls. All he could think about was the approaching arm of the law. They would catch Abe Jenson downstairs as he made off across the car park.

The living room door opened cautiously and Thea peered into the hallway.

"My God, what's he done to you?" she gasped, kneeling down to better inspect him.

"Don't ask," he groaned, wiping a trickle of blood seeping from between his fast-swelling lips.

"Can you stand up?"

"I don't know." He glanced towards the front door. "The police will be here soon."

Thea and Clelia exchanged a glance. Then Thea said, "They won't."

"What d'you mean?" he muttered. "They're on their way; I heard the siren."

The girl shook her head. "We didn't call them. They must be after someone else."

"What?" His voice rose in astonishment.

Thea's lip trembled as she went on, "The Police only make things worse."

A surge of fury overrode Reece's pain. He struggled up onto his good foot and faced the girl. "You unfeeling bitch, don't you realise he could have killed me?"

"I'm sorry," she whispered, looking down at the floor, unable to meet his gaze. "But last time ..."

Clelia came out into the hall. Sizing up the situation, she firmly placed a hand under Reece's elbow and helped him into the living room where he gingerly lowered himself into an armchair.

"Let me look at it," she said. "I'm training to be a nurse."

His left foot was swelling rapidly. Clelia crouched down beside him and tentatively touched it. "Ouch! That hurt. It may be fractured; you'd better get an ambulance."

"Not an ambulance," protested Thea.

"Christ!" shouted Reece angrily. "Why not?"

Ignoring his outburst, she and Clelia conferred quietly together, sometimes nodding, sometimes shaking their heads. He heard the whispered words: "I think it's only badly bruised."

Irritated by their procrastination, he snapped, "What's keeping you?"

Thea turned back to him. "Don't worry, we'll get you to A&E. Picking up the telephone, she ordered a minicab and, in answer to his glare of protest, said in appeasement, "It'll be quicker this way. The ambulance can sometimes take ages."

"What about all those stairs? The lift's out of order."

Her mother intervened. "Der sweet boy's right. He need be carried down." She bore down on Reece, grasping his wrists with her warm plump hands, squeezing and shaking them so hard he felt his arms must come loose. "Tank you, tank you fer dat. Tank you fer being strong for us."

Reece found her gratitude embarrassing. He stared back at her in modest silence, not knowing what to say. Abruptly, she let go of his wrists. Placing her hands on her bountiful hips, she swung around with surprising agility and jerked her head in the direction of the kitchen.

"You, Clelia, get brandy from dat cupboard; you, Thea, be a sweet sensible girl, call der ambulance."

"No Ma," retorted the latter, her face set in an expression of ferocious determination. "When the cab comes, Clelia will help me get him down the stairs."

A voice from the hallway took them by surprise. "Bloody hell, looks like I've missed the frigging party. Has that son-of-a-bitch been here again?"

All heads turned to see Ben standing in the doorway.

"It's badly bruised and there are some nasty abrasions. I'm afraid the swelling will take a while to go down. How did you say this happened?" The young intern tending Reece looked up and scrutinised him, his eyes squinting with curiosity.

"I dropped a sledgehammer on my foot," said Reece, his reddening face, betraying the lie.

The doctor gave a chortle. "Sledgehammer eh! Have you escaped from a penal colony?"

"What? Oh sorry, missed the joke."

The doctor became serious. "Rest the foot for a couple of days and be more careful in future when you carry out building work." He turned to the nurse and said. "Please get this young man a pair of crutches from Infirmary."

Reece looked alarmed. "No crutches." The very idea of such undignified assistance filled him with dismay. "Don't worry, I'll manage. Got to, I'm due back at work tomorrow."

"What do you do for a living?"

Reece told him.

"Forget work for a few days," advised the doctor. He gently touched the rapidly bruising jaw-line. "The jaw won't take long to heal. Go home and rest, then check with your GP in a week's time."

"I haven't registered with a GP," Reece started to explain, but the doctor had already turned his attention to another patient.

The nurse returned with a pair of crutches, forcing them on him.

"You'll manage much better with these," she said. "You'll only need them for a few days."

Reece turned to Ben who was sitting on a chair opposite him, grinning. "Just look at the mess you've got me into," he mumbled. "You shouldn't have made off like that."

Ben shrugged. "You'll be okay. Medics are always over cautious. Come on! Let's get out of here. Hospitals give me the creeps."

Now that he knew the injury was no more than a bad sprain, Reece's confidence began to return, bringing with it a surge of anger at Ben. The seething reached exploding point as they made their way along the hospital corridor.

"Why the hell did you go off leaving me in the shit?" he demanded.

Ben shrugged his heavy shoulders and grinned. "Does it matter? You managed."

"Your family's your responsibility, not mine," snarled Reece, quite forgetting that he had been the one to insist on travelling up to Birmingham.

"No-one asked you to come."

"Is that all the thanks I get."

"What d'you want, a medal?"

This was too much for Reece. The crutches fell with a clatter to the floor as he forgot all about his injured foot. He launched himself at Ben, forcing the black man up against the wall. Raising his fist, he started to take a swing at him. An angry shout stopped him. "Hey, what do you think you're doing? This is a hospital. Get out of here before I call Security."

A young nurse ran towards them along the corridor. She stopped several feet away, clearly uncertain of her own safety.

"Sorry," they both mumbled.

At this sign of contrition, she cautiously approached them and, picking up the crutches, handed them back to Reece. Shame brought a flush of colour to his face.

"Sorry," he said again. "I hope we didn't frighten you."

Her expression softened. "Off you go," she said. "The Exit is round the next corner and there's a taxi rank across the road if you haven't got your own transport." She pursed her lips primly although he could see that a smiled lurked at her eyes. "Don't ever do that again."

During the taxi ride home, Reece's thoughts turned to the Jenson women. "You should have stayed with the girls, Ben," he said.

"Don't worry, they're all right. Before we left for the hospital I got a couple of my mates to come round and board up the door. They'll keep an eye on things."

It took the pair over fifteen minutes to reach the sixth floor of Martin Luther King Mansions.

"Your Pa could be lurking on any of these landings," said Reece apprehensively as, with Ben's assistance, he struggled up the stairs. "Aren't you worried?"

"He won't come back tonight."

"How d'you know?"

"You put the frighteners on him."

Reece gave a snort of derision. "That police siren put the frighteners on him. He's a really strong bloke, he could have finished me off."

Ben's next words were rank with bitterness. "Nah! Pa's all mouth."

All mouth and feet, thought Reece, recalling the size twelves that had landed on his toes.

"Has he always been like that?" he asked.

Ben pulled a face and, for once, gave more than a monosyllabic reply. "It happened slowly, no-one noticed at first. He used to be a good dad. I can remember him playing football with me on the beach."

"Back home in Jamaica?"

"Yeah." Ben shrugged. "I remember him holding Clelia when she was just a few hours old. Gentle as a woman, he was. I guess he got disillusioned: came over here full of hope, found work, a council flat, then Ma had the girls, one after another. The rot set in when he lost his job; couldn't hack being on the dole. Ma's so uncomplaining yer see, never wants anything for herself ..." He paused, looking reflective. "It's hard living with someone as saintly as Ma. She stood by him even when the booze mangled his brains."

Turning to face Reece, he shook his head and finished, "Nah, he wasn't always such a heavy-fisted bastard. S'pose you could say, life's done it to him."

The front door of the flat was well and truly boarded up. Ben thumped on the wood and shouted, "It's us, Thea!"

It took the girl some minutes to open up. "Stop hollering," she ordered as she let them in. "You'll wake everyone up."

Relief showed in her eyes when she saw that Reece seemed to be recovering from her father's attack on him. "Are you okay?" she asked anxiously. "No broken bones?"

"Clelia was right," he replied. "It's just badly bruised. What about you, has everything been quiet here?

"Yes," She turned to her brother, her chin thrust out indignantly, "But it's no thanks to your chums."

"They turned up, didn't they?"

"Yeah, boarded up the door, then legged it. Nice way to look out for us!" Her tone was rife with sarcasm.

Ben gave the boarded-up door a cursory inspection. "Don't know what you're moaning about, they made a good job of the door," he said. "No-one could get through that without a hatchet."

While brother and sister continued to squabble, Reece stood listening. Then Thea remembered him. The angry frown vanished from her features, replaced by a concerned smile.

"Come and sit down, Reece," she said, taking the crutches away and leading him to a frayed Parker Knoll with scuffed wooden trims. "I can't thank you enough for what you did for us."

"I wasn't much help," he mumbled modestly.

"Yes you were. You were great. We're in your debt."

He shrugged off her gratitude. "It was nothing."

"Hannah and Naomi think you're a real hero," she chuckled.

He gave an embarrassed snort and felt his colour rise. Studying Thea for the first time, he saw that she was an attractive girl. Now that the threat of Abe coming back had diminished, the tension had fallen away from her and he realised that fear had been responsible for her aggression when Ben had first introduced them.

"I'll get you a drink," she said. "Tea, coffee?"

"Tea please."

"Something to eat?"

Ben butted in. "I'm going out again. Lock up after me."

"What?" shrieked Thea in alarm. "You can't leave us here alone. Pa might come back."

"Of course he won't. He'd never get through that door and besides, by now, he'll be lying paralytic in some doorway."

As he started toward the door, Thea rushed after him. "Ben please don't go, not tonight."

"Got to," he said. "Things to do. You'll be all right."

Reece struggled out of the armchair and hobbled across the room. "Ben, don't be a fool. You'll never forgive yourself if he turns up again and you're not here to sort him out."

Thea lost her temper. Clenching her fists, she cried, "You can't go. We need you here." When she snatched at Ben's sleeve, he roughly twisted her hand free. She let out a cry of pain, tears smarting at her eyes. Still unwilling to see him go, she shrieked, "You don't care about us, you don't give a damn about anything."

For a moment, Ben remained motionless. Then, as if they were parting on amicable terms, he flashed a smile and said confidently, "He won't turn up. I know where he's gone."

He strode out of the flat before either his sister or Reece could stop him. As the clatter of his footsteps died away, Thea turned to face Reece. "How could he be so heartless," she cried, tears of anger and frustration streaming down her cheeks.

"What the hell did he mean about knowing where your Pa's gone?" asked Reece.

Thea shrugged. "I don't know."

Thea locked the door and came back into the living room to slump into a chair, her head in her hands. All at once, she looked up with a start. "What was that?"

"I didn't hear anything."

"I heard a sound outside."

"It was nothing. Don't let your imagination run away with you. "

"I did hear something."

"A cat perhaps."

She sighed. "You're right. I'm getting paranoid. I'd better go and make that tea."

She disappeared into the kitchen and Reece could hear her slamming cupboard doors and he figured that rather than allaying her anger, her jaunt into domesticity had fuelled her resentment against her brother.

Returning with a tray loaded with sandwiches, biscuits and tea, she burst out, "I can't believe Ben's gone off like that. And where the hell was he when Pa burst in?"

"He told me he was going out to look for him."

"That was a pack of lies," retorted Thea. "He probably went down the boxing club."

She passed him a mug of tea, thumping it down so hard that it spilled on the table. Without thinking, she leant over and vigorously wiped up the spillage with the sleeve of her cardigan, ranting all the time about how awful her brother was. From time to time while they were tucking into the sandwiches, she would tense and listen: "Shhh!" Then grin self-consciously, saying almost apologetically, "Thought I heard something."

The girl's mixture of fury and nervousness had a soporific affect on Reece, dampening his own anger. He could see that, deep down, she nursed a great fondness for her wayward brother.

"Ben does have his good points," he ventured.

"Good points!" snapped Thea. "I've yet to see them."

He touched her hand. "Calm down. I can see you take responsibility for the whole family. Give yourself a break, lean on your sister. Is she a lot younger than you?"

"Clelia? She's older if you must know, but she's useless in a crisis."

"Let Ben take charge, but let him do things his way. You know what he's like, maybe he thinks you're too..."Valiantly he tried to find a suitable adjective. "...organising."

Thea snatched her hand away. "Bossy, you mean. You don't know Ben; nothing would get done if he was in charge."

"He manages very well down in London."

The girl looked puzzled. "What do you mean?"

"He's the most respected manager at McDonalds and he won't take any nonsense at the night-club."

"What night-club?"

"Deceptions, he started off as a bouncer. Now he's beginning to take over the running of the place. I think he's saving hard."

"Do you mean he's got two jobs?"

"Yes, didn't you know?"

"No, I didn't," she said sharply.

Reece began to feel uncomfortable. Why was he sticking up for Ben when he was so angry with him? Yet something told him that there was another side to the West Indian that even his sister didn't know about.

Snippets of dialogue came back, muttered words registering only distantly during an evening spent sharing a joint with a group of pals…

Ben's voice: "I'll have enough by the end of the year. Symonds has promised to let me buy into Deceptions, then it's goodbye McDonalds."

Another: "You'll never make it. You're always playing the horses, losing the bread as soon as you've earned it."

Ben: "I never get carried away, always bet on a dead cert."

The other: "Where have I heard that before? Listen, mate, they're all dead certs."

Ben's snarl: "Shut your frigging face, I'll make it. I know what I'm doing. My family's not going to live on the bread-line for much longer. My ma didn't come over here to work her fingers to the bone."

The rest of the conversation had become a mumble as the grass had taken its effect, but Reece could dredge enough from his memory -- and from his daily observation of Ben -- to know that his friend meant business.

"Can I trust you to keep this under your hat?" he said confidentially.

"What?" The girl's hostility showed no signs of diminishing.

"Can I trust you?"

Reluctantly she nodded.

"I think he's planning to invest in a business. He's keen to make money and believe me, Thea, he's truly concerned about your mother. He often says he wishes she'd come down to London."

"He doesn't mean it. He'd have a fit if she decided to move in with him."

"Maybe so, although I think you judge him too harshly."

"You don't know him like I do."

Reece shrugged. There was no arguing that point. All at once, the girl's expression began to soften. "Well -- I suppose if you think he's saving up to do something sensible with his money it does throw a different light on things. Maybe he wants to see how it goes before telling us."

Reece relaxed. The girl seemed satisfied; he'd managed to pull his friend out of a tight hole. Maybe, just for once, he'd successfully played peacemaker. If so, it would be a first. He couldn't think why it had become imperative to reconcile brother and sister. Envy perhaps!

His thoughts flew back a few years, to when his own beloved sister, Mary, had died so tragically. Neither Ben nor Thea really understood the importance of family, of being surrounded by squabbling siblings. His own youth had been chequered with loneliness and change: his incompetent mother forced to pack up their shabby belongings time and time again to move to yet another squalid backstreet bed-sit because her latest meal ticket had walked out on her and the bailiffs were on her tail. At school, he was always the new boy, the one wearing the wrong uniform. No wonder Mary, ten years his senior, had run away from home at fourteen. He gave a silent sigh. It was years before they met up again, but once they did, she had taken him under her wing providing, for a few years at least, a proper home and family. Her death at only thirty-two had come as a terrible blow. That was when the travellers had beckoned and he had taken up the pennant of their crusade: planting trees, saving whales, protecting the environment. It had given him both a purpose in life and a surrogate family. As for his mother, all ties with her were broken the moment he met up with his sister again. He had no idea what had happened to her after that.

Thea broke into his meanderings. "You must be exhausted. Why don't you hit the deck? You could still get in a few hours sleep before morning."

Reece nodded. "I think your Pa would have come back by now if he was coming, don't you, but what about Ben? He won't be able to get back in."

The girl frowned defiantly. "I'm not staying up for him. If he turns up again, he'll just have to kip down on the landing outside."

Reece gave an amused chuckle and asked, "Do you feel safe? I don't mind sleeping in here, nearer the front door, if you'd prefer me to."

"I wouldn't hear of it," protested Thea. "You take Clelia's bed like you did before." She gave him a brief smile. "I'm all right now, honestly!"

"What time do you go out in the morning?"

"Half eight."

"Can you wake me before you go?"

"Yes, but you don't have to leave tomorrow. You can stay over for another night if you like."

"Thanks," he said. "But I'd better get back."

She reached out a hand to assist him from the chair.

"I'm okay thanks."

Initially, he dismissed her help, but when he went to stand up, he found he was shakier than he'd thought. He tried to balance on his good foot, stumbling against the girl. For a moment, they were locked together in an accidental embrace. "Sorry," he apologised.

She looked embarrassed, then said, "No, I'm the one who should be apologising. I'm sorry I lost my temper earlier this evening. It's just that things get on top of me sometimes." After making sure he was steady on his feet, she collected the crutches from the corner of the room and handed them to him.

"Thanks," he said. "And Thea, I think you're great."

She gave him a wide grin, reminding him of her brother when he was in a congenial mood, and said simply, "Thanks, Reece," before disappearing through the door.

Ben turned up early next morning. Reece experienced a rush of anger, but the tenderness of his jaw and the shooting pain in his foot denied him the opportunity of giving vent to it. They travelled back to London in silence, and as they drew closer to their destination, Reece's temper began to simmer. Ben slouched in the seat opposite him; sometimes nodding off until a gentle snore woke him up, sometimes staring into space with an amused smirk lingering at his mouth as if he were dwelling on an enjoyable memory.

With his nerve-ends twitching and his temples throbbing with the roar of the train, Reece could no longer stand the tension between them. "I don't know what you've got to smile about," he snarled.

Ben looked at him in surprise. "Why, what's up?"

"You are. I hope you apologised to your sister before she left for college this morning."

Ben raised an eyebrow. "What for?"

"For walking out on your family, you prize moron."

"Why? Did something happen after I left?"

"No, but it could have done. What was so bloody important that you had to leave?"

"None of your business," came the short reply.

"My coming up here made it my business," retorted Reece. "What did you mean, you knew where your Pa went to?"

"I didn't know, I just said that to keep Thea quiet."

"You did what?" Reece's face reddened in anger. "How can you treat your sister like that? She was terribly worried about you. She really cares, you know. Why do you treat her like shit?"

Ben's lip curled. "She deserves it. We're always fighting, never see eye to eye. She can't stand the sight of me."

When Reece opened his mouth to protest, Ben cut him short. "Keep out of it, Reece."

Settling himself more comfortably in his seat, he closed his eyes on the discussion. This was too much for Reece. A surge of rage coursed through him. Leaning over, he snatched Ben's jacket, yanked him forward and took a swing at his jaw. Instinctively the black man averted his face so that the punch barely glanced his chin. Before Reece could strike again, he grabbed his wrists and twisted his arms downwards.

"Don't ever try that again." The black man's voice was husky with menace.

Reece blinked, quickly realising that Ben had the advantage. With a hiss, he drew away, trying not to wince as Ben's grip on his wrists loosened and the blood rushed back to his hands.

"You've got one over me this time," he muttered. "But I'll not forget this."

Ben adjusted his jacket and sank back into his seat, his mouth widening into a smile, his teeth sparkling with almost unnatural brilliance.

"No-one messes with me," he said in a companionable tone and promptly closed his eyes again.

Reece felt foolish. There was no way he could match Ben in a fight. He sat glaring at him, cursing under his breath until the train pulled into Euston.

As he followed Ben to the Underground, he was reminded of Thea and experienced a surge of indignation on her behalf. On first meeting her, he'd formed the impression of a forthright belligerent know-all, a girl who was distrustful of the white community. Later, her behaviour had negated this impression. She had softened towards him and was apologetic about her brother's conduct. Clearly, she was devoted to her mother and was doing all she could to look after her sisters, but she was young and attractive and it was unfair that she should be obliged to carry all that responsibility on her shoulders.

When they reached Twickenham Ben shouted a casual 'cheerio' and made off leaving Reece to struggle into a taxi. As it deposited him outside the house in Tennyson Avenue, he came face to face with Connie.

"What the hell's happened to you?" she gasped.

"I met with an accident."

"A likely story! It was Ben, wasn't it?"

"Not exactly."

"What happened then?"

He heaved a sigh. "It's a long story. Look, I'll tell you later; right now, all I want is a bit of shut-eye."

Connie stared at him, blinked, then got out of his way. "Sure, we'll talk later."

CHAPTER FOUR

Megan was depressed. The visit to Thames Ditton hadn't gone well. The next day she telephoned Connie.

"Can we meet?" she burst out without preamble. "Only I don't know what to do. I left my telephone number with Christopher's mother. He hasn't rung up. I don't think she's passed it on to him because I'm sure he'd want to see me." She smothered a sob. "His mother's turning him against me."

Connie's heart sank. To have Megan pouring out her troubles was the last thing she needed. She had a heavy day of classes ahead of her, followed by an evening shift at McDonalds. "Sorry Megan, I can't meet you today. I'll give you a ring tomorrow."

Panic rushed to Megan's voice, bringing out the Welsh lilt. "Not tomorrow. Today, I'm free at half four, can't you meet me for half an hour? Please."

"I'm very busy."

"Please, Connie."

Connie gave a shrug. If she skipped her mime class she could spare the time, but the assessments were due and she was beginning to wish she hadn't got herself involved with Megan.

"All right," she reluctantly agreed.

Megan was waiting for her when Connie left the college. "Let's walk and talk," she suggested. "Only I haven't got much time. Tell me, what exactly did Mrs Mills say?"

"She said Christopher had been very ill and that he wanted to be left in peace; she said he didn't want anything to do with me." Megan shook her head vehemently. "It's not true, I know it's not. She's not being fair to him." She gripped Connie's arm. "Don't you think that it's only right he should get to know his own child. Why is his mother being so hateful?"

Connie pulled herself free from Megan's clasp and said, "I expect she thinks you'll demand money."

Megan's blue eyes widened in astonishment. "I'd never do that," she gasped. "All I want is to show Calum off to Chris, let him get to know his son."

"I know," replied Connie. She glanced at her watch. "I've got to run now. I'll have another talk with Daniel."

"I'm looking for Daniel Mills, do you know where he is?" Connie asked one of the girls she had often seen in Daniel's company.

"Sorry, don't know."

Connie looked at her watch; she was late for class.

"Did you say you were looking for Daniel Mills?" said a voice behind her.

Connie spun round to face a fresh-faced lad carrying a bundle of books under one arm. "Yes," she said. "Do you know where he is?"

"On the playing field, I expect, that's where he usually hangs out. Or down the pub."

"Which pub?"

"I dunno, different ones."

"Which ones?" countered Connie impatiently.

The youth wrinkled his nose. "I dunno, he's not a mate of mine," he protested.

Disappointed, Connie shrugged and turned away.

"Don't take the hump with me. I used to hang out with his brother Chris, that's how I know him."

"Chris? You're a friend of Christopher Mills?"

"Yeah, we used to be good mates only I haven't seen much of him since the…the incident." He started to go through the door into the college.

"Wait!" cried Connie. "What incident?"

The boy tensed, his unwillingness to continue apparent. "Must go, got a lesson in five minutes."

"So have I," snapped Connie. "But it's very important that I speak to Chris. What happened to him? What's this incident you mentioned?"

"I shouldn't have said anything," muttered the boy. "Got to go now."

Connie wasn't so easily put off. Stepping in front of him, she took hold of his arm and said, "What's your name?"

"Robert Parkes."

"Mine's Connie Dixon. Let's meet after college, say four o'clock at the gate."

"What for?"

"I need to find out about Christopher."

"I dunno about that. His parents wanted the whole thing hushed up."

An idea dawned in Connie's mind. Teenagers liked to swank about their conquests, didn't they? Maybe Christopher had bragged to Robert about Megan.

"I'm looking for Christopher for my friend, Megan Hughes," she said casually.

"Megan?" Clearly the name meant something to the boy.

"So he mentioned her to you?"

"Chris talked about her a lot last year," he replied, gaining interest. Then he frowned in puzzlement. "Why? How do you know her? I thought she lived in Wales."

"She used to, but now she's here in Twickenham. Do you think Chris would want to see her?"

The boy looked thoughtful. "He might."

"Look, Robert, it won't matter if you miss your class for once?" said Connie.

"I never skip college," he replied piously.

Connie suppressed a giggle and adopted her most persuasive manner. "Come on, just for once. I'm due in Theatre Studies, so you wouldn't be the only one."

"No," he said firmly.

"After class then. We can go to the café, I'll buy you a Coke."

He grinned. "Okay."

Robert met Connie at the college gates after class. She'd seemed desperate for information and during the lesson he'd thought it through. He would give her the low-down although she would have to pay for it. They walked along the road in silence. He deliberately lengthened his pace but, to his chagrin, Connie was well able to match his stride.

At the café, he let her go in ahead of him. "Two Cokes?" she said to the girl serving them.

"And a large sausage roll and chips," added Robert.

Connie threw him a frosty glance, but when the girl behind the counter looked uncertain, she said, "Go on, give him what he asked for."

They sat down opposite one another across a melamine-topped table, and again Robert had doubts about talking to her.

Connie broke the ice with, "You must be a really good pal of Chris's for him to confide in you about Megan."

"Chris and me have always been close."

"I can understand you not wanting to betray his trust. I promise you anything you tell me is only between you, me and Megan."

He frowned. Was she sending him up? He could feel her gaze on him and felt uncomfortable.

"Did he tell you about Megan when he came back from Swansea?" she asked.

"Yeah." Robert was guarded. "But his mum didn't want them to stay in touch."

"Why not?"

"How should I know?" he mumbled defiantly. "She treats him like a little kid. If it was me, I wouldn't stand for it."

"He was down there while his mother was in hospital, wasn't he?"

"Yeah."

"What was wrong with her?"

"Woman's troubles, you know, but she's always been a bit funny, sort of neurotic."

"So was Chris upset about this veto?"

"Veto?"

"The ban," expounded Connie.

"He sure was. Sulked for weeks just to spite his mother, said he wanted to go back to Wales. Hung around the house getting under her feet. Didn't go anywhere until the weekend of that party."

"What party?"

Robert crammed another mouthful of sausage roll into his mouth and shook his head, mumbling as he ate, "I shouldn't be telling you this."

"Why not, you've come this far, tell me the rest."

He shrugged. "A crowd of us were asked to a party in Shepherds Bush. It was all because of Jason."

"Who's Jason?"

"A schoolmate. He said it was going to be a riot. You know, booze, girls…" He lowered his voice. "A snort or two, nothing heavy."

"This Jason, how did he come to hear about it?"

"His cousin, Nick, was throwing the party while his parents were away. At first, Chris didn't want to go, but things weren't going well at home. His mum and dad were rowing a lot and Chris got caught up in the middle. Daniel's his dad's favourite, you see - always has been - because he's good at sport and pulls the birds. Chris isn't like that. His dad started taking it out on Chris, said he was a wimp. His mum stuck up for him. That made things even worse. Anyway, that weekend, they were really laying into one another. In the end, Chris came with us just to get out of the house."

"What happened when you got there?"

"Nothing much, just the usual disco and dancing."

He knew this wouldn't satisfy Connie. He was stalling for time, trying to marshal his thoughts.

Connie flicked an impatient hand at him, "Go on!"

He stopped cramming food into his mouth and stared at her as it dawned on him that he didn't want to relive the event all over again.

Connie recognised his discomfort. "It's very important to Megan," she urged.

Still he hesitated.

"Well?" encouraged Connie, adding, "I'll make it worth your while."

He was always short of the readies. The monthly allowance his estranged father sent him was invariably spent in the first fortnight. Extra money was tempting and, with the adolescent's aptitude for self-justification, he snatched at the chance to salve his conscience, telling himself that bringing Chris and Megan together again through Connie would be doing them a favour. The fact that it would line his pockets at the same time was beside the point.

"How much?" he asked.

"A tenner?"

"Nah."

"Twenty?"

Keeping his gaze fixed on the floor so as not to show his surprise, he mumbled, "That'll do."

She pulled a note out of her purse and shoved it towards him.

"A fiver!" he exclaimed.

"It's all I've got until tomorrow."

He was trapped. Hoping that Connie would be satisfied with a brief resume rather than a long-winded account, he said, "After all this time, the details are a bit hazy."

In fact, the details were as starkly clear now as they had been then. Connie said nothing, yet he could sense her willing him to get on with the telling of the story.

Pushing aside the fog of reluctance, he started speaking in the present tense, as if the events were happening to him all over again ...

"'Look, there's the house, Chris! Wow, this is going to be some party!'

'Bienvenue!' Some guy greets us, throws out his arms, bows low, theatrical-like. 'Entrez!' he says.

'Who's that moron?' mouths Chris.

'Hi there, you two!' calls a voice. Jason pushes his way through the hall, nudges the idiot aside and says, 'Leave off, Nick, they're friends of mind.' Jason ushers us inside, loads of kids dancing and smoking."

Robert paused to gather his thoughts. Connie urged him on. "What happened next?" she asked.

Doubts began to crowd his mind. "I'm not sure about this," he muttered.

"You can't stop now," hissed Connie.

It was like a game of cat and mouse. Reluctantly, he resumed his story...

"Jason gives us the run-down and leaves us to it.

'I haven't seen any of the kids from school yet?' says Chris. 'Let's go and look for them.'

I don't like this much but I follow Chris and we find the others. That makes me feel better. There's Stephen Buchan, Paul Strang and Andy Maples with two of the girls from our class. And there's two girls I don't know.

'Hiya!' calls out Paul and rolls his eyes. 'Dig this place! They've got everything.'

Hours pass, the music gets louder, the kids go mad, Chris is out of his head, I try to calm him down. 'Some of these guys look really spaced out, Chris. S'pose the police raid the place, we ought to get out while we can.'

'Don't be such a dork, Rob,' he says."

Robert scowled at Connie and muttered indignantly, "You know, when we started out it was Chris who wasn't keen. It just goes to show, you can never tell with people."

Connie gave him a sympathetic smile. "I know, you can't count on anybody."

"After that I lost sight of him ..." Robert's eyes glazed over as he drifted back into the scene ...

"There's this blond chick, she pulls me onto the dance floor; she's quite pretty, but she's wearing horrible scent ..."

He stopped abruptly. "I can't remember any more."

"Liar!" cried Connie, her eyes narrowing. "You mean, you don't want to remember any more."

He stared at her in surprise. How right she was! In fact, this part of the evening was very clear to him. The skinny girl had led him upstairs, retrieved a beaded drawstring bag from one of the bedrooms and offered him a small capsule. With a shrug, he resumed his story ...

"'Want to try it?' she asks.
'What is it?'
She clucks her tongue and says, 'It's E-static!' She thinks she's real clever. Me...I don't want to look like a dork."

"What happened next, Robert?" asked Connie.

"I don't remember anything else until I woke up in the morning. I went to look for the others, couldn't find them. I was dead worried, felt sick, my head ached..."

"In other words, you had a hangover. What did you do then?"

"Well, Nick turned up, remember Nick - Jason's cousin. He said the others had left, so I came home."

Connie looked puzzled. "What's all this got to do with Christopher's illness?"

Robert gave a swallow, seeing a clear picture in his mind's eye of a scene he had not mentioned: drawn blinds; brain-dead music; strangers - North African-looking; handing something out. He'd felt sick, made a dive for the bathroom. They'd gone when he got back.

Connie glowered at him. "Well?" Still, he kept silent. She lost patience. "You've come this far, you may as well tell me the rest. Besides, Megan has the right to know what's happened to Chris." Her words tweaked his conscience. He knew his friend still cared for Megan. Unwillingly, he mumbled about the fleeting appearance of the North Africans.

Connie looked puzzled. "Was Chris at home when you got back?" Robert shook his head. "Where was he?"

"No-one knew."

"What do you mean, no one knew? What about Chris himself?"

"He can't remember."

Connie began to lose patience. "You're not making sense, Robert," she said. "Did you phone Chris when you got home?"

"Course I did. He hadn't got home. To keep my mum quiet, I made up a story about the party, but later that day, Chris' mother phoned my mum saying that he was still missing. Then they all descended on me, asking awkward questions. It was hell." He jutted his chin defiantly. "I honestly thought Chris had left with the others; no-one believed me."

"What about the North Africans? How do they fit in?"

"I dunno. At first I thought I'd dreamt it; the dope and the booze, you know."

"You can't have dreamt something like that. You must remember."

"I don't."

He dried up, feeling angry with himself for agreeing to confide in Connie. He didn't want to fill in the more gruesome details. His thoughts flew to his large airy bedroom with the state-of-the-art playstation his father had recently given him. The constant vying for his favour was the up-side of being the only child of divorced parents. All he wanted to do was go home and lose himself in a world of techno-fantasy.

Pushing back his chair, he picked up his school bag and muttered, "I've got to go now."

"Wait a minute!" snapped Connie. "You haven't told me what actually happened to Christopher. You *do* know, I can see you do."

When the waitress came to clear the table, Robert saw his chance to sneak away.

"See you around," he said, making for the door.

Connie was too quick for him. Catching hold of his sleeve, she shouted, "Hang on, you little toe-rag, you've only told me half the story. That wasn't the agreement."

"Well, you've only given me a quarter of the money," retorted Robert.

"Stop being picky."

Robert dropped his schoolbag to the floor and sat down again.

"Come on, out with it?" she insisted.

"Not until you cough up the rest of the dough."

"Don't be such a bean-head, Robert, I told you, you'll get it tomorrow."

Robert gave in under his interrogator's grilling. "Chris was missing for two days," he mumbled.

"Speak up," ordered Connie, pulling her chair in and leaning across the table.

"Mr Mills called the Police, Jason's parents were contacted. No one knew what had happened to Chris. His mother was frantic."

"I'm not surprised' gasped the girl. "How long ago did this happen?"

"Getting on for a year."

"Wow! He could only have been about 16 at the time."

In a perverse way, Robert began to enjoy the drama of the situation. Resting his elbows on the table, he too leant forward until his head was almost touching Connie's. If the end of the story were going to be told, he figured, it may as well be told with a touch of the theatrical. Speaking conspiratorially, he went on: "His father stayed home from work for two days, waiting ..." He paused for effect. "Then, on the third morning, the phone rang. Guess who it was?"

Connie's eyes widened. "Christopher? Where was he phoning from?"

"From a phone box on the edge of Hampstead Heath; begged his father to go and pick him up; couldn't explain where he'd been." Their heads were so close now that when a lock of his hair fell forward it brushed against Connie's wiry fringe. "He'd completely lost two days."

"What happened then?" breathed Connie. The mystery of the situation was beginning to make her think that perhaps it was worth the money. She hoped Megan could fork out twenty pounds.

"His father drove up to London, found him collapsed, rushed him to hospital. Guess what they found?"

Connie banged the flat of her hand on the table. "Bugger the guessing game?" she exploded. "Just tell me."

"He'd had a kidney removed!" Robert was jubilant now. He'd completely dismissed his earlier reluctance to tell the story. "Those North Africans, you see, they were body part racketeers. 'Course, Nick and Jason denied any knowledge of them, said they'd gate-crashed the party."

"What happened to Chris?"

"He nearly died. They kept him in the ICU for weeks. They made another discovery you see ..." Again, he paused for dramatic effect. "Guess what?"

"Not again!" Connie cast her gaze heavenwards in exasperation.

"They found out his other kidney wasn't working properly."

Now she looked shocked. "Surely even unscrupulous villains like that wouldn't have chanced taking both kidneys? They could have ended up on a murder charge!"

"The hospital said he must have been born with one faulty kidney, but because the other one was working properly nobody knew. Now, he's waiting for a transplant, goes on dialysis three times a week."

Connie sank back in her chair. "My God, no wonder his mother's so protective!"

Robert left the café in a mood of exhilaration. Connie had been well impressed. It wasn't very often that girls listened to what he had to say, especially girls who were older than him. And he was better off by twenty quid, or he would be when Connie got back to him with the rest of it.

But his mood changed as he walked along. The unpleasant taste of disloyalty filled his mouth. The Mills family hadn't wanted the story spread around. In fact, Mrs Mills had been reluctant to let him visit the house afterwards even though he'd always been welcome there before. When he did start seeing Christopher again his friend seemed different: lifeless, drained of spirit. He recalled a confidence Chris had shared with him. "I like Megan a lot, Robert. I wonder what she's doing now. She promised to try and get a university place in the London area if she got good enough A-Levels."

This memory helped to restore Robert's self-esteem. Connie, he reasoned, had given him the opportunity to make amends. Megan's presence in the area might somehow aid Chris's recovery.

CHAPTER FIVE

"Connie!"

Startled, Connie looked around and saw a woman standing a few feet away. She knew the voice at once.

"Auntie Della!" Her eyes widened in amazement. The woman looked chic in a stylish suit and high-heeled sandals, an expensive crocodile bag slung over her shoulder.

She stepped forward, a hand outstretched and said, with a pronounced lisp, "So you still remember me, the black sheep of the family!"

"Of course I remember you," gasped Connie. "But where have you been all this time? I thought Mum lost touch with you years ago."

"Well," grinned the woman. "Just like the proverbial bad penny, I've turned up again."

"Did Mum tell you where to find me?"

"No, I phoned your brother at school."

"Tim? So you must have been in touch with Mum too?" She smiled happily. "I bet she was thrilled to hear from you."

"I'm not so sure about that."

A questioning frown drew Connie's brows together. "What d'you mean?"

Her doubts were swiftly swept aside as Della threw open her arms and cried out, "Come and give your long-lost Auntie a hug. The last time I saw you, why, you were barely knee-high to a grasshopper. Now look at you!"

Laughing, they hugged one another and as they drew apart, Della said, "Where's the nearest pub? Let's go and have a drink."

Linking arms, they headed for the pub where, over a ploughman's and a couple of glasses of wine, Connie found herself warming to her unexpected visitor. As the lunch-time regulars began to leave, Connie glanced at her watch. "I must go, I've got at least two hours study ahead of me. It's been so nice seeing you. Where are you staying?"

Della pulled a face. "That's the trouble," she said. "I haven't found anywhere yet."

"Don't worry, there's a nice hotel down by the river, and it's quite reasonable by all accounts."

Della's gaze shifted away from her niece's candid scrutiny. "I was wondering," she ventured. "Whether you could put me up for a night or two."

Connie gulped back her dismay. "I'd love to, but my digs are awfully cramped and..." She hesitated in embarrassment, wondering how with such a fun-loving relative in situ, she would find time to do any studying. "Honestly, there's hardly room to swing a cat."

Della's pout of disappointment was only fleeting. Switching to coercion, she mewed, "I wouldn't get in your way. I'd be as quiet as a mouse. I wouldn't be a chatterbox or leave my undies all over the place. Please, Connie darling, please."

"It's not that you wouldn't be welcome," Connie rushed to explain. "But I need time to study. I can't afford distractions. I'd have to leave you to your own devices. You'd be awfully bored."

"No I wouldn't, just sit me in the corner in front of the TV."

"Della, I can't study with the television on."

"I'll read a magazine or something."

"Can't you book in at a hotel. We can meet up again for a meal?"

Della sniffed and drew out a crumpled tissue from her bag. "I haven't any money."

"What?"

"It's only temporary," she lisped. "The cheque's due in a day or two."

"The cheque?"

"The alimony."

"You're divorced?"

"Twice wed, twice divorced."

The determination to spend the afternoon studying had by now been mentally cancelled from Connie's schedule. "Twice married and divorced?" she gasped.

Della brushed her matrimonial disasters aside. "They were both useless guys." She leant towards her niece. "Please let me stay, Connie. I've been doing a lot of travelling lately. I'm fed-up with always being on the move."

The pleading tone made Connie feel guilty. After all, Della was her mother's sister. She could hardly turn her away. Besides, her aunt's history was beginning to intrigue her. She caved in. "In that case, there's no question of your looking for somewhere else to stay. Come home with me; I'll sort something out."

Della's mascara-fringed lashes widened, "Are you sure?"

"Yes, of course."

"I promise I won't be any trouble."

With a sigh of resignation, Connie cast her long-lost relative a sideways glance, instinct telling her that Della could not be relied upon to keep her promise.

As they went into her room Connie experienced a rush of shame. The place was untidy with dirty laundry strewn across the unmade bed and unwashed mugs adorning every available surface. The tattered curtains were faded, their original pattern barely recognisable; cobwebs had gathered high up in the corners forming a network between the holiday postcards stuck on one wall and the *avant-garde* posters pinned to its neighbour. Judging by her aunt's appearance, she wouldn't be used to slumming it.

"Sorry about the mess," she said apologetically, dumping down her rucksack and showing concern for her visitor by sweeping the contents of the armchair onto the floor with one arm, whilst kicking a pile of magazines and cushions aside with her foot.

"Don't worry on my account," replied Della.

Connie switched on the television, then hurried to put the kettle on. "Tea or coffee?" she called from behind the curtain partitioning off the kitchen.

"Tea please."

"Where have you left your luggage?" asked Connie emerging again, a mug in each hand.

"In a locker at the station. I'll have to go and get it after I've drunk my tea." She favoured Connie with a coy smile. "Don't let me stop you studying. Hand me the remote, I'll turn the TV right down low."

"Never mind," replied Connie. "I'll get some work done while you're out collecting your luggage."

Connie's hint brought no move from Della. She seemed in no hurry to claim her belongings. Instead, she continued to chatter inanely until, worn out, she dozed off in the armchair. Sleep makes no allowance for age, thought Connie wistfully as she studied her aunt in slumber. Della's baby-pink mohair sweater had parted company at the waist, revealing a spare tyre as her bosom rose and fell with each shuddering breath. From above her head, Connie could detect a trace or two of grey in the flaxen hair. Poor Auntie Della was sure as hell putting up a brave fight against the onset of middle age, she mused. Her thoughts turned to her mother. Ten years older than Della, Linda was far less absorbed with her appearance, yet she always looked good.

How lucky she'd been! Connie lost herself in reflection. Adopted as a baby by Linda and Steve Dixon, she had known nothing except love and stability. Even when Tim came along, her adopted parents had continued to lavish affection on her. She'd often wondered why they'd chosen to adopt a baby of mixed race rather than an English child.

She studied her aunt and felt puzzled. She'd always been a bit of an enigma, coming and going in her life until she had reached the age of nine, then one day, she'd vanished altogether. Linda had met her daughter's questions with: *Aunt Della's gone away to a far off country.*

Her visitor gave a grunt and blinked. "Sorry, did I drop off?" She rubbed a fist across her eyes, then noticing the mascara smudge on her knuckles, delved into her bag and hastily repaired the damage.

"You'd better go and get your luggage," said Connie. "I'd come with you, but I must get some work done."

Della stood up and smoothed her short black skirt down over her thighs. As she wriggled her feet back into the stilettos, Connie saw she had good legs. Still half asleep, she tottered to the door and, with a desultory wave in Connie's direction, made her way carefully down the wooden staircase.

Reece passed her coming up, both of them squeezing flat against the banisters as they met. Connie saw her aunt flutter her eyelashes at him and felt sickened. How could this middle-aged woman dress like a 20-year-old yet employ the flirting techniques of the 1950's? Despite her up-to-date gear and her spiky hairdo, Connie couldn't see Della as a ladette, knocking back the pints of lager. No, she would perch on the bar stool and demand g&t's.

Quickly closing her bedroom door, Connie leant her back against it, hoping that Reece would be discreet enough not to disturb her. It was not to be. Seconds later, she heard his tap on the door.

"Go away, I'm busy." she called out.

"Who's the visitor?" asked Reece.

"My long-lost aunt."

"You must be joking. Open up, and tell me about her."

"Piss off!" she started to say, then checked herself. If Reece really was still on speaking terms with Ben, perhaps he could be persuaded to shack up in his flat for a couple of days so that Della could use his room. She'd even shift the television set in there for her.

Flinging open her door, she caught Reece just as he was about to shut his.

"Sorry, didn't mean to snap at you," she said contritely. "How's the foot?"

"Not too bad."

"Good. Actually, I wanted to ask you a favour."

"Yes?"

"My aunt's got no-where to stay so I wondered if she could use your room."

"Where am I supposed to sleep? Oh, you mean ..." He raised his eyebrows hopefully.

"No I don't! I mean, you could bunk down with Ben for a few days."

Reece's mouth dropped open. "But, but ..." he started to say.

"You said the fight wasn't with Ben."

"It wasn't really."

She glared accusingly into his eyes. "Then you're still speaking to him?"

His denial was half-hearted. "Sort of."

"Come on, out with it."

Briefly, Reece recounted the sequence of events that had taken place in Birmingham. When he'd finished, Connie nodded wisely. "Ben's like that. He'll have forgotten about your little fracas by now."

"But I haven't," snapped Reece.

Connie assumed a pleading air. "Come on, Reece, it's not like you to bear a grudge."

"Suppose he says no."

Connie smiled confidently. "He won't."

Reece scratched his head thoughtfully, then reluctantly agreed. "Okay, but just for a day or two." His mood changed. "Wow! I still can't believe she's your aunt; she doesn't look much older than you."

Connie felt insulted and protested indignantly, "She's in her late forties with two failed marriages behind her. If you were to take a closer look at her, you wouldn't be so enthusiastic."

"She looks a right little raver to me."

"Appearances can be deceptive," hissed Connie. Then as if to counter an unspoken criticism of her family, she rushed on with machine-gun rapidity, "Of course, my mum isn't a bit like Della. You'd never believe they were sisters. Mum's got her feet firmly on the ground and she and Dad are really happy together."

Reece looked taken aback. "I wasn't suggesting ... only, this is the first time you've ever mentioned your parents and when you told me you'd left home at sixteen, I rather assumed you'd left in a huff."

"Not at all," declared Connie. "I had to leave because Dad got a job abroad, and with my brother at boarding school, there was really no point in staying on in Steyning."

She started to busy herself, collecting up the dirty mugs, and making it clear that she wanted him to leave. When he didn't take the hint, she said, "I'm afraid you'll have to go now. I've got absolutely loads to do before Della gets back."

After he'd left, Connie re-ran their conversation. She'd been completely taken aback by her aunt's arrival and had ended up telling Reece more than she'd intended to. Of course, she'd been thrifty with the truth but, nonetheless, she had unwittingly allowed this warm-hearted Canadian red head to prise open a little chink in her protective armour. A string of nostalgia wound itself around her heart, pulling tighter the knot of guilt which had been with her since the death of her paternal grandmother a year earlier. Instead of knuckling down to her course work, she allowed her thoughts to wing back to when, at sixteen, she'd been left in Grannie Vera's care after Steve and Linda had departed for the Middle East. She remembered how she had rebelled against the out-dated discipline meted out by her elderly relation. The business study course, in which she had been persuaded to enrol, had proved too humdrum for her lively temperament and, after a row with her grandmother, she had stalked out of sixth form college half way through the term and run away to London.

Linda had made an impromptu visit to the UK in an attempt to urge her back to the safety of Sussex, Grannie Vera and the college course, but Connie had resolutely refused to return to her former life. Although hurt and concerned, her mother had had no choice other than to return to Bahrain, leaving her headstrong daughter to sort out her own life in the big city.

Poor Mum, thought Connie, I really wasn't fair to her when I decided to make my own way. But full of the self-confidence of youth, she'd found work, first as a waitress, then as a barmaid -- lying about her age -- and, eventually, when a photographer with suspect credentials spotted her at a disco, as an artist's model. Older and wiser now, she reflected that, in retrospect, the chances she'd taken were a recipe for disaster. She gave a little shudder recalling that, as the poses expected of her became more pornographic and less artistic, she had pushed doubts aside deciding that the money was good and it enabled her to move into better digs, buy the latest fashions and try out the most outrageous cosmetics. She'd persuaded herself that most actresses started out as models; that the catwalk was the gateway to a career on the stage.

It wasn't until the day a male model was introduced into the shooting that she decided enough was enough and, hurriedly grabbing her belongings, she'd headed for the door, still zipping up her jeans and pulling on her sweatshirt.

Toby, the photographer, had run after her pleading, "Come back, Connie, it'll be all right. You'll get used to it. The pay's good, far better than modelling on your own."

"Stuff the pay," she'd called back.

"You're making a big mistake, girl. You don't get opportunities like this everyday."

She'd made an obscene gesture, making Toby lose his temper. "Okay, piss off then, you silly cow. I never thought much of you any way. Too skinny, no tits!"

Fury kept her going for the rest of the day, until by late afternoon, practicalities had begun to worm their way into her mind. The rent was due, so was her Visa account, the gas bill, the telephone account, to say nothing of the next catalogue payment. She hadn't any ready cash and hunger pangs gnawed at her stomach.

Searching in every nook and cranny of her room, she had managed to salvage three pounds fifty. It had seemed like a fortune. Her spirits had soared. If she'd managed to hang out in the big city thus far -- she'd left college with only £50 in her purse -- then she could and would do it again. What was to stop her finding a job as a proper fashion model? Of course, it hadn't worked out that way. She'd ended up down-grading her digs and working at McDonalds, which is where she had met Ben. It was Ben who encouraged her to enrol in the Drama Course as a mature student.

Three hours elapsed before Della returned. Connie was beginning to think that her wayward aunt had disappeared from her life as suddenly as she had come into it. She couldn't make up her mind whether she was relieved or disappointed.

"Sorry I've been so long," sang out Della as she breezed through the door.

"Where's your luggage?" asked Connie.

"Downstairs in the hall. I thought that nice young man might be persuaded to carry it upstairs for me. Is he your boyfriend?"

"The answer's no, he isn't my boyfriend and he's got an injured foot so he can't carry it up for you."

"Oh dear, what am I going to do?"

"I'll fetch it," said Connie with a resigned sigh.

She ran downstairs and heaved her aunt's bulging suitcase up to the top floor, dumping it down outside Reece's bedroom.

"You'll be sleeping in here," she said. "Reece has agreed to move in with a mate for a couple of nights."

"Gee, that's real swell of him," replied Della and, with her slip into Americanisms, Connie realised that her aunt was well and truly tanked up. No wonder she had taken so long to collect her luggage! She swallowed her irritation: drink cost money, money that could have been spent on a hotel room.

She nudged the suitcase into Reece's room and, taking Della by the elbow, propelled her into the armchair in her own bedroom. "I'll make some coffee, you look as though you could do with it," she said pointedly, not objecting when her aunt snatched up the remote and switched on the TV. "You can take the television in the other room with you this evening. I won't be needing it, what with all the reading I've got to catch up on. I'll fix us an early meal, nothing fancy, something out of the freezer."

"Oh," called back Della. "I forgot to tell you, I'm a vegan."

"What?" shrieked Connie.

"It's all right, honey, I can make do with beans on toast."

A rush of anger made Connie bite her lip. Count to ten, she told herself.

"Did you say something, hon?"

"No," groaned Connie.

At half past seven, Della yawned and obligingly went into the adjoining bedroom to sink onto the bed fully clothed. After she'd gone, Connie found it difficult to concentrate. The elation with which she had originally greeted her long-lost relative had waned. Della was proving to be a nuisance. At ten o'clock, she gave up trying to study and closed the book, wishing now that she hadn't so readily handed over the television.

She fed a Cher CD into the stereo and flung herself onto the bed, hands laced behind her head. Just as she was dosing off, there was a knock on the door.

"Come in," she called.

Della stood in the doorway. She was wearing a lilac satin dressing gown; her feet were bare. "Fancy a nip before bed-time?" She winked and brought out a bottle of red wine from behind her back. "We can have a girlie chat."

"I'm awfully tired," protested Connie, sitting up and dangling her legs to the floor. "I really need to get some kip."

Disappointment clouded Della's brow. "What a shame! We need to get to know one another, don't we?"

"There's time for that."

"Come on, Conchita."

Connie noticed that the American accent had vanished with her aunt's return to sobriety.

"Don't call me Conchita."

"Sorry."

Unwillingly, Connie yielded to the inevitable: a girlie chat heavily weighted on her aunt's side. During their entire conversation, Della kept topping up her own drink, but omitted to replenish her niece's. Connie's reactions were swift enough to forestall her.

"Are you a lady of leisure now?" asked Connie once she could get a word in edgewise.

"Lady of leisure? Chance would be a fine thing! I could teach you a lot about forging a good career for yourself, Connie. D'you know, I've worked in advertising, sales, tourism, waitressing..." The list continued, interrupted only by the occasional gulp of wine.

As the evening wore on, Connie grew more and more impatient as, through a stream of increasingly incoherent sentences, she learnt that neither of her aunt's marriages had lasted more than a few months, that the errant husbands were both Americans and that before, during, between and after the divorces, she had gone through a succession of boyfriends.

"Men!" sighed Della. "If only we could do without them!"

Connie allowed the yawn she had been stifling to overwhelm her. Della didn't appear to notice. When her head started to droop forward onto the collar of the satin robe, Connie pinched her arm. "Wake up, you can't go to sleep here. Come on, I'll help you into bed."

Della's eyes blinked open. "I'm not tired," she protested, putting out a hand for the wine bottle. Connie deftly swept it out of her reach.

"You sure are a chip off the old block, Conchita baby," chuckled Della.

Connie looked startled. "What d'you mean?"

Della flicked a limp wrist. "Nothing, I didn't mean anything."

Feeling agitated, Connie plucked at her aunt's sleeve. "Yes you did."

"It was nothing, a slip of the tongue."

But Connie wouldn't let the matter rest. "You know my real parents," she accused. "You know who my biological parents are. Why else would you have said that?"

"Stop going on about it."

"I can't. If you know, you must tell me."

All at once, Della's lethargy evaporated. "I suppose you have a right to know the truth," she said. Her accent was English again, although the irritating little girl lisp was still there. "I don't know how you're going to take it." She looked up at Connie through half-closed lids. "But...now you're all grown up, you should be told the truth."

Connie could hardly control her curiosity. She sprang up and stood towering above her aunt, her fists clenched down at her sides and shouted, "For God's sake, tell me!"

"There's no need to shout."

Della wriggled awkwardly and Connie saw indecision flicker across her face. "I can't tell you, Linda would never forgive me," she muttered. "I promised never to tell you."

Seething with anger, Connie grasped her aunt's wrists and shook her vigorously. "You can't leave it like this. If you don't tell me, I shall email Mum," she shouted.

"Don't do that!" Della's eyes widened in panic.

"Well then?"

Della straightened her back as she prepared herself to drop her bombshell. "Would it surprise you to know that I'm your real mother."

It took Connie several seconds to take in this revelation. She leapt away as if stung. Within two feet of her sat a blowsy forty-five year old clinging desperately to her youth. Nervous red-tipped fingernails stroked ridges into the pancake make-up as tears welled and mascara began to trace rivulets down the beginning-to-sag cheeks. Connie shook her head in an attempt to clear her mind. Her mother, her real mother!

"I don't believe you," she gulped at last.

"I knew you'd be surprised."

"It can't be true."

"But it is," insisted Della. "You see, Linda and Steve adopted you as a tiny baby."

"Why?"

"To hush up the scandal. I can show you the adoption papers if you like."

Any warmth Connie might have felt for this pathetic creature was crushed under an overwhelming weight of hatred. Pointing at the door, she screamed, "Get out!"

Looking scared, Della scrambled to her feet and fled from the room. Connie slammed the door shut after her and stood staring into space. All her life she had planned to one day look for her real parents, but love and respect for Linda and Steve had held her back. Out of the blue, the past had reared its ugly head and slapped her in the face.

Her wayward aunt had suddenly become her mother. Instead of filling her with joy, the knowledge almost choked her. With a howl of despair, she threw herself on top of the bed and wept. But as the sobs subsided, curiosity began to take hold. If Della was her mother, then her father must be black. Who was he?

Without thinking, she barged into Della's room and shook her awake.

"What's the matter," she mumbled. "Don't you know it's the middle of the night?"

"I need some answers...and you're going to give them to me. You owe me that much," retorted Connie.

"I shouldn't have told you,"

"Well you did, so now you can tell me the rest. Who's my father? Where is he?"

"What d'you want to know about him for?"

Connie clenched her fists, trying to remain calm. "Because I have a right to know."

"Can't it wait until the morning?"

"No, it bloody well can't."

Realising there was no way she could get out of the situation, Della sat up. "Let's be civilised about this, talk over a drink. Is there any of that wine left?"

"A cup of tea, in my room," snapped Connie.

Given no choice, Della got out of bed and followed Connie into the next room.

An uneasy silence hovered over the two women as Connie set about making tea. As she poured the boiling water onto the tea bags, she tried to formulate her questions. She remembered snippets of conversations from the past, when Linda had remarked to Steve that Della was the most unpredictable person she had ever known.

Handing her the mug of tea, she said, "Tell me how it all began."

Della brushed a hand across her face. She looked terrible. Traces of make-up combined with tearstains had given her pert prettiness a blotchy slackness. Her bleached hair stood on end.

She prefaced her explanation, with, "I was very naive, you know."

"How old were you?"

"Eighteen."

"Go on."

"When my boyfriend, Lenny, asked me to go on holiday with him to Rio de Janeiro -- he'd had an unexpected windfall, you see -- naturally I wanted to go. What an uproar that caused! Your grandparents were furious, but the more they tried to stop me, the more determined I was." She glanced at Connie, realising the need for further explanation. "Back then, it wasn't the done thing for a teenager to go half way across the world with her boyfriend. Nowadays they are much more streetwise. Where was I? Oh yes, I wouldn't let that stop me." She gave a lop-sided smile and said defiantly, "Nothing will stop me once I've made up my mind."

Connie experienced a flicker of conscience, recognising her own stubbornness. "Go on," she urged.

"Everything was fine at first, but when Lenny started giving those bikini-clad Brazilian girls the eye - with their fantastic figures and lovely skin -- I couldn't take any more. Well ..." She threw out an arm. "Look at you!"

Connie wrinkled her brow. "Get on with it."

"We had the most awful row. I stalked out and went for a walk along the beach and...that's how I met your father."

"On the beach? Just like that?"

"We were attracted to one another at once."

"What was he like, this beach bum?"

"He wasn't a beach bum and he was tall and good-looking!"

"Tall, good-looking! For God's sake, Della, what else? What was his name?"

"Javier de Oliveira Figueres."

"Javier de ... ?"

"It's Portuguese, that's what they speak in Brazil."

I know that," blinked Connie indignantly. "But who was he, what did he do for a living?"

"He was a famous footballer. Well, not famous then, but he became famous later."

This fairy-tale description of her father left Connie breathless. "Where is he now?" she gasped.

"In Rio I suppose."

"Is he married?"

Della shrugged. "I don't know."

Connie lost patience. "Don't you care?"

Della dropped her gaze and began to fiddle with the edge of her dressing gown. She seemed to have lost the urge to confide. Was her conscience tweaking her, thought Connie, after all, she had broken her promise to Linda.

"Well?"

"We didn't get around to exchanging confidences."

"Della, for God's sake explain," cried Connie.

"We met on the beach. It was a beautiful moonlit evening. We started talking ..." She uttered a dreamy sigh. "He was so attractive, had a fantastic body. Where was I? I told him I'd quarrelled with my boyfriend so he offered to take me to a nightclub. I wouldn't go at first, although he was very persuasive. We danced until the early hours, I drank a bit too much, then ... we made love."

"Where? Where did you make love? In a hotel room, in his house?"

"Stop badgering me."

"I must know. You don't seem to realise what a shock you've given me. I never expected to meet up with my real parents. I was totally unprepared..." croaked Connie.

"I don't remember where."

Connie sprang up and stamped her foot on the thread-bare carpet. "Don't lie, you must remember."

"For Christ's sake, give over. It was on the beach, if you must know. It was very romantic, with waves gently lapping the shore and a starry sky above."

"How could you?"

"It wasn't my fault. He got me drunk."

"Haven't you got any self-control?"

"I was young and impressionable. Look, I'm tired, let's talk again tomorrow."

But nothing was going to stop Connie from hammering on with her questioning. "What did you do about Lenny?"

"I went back to him. We made it up and spent the rest of the holiday together."

"What about this other man, my father?"

"I never saw him again."

"So you're saying I'm the result of a one-night stand!" gulped Connie, stifling back the tears. "What happened when you found out you were pregnant?"

"I assumed it was Lenny's, only by then we'd split up." Della leant forward and grasped Connie's hands. "Linda was marvellous," she gushed. "She and Steve stood by me. Even when you were born and it was obvious Lenny wasn't the father, Linda refused to let you go to strangers."

Connie felt mesmerised. She could hear Della's voice droning on, but the words made no sense. Shaking her hands free, she shouted. "For heaven's sake, shut up!"

"I thought you wanted to know everything. Can't you see, I couldn't do anything else, I couldn't bring you up myself, could I?"

"You could have stayed around to see how I was getting on," she shrieked. "You could have taken an interest in me even if it meant keeping up the pretence; come to see my school plays, turned up on my birthday parties, brought me Christmas presents."

"I did what I could. It wasn't easy for me." Della pouted defiantly. "I wish I'd never told you."

"So do I," snapped Connie. "You're twenty-six years too late with your mothering instincts. You've turned my life upside down and I hate you for it. I wish you'd had a termination."

"Don't say that, Conchita."

"Stop calling me Conchita!"

"It's your name."

"I hate it, especially now I know why I've got a foreign name. I bet it was your idea!"

"It was as a matter of a fact. It was the one thing I insisted on." Della shrugged. "But, of course, it got shortened to Connie."

"My whole life's been a lie," wailed Connie.

"It hasn't, nothing's changed. You're still the same person; to you and the world Linda and Steve will always be your mum and dad."

This was the first piece of commonsense Della had uttered. It wrenched Connie from emotional turmoil, turning acute pain into a throbbing ache. All she wanted was to be left alone to nurse her wounds. "Get out! I never want to see you again. Get out of here tomorrow morning; leave while I'm at college."

When Della didn't move, she took her arm in a strong grip and propelled her to the door.

Della's tears flowed uncontrolled. "Please, Connie, please," she begged. "Give me a chance. Let me make it up to you. All those lost years..."

Connie hardened her heart. Pushing her outside, she didn't even wait for Della to go into the other room before closing the door and ramming a chair up against it. The expected attempt at re-entry came.

"Go away," called Connie.

"Please, baby, let me in."

The timid tapping became a hammering.

"Stop it, you'll wake the rest of the house."

"How can you be so cruel after all I've been through," wept Della, her voice filled with dramatic pathos. Through her pain, Connie gave a bitter smile, recognising where her own acting ability had come from.

CHAPTER SIX

Connie moved through the next day in a trance. After a sleepless night, she got up early. Somehow she managed to communicate with her college friends, but she couldn't concentrate on the lectures. She didn't leave the college premises at lunchtime afraid that Della would be waiting for her at the gate. At four she sneaked out under cover of a group of second-year students and headed for McDonalds, unwilling to go straight home in case Della had put off leaving. To encourage her aunt's departure, she had added to her overdraft by drawing out thirty pounds and slipping it under Della's bedroom door.

In the restaurant doorway, she came face-to-face with Reece.

He scowled at her and said, "Where've you been? Everyone's been looking for you."

"Who?"

"Ben, for one."

"What does he want?"

"A shift change I think."

"Is that all?

"No."

"Who else?"

"Some girl. She's still in there. Says you promised to meet her yesterday."

"Megan! Hell's teeth! I completely forgot about it."

"You'd better not keep her waiting any longer; she looks pretty upset."

"I can't see her now." Without explanation, Connie turned her back on Reece and began walking away.

He hobbled after her. "Wait a minute, I haven't finished. When can I have my room back?"

"Tonight with any luck."

"Connie," he called as she started to walk away again. "What's happened? You seem upset."

Half-turning, she brushed off his concern by retorting, "It's nothing."

Reece wouldn't let her go. "What about that girl? She's quite pathetic. If she's one of your lame ducks you can't just abandon her."

Connie stopped mid-stride, remembering the awful disclosure she had heard from Robert. She owed it to Megan to put her out of her misery.

However terrible the news was, she would at least know that circumstances beyond Christopher's control had been the reason for his unwillingness to see her. She wouldn't be left harbouring the belief that he didn't care about her.

"Look, Reece," she said. "Do me a favour, tell Megan I'll meet her tomorrow without fail."

Reece looked puzzled by her change of attitude. "Okay," he agreed, then added diffidently, "You're very on edge. What's up with you?"

She shrugged. "I told you, nothing. Why should there be?"

Megan Hughes twisted the corner of her paper napkin as she waited in McDonalds for Connie. All her hopes were pinned on what her friend had been able to find out. She'd been desperate the day before when Reece had told her Connie wasn't coming.

"Hello, Megan." This time, Connie arrived as promised. "Sorry about yesterday. Look, we can't talk here; it's far too noisy. Let's go along to that pub down the road."

Megan felt alarmed by her friend's serious expression. "What have you found out?" she begged, as soon as they sat down in a quiet corner of the pub.

"It's not good news, I'm afraid," replied Connie.

Megan clapped a hand to her mouth.

Connie swallowed hard before giving the girl a potted version of her conversation with Robert, the narrative frequently intercepted by Megan's smothered gasps of "No, please God, no."

When she'd finished, Megan shook her head in disbelief and muttered, "It can't be true. It's like a TV drama. Things like that don't happen in real life."

"That's what I thought at first," agreed Connie.

"But you believe it now?"

"Christopher's state of health bears out Robert's story."

"But it's terrible. They shouldn't be allowed to get away with it. Surely the Police can do something."

"According to Robert, they're looking into it. These cases are almost impossible to follow up unless the victim can remember some of the circumstances."

"Surely an operation like that had to be carried out in hospital! Which one did they take him to?"

"Your guess is as good as mine," shrugged Connie. "It must have been somewhere in the London area."

"Ask Robert, he might know," implored the Welsh girl.

"I don't think so. He said the Police know there are illegal clinics set up in various parts of the country, but it's difficult to track them down. These body-part dealers are very clever."

"Body-part dealers!" Megan's features screwed up in disgust. "That's dreadful, that makes Christopher sound like a piece of meat."

Connie sighed. "To tell you the truth, Megan, Robert is as upset as you are."

The other girl cast her a scathing glance. "He's only a mate, and not a very good one by the sound of things. He doesn't love Chris like I do."

There was no answer to that. After a moment's silence, Connie said, "Robert told me he didn't see what went on because he felt sick and had to make a dash for the loo."

Megan accepted this with ill-disguised distrust. "Why Christopher? Why not one of the others?" she muttered.

Connie's heart convulsed. She'd asked herself the same question. "He was unlucky," she replied. "After all, they could have chosen any of the people at that party. Perhaps Chris was more out of it than the others, easier to coerce into going with them. Was he into drugs?"

Megan's mind flew back to their idyllic days in Swansea. Christopher was always in the front line for a snort, and he got drunk easily. She gave an inward shudder. Wasn't it the drink that had landed her in the club?

"I must see him," she gasped. "I'll go tomorrow."

"Don't be too hasty," advised Connie. "I think you should phone his mother first, or maybe write her a letter, make friends with her. Show her you're truly concerned."

"What makes you think she'll believe me?" Megan shook her head. "No, I've got a better idea. I'm going to watch the house, wait until she goes out, then pounce. She's not going to stop me seeing Chris this time."

"You don't know how this experience has affected him. You'll have to be careful how you break the news. He may not take kindly to fatherhood," warned Connie.

"Nonsense, he'll be delighted." Megan looked defiant. "He really loves me, you know."

"I don't doubt it," fibbed Connie. "But after the terrible experience he's had this added shock might prove too much for him."

They argued for half an hour, but no amount of counselling would deter Megan. Shedding her little-girl-lost apparel, she donned the robe of determination and brushed off Connie's well-intentioned advice. "Don't think I don't appreciate what you've found out, but now it's up to me."

"Okay, do things your way. Don't come crying to me when you fall flat on your face," warned Connie, adding with a touch of sarcasm, "What do you intend to do with the babies while you're spying on the Mills family, trail them along with you?"

Megan pouted. "I'll think of something."

It was only after they'd separated that Connie remembered she hadn't asked Megan for the twenty pounds.

By the time Megan got back to Strawberry Vale, her confidence had ebbed. Connie was right. It simply wasn't practical to carry out a watch on Mrs Mills' movements.

To her surprise, Connie phoned the next day. "If it's any help," she said. "I bumped into Robert at college this morning and he said, Mrs Mills works each morning from nine to mid-day. You'll probably find Christopher on his own then." She paused, before adding, "I'm not sure my telling you this is a good idea, although I suppose you would have found out in the end anyway."

"Thanks, Connie," said Megan.

Luck played into her hands. Lorraine Goddard had taken a few days off work so Megan was able to make her way to Thames Ditton with Calum in the single pushchair. It was mid-morning when she arrived at the house. She rang the bell several times before the door was opened. When it was, she almost recoiled in shock. Christopher stood facing her. But this Christopher wasn't the tall, healthy sun-tanned teenager with sparkling eyes and a ready smile. This Christopher was thin, pasty-complexioned and dull-eyed. At first, he didn't seem to know her.

"Hello Chris," she said.

It must have been her lilting accent which stirred recognition. He gasped in surprise and leant against the door jamb.

"Can I come in?" she asked, taking the initiative.

"Yes, of course."

He stepped back and watched while she struggled to haul the buggy over the doorstep. He seemed completely mesmerised by her unexpected appearance.

"In here," he said, pushing open the door to a large kitchen/breakfast room and inviting her to sit down at a table in the centre. She pushed the buggy through and removed the dummy from Calum's mouth.

For the first time, the hint of a smile showed on Christopher's lips. "He's a nice little lad," he said. "Are you looking after him for someone?"

Megan swallowed. Clearly his mother and brother had not told him about Calum.

"He's mine," she replied hesitantly. "Well, actually, he's ours."

This information didn't register with Christopher. He appeared vague and preoccupied. Connie's words of warning came back, prompting Megan to tread carefully. Although she longed to question him about his terrible experience, she held back, asking tentatively, "How are you, Chris? I heard you'd been ill?"

Once the conversation was focused on his own welfare, Christopher came to life. "Kidney trouble," he said. "I'm waiting for a transplant."

"I'm sure they'll find a suitable donor soon."

"When someone dies," he replied sourly.

"Not necessarily," she rejoined, shocked by the malice in his tone. "A relative might be found to be suitable."

As if talking to himself, he went on, "They stole my kidney. If they put it into someone else and that person dies - meets with an accident, or something - who knows, I might get my own kidney back. What a hoot!" He gave a short embittered laugh.

Megan shivered. This wasn't what she had expected. How was she going to tell this shell of the person that the child gurgling happily between them was his son?

"Don't talk like that," she said. "You're only young. Once you've had the transplant, you'll get better quickly and before you know it, you'll be as good as new."

"Oh yeah!" he retorted.

For several seconds, neither of them spoke. Beyond the kitchen window, skylarks chirped as they dive-bombed the bird bath, the distant hum of a washing machine could be heard through a closed door, a clock on the wall ticked steadily.

Calum broke the silence between them. "Mummy," he cooed.

"He's yours?" said Christopher in surprise.

"I told you he was."

"I didn't hear you."

It's now or never, thought Megan. Christopher's gaze was trained on Calum. He hadn't sat down. He was standing by the fridge, one elbow resting on top of it.

"His name's Calum and he's not just mine, he's yours too."

"What do you mean?"

Megan felt her heart begin to beat rapidly. What was the matter with Christopher, why couldn't he take it in? "He's a year old, work it out," she burst out.

The boy's fists clenched and unclenched and he swayed against the fridge. Megan leapt to her feet and went to steady him. Taking most of his weight, she managed to lead him to a chair and help him sit down.

He stared at Calum and then gasped, "You're serious, aren't you? But we only did it once."

Megan gave a short laugh. "That's exactly what I said."

A patch of colour began to return to the boy's cheeks. He leant forward to take a closer look at the baby, who obligingly snatched at his little finger. Megan watched as father and son studied at one another for a few moments."

"Would you like to hold him?"

Christopher frowned doubtfully, then nodded. She released Calum from his harness and handed him over.

"Shall I make some coffee while you play with him?"

"Yes, you'll find everything in that cupboard over there."

For about fifteen minutes, the scene was one of perfect harmony. Megan could hardly believe it. Calum had met his father and there was already a bond forming between them.

Without warning, Christopher's mood changed. Clasping the baby round the waist, he thrust him out at arms length towards Megan. Hastily she put down her mug of coffee, spilling most of it on the table as she reached out to catch the child.

"Be careful!" she gasped.

"What have you come here for?" demanded Christopher. "I can't do anything for you." With panic glinting in his eyes, he glanced up at the clock. "You've got to go, Mum will be home soon. This will kill her." He rose abruptly to his feet. "Leave. She mustn't find you here." His voice rose an octave. He pointed at the door. "What are you waiting for? Go!"

Megan stumbled out of the house and ran all the way down the road to the bus stop, bumping the pushchair down the kerb and up again. It wasn't until she was on the bus and Calum started whimpering that she realised she had left his dummy behind. Tears of self-chastisement rushed to her eyes. How badly she'd handled the meeting. Connie had been right all along. She should have done things differently. Christopher's mother would find the dummy and draw her own conclusions. Mrs Mills would never accept her now.

Hiding her tear-stained face behind the hood of Calum's cotton jacket, she dandled him on her knee so that he could look out of the window. The baby soon forgot about the missing dummy and started gurgling happily. He wasn't a difficult child to placate.

On reaching the house in Strawberry Vale, she rushed straight upstairs to her room, relieved that Lorraine was in the garden entertaining some of her friends. She shoved a spare dummy into Calum's mouth, sat him on the floor with some toys and collapsed onto the bed in a heap. Tears of humiliation and despair gushed forth and, for the first time since leaving Swansea, she yearned for her mother.

CHAPTER SEVEN

Since his return from Birmingham, a cloud of despondency had settled on Reece. He had been able to carry on working by doing lighter shifts and taking a taxi home afterwards, but once he'd taken off his shoes -- stiff black brogues were the regulation footwear -- the pain rushed to his injured extremity and all he wanted to do was sink into a pain-free sleep.

Connie knocked on his door late one afternoon and found him stretched out on the bed, hands behind his head, a frown creasing his forehead. "What's the matter with you?" she asked.

"What d'you think?" he snarled. "I've just finished a seven-hour shift, my foot's giving me hell and if I'm going to get anything to eat this evening, I'll have to drag myself down to the supermarket." He gave her a ferocious glare. "Need I say more?"

Connie burst out laughing. "Is that all? Cheer up, if food is all you need, I can provide that. What d'you fancy? My treat."

Reece's expression brightened. Lifting himself up onto one elbow, he grinned. "You're an angel. How about an Indian?"

Connie pursed her lips. "I meant ... " she said purposefully. " ... that I'd cook you something. I can't afford a take-away."

"Oh," he said, dropping back onto the pillow.

She turned to leave the room. "Well, if you're not interested ..."

Reece jerked himself up again. "I am," he replied. "How about Chicken Kiev and chips followed by a nice big jammy doughnut?" Since working at McDonald's he'd given up being a vegetarian.

"Sure thing," she said and disappeared out of the door.

After she'd left, he dozed off, drifting into a dreamlike state in which Connie played a major role. The fantasy was just getting exciting when she shattered his dream by throwing open the door and calling, "Grub's up."

He forced himself back to reality, although he couldn't help wondering whether she ever thought about their one-night stand. She'd never referred to it since then. At first, he had found her lack of concern unflattering as, clearly, there was never going to be a repeat of the incident, he decided it would be best to forget all about it. He hobbled into her room on bare feet.

"Look," she said, "I've moved the armchair up close to the bed so that you can rest your foot."

"Thanks Connie."

The chicken kiev and chips turned out to be cod steak and boiled potatoes; the doughnut, natural yogurt.

"Yogurt's much healthier for you," she said when he commented on it. Licking the last trace from her spoon, she asked, "What else happened in Birmingham?"

Reece filled her in, telling her about his confrontation with Abe, his visit to Casualty, his anger at Ben. When he mentioned Thea, Connie began to fidget. Leaning across to the dressing table, she picked up a hand mirror and inspected her reflection, delicately tweaking her hair with long slender fingers. Her behaviour triggered Reece into describing Ben's sister as very sexy, letting drop that they intended to keep in touch. They had made no such arrangement, but talking about the girl conjured up her image and he wished now that he had asked for her telephone number. Intuition told him that asking Ben for it would be unwise.

All at once, Connie swung her legs off the bed, gathered up the dirty dishes and disappeared behind the curtain into the kitchen. On her return, she enquired about his foot, was it terribly painful, did he want a cold compress?

"The pain's easing off a bit now," he said.

"I've got an idea," she exclaimed. "Wait here, I'm just going to see Jamie downstairs."

Reece looked surprised. She rarely had anything to do with the tenants on the lower floors. Ten minutes later, she came back, her face wreathed in smiles.

"This will help," she said and deftly proceeded to roll a joint.

Reece's thoughts flew back to France. He'd sworn to Chantal that he'd given up grass, but since arriving in England, he'd twice gone back on his word. He gave a mental shrug. Chantal was out of his life forever now. She belonged to a different Reece, a different existence. She'd always been a bit of a goodie-goodie. A little puff when you fancied it did no harm.

"Great," he said, banishing guilt and taking the joint from Connie.

He waited for the dizziness of the first draw to diminish, observing her as she squatted on the end of the bed, her legs tucked under her.

"Ever been to a nudist camp?" she asked him unexpectedly.

Reece gulped and spluttered. "No, why should I?"

Connie twiddled with a large jade ring on her finger and giggled, "Well, you being a nature lover, I thought perhaps ..."

"No way," said Reece, handing the shared joint back to her. "Have you?"

"I went on a nudist weekend once," she replied. "But I left after the first day."

Reece grinned cheekily. "Couldn't hack it, eh?"

"You must be kidding. It was too bloody chilly in North Devon, even in June." She burst into a fit of giggles. "You should have seen them all. They were covered in goose pimples." The giggles gained momentum. "That is, everyone except for me and a guy from Mozambique. Didn't show on our skin. There are some compensations for being black."

Picking up on the bitterness in her tone, Reece sat up straight and reached for her hand. "Connie, don't you realise how attractive you are," he exclaimed.

For a moment, Connie looked at him in surprise. Snatching her hand away, she said curtly, "You misunderstood me; I'm proud of who I am."

"I never doubted that," mumbled Reece.

She went on, "I wouldn't mind trying nudism somewhere hot, somewhere like the Bahamas or Jamaica."

"Is that where your father comes from?"

"No, he's from South America."

"Do you ever see him?"

He watched her take a slow draw from the joint, waiting for her reply. "Never," she said.

Instinct told Reece to curb his curiosity and, to cover the awkward moment, he said, "I'm thinking of quitting McDonalds."

"Why?"

"It's time to move on."

"Where will you go?"

"I dunno, but I do know the fast food industry isn't for me. Who knows, I might even go back to being a vegi."

Connie's eyes twinkled. "Don't kid yourself. I've seen how you tuck in to those beef burgers."

"Only because there's nothing else to eat," he protested. "What about you? What are you going to do when you've finished college?"

Connie flung out her arms and sang out, "I'm going to be a star."

Reece laughed. "And I'm going to win the lottery!"

"I mean it. One day, you'll see my name in lights: Conchita de Oliveira Figueres."

"That's a bit of a mouthful!"

"I know," she said frowning. "But that will show them, especially him."

"Your father?"

She nodded, then said, "I suppose I could shorten it to Conchita Figueres."

"That would be better," agreed Reece.

Abruptly Connie changed the subject. "How's the foot?"

He lifted his leg into the air and mumbled, "'Scured."

"Skewed! You've got meat on the brain, you idiot. What did I tell you, I knew you wouldn't be able to give it up."

For several minutes they giggled companionably, gradually subsiding into silence.

They each took a last draw on the joint, then Connie said, "What brought you to Europe?"

"Chantal did."

"Are you still pining after her?"

Reece shook his head. "Not any more." The words came out spontaneously, but he wondered whether he had, in fact, got over her. "We parted on friendly terms. By now she must be married to that French lawyer."

"She may not have married him, why don't you try getting in touch with her again?"

"There's no point."

Connie gave a sniff. "You give up too easily."

"*C'est la vie!*" he mumbled in reply.

"Will you go back to Canada?"

"Shouldn't think so. There's nothing there for me."

Connie raised an enquiring eyebrow. "No family?"

Before he could stop, Reece found himself telling Connie about his chequered childhood: his mother's succession of lovers, the shock of his sister's death, the loneliness which drove him to join the travellers. "Chantal hated them," he said. "At first, she pretended to enjoy the Commune's way of life, although she never really settled in. I was forced to make a choice: Chantal or the Commune. After we left, I sometimes went back to see them, but I felt like an outsider." A hint of bitterness crept into his tone. "She swore she'd do anything for me, but she lied. She couldn't give up civilisation in order to free the inner spirit. I can hear her now: 'What's so wonderful about living close to nature, Reece? No privacy, no home comforts. Why squat over a hole in the ground, when modern plumbing's available?'"

"What took you to Paris?" asked Connie.

"Chantal was called to France, something to do with a legacy from her French mother." Looking up, he went on with a touch of dry humour, "I followed her, thought I'd be able to re-kindle the flame of love by giving her a surprise. Instead, she gave *me* a surprise. I found a different Chantal: a smart Parisian in stylish suits. Indian cotton and baggy sweaters had gone out of the window. But it wasn't only her appearance. She'd completely changed, seemed more mature, more conventional." He gave a shrug of hopelessness. "Made me feel like a country bumpkin."

"You were drawn together in the first place so you must have had some good times," said Connie gently.

Reece gave a brief smile. "We'd both had a lonely childhood; we shared the same taste in music and books; laughed at the same jokes. It was wonderful being together every evening -- exchanging trivia about the day -- after she got home from her job at Meldrew's. That was another thing: she insisted on having a regular job while I was happy to take whatever work came along, whether it lasted for a day, a week or a month."

He was so completely lost in reflection that he didn't notice Connie was asleep until she let out a noisy snore.

After the meeting with Christopher, Megan spent a sleepless night. To make matters worse, Jessica was fretful and it took all the teenager's self-control not to scream at the teething baby. Calum had never been like that. He had slept through the night even when cutting a tooth.

By six in the morning, Jessica had slipped into a peaceful sleep and Calum had woken up. She left him playing in his cot for an hour, cooing happily to himself. She was desperate to talk to someone and, at seven-thirty, she phoned Connie.

"Hello, oh it's you!" grunted Connie, rubbing a fist over sleeping eyes and silently cursing the ill-timed Saturday morning call.

"I've seen Chris," announced Megan.

"Good, look Megan, I'm having a lay-in. I'll speak to you later on."

"Don't hang up, Connie!" cried Megan.

"I'll phone you back later."

"Please, Connie, listen. You were right. Chris's mother is keeping us apart. He's terribly ill. I hardly recognised him. Worst of all, he's ever so depressed. It's as if he's lost hope..." She faltered. "...it's as if he's lost the will to live. I'm so frightened."

By now, Connie was wide awake. Warning signals flashed through her mind. "I think you ought to keep out of this, Megan," she advised.

"I can't, Calum's Chris's son." Her voice bordered on hysteria. "I must see you; when can we meet?"

Connie heaved a sigh. There was no reasoning with Megan, "This afternoon down by the river at half two. You know, the seat where we met before."

"Thanks, Connie," whispered Megan.

When Michael Goddard answered the front door, he was confronted by a tall, slim girl wearing a pair of frayed denim hipsters, colourful espadrilles and sporting an afro hairstyle. His eyes were drawn to her navel, which was adorned with an ornate metal stud. His gaze travelled upwards, focusing briefly on the outline of her nipples through her thin Indian cotton top. Her face was striking, her eyes compelling.

"Michael Goddard?" she enquired with a slight raise of an eyebrow. When he nodded, she went on, "I'm sorry to bother you. I'm looking for Megan Hughes. Is she at home?"

Michael was taken aback. The girl spoke politely, in an educated tone. He wouldn't have expected that.

"I'm afraid not," he replied.

She frowned. "Megan was supposed to meet me an hour ago, but she didn't turn up."

Michael was still recovering from his surprise. Although she was the type of girl he might have lusted after in his dreams, she wasn't the type he would have expected to be acquainted with Megan, a minister's daughter, whom he'd always considered to be rather straight-laced and conventional despite the illegitimate child.

"Well?" said the girl, nudging him into a response.

"She left the house a while ago; she didn't say where she was going." Starting to shut the door, he added, "I'll tell her you called."

The girl was persistent. "Do you know where she's gone?"

"Sorry, I've no idea where she goes on her day off."

This time, he managed to shut the door.

Connie made her way back to the riverside, annoyed at being stood up, but worried too. When she arrived at the meeting place, she was relieved to see Megan waiting at the appointed seat staring down at the grass as if studying the insect life. Calum was playing at her feet.

Relief gave way to annoyance and she rounded on Megan with, "So you've deigned to arrive! It's four o'clock, our meeting was for two-thirty."

Taken by surprise, Megan gave a start and looked up. Her face was blotchy, her eyes red-rimmed. She dabbed an already damp tissue to her cheeks, looking utterly crestfallen.

Forgetting her annoyance, Connie sat down and slipped an arm round her shoulders. "What's happened?" she asked.

Megan gulped and mumbled, "I phoned Christopher and his mother answered ..." A surge of indignation gave spirit to her explanation. "Stupid old cow -- she wouldn't let me speak to him. She put the phone down on me." The tears gushed forth, streaming unchecked down her cheeks.

Connie hugged her. How thin she was! She wondered whether she was getting enough to eat chez the Goddard's.

Megan's muffled voice rose from the depths of a Connie's shoulder. "Chris's mother's a witch. There's not a sympathetic bone in her body."

The older girl couldn't help seeing Mrs Mills' point of view. Wasn't it enough that her beloved son had been struck down by a ghastly illness without being stalked by a teenager with claims of paternity?

"Where have you been all this time?" she asked.

"I walked to the next phone kiosk and rang up again, same thing. After that, I just kept walking. I can't understand how anyone can be so cruel, so uncaring." Dropping her head into her hands, Megan burst into another spasm of sobs.

Connie delved into her bag for a clean tissue. Suddenly, she noticed that Calum was eyeing the ducks at the water's edge with great interest. Springing to her feet, she scooped him up and put him back in his pushchair.

"Let's go and have a cup of tea," she suggested. Wasn't tea considered to be the antidote to an emotional crisis?

Megan shook her head. "I can't face people looking like this."

Connie was at a loss. She had warned Megan of the consequences of rushing in at full throttle. It would be easy to say I told you so, but she held back. Stage-struck for as long as she could remember, becoming a star had been Connie's sole aim in life. Falling in love had never entered into the equation. The first sign of commitment in a relationship sent her into a shuddering panic, prompting a swift brush-off for the unfortunate young man. With a start of surprise, she realised that despite Megan's immaturity, the teenager's experience of true devotion was greater than hers. She had never felt that overwhelming, gut-rending sense of loss when lovers are parted; she had never been motivated by anything other than her own selfish desires. Despite her efforts to remain detached, her friend's dilemma touched her deeply, bringing a rush of tears to her eyes. Megan's despair became her despair. "You poor dear," she whispered, hugging the little Welsh girl and rocking her gently.

"What can I do?" wept Megan. "His mother won't let me anywhere near him now." She sniffed into the tissue. "She knows I called at the house the other day. She forced the truth out of Christopher when she found Calum's dummy on the kitchen table."

Against her better judgement, plans began to form in Connie's mind. "Robert might be able to help," she suggested. "I'll have a word with him. Maybe we can set up a courier service on the quiet. I'm sure Chris's mother could be persuaded to let Robert visit the house."

Connie's plan worked and, within a few weeks, Robert had become a regular go-between for Megan and Christopher. The young mother borrowed a camera and took photographs of Calum, sending new ones with Robert each time he visited his friend.

One week in early September, two things happened. The first started insignificantly, but had far-reaching consequences; the second should have been anticipated, but wasn't.

Lorraine Goddard went away on business for a few days leaving Megan in charge. It was during a period when Michael Goddard was very busy, getting to grips with the new computer system on which his engineering company depended. Consequently, he arrived home late every evening after the children were in bed. Jessica began to miss her parents. She was still teething and Megan found herself frequently having to comfort her small charge. Calum, amiable as ever, was left to his own resources. He was several months older than the baby girl; he walked with confidence whereas Jessica was still only just able to stand on her own. Also, he was a very inquisitive child.

One afternoon, Megan spent an hour trying to rock Jessica to sleep. All at once, she realised that the nursery door, which had been slightly ajar, was now wide open and Calum was no-where to be seen. Putting Jessica back in her cot, she dashed out of the room.

"Calum, Calum, where are you?"

'She ran to the top of the stairs and, to her relief saw that Calum wasn't lying in a crumpled heap in the hall below. The door to the master bedroom was open. She rushed in. Calum gurgled happily when he saw her, reaching up for a cuddle. Laughing with relief, she bent down and picked him up from the pale beige carpet, realising as she did so that the baby had managed to pull open a small drawer at the bottom of the dressing-table. The contents were strewn on the carpet.

"Naughty boy," she scolded, half teasing. "We'd better put these things back where they belong, hadn't we?" He gave her a toothy smile.

She put him down and started clearing up the collection of items he had pulled out of the drawer: a pair of tights, thankfully un-snagged; a make-up bag, thankfully still zipped up; a bottled of perfume, thankfully still intact; a beautiful gem-encrusted pendant of Venetian design. Megan held it up to the light. It must have cost a fortune. Then she gave a gulp: the chain was broken. Kneeling down beside Calum, she tried to question him.

"Did you play with this pretty necklace, Calum?" He gurgled and tried to snatch it from her. She dangled it just out of reach. "Did Calum play with it?" He reached for it again and when she held it away from him, his mouth puckered and he started to cry.

She hugged him to her. "It's all right, darling."

Taking another look at the chain, she saw that it was extremely delicate, easily breakable. Maybe it was already broken when Calum spilled out the drawer's contents! Then, in a flash of sunlight, she noticed something glinting in the deep pile carpet. It was a link from the chain. Her hand flew to her heart. Thank God Calum hadn't swallowed it!

She wondered what to do. If she replaced the pendant in the drawer with all the other things, Lorraine would eventually discover it was broken. Was there time to get it repaired? Lorraine was due home the next day. There was nothing for it: she would have to own up and offer to pay for the repair.

She found a pencil and wrote a few words of explanation on a scrap of paper, placing it with the pendant in a prominent position on the dressing table. Then, gathering Calum up from the floor, she took him back to the nursery.

The second incident drove the first incident out of Megan's mind.

Several weeks had passed since Connie had set up the go-between arrangement with Robert, and Megan had fallen into the habit of meeting him once a week. On this occasion, he had some really exciting news for her.

"Chris wants to see you," he said. "He suggests, as the weather's nice, he'll come down to the park this afternoon. He wants you to bring Calum."

Megan's eyes lit up. "That's wonderful! He must be feeling better."

"Umm," grunted Robert.

"What's that supposed to mean?" demanded Megan.

Robert shook his head. "He still looks pretty groggy to me."

"What time does he want to meet?"

"Three o'clock."

"How's he going to give his mother the slip?"

"She's gone out for the day."

Megan could hardly contain her excitement. The hours dragged until three o'clock. She washed her hair and deliberated over what to wear, opting finally, for her newest jeans and an azure vest top, which reflected the colour of her eyes. Last of all, she dressed Calum in his best outfit, a pair of green and white striped shorts and matching top that made him look really cute.

When she got there, Christopher was waiting for her. He greeted her shyly, crouching down awkwardly to talk to the baby. Calum responded warmly, pleasing both his teenage parents. Megan's heart lifted. Things were going to work out well.

"It's lovely to see you, Chris," she said.

He grinned. "Mum doesn't know I've come out. It's the first time I've walked this far for ages. Shall we take Calum to the swings?"

Megan glanced across the grass to the children's play area. "It's a long way off. Are you sure you want to go that far? Let's sit here and chat."

He nodded and, pointing at the baby, said, "He looks just like you."

"No he doesn't, he's the image of you."

The boy shook his head. "He's got your blond hair and blue eyes." He paused to think. "Although, come to think of it, Mum says I was blond as a baby."

"There you are then! He's going to grow up just like his dad."

This made Christopher laugh, reminding Megan of the carefree schoolboy she'd known in Swansea.

He became serious again. "How do you manage? Do you earn enough to live on?" he asked.

"Why do you think I chose to be a live-in nanny?" replied Megan.

He looked embarrassed. "I'd help you if I could, but you can see what a spot I'm in. Besides, even if this kidney trouble hadn't blown up Dad would never let me leave school. He's got plans for me to go to university." He shook his head. "I don't know about that; after this set-back I'm not sure I want to go on to further education."

"But Chris, you must," insisted Megan. "Why, you were top of the class in Swansea!"

"That's because I'd already covered that part of the curriculum in London."

"Your dad's right," went on Megan. "You've got it in you to go far. After you've had the transplant, things will seem less complicated. I've got faith in you, Chris."

He bit his lip. "But you can't bring up Calum all on your own. He's my responsibility too."

Megan's eyes lit up. These were the words she had longed to hear; not because she wanted help, but because she desperately wanted her son to know both his parents.

Christopher went on. "Once I'm well again, I'll leave school and get a job, then I can help you out with money."

"I don't want it," she shouted. "All I want is for you to get better and continue your education. You said you wanted to study law. Well, get on with it, and when you've qualified, then, and only then, I might let you help." She dropped her voice and added firmly. "Not before."

The boy smiled and changed the subject. "How are your mum and dad?"

"Fine."

"You're being an unmarried mum must have shocked your father."

Megan gave an impish grin. "It certainly wiped that self-righteous smirk off his face."

"I'm surprised your parents let you move away."

"I didn't tell them I was going; just packed my bags and left." At Christopher's gasp of dismay, Megan hastened on, "It's all right, I've been in touch. I phone them regularly." The tailpiece was an exaggeration. However, it satisfied Christopher.

They exchanged a smile when Calum began oohing and aahing at the ducks. Megan said: "I forgot to bring the stale bread for him to feed to them."

"He seems very bright for his age."

"He's ahead," replied Megan proudly. "Lots of babies his age can barely walk let alone talk, but Calum's been saying words for over a month." She turned her head and addressed Christopher directly. "You look much better than when I last saw you."

"I feel better," he replied. "It was a terrible shock learning about Calum. Since then, I've had time to think. In a way it's made things easier. I've got to get better now, haven't I?"

Impulsively, Megan leaned over and planted a kiss on his cheek. Taken by surprise, the boy blushed and glanced around to see if anybody was looking at them. She felt as if she were on a first date. It was hard to believe that they had made love. She glanced down at Calum, seeking confirmation.

All at once, Christopher began to wilt. "I think I'd better be getting back. The last thing I want is Mum finding out that we're seeing one another."

"It's all thanks to Robert."

"Yes, he's a good mate."

"I'll come part of the way with you."

He shook his head. "Better not."

Rising rather unsteadily to his feet, he patted the baby's head, fidgeting a little, not quite knowing how to make his departure. Megan stood up, placed her hands on his shoulders and kissed him firmly on the mouth.

"Take care," she whispered.

Christopher caught her hands and held them. Megan smiled back at him. He seemed more like a little boy than a youth on the verge of manhood. For 30 seconds he clung to her hands, his grip slowly loosening until, at last, their fingers slipped apart.

"Good-bye, Megan," he murmured.

Turning around, he shuffled up the grassy incline, dragging his feet as if his shoes were loaded with lead. On reaching level ground, he turned and waved before covering the last 50 yards. She noticed how hunched he was, how unhappy he seemed, and felt the prick of tears at her eyes. "God bless and keep you, Christopher," she whispered aloud, and resolved to say a prayer for him in church on Sunday.

CHAPTER EIGHT

Reece's foot improved, but his attitude towards Ben didn't. When their paths crossed at McDonalds, he hid his antagonism; outside work, he avoided him. He couldn't get the memory of Ben's uncaring behaviour towards his family out of his mind. He wondered how Imelda and the girls were doing, especially Thea.

The weekend spent in Ben's flat had worked out satisfactorily simply because the Jamaican had spent most of his time at Deceptions. Reece was forced to acknowledge that Connie was the only person who could have persuaded him to spend two nights under Ben's roof and part of his anger was against himself. How could he have allowed himself to be so easily persuaded?

But as time moved on and he found himself seeing more of Connie, his recollection of the Birmingham episode faded. To his surprise, she sometimes invited him into her bed. It was as if her aunt's visit had unleashed friendliness towards him and he could only put it down to the willingness with which he'd complied with her wishes over the room.

Getting up one day after a late shift, he ambled onto the landing and was startled to hear voices coming from Connie's room. Rubbing a fist over his sleepy eyes, he held his breath and listened. Connie's infectious laugh rang out, then Ben's unbridled guffaw. He felt his hackles rise. What was Ben doing there at eight in the morning? Again, Ben's laugh, then the words: "You sexy bitch!"

Jealousy surged through Reece's veins; he reached for the door handle, but his hand met a void as Ben flung open the door and strode out, wearing nothing more than a pair of underpants.

"Hi ya," he said casually as if such a meeting there were a daily affair.

"What the hell are you doing here?" demanded Reece.

The black face creased into a wide grin. He shrugged his massive shoulders. "Just visiting. What's it to you?"

Ben's arrogance infuriated Reece. Rising to the bait, he took a swing at Ben's jaw. Connie dashed out onto the landing, hastily tying the sash of a towelling robe round her waist.

"What the hell are you two up to?" she cried.

"Out of the way, Connie," yelled Reece as he took another swipe at Ben.

But the other man had recovered. Despite his bulk, he was extremely light on his feet. A trained boxer, he dodged swiftly aside, easily warding off Reece's clumsy blow. Reece backed to the top of the staircase, but in his irrational frame of mind, he missed his footing. Ben was already grappling with him as he wobbled precariously on the top step.

"Stop it, you idiots!" shouted Connie, her eyes widening in alarm.

There was a loud crack and the flimsy banister rail splintered under their combined weight. Arms and legs flailing, the two men rolled down the narrow flight of steps to land with a thump on the next landing. Reece landed on top. Believing he had the upper hand, he laid into Ben.

Beneath him, Ben shook his head as if to clear his brain and, before Reece knew what was happening, he had turned the tables, twisting the taller man's punching arm behind him and rolling him over. As he knelt across Reece's chest to deliver the knockout punch, he felt a blow on the back of his head. It wasn't enough to black him out, although it was sufficient to stop him in his tracks. He looked up. Connie stood over him with a large chunk of the broken banister rail in her hands. She lifted it as if to strike again.

"Stop it, you silly cow!" spluttered Ben.

Reece lifted his head, his eyes almost popping out at the sight of Connie above them. The robe had slipped open and he saw that she was naked beneath it. Following his gaze, she tried unsuccessfully to adjust the sash without dropping her makeshift weapon.

Ben broke the deadlock. With a burst of laughter, he got to his feet, put out a helping hand and said, "Get up you son-of-a-bitch, let's call a truce."

Reece got up and swayed uncertainly, reaching for the wall to steady himself. Ben slapped him on the shoulder. "You put up a good fight, considering," he said, the corners of his eyes wrinkling in amusement.

Reece found his voice. "What the hell's going on?" he gasped, wiping a trickle of blood from the side of his mouth. He turned to Connie. "I thought you said there was nothing going on between you two."

Connie exchanged a glance with Ben, who smothered a chuckle. "There's not," she said.

Reece frowned. "I don't get it."

The other two burst out laughing. "Chill out, Reece," said Connie. "Surely you know by now, I don't belong to anyone."

At Reece's blank expression, Ben's mirth increased. "We've been at it for months," he said. "It passes the time."

"But, but..." stuttered Reece.

Connie lost her temper. Tossing the chunk of banister rail onto the floor, she snapped, "For Christ's sake, grow up, Reece." Spinning on her heel, she ran upstairs, shouting back at them. "You two are going to have to pay for the banister. God knows how I'm going to explain it to the landlord."

As Connie made her way upstairs, Ben asked, "Where is everybody?"

She stopped at the top and snapped, "Gone out or terrified to show their faces. luckily for you the landlord's away, otherwise he would have got you both jugged up. Now, get out of my sight, I need some space."

The two men looked at each another, then slowly shook hands. Ben was smiling broadly, Reece's perplexed features gradually softened into a matching grin. They went upstairs and Ben knocked at Connie's door.

"Go away," she yelled.

"I can't without my clothes."

The door opened and a pair of jeans and a T-shirt were thrust out.

"Shoes!"

The door opened again and a pair of trainers landed with a thump on the wooden floor. Ben picked them up.

"You'd better come in here," said Reece going in to his own small cubicle.

"For fuck's sake, how can you live in this rat hole?" exclaimed Ben.

"It's convenient."

The West Indian pulled on his jeans. "Why don't you move in with me," he suggested. "I've got plenty of room and I could do with some help with the rent."

Reece looked startled. "What about Connie?" he asked.

Ben raised a surprised eyebrow. "What about her?"

"Well ... where do we go from here?"

The other man finished tying his shoe laces and straightened up. "Connie's her own person, she'll call us when she wants us."

"You make her sound like a pro."

Ben's expression hardened. "Pro's don't call the shots," he said. "Connie does."

So Reece moved in with Ben and, for the first time since leaving Canada, he felt as if he had found a base. It was a mock Tudor house on a corner site, converted into two flats with the entrance to Ben's flat at the side. There was parking space for several cars and a high hedge surrounded the property. A staircase led up to the living accommodation with all rooms leading off a narrow passage.

Reece's bedroom was large and airy with plenty of cupboards, a luxury for him. Ben's room, equally large was next door with the bathroom situated on the other side. By comparison, the kitchen was a mere pigeonhole, although it was well laid out and had everything the two young men needed, including a dishwasher and a microwave.

The shared living room was also spacious. It was sparsely furnished; Ben had purchased a couple of large beanbags to serve for extra seating. The room was painted red, a colour that didn't go too well with the maroon and yellow carpet. Nevertheless, it was pleasant enough. In the corner there was another staircase leading to the roof space.

"What d'you think?" asked Ben.

"I've seen it before."

"I know, but now you'll be living here, what d'you think?"

"It seems fine."

"Really?"

"Yeah, 'course."

"The bedrooms and hall could do with a lick of paint. Maybe you could give me a hand with that."

"Sure," agreed Reece, feeling puzzled by his friend's interest in freshening up the place. "Have you checked with the landlord about sub-letting? He won't chuck me out will he?"

"Not if you behave yourself." All at once Ben roared with laughter. "I'm the landlord, I've bought the fucking place."

Reece's eyebrows shot up. "Holy mackerel! That's a big step, isn't it? "

"Always wanted my own place."

"I hope you know what you're doing? What about the Deceptions deal?"

Ben's eyes narrowed. "How do you know about that?"

"I keep an ear cocked."

The other man shrugged. "It might come to something, it might not." He tossed Reece a set of keys and started to run downstairs, calling back, "There's only one ground rule."

"What's that?"

"No women." At the sight of Reece's pained expression, Ben burst out laughing. "Just kidding. Ciao!"

"Wait!"

Ben hesitated at the bottom of the stairs. "What is it?"

"No overnight visits from Connie," shouted Reece. "We only crash at her place."

Ben nodded. "Sure thing."

The meeting with Christopher upset Megan. It had gone well, yet she couldn't help worrying about him. This was the first time she had come across serious illness. Her parents were in the best of health, she herself had never been afflicted with anything more serious than chickenpox or mumps. Calum's birth had been unremarkable and she had slipped easily into motherhood, breastfeeding without problems and not experiencing the post-natal depression that some young mothers experience.

She tried to brush her concern aside, telling herself that Christopher was young and strong and that, as soon as the operation had been carried out, he would be as good as new. Her anxiety drove the incident of the broken pendant from her mind until several days later when she heard the Goddard's quarrelling.

Michael's voice reached her first, through two closed doors. "Where did it come from?"

His wife's reply was inaudible.

"What's his name? Tell me, I demand to know!"

Lorraine's voice, louder now. "You can demand all you like, there's nothing to tell."

"Lover boy gave it to you, didn't he? Come on, own up."

"You don't know what you're talking about. You've been hitting the bottle again."

"I have not!" Michael's voice was loud enough to be heard all over the house now. "It's an expensive piece of jewellery. If you came by it innocently, how come you've never shown it to me?"

"Shhh! She'll hear you."

"I don't give a shit who hears me."

"You'll wake the children."

"Don't evade the issue, Lorraine. I know you've got a bit on the side."

Lorraine gave a snort of derision. "You're talking through the top of your head."

"Am I, heck?"

"Yes you are," annunciated Lorraine. "Watch my lips, there's no one. The pendant was a 'thank you' gift from a client."

The colour drained from Megan's cheeks. She ran a nervous tongue over her lips. Why oh why had she left the pendant on the dressing table? Why hadn't she kept it safe and told Lorraine about it on the quiet?

"Clients don't give 'thank you' gifts of this quality. It must be worth £1000 or more."

"You're exaggerating. It's not worth anything like that. Hand it over, Michael."

Megan pressed her ear close to the door. Suddenly, she heard a thump and a cry, then silence. My God, she thought in panic, he's killed her. Spinning round, she ran back to her own room. A moment later, she heard the Goddard's bedroom door open, followed by Michael's footsteps on the stairs. The front door slammed shut after him.

After a few minutes, Megan crept out of her room and tip-toed along the landing. Suppose he had really killed Lorraine! Then she heard the sound of sobbing. Nervously, she tapped on the door. There was no reply.

"Go away Michael," called Lorraine.

"It's not Michael, it's me, Megan."

The door opened and she found herself face to face with her employer. She had never seen her look so awful. Her hair was dishevelled, her make-up a mess. There was a red streak across her left cheek. Before she could say anything else, Lorraine thrust her face close into hers and shouted, "This is all your fault. Just get out! Take that bastard brat of yours and get the hell out of my house."

"But, but ..." stuttered Megan.

This fuelled Lorraine's anger. With eyes blazing she pointed an accusing finger at Megan. "Do you know what you've done, you stupid little idiot? You've ruined my marriage; that's what. He'll never trust me now. It's goodbye to all those trips ..." She dissolved into a flood of tears. "You stupid little cow, you've ruined everything."

Megan backed away. "I'm so sorry," she whispered.

"Sorry! Is that all you can say? Get out of my sight. You can leave first thing tomorrow," she screamed, then slammed the door in Megan's face.

Megan barely slept all night. In the morning, she got up and looked at herself in the mirror. Crying into her pillow had produced puffy eyes and a red nose. Ignoring the children's calls, she took a hurried shower and washed her hair. If Lorraine Goddard was going to fire her, then she'd at least confront her employer looking half-decent. A facial scrub did wonders for her complexion and, on leaving the bathroom, she felt ready to hear the worst.

By now, both babies were yelling. She pulled on a bathrobe, lifted Calum out of his cot and ran into the nursery to find Lorraine cuddling Jessica.

"Where have you been?" she demanded as Megan came in. "Do you realise Jessica's been crying for over an hour."

This was gross exaggeration, but Megan decided not to argue. "I needed to take a shower and get my things together if I'm to leave today," she said, a surge of courage lending petulance to her tone.

"You can stay until the end of the week. I've got to find a replacement," retorted Lorraine.

Megan would have given anything to shout back: *no thanks, I'll go now,* but fear of homelessness and the unknown had snuffed out her earlier spark of defiance. She nodded her head in agreement.

It was only when she found a quiet moment during the children's mid-morning nap that it occurred to her that legally the Goddard's had no grounds for dismissing her. She had not been negligent and Lorraine had not given her the opportunity to explain about the broken pendant or to offer to pay for its repair. This injustice made her bristle, bringing a return of defiance.

She went downstairs and sought out her employer, who was watching a video. Tapping on the door, she called, "Excuse me, could I have a word please?"

"What is it?" Lorraine looked over her shoulder from her stretched-out position on the sofa, simultaneously pressing the pause button.

"I want to tell you what happened about your pendant."

"It's obvious what happened; you were snooping around in our bedroom."

"No," protested Megan. "You've got it wrong. I wasn't prying, really I wasn't."

Lorraine swung her legs round and placed her feet on the floor. Even when relaxing at home, she dressed with the utmost care, never failing to apply make-up and curl her hair with the hot brush. "Well," she said tartly. "I'm waiting."

She was wearing an expensive catsuit and to disguise the slightest hint of a spare tyre, she held herself unnaturally erect, twisting from the shoulders to face the embarrassed teenager. Clumsily, Megan tried to explain that Jessica had needed coaxing to sleep and that Calum had run into the master bedroom unnoticed. "He's too young to know where he can or cannot go," she said, ending timidly, "You must have left the door open."

"I always close it. You should have been watching that brat of yours."

Memories of the hours spent rocking Jessica to sleep inflamed Megan's temper. Somehow, she managed to remain calm. "Calum pulled the drawer open and emptied out the contents. I caught him playing with the pendant and when I saw that the chain was broken I wasn't sure whether he had done it or whether it was like that before. I'm very sorry if it was Calum's fault and, of course, I'll pay for its repair."

Lorraine's lips tightened into a straight line. Her eyes flashed. "You stupid girl, you still don't understand what you've done, do you?"

The door behind them opened and Michael Goddard came in. "What's going on?" he asked.

His wife gave him a haughty glare. "Megan's leaving at the end of the week; we were discussing her severance pay."

Michael's mouth gaped in dismay. "Oh no," he said. "Don't leave us, Megan, you're the best nanny we've ever had."

"Huh!" muttered Lorraine, casting her gaze to the ceiling.

Realising that the desire to curtail the employment was not Megan's, Michael's attitude changed. Choosing his words with care, he said mocking, "Jessica adores you. She loves having Calum to play with. Isn't that true, Lorraine my dear?"

His wife's reply was no less sarcastic. "She wants to leave, don't you, Megan?"

Megan looked from one to the other. The focus of disagreement had moved from Lorraine's indiscretions to her own departure. Lorraine wanted her to go; therefore Michael wanted her to stay. She had become a pawn in a battle of wills. It was a situation far beyond the teenager's experience. She simply did not know what to do.

Lorraine and Michael continued to glare at one another until the squeal of the telephone startled all three. When Lorraine went to answer it, Michael turned and smiled at Megan. Her bewilderment must have been apparent because he walked over and slipped a fatherly arm around her shoulders, saying, "Don't worry, I'll talk my wife round. She's upset." He checked his watch. "Time for the children's tea, I think. Cheer up, this will soon blow over."

The weekend came and went and still Megan was uncertain of her future. Both the Goddard's were back at work and, as far as she could tell, Lorraine had not as yet interviewed any potential replacements.

Whenever she bumped into Michael he treated her with excessive courtesy; Lorraine took pains to ignore her. Unable to bear the tension any longer, Megan eventually spoke to Michael. He got up from behind his desk in the study and came towards her. "Stop worrying, my dear, I told you I'd sort it out. Your job's secure." Again, the arm went round her shoulders. He winked. "Between you and me, my wife can be hot headed at times. Pressure of work, you know. She's got a very high-powered job."

Relief flooded over Megan. That was it. Lorraine's attitude was due to business worries. There was nothing to fear: she and Calum were safe. But despite Michael's assurances, the misgivings kept coming back, intensified by a stream of telephone calls for Lorraine, which she always made a point of taking either upstairs in the bedroom with the door firmly closed or in the garden on the cordless. Once, when Calum's ball rolled down towards the greenhouse, Megan surprised Lorraine behind the six-foot hedge that shielded it. She was murmuring into the phone in a foreign language, a smile playing at her lips. On catching sight of Megan, she frowned furiously and, covering the mouthpiece, shooed her away with an impatient flick of the wrist.

Red-faced, Megan picked up the ball and hurried back up the garden, collecting the children on the way and taking them into the house. Reflecting afterwards, she realised that these secret calls were nothing new. They had always been going on, but lack of observation on her part had made them indistinguishable from the genuine business calls Lorraine habitually received.

She tried to push aside her concern, reminding herself that she would be seeing Robert again soon and he might have good news from Christopher. On the following Friday, she waited at the appointed meeting place for over fifteen minutes before Robert turned up. At last, he sauntered into view.

"I'm going on holiday next week," he informed her.

Panic rose. "How will I keep in touch with Christopher?"

"I'll only be gone for two weeks. Surely you can survive that long!"

Without another word, he turned on his heel and loped off, leaving her feeling slighted and not a little alarmed. Understandably, Robert was getting tired of his role of go-between. Suppose, after he returned from his holiday, he decided not to continue!

Filled with dismay, Megan walked along the tow path, pushing the double buggy over potholes and through puddles, not even stopping to let the babies feed the ducks, until she arrived, panting, at the path which led up to the road. She needed to talk to Connie.

Her despair mounted and by the time she gained the main road, dread for Christopher's welfare and a sense of utter loneliness had gripped her so tightly that she drove the pushchair between the shoppers, refusing to give way and angering passers-by. She stopped at the entrance to McDonalds. Connie was on duty and the restaurant was packed with foreign students, who were using the college facilities during the summer vacation. All of them, it seemed, had decided to buy their lunch at McDonalds. She stood at the window looking in, trying to catch Connie's eye, but her friend was too busy to notice. Losing patience, she went inside.

All the tables were occupied. Megan fought her way through and joined the end of the queue, scowling as people bumped into the buggy. Ten minutes later, Connie's surprised grin met her troubled gaze. Megan placed her clenched fists on the counter and gasped, "I must see you."

"What's happened?" Megan started to explain. Connie cut her short. "It'll have to wait."

"Five minutes, that's all it will take."

"Can't you see I'm busy?"

"Five minutes, Connie?"

Connie glanced around in alarm. "For God's sake, Megan, order something or you'll get me the sack."

"Regular French fries and a banana milkshake," stuttered Megan, rapidly calculating the money left in her purse.

Connie relented. "I'll be finished soon. Meet me outside at five past two."

Balancing the tray with her meal on top of the pushchair, Megan adjusted her shoulder bag and manouevred her way to a table that was just being vacated. Ramming the buggy ahead of her, she resolutely staked her claim from under the noses of a couple who were also making for it. Dumping her bag down on the seat, she wedged the buggy into position and sat down, ignoring the grunts of protest from other customers.

Studying the bag of chips in front of her, she realised she had bought nothing for the babies to eat. Jessica started to whimper and, remembering the child's bottle, she got it out from under the pushchair and jammed it into her mouth before the child could give vent to her demands for nourishment. Calum looked up at her, his eyes wide with expectation. With a shrug, she relinquished the banana milkshake to her son, wondering how he would cope with a straw. He examined it for a few moments, tried to suck, got the hang of it and gulped the banana-flavoured liquid down, clearly pleased with the taste. This was much nicer than his usual warm milk.

Megan picked at the French fries, gazing vacantly at the wall in front of her. After a few minutes, she checked on the children. Jessica was still sucking at her bottle; Calum was gurgling happily as he drank the milkshake.

"I think that's enough for you," she said, reaching for the carton. The baby turned away, the milkshake still clutched in his chubby hands. "Calum," said Megan warningly. "You've had enough. You must leave some for Mummy."

She started to take it from him, but his eyes screwed up in defiance, his grip tightening round the carton. "Let go, you naughty boy," she scolded and plucked the milkshake from his hands. For a couple of seconds, he looked up at her imploringly, but when she put the flattened-out straw to her own lips, he opened his mouth and let out an ear-splitting yell.

"Stop it, Calum," she said sternly, glancing around in embarrassment.

"I want, I want..." he screamed, his face bright red, his arms stretched out in demand while, beside him, Jessica sat drawing at her bottle in angelic innocence.

"Shut up, Calum," she shrieked. His screams got louder.

She unfastened his harness and took him onto her knee. Calum always responded to a cuddle and, for several seconds, the noise abated. But as soon as she put the milkshake to her lips, the screams began again.

"That's enough," she snapped and, thumping the milkshake down on the table, she tried to put him back in the buggy.

His screams became even louder as he arched his back and kicked. A hush fell over the restaurant. Everyone's attention was focused on the warring mother and child. Out of the corner of her eye, Megan saw enquiring eyes, some hostile, some sympathetic, some simply amused. The colour rushed to her cheeks. She lost her temper and shouted, "Shut up you little monster!" And for the first time ever, she smacked her son.

The shock took his breath away. Hastily, Megan shoved him into the buggy, fumbling to fasten his harness. Abandoning the now cold French fries and the half-consumed milkshake, she blindly thrust the pushchair ahead of her to the exit. Two youths sprang up and held the door open and, as it closed behind her, she heard the interrupted conversations take up where they had left off. Trembling with anger and embarrassment, she slipped round the corner to wait for Connie.

"Well," said Connie teasingly when she joined Megan later. "That was a show-stopper!"

"I didn't enjoy it," complained Megan.

"I thought Calum was always such a good baby."

"He is," claimed his mother defensively.

"What's all this about? Why did you want to see me so urgently?"

Stumbling over her words, Megan explained about Robert.

"Is that all?" said Connie when she'd finished. Megan turned away, clearly hurt. Connie went on, "I mean to say, two weeks isn't a lifetime."

The Welsh girl frowned at Connie. "How can you be so hateful?" she gasped. "I really thought I could rely on you. No one understands. Well, I can do without you, without anybody. Calum and me, we'll make out all on our own. I'll force Christopher's mother to let me see him." With that, she swivelled the pushchair round and strode off.

Connie stiffened with indignation. "Is that all the thanks I get for being your nurse-maid?" she called after her, but Megan was out of earshot.

Things were looking up for Reece. After moving in with Ben, he left McDonalds and found a job at a garden centre. It didn't take him long to realise that he had at last found his niche.

His interest in plants and trees dated back to the period he had spent with his sister and her husband. His brother-in-law had run a market gardening business and during the school holidays Reece had helped out with the donkey-work. If Howard hadn't gone to pieces at Mary's death, the boy would no doubt have gone on his payroll after leaving school. Unfortunately, her husband had been as much affected by his wife's untimely demise as her young brother had been. Losing interest in his booming business, he had sold up and returned to his home town of Vancouver, leaving the teenager alone once more.

Reece's new employers were surprised by the extent of his knowledge and he was quickly given more responsibility. It didn't take long for the word to get around and soon customers were regularly seeking him out for advice.

Several weeks after he'd moved in with Ben, Thea Jenson paid her brother a visit. Reece was delighted to see her, and she seemed equally pleased to see him.

"How long are you staying?" he asked her.

"Just for a week."

Ben explained. "Our pa's been banged up for six months, that's why she's come."

Reece was surprised. "That's a short sentence. With remission, he'll be out in four."

"Yeah," agreed Ben. "That's justice for you."

"I shall be making the most of my time down here," said Thea. "Up at the crack of dawn tomorrow to do some exploring."

"Tomorrow's my day off, I'll show you around if you'd like," offered Reece.

"Would you?" She smiled with pleasure, displaying her large slightly protruding teeth, and added pointedly. "Ben certainly won't bother."

Her brother grinned in his turn. "I'll let you two get on with it. I'm warning you, Reece, she'll run you off your feet."

"That reminds me," said Thea. "How's the foot?"

"Good as new," replied Reece. "Now, about tomorrow, where would you like to go?"

"London."

"It's a big place. What do you want to see?"

"Everything," said Thea. "This is my first time in London."

Next morning, they got up early and made for the Tower of London. Thea was as excited as a little girl, pointing at everything and asking the Beefeaters lots of questions.

"I can't get over this, Reece," she said. "I would have come down to London before if I'd known it was going to be such fun."

The fun for him was being with her. She was a lively companion, game for anything and full of energy. As Ben had predicted, she practically ran him off his feet. St Paul's was scheduled for the afternoon so their stop for lunch was hurried.

"Get a move on, we can't waste time eating," said Thea, shovelling the last piece of pizza into her mouth. "We've got to cram in as much sightseeing as possible."

"Why don't you move down here?" Reece asked her.

"I might once I've come to the end of my course," she said. "That is, if Ma's okay."

"Clelia will look after her; you said, yourself, she doesn't want to leave Birmingham because of her boyfriend."

"Nathan? Yeah..." said Thea reflectively.

The day ended with a visit to the cinema. Once they were comfortably settled in their seats and the lights dimmed, Reece slipped an arm round Thea's shoulders. She didn't object, and when he kissed the nape of her neck, where her shiny black hair stuck out, she giggled and whispered, "Naughty."

Ben wasn't around when they got home so they made a cup of tea and sat down on the beanbags in front of the television. Neither of them wanted the day to end. Thea glanced around the sparsely furnished room and said, "I'm not sure I like Ben's taste in decor."

"He hasn't finished it yet," replied Reece in his friend's defence.

To his surprise, Thea sprang to her feet. Going to the centre of the room, she stood akimbo pointing out the things she particularly didn't care for. "For starters, I'd get rid of those kettledrums and that leopard-skin rug would have to go. Where on earth did he pick them up?"

"In a market somewhere I'd say."

"They're too African, out of place in Twickenham."

"How would you decorate this room?" asked Reece.

"Umm! It would have to be light and bright because the room faces north. I'd put back the original fireplace, restore the ceiling rose, rub down the floor to its pine finish, reinstate the door furniture..."

"Hey, wait a minute," cried Reece. "That would cost a fortune."

She laughed. "I know."

"You seem really interested in decorating."

"During the holidays I did a stint at Habitat."

Sighing contentedly, she returned to sit next to him on the beanbags and, without invitation, rested her head on his shoulder, whispering, "I've had a lovely time today, Reece."

"Me too," he whispered back and, tilting her chin, kissed her.

He was surprised at the strength of his feelings for her. They kissed and hugged, although both knew instinctively that things would go no further. Reece didn't mind. Sex with Connie had been exciting; making love to Chantal had been a learning process. He wanted it to be different with this girl. With Thea, he wanted to proceed slowly and he was pleased to see that she, too, had no wish to rush into a relationship.

For the rest of her stay, they met each evening after he'd finished work and Reece was surprised to discover that, despite her forthright manner, Thea was a shy girl. She wasn't anxious to meet Ben's buddies at Deceptions, was even hesitant about meeting his colleagues at McDonalds although Connie soon put her at her ease. On her last night Connie joined them at the flat and, together with Ben, they spent the evening watching a video. When her brother brought out a shag of cannabis and started to roll a joint, Thea refused it.

"Suit yourself," said Ben and offered it to the others. But Thea's refusal influenced Reece and he shook his head. The four relaxed into comfortable companionship: Thea and Reece opposite one another on the only available easy chairs, Ben and Connie sprawled out on the beanbags. The dope had its effect. Before long, Connie was half-asleep, her head resting on Ben's lap while he followed the images on the screen through half closed eyelids. Occasionally, Connie gave a giggle and reached up to tweak the shared joint from his stubby fingers.

After half an hour, Reece looked across at Thea. "I don't think much of this film, do you?" he said. Nodding towards the other two, he went on, "Those two are out of it. It's a lovely evening. Do you fancy going for a walk?"

"Yes," smiled Thea.

They got up and crept out of the room, hand-in-hand.

"Where did you two get to last night?" demanded Ben when he met Reece in the narrow hall next morning.

Reece didn't like the challenge in his tone. "We went for a walk, why?"

Ben glowered. "Don't get too friendly with my sister." Turning his back, he disappeared into the bathroom, slamming the door after him.

Reece shrugged and went on his way. There was no point in making an issue of it. These were early days. He'd said goodbye to Thea the night before because he'd guessed she'd still be asleep when he left for work in the morning. He knew he'd miss her and had every intention of accepting her invitation to visit the family in Birmingham.

"Ma and the girls would love to see you again," she'd said. "And next time, you won't be on sentry duty. We'll be able to go out and have fun. I'll show you the high spots."

Carrying her promise in his thoughts, he left the flat with a spring in his step, but when he got to work, his spirits sank.

"The boss wants to see you in his office," said his supervisor as soon as he arrived.

What have I done now, thought Reece as he checked his bottle green and orange uniform for stains and creases. In the staff washroom, he smoothed his beard and splashed water on his hair, acknowledging that it badly needed a trim.

To his surprise, the boss's opening words were welcoming. "Reece! Morning, take a seat. I'll be with you in a minute. Just got to finish off here."

"Good morning, Mr Randle."

The formality of his superiors at the garden centre had disconcerted him at first. He had never before worked for a company with such regard for rank. The friendly greeting made him suspicious. It could mean anything: promotion, a transfer, the sack. He sat down in the chair offered him and tried not to look ill at ease. To while away the time, he studied his boss, a self-important, vertically challenged character. He could hear him muttering to himself from behind the computer.

Randle looked up. "Sorry about this, just something I had to sort out." Finished at last he swivelled his chair round to face Reece and said, "Well, my boy, I've heard glowing reports about you. Are you happy at Gardens Unlimited?"

Taken aback, Reece blinked and said politely, "Yes, very."

"What are your career intentions, Reece?"

"I'm not absolutely sure, although I feel at home in this environment."

Randle relaxed back in his black leather chair, his fingertips pressed together, his bushy brows drawn into a thoughtful frown. "Well, Reece ..."

The continual use of his name began to irritate Reece. Get on with it you pompous moron, he thought, if you're going to tell me how much you value my services, but find you can't keep me on, get on with it and say so.

" ... we've decided to chance a little investment in you, that is, of course, provided you're prepared to make a commitment to the company." Randle looked up enquiringly. "Would you be interested?"

Alert now, Reece leant forward. "What have you got in mind, Sir?"

Randle tipped the adjustable chair forward, leant his short arms on the desk and said confidentially, "We'd like to send you to college, part-time of course, with a commitment from you to stay with the company for at least a year. You'd come out of it with a respectable qualification."

Reece was stunned. This was the last thing he had expected. "Would it mean a drop in salary?" he gasped before he could stop himself.

"On the contrary, it could mean a rise."

Enthusiasm lit up Reece's face. "It sounds great, but I need to know more about it. When would I have to start this course and what would it involve?"

"Commitment, my son, that's what it would involve." Randle clearly felt at home with 'commitment'. In contrast, it was a word, which Reece had always shied away from. "Starting October, college three days a week, your duties here three days, including weekends. Wednesday's off. There is one thing though ..." He paused, a smile twitching at his lips.

Here comes the catch, thought Reece dolefully.

"The whiskers will have to go. For our image, you know. We're a mite conventional here at Gardens Unlimited ..."

At the mention of his beard, the rest of Randle's words were lost on Reece. Shave off his beard! Instinctively, his hand went to his jaw line. He'd had the beard so long he couldn't remember what he looked like without it.

"I can see you're surprised by this opportunity ..." Randle's voice penetrated his thoughts. "...and as, I told you, we don't usually make offers like this."

Reece gulped. The beard was the essence of his personality. Without it, he became Everyday Joe, an ordinary bloke with very little going for him. It made him different. With a jolt, he realised that for years, he'd used the striking auburn growth to hide behind. Would shaving it off expose his shyness, his vulnerability?

"Well," finished Randle. "I can see I've taken you by surprise."

Reece managed a smile and got to his feet as Randle came around from behind his desk. "Congratulations my boy, no need to give an answer now. Think about it, think about it very seriously."

Minutes later, Reece found himself walking back to his post still fingering his beard. Maybe it was time to shave it off, to move on.

"Go for it!" cried Connie when he called in to see her later that day.

He'd sought her out because who else did he know with such commonsense, such a capacity for solving other people's problems?

"But a year's a heck of a long time," he protested. "Normally, I never plan more than a week ahead."

"It'll fly past." She gripped him by the wrists. "You must do it, Reece, chances like this don't turn up every day. It will give you a goal to work to."

His thoughts flew to Thea. Weekend visits to Birmingham would be out of the question. Maybe she could be persuaded to come down South!

"It means shaving off the beard," he said ruefully.

"Good riddance I say; it makes you look like Rasputin."

"And I'll have to get a haircut," protested Reece.

"About time too."

"Look who's talking?" he gasped. "You're the last person to advocate convention."

She laughed. "This opportunity's worth the sacrifice."

There was no arguing with Connie. She spoke good sense and confiding in her brought him to a decision. He would accept the offer. With a valid piece of paper in his hand, in a year or two, he could move on, make a career for himself. Maybe, Chantal... Brusquely, he pushed aside the girl's image. Chantal was history. Thea was the present, a real live girl who'd shown an interest in him; but would she like the clean-shaven version?

Brushing aside last-minute doubts, he grinned at Connie and said, "You're right. Tomorrow, I shall tell Randle I'd like to go for it."

CHAPTER NINE

Megan sat on the bench beside the river drumming her fingertips on its armrest. It was a blustery yet warm afternoon. The surface of the water leapt and foamed, tossing the moored boats about like paper replicas. Calum and Jessica were contentedly watching a group of swans swimming close to the towpath.

"Where are you, Robert?" she muttered to herself, glancing yet again at her watch.

This was the third afternoon she'd spent waiting for him. It was over three weeks since they'd last met and she knew, in her heart, that the holiday excuse had been the thin edge of the wedge. He wanted out, he was fed-up with playing messenger boy. A surge of impatience made her jump to her feet. Swivelling the double buggy around, she pushed it across the springy turf, blinded by tears.

Lorraine met her at the front door. She seemed to be in a good mood. "Take the evening off, Megan," she said, releasing Jessica's harness and lifting her out of the pushchair. "I'll see to the children's tea and put them to bed."

Megan was puzzled. Although the pendant incident seemed to have been forgotten, she felt suspicious.

Lorraine flashed her a dazzling smile. "Go off and have fun."

"Thanks, Lorraine," said Megan and, after giving her son a goodnight kiss, she went upstairs to change, still dogged by misgivings.

In the bedroom, she rummaged through her few clothes hanging in the wardrobe, finally choosing a short denim skirt and a white T-shirt. As she changed, she made plans: she'd go to Thames Ditton and seek out Christopher. Without Calum in tow, Mrs Mills might not be so hostile towards her. She marshalled her thoughts. What if his parents were out for the evening and Christopher were on his own! This possibility lifted her spirits. She turned her attention to footwear, deciding against wearing her new high-heeled sandals, since she wasn't yet used to them, opting instead for her comfortable navy canvas kickers. They were dusty from her frequent treks in the park, but a quick wipe with a damp cloth brought them back to life and the thin patch where her toe was nearly poking through was hardly noticeable. At the last minute she snatched up a cardigan in case it turned chilly later on.

Feeling elated, she left the house. Her imagination took off: Christopher had had his operation and was convalescing in the garden. She pictured the dusk of an Indian summer, saw herself sitting beside him under an apple tree, holding his hand, stroking his forehead, pouring him refreshing glasses of lemonade.

The bravado that had propelled her from Strawberry Vale to her destination had waned by the time she reached Thames Ditton. Getting off the bus, she adjusted her shoulder bag and took a deep breath. Christopher's house was only a few yards from the bus stop; it was broad daylight and there was no way she could hide her approach from anybody watching at the window.

She crossed the road on trembling legs, misgivings looming larger with every step. Suppose his mother still wouldn't let her see him! She recalled, with trepidation, that his brother, Daniel, disliked her. Could he have sewn the seeds of hate in his mother's heart? Hesitating at the gate, she considered her chances: one in three that Christopher would be the one to open the door.

She rang the bell. A woman she'd never seen before greeted her.

Megan was taken aback. When she failed to speak, the woman asked, "What do you want?"

"Er, er, is Christopher in?" mumbled Megan.

"Christopher who?"

"Christopher Mills, he lives here."

"Oh you mean the lad who's poorly. He's gone, I'm afraid."

The colour drained from Megan's face. "Gone?" she gasped.

The woman edged back into the house, half closing the door. "Yes, the Mills family moved out two weeks ago. I've had lots of callers ever since." She threw up her hands in exasperation. "And the phone never stops ringing. We're having to change the number." She gave an indignant sniff. "At great expense, I might add."

Megan's relief was so great, she could hardly breathe. She'd misunderstood the woman. Christopher had gone away, he hadn't died. The woman started to close the door. Megan stopped her. "Please, have you got their new address?"

"No. I keep telling people." She frowned impatiently. "These enquiries about the boy are endless. I really can't be held responsible for his whereabouts. You'd better ask the Post Office."

"Is Christopher all right? Has he had the transplant?"

"I've no idea." The woman glanced back over her shoulder. "Sorry, I've got to go. My cakes are burning."

The door shut and Megan was left staring at its dark green paintwork. She leant against the wall and tried to take in the news. Her breath came in short bursts; her heart pounded erratically. The woman was lying, of that she was certain. She must know the Mills' new address.

She rang the bell again. The woman answered it at once, rubbing floury hands down her apron and brandishing a rolling pin. "You again!" Megan drew back in alarm. Realising that she had startled the girl, the woman went on in a more kindly tone. "I'm sorry I can't tell you any more than I've already told you. Now please go, I'm very busy."

"Wait!" cried Megan as the door began to close. "Please give me just a few minutes of your time, then I promise I'll leave."

The woman heaved a long-suffering sigh. "Well?"

"When you bought the house from the Mills', they must have given you some idea of where they were going."

"We're renting. It's all above board, through an agency. We've never met or spoken to the owners. I really must get on with my baking. I've got the in-laws coming tomorrow."

"Thank you for your help," muttered Megan to the closing front door.

Megan stumbled down the path to the road. Had Robert known that Christopher had moved away? Was that why he hadn't bothered to meet her? A multitude of questions careered across her mind as she ran all the way to the bus stop. She was panting for breath, just the way she used to on school sports day when she put all her effort into pleasing her father by striving to come first in the 300 metres. An elderly couple joined her and the woman, showing concern, touched her arm. "Are you all right, dear?" she asked. "Only you look rather flushed and out of breath."

Does it show that much, thought Megan, politely thanking the woman and hastily fabricating a story that she had run and just missed a bus.

"Don't worry," said the woman. "There'll be another one along in a minute. You're not from around here, are you?"

Megan shook her head.

"Thought not." She raised an enquiring eyebrow. "Welsh? Which part do you come from?"

"Swansea," supplied Megan, wishing with all her heart that the woman would stop her chatter.

"We had a holiday down there once, didn't we George?" she said, nudging her husband with her elbow.

"What, my dear? Oh, yes, we did. Very nice part of the world, if I might say so."

Praise for the natural beauty of Swansea and its surroundings continued for several more minutes, mostly coming from the woman with her husband nodding in agreement.

At last the bus came into sight and they all boarded it. Megan made a point of going upstairs in order to get away from the over-friendly couple.

"Goodbye, my dear," called out the woman. "Nice to have met you."

But the incidental conversation brought Megan to her senses. The Mills family had moved away, she reflected. So what? It couldn't be that difficult to trace them. There was the letting agency. She wished she had thought to ask its name. Then, there was the college Daniel attended; they would know. By the time she reached Strawberry Vale, she had managed to convince herself that all was not lost and that it was only a matter of time before she would see Christopher again.

Letting herself into the house, she ran upstairs before Lorraine could accost her. Calum was in his cot, almost asleep. She glanced at her watch. It was only six o'clock. He didn't usually go to bed until seven. Not wanting to disturb him, she crept out of the room and peeped into the nursery. Jessica, too, was already in bed. Tears smarted at her eyes. She desperately needed time on her own, but with the children just dropping off to sleep, there was no-where to go. She would just have to go downstairs and face Lorraine's patronising waffle.

It was as she was going back out onto the landing that she heard noises coming from the Goddard's bedroom. Hesitating, she couldn't help giving a small snigger. Michael must have got back from his trip earlier than expected and, by the sound of things, they had patched up their differences.

Running lightly downstairs, she was startled when the front door started to open. Michael walked in and dumped an overnight bag on the floor. "Hello Megan," he said. "Is my wife home yet?"

Megan felt the colour rush to her cheeks. "I don't know," she stuttered. "I didn't think you were due back until tomorrow."

"The meeting was cut short," he replied and, much to Megan's relief he went into the sitting room, switched on the television, poured himself a whisky and sat down in an armchair.

Megan was dumbfounded. Who was in the bedroom with Lorraine? Should she go and warn her? She gave a gasp. Perhaps she'd misunderstood and Lorraine was ill, moaning on her sick bed.

Hardly daring to let Michael out of her sight, Megan lingered just inside the room playing for time by making small talk. "The weather's been nice," she ventured.

He glanced over his shoulder at her, seeming surprised that she hadn't moved from the doorway and said, "Has it? It's been raining in Carlisle."

"Is it a nice place?" She enquired, addressing his back. She felt compelled to stand guard at the door, barring his exit.

Again, he turned and glanced at her. "Is what a nice place?"

"Carlisle."

He looked puzzled. "Why, are you thinking of going there?"

Megan shuffled from one foot to the other, her colour deepening even more. "Oh no, I was just interested."

"Why don't you come in and take a seat?" he said. "No point in hovering about in the doorway." He pointedly pressed the volume button on the remote control. "I'd rather like to watch the News."

"No, I won't join you if you don't mind. I've got things to do," replied Megan, sighing with relief. The News would keep him occupied for at least half an hour.

As she turned to leave the room, Michael called her back. "Check to see if my wife's upstairs will you?"

With her cheeks flushed bright scarlet, Megan swivelled on her heels and left the room pulling the door to after her.

Taking the stairs two at a time, she paused when she reached the landing. Apart from Jessica's gentle snoring, there wasn't a sound coming from any of the bedrooms. I must have imagined it earlier, she thought and, feeling calmer, walked along the corridor to the master bedroom. Stopping at the door, she raised her arm in readiness to knock. Before she could do so, the door swung open and, for the second time that day, she found herself face-to-face with a stranger.

The man facing her was not very tall. In fact, Megan found herself looking him squarely in the eyes - dark brown, expressive eyes. He was as surprised as she was. Stopping in his tracks, he clamped his mouth shut mid-sentence and stared at her, clearly embarrassed by having been caught with his trousers down.

"What is it, *tesoro*?" called Lorraine.

The man spun round and snapped, "*Idiota*! You said we had the house to ourselves!"

There was a rustle of sheets and Lorraine ran to stand beside him, a robe hastily thrown over her nakedness.

"Megan!" she exclaimed in surprise. Surprise changed to anger. "I thought I told you to take the evening off."

Megan's legs began to tremble. Pressing a finger to her lips, she frowned earnestly at her employer and whispered urgently, "Your husband's downstairs."

Lorraine's hand flew to her mouth. "My God! Quick, Luca, hide!"

Luca's eyes flashed. "Hide?" He spat out the word with utter disgust. "Are you suggesting that I cower in a corner!"

Megan's gaze darted towards the staircase. "Quick," she pleaded. "If you hurry, you can sneak out while Michael's watching the News."

The man's indignation mounted. Drawing himself up to his full height, he said indignantly, "*Madre di Dio*, Luca Marotti no hide from nobody!"

Lorraine cut short his protestations. Kissing him briefly on the cheek, she thrust an armful of clothes at him, coaxing him towards the door with, "Go quickly. Please, *amore*, for my sake. I'll ring you tomorrow."

Megan saw that the sitting room door was still slightly ajar and, while the Italian was pulling on his trousers, she ran downstairs and slipped into the room, closing the door behind her.

Without taking his gaze from the screen, Michael said, "Well?"

Megan gave a start. "Well what?" she gasped.

"Is my wife upstairs?"

"Yes ... yes," stuttered Megan, adding the first thing that came into her head. "She's not feeling well. She's gone to bed with a migraine."

"What brought you home early?" enquired Lorraine later that evening after Michael had disappeared into his study to catch up with some paperwork.

"I forgot something," lied Megan. "It was lucky that I was able to distract your husband."

Lorraine threw her a sharp glance. "You didn't see anything," she said pointedly. "There was no-one here. Just remember that."

Megan gulped and stared back at her. No word of thanks, no hint of gratitude! Furiously, she turned on her employer. "I helped you out, remember that!" she retorted.

Lorraine gave a disdainful look. "Careful, don't forget you're still under threat of notice."

"What?" shrieked Megan.

"Keep your voice down," cautioned Lorraine. "Let's come to an agreement, shall we? Don't make trouble for me and I won't make trouble for you."

Megan's fury mounted. It would be wonderful to spill the beans, to bring Lorraine down a peg or two. However, the thought of Calum asleep upstairs made her bite back an angry riposte.

The uneasy truce between the two women endured into its second week, although Megan didn't have time to dwell on it because her thoughts were filled with more pressing worries.

She phoned Robert on numerous occasions and, on getting no reply, left explanatory messages on his answer-phone. She tried the college, only to discover that the office was closed for the summer vacation. At last, one afternoon after settling the babies down for their nap, she went downstairs to the phone in the hall, picked up the receiver and tried Robert's number again. This time, she managed to catch him.

His unwillingness to continue with his involvement was evident. "I don't know where they've moved to. Christopher didn't mention anything to me when I last saw him."

"He must have said something, dropped a hint at least."

"He didn't," growled Robert. "Don't be so impatient. He's not been gone long, I expect he'll write to you once he's settled down."

Megan's voice rose in panic. "But suppose he's gone into hospital for a transplant."

"Why don't you phone the hospital?"

"Which hospital?"

"Try Kingston for starters. Listen, Megan, I've got to go now. See you around."

Before she could reply, the line went dead. Megan replaced the receiver and stood trembling with anger and frustration. How could Robert be so offhand? Surely he understood how ill Christopher was! Surely he knew how much she cared! With a sigh of despair, she reached for the telephone directory and thumbed through it for the number of Kingston Hospital.

"There's no one here of that name," came the receptionist's reply.

"Has he been in and gone home again?" asked Megan. After all, several weeks had elapsed. Enough time for the whole dreadful thing to be over and done with.

"Not that I know of."

"Can you put me through to someone on the Surgical Ward?" she insisted.

"It won't do you any good," replied the girl tartly. "They won't tell you."

Megan's spirits sank. It was hopeless. No one cared. She longed to talk to Connie. Pride wouldn't let her, not after their recent disagreement. Everybody had let her down. Overwhelmed by self-pity, she flopped onto the bottom stair, lowered her head into her hands and sobbed.

That was where Michael Goddard found her.

"Whatever's the matter, my dear?" he asked, putting out a hand and helping her to her feet. With a flourish, he withdrew a folded handkerchief from his pocket and offered it to her.

Megan took it and dabbed her eyes, muttering, "Sorry, you must think me awfully silly."

"I hope my wife hasn't torn you off a strip."

Megan shook her head. "Of course not. It's just ... just something personal."

"Come and sit down in here, you look really upset."

He led her into the sitting room and poured her a brandy. "This will help to calm you."

Megan looked at the glass warily, but she took it from him and obediently took a sip. The burning liquid trickled down her throat nearly choking her. She had never tasted brandy before. The product of strictly teetotal parents the most she'd ever had was half a pint of cider or the occasional glass of white wine with her school chums. She knew her father would be shocked if he could see her.

With her chest still heaving with the occasional sob, she tried to marshal her thoughts. Michael's kindness made her even more emotional.

"My dear, come here." Before she knew what was happening, she was wrapped in Michael's embrace.

The comfort of his arms was almost too much to bear. Since Calum's birth, she had fought against breaking down, had struggled to maintain a stable routine for her child. Not once, had she asked for help from her parents. They had, of course, kept her and her baby during the year before she'd left home, although she had never asked them to baby sit or requested any extras. The help they had given her had been entirely of their volition. Now, in the arms of this good-looking man of the world, the feelings she had resolutely suppressed since the discovery of her pregnancy rushed over her like a giant tidal wave, draining the energy from her limbs, sucking the air from her lungs. Her only recourse was to cling feebly to Michael's strength. If he let her go, she would drown in a flood of unutterable despair.

"I've tried, I've tried..." she sobbed. "But no-one will help me."

Michael held her tightly, gently pressing his lips to her blond hair. As she quietened, he ran a light hand down her spine, stopping in the hollow of her lower back, pulling her towards him. She was acutely aware of his masculinity, knew that what was happening wasn't right yet couldn't bring herself to draw away. It was Michael who withdrew.

"Another drink?" he enquired, deftly bringing normality back to the scene.

Why not? she thought, the effects of the first drink beginning to relax her. Giving her eyes another dab with his handkerchief, she nodded "yes". Michael set two drinks down on the glass-topped coffee table, then guided her to the sofa, sitting down opposite her and holding her hands loosely in his. Between diminishing sobs, she found herself opening up, telling him her troubles. His quiet sympathy moved her deeply. If only her father were like this!

A pleasant drowsiness crept over her, making her surroundings seem surreal. She heard Michael's voice as if from a distance: "I think you need to lie down. I'll help you upstairs."

She let him lead her, giggling when he stopped her from stumbling on the stairs. Opening the door at the end of the landing, he gently pushed her onto the bed.

She blinked and mumbled, "This isn't my room."

"I thought you'd be better in here. You don't want to wake Calum, do you?"

She smiled sweetly at him. How kind and thoughtful he was!

Resting her head back on the pillow, she allowed Michael to remove her shoes. When he started to unbutton her cardigan, she demurred and he stopped at once.

"Are you comfortable?" he asked.

A feeling of well being superseded her earlier distress. She felt cosseted, safe. Michael sat down on the edge of the bed and gently stroked her head, pushing a long strand of hair behind her ear. His hand was soothing. She shut her eyes and gave herself up to his pleasurable caresses.

His lips brushed her cheek, but she wasn't shocked. It seemed quite natural, to resist would seem ungrateful. He was only being kind. With his free hand, he slipped off her cardigan and tweaked the ties of her halter necked top.

"No bra," he whispered approvingly. His words startled her; somewhere in the depth of her being she knew it shouldn't be happening, but the brandy had deadened her senses. She couldn't summon the willpower to tell him to stop.

"What the hell's going on?" Lorraine's voice sliced through the web of sensuality in which Megan was ensnared.

Michael straightened up and, with amazing presence of mind, placed himself strategically in Lorraine's line of vision so that Megan could adjust her clothing. "Megan isn't well," he said. "I was feeling her forehead to find out whether she had a temperature."

Lorraine was beside herself. "Feeling for her temperature," she shrieked. "Do you take me for a fool?"

Michael got up and crossed the room, a smile on his face, his arms outstretched, but Lorraine side-stepped away from him. With a haughty lift of her shoulders, she pointed at Megan and hissed, "Get out, you man-eating little vixen, get out of my house!"

Megan shrank back into the pillow. The colour drained from her cheeks. She felt nauseous with shame. What had come over her? How could she have let things go this far?

In contrast, Michael had completely recovered his composure. "Tut tut, my dear," he said, putting a hand on his wife's wrist. "The child's not well. Leave her to rest. Talk to her once you've calmed down. This is all a terrible misunderstanding."

Lorraine shook her arm free and, before Michael could stop her, she launched herself at Megan and slapped her face.

Michael's placating manner vanished. Seizing Lorraine's wrist, he pulled her clear of Megan, who was curled into a foetal ball, sobbing in terror.

Dragging his wife into the hall, he marched her along to the master bedroom and shoved her inside. Megan could still hear her yelling insults. She knelt up on the bed, hugging herself to stop the trembling and tried to shut out the sounds.

"How could you, Michael," screamed Lorraine. "How could you deceive me with that little tart?"

"She's not a tart, as well you know."

"The conniving cow ensnared you, trapped you with her innocent ways."

"Stop it, Lorraine," shouted Michael. "You're in no position to point the finger. What about *your* catalogue of peccadilloes? Don't think I don't know what's going on?" He gave a hoarse laugh. "What's good for the goose is good for the gander!"

Megan could barely breathe. Her heart thumped almost as loudly as the slanging match taking place down the hall. But through her distress, a baby's cry penetrated. The shouting had woken Calum. Springing to her feet, she raced along the corridor and flung herself at his cot. On seeing her, he stood up and reached out his arms. Lifting him up, she held him tightly and paced the floor until his sobs had subsided. When he became quiet, she put him down on the floor with some toys and, pulling out her suitcase, started to fling clothes into it. It was soon bulging and, not bothering about the things that wouldn't fit in, she changed Calum's nappy, collected his buggy and, picking him up, struggled towards the door.

On the landing, all seemed quiet. The fighting had ceased. Creeping past the master bedroom, she hesitated outside the door, almost frozen to the spot with dread. There wasn't a sound. She took a tentative step, wary of the creaky floorboard at the top of the stairs. A rustling noise reached her, then Lorraine's voice: "Oh Michael, you are a naughty boy!"

It seemed the battle was over, but Megan wasn't going to wait to discover her fate. Michael had persuaded his wife to keep her on once, but even if he were clever enough to talk his way out of this compromising situation, she knew she couldn't stay there. Lorraine would never trust her or Michael again. She couldn't blame her. It was time to leave the Goddard's household. With a heavy heart she went downstairs and let herself out of the front door.

There were no tears left now, only a gut-wrenching fear. She had no friends, very little money, a young child to care for and she was homeless. There was only one course of action. She would just have to throw herself on Connie's mercy.

It was a long walk to Tennyson Avenue, made difficult by the bulky suitcase and the buggy, whose swivel wheels refused to swivel. With a sigh of relief, she knocked at the front door. Even if Connie wasn't there, she was confident that someone in the house would be sympathetic enough to let her wait inside for Connie's return. There was no answer. Sinking down onto the doorstep, she decided to wait.

After half an hour, the next-door neighbour arrived home. Stopping at the gate, she said not unkindly, "You'll have a long wait, love, all the students have gone home for the summer vacation. They're not due back until the middle of the month."

"My friend hasn't gone home," said Megan. "She's staying on over the summer."

"If you mean Connie Dixon, I'm afraid she's gone too."

Megan jumped to her feet in alarm. "What?" she gasped.

"She's gone abroad."

"Gone abroad? When will she be back?"

"Lord knows! These students come and go as they please these days." Seeing the look of dismay on Megan's face, the woman added, "I'm sure she'll return in time for the start of term."

The start of term! That was weeks away. With a shudder of dismay, Megan thanked the woman, who smiled, "You're welcome," before going into her house and closing the door.

Left alone on the doorstep, Megan almost gave way to despair. It was getting dark, the air was chilly and, although Calum had fallen asleep, he didn't look very comfortable with his head resting on the side of the pushchair. She pulled out a blanket from her rucksack and wrapped it around him, then delved into the suitcase for a jumper for herself.

With her heart pounding, she glanced around. What was she going to do? If only she could find a way into the house. Connie wouldn't mind if she and Calum took up residence for a few days until she had time to sort something out. But all the windows were securely shut and, since the house was mid-terrace, there was no way of getting into the back garden where she could have found temporary shelter in the shed.

She glanced down at her sleeping child and felt panic rise, shame too. This was exactly the gloomy prediction her father had made. "Stay here with us," he'd argued when she'd tentatively put forward the suggestion that she and Calum would be better off living independently. "You're still only a child yourself. If you leave our protection, you'll end up on the streets. You've seen those TV pictures of homeless youngsters living in a cardboard box." It was her father's inflexibility that had driven her to leave home secretly, unavoidably hurting her mother's feelings.

Opening her purse, she counted the money she had left, realising with a groan of regret, that pay-day fell at the end of the week. She could have done with the extra few pounds. Her tummy rumbled and she remembered that she hadn't had anything to eat since breakfast. At lunchtime, going to look for Robert at their riverside meeting place had driven everything else from her mind. She counted the money again. There was enough left for a big mac and fries and a milkshake to share with Calum. Collecting her belongings together, she embarked on the long walk to York Street and McDonalds.

The restaurant wasn't busy. Megan soon made her purchases and settled Calum into a quiet corner. Although she was ravenous, she deliberately took a long time to eat the food, studying people as they came and went, envying them. They had a warm house to go home to. But gradually a strange calmness came over her. The prospect of homelessness no longer frightened her. Her mind skipped back over the episode with Michael. She saw now that he'd played with her to get back at his wife. In many ways, freeing herself from the clutches of that self-indulgent, bickering couple with their obnoxious child, was a relief. The most important issue was Christopher's whereabouts. There must be a way to track him down. Whole families didn't just disappear into thin air.

"Excuse me, don't I know you?"

Megan looked up and met the amber eyes of a tall auburn-haired young man. He looked vaguely familiar.

Frowning in puzzlement, she said, "I'm not sure."

He sat down uninvited at her table and said, "You're a friend of Connie Dixon's aren't you? We met a few weeks ago. Don't you remember?" He fingered his chin. "I've shave off my beard since then."

"Oh yes," gasped Megan. "But I don't remember your name."

"Reece Cassidy," he said, taking her hand in a firm grip. "You are ... ?

"Megan Hughes," she supplied.

"I hope you don't mind me joining you," he said. "The girl behind the counter is going to call me when my burger's ready. Can I share your table?"

"If you like," muttered Megan begrudgingly.

"We're both strangers to these parts, I think," said Reece. He seemed intent on making conversation.

"Strangers?"

"I'm from Canada, and you're from Wales, aren't you?"

"Yes."

"What are you doing in Twickenham?"

Megan looked down at her hands and mumbled, "I was working as a nanny."

"Did I detect the past tense?"

Megan nodded and said curtly, "I walked out today."

Instinctively, Reece's gaze dropped to the sleeping baby in the pushchair. For a moment, he looked alarmed.

Megan gave a gasp and hastened to reassure him. "No, I've done nothing wrong. Calum's mine. I was looking after the Goddard's baby girl, Jessica."

Relief flooded Reece's features. "You must have been living-in; where are you going to stay tonight?"

"No-where."

Now he *did* look shocked. "That's impossible. You can't sleep out in the open."

Megan shrugged. "I've no money, and apart from Connie, who's gone on holiday, I don't know anybody around here." She paused before adding with a touch of bitterness, "There's Robert of course, but he wouldn't want to know about my problems."

Reece turned his head as he heard his name being called. "Don't go," he ordered her. "I'll be back in a minute."

When he returned with his burger and fries, he said, "Have you had enough to eat? I'll get you another burger if you like." Pointing at Calum, he added, "What about him, is he hungry? What do babies eat?"

Megan couldn't help smiling. "He's had his tea," she said. "He'll probably sleep through until the morning."

The conversation seemed absurd. After everything that had happened that day, this talk of feeding Calum seemed too mundane to be real.

She realised that Reece was staring at her. "Listen," he said. "We can put you up tonight."

Megan tensed. "That's very kind; I wouldn't hear of it," she replied. After her recent experience, she knew that kindness had a way of turning sour.

In an effort to persuade her, Reece leant across the table and touched her wrist. With a startled gasp, she brushed his hand aside. He noticed her inflamed cheek and exclaimed, "Your face! Has someone slapped you?"

Megan blushed. So Lorraine had left her mark! "It's nothing," she muttered, putting up her hand to hide the blemish.

Reece sank back in his seat. "Look," he said. "As I see it, you don't have much choice. It's either a doorway, or a mattress on the floor at our place. I know which I'd choose." When she still looked doubtful, he said, "Connie would approve?"

"What do you mean?"

With a grin, he went on to describe his first meeting with Connie, how she'd rescued him from Ben and given him a bed for the night.

"You said we," said Megan. "Won't your flat-mates mind?"

Reece gave a laugh. "No," he said. "It's only Ben and with him, anything goes."

"Ben? You mean the guy who beat you up?"

"Yeah," nodded Reece with a grin. "Don't worry, he's quite friendly really and I've never known him beat up women and children. He only picks on his own size, or bigger."

Realising he was teasing her, Megan began to smile. This auburn-haired Canadian with his ready humour wasn't easy to refuse. Besides, as he'd pointed out, she really didn't have a choice.

"Thanks, Reece," she replied, impulsively touching his hand. "It would be such a relief to have a roof over our heads tonight."

CHAPTER TEN

"What's brought you home, Ben?"

Thea greeted her brother with a mixture of surprise and pleasure.

"Aren't you pleased to see me?"

"Of course I am, but normally, you only come home if there's a crisis."

"This time it's different," replied Ben giving his sister a broad grin. "How's Ma?"

"Ma's fine. She's gone out shopping with Naomi and Hannah."

She took her brother's hand and pushed him into a chair. "I was just making some tea, do you want a cup?"

"That sounds good."

"Strong and sweet?" she called from the kitchen.

"You know me," he called back.

Thea came back in with a tray of tea and biscuits. "How's Reece?" she asked.

"It's Reece I've come about," replied Ben.

Thea's hand shook slightly as she handed her brother a large mug with Bart Simpson's face on it. "Why, has something happened to him?"

Ben set the mug down on the coffee table and leant forward, his hands clasped together between his knees. "Look sis, I want you to stop writing to him."

Thea bristled. "Why?" She frowned. "How do you know we've been writing to one another?"

"I catch the post some mornings, recognised your handwriting."

She picked up her mug of tea and sat straight-backed in her chair, her attitude unyielding. "It's got nothing to do with you."

"He's no good, a drifter. D'you know, he spent three years with the travellers in Canada?"

"He told me."

"He's still pining for some girl in France, he's got no money, he's never had a steady job."

"He's getting on fine at the garden centre, and as for that girl, it's all over. He told me so."

"That's not what Connie told me."

"How does she know?"

"He tells her things."

"What things? I didn't think they were particularly friendly."

"He's been shagging her."

"Who? Connie? I don't believe you."

"Ask her yerself. Connie won't lie about it. She's up front about everything."

Thea thrust out her chin. "What does it matter? Reece and I are just friends."

"It's a dangerous friendship."

"No it's not."

Thea thumped her mug down on the table, looking angry.

"He's not our sort," insisted Ben.

Thea jumped to her feet. "Why, because he's white? Ben Jenson, you're no better than Pa with your bigoted opinions, your out-dated ideas, your prejudices. If this is what brought you up to Birmingham, you needn't have bothered. Reece and I are good friends and I'm not going to stop seeing him because of you." Spinning on her heel, she flounced out of the room.

Ben gave a swallow. He'd wanted to test the waters, to find out how his sister felt about the Canadian. Her reaction had said it all. Hating himself, he resolved to do his utmost to break up the relationship. It was only right that Thea should stick to her own kind.

A rattling at the door pushed the dilemma from his mind. Imelda Jenson and his younger sisters rushed in and he found himself swamped by affectionate hugs.

Reece woke up with a start, struggled to his feet and, still swathed in his sleeping bag, hobbled to the living room door. It burst open before he had time to reach for the handle.

"What the hell are you doing kipping in here? What's wrong with your bedroom?" asked Ben in surprise.

"I'll explain if you'll give me a chance," replied Reece.

Ben gave a snort. "I suppose you brought a girl back and now she's had the cheek to turf you out of your own room."

Reece gave a weak smile. "That's about the size of it."

Before he could explain further, Calum's cry reached them from along the hall.

"What's that?"

Reece hopped across the room again and closed the living room door. "Listen Ben, you're not to get the wrong idea. This kid's got a baby…"

Ben's eyes widened. "It's not that Welsh kid Connie's taken up with?"

Reece pointed to a six-pack stacked in the corner of the room. "Grab us a beer and I'll explain," he said.

The pair sat on the beanbags in front of the television while Reece described how he had met Megan in McDonalds and had impulsively invited her back for the night. He shrugged and said, apologetically, "One night somehow stretched to three."

"No wonder you look done in!" said Ben. "I suppose you've been sleeping on the floor since she arrived."

Reece nodded. "I'm afraid we're stuck with her."

"Stuck with her? You must be joking. It doesn't sound like she's got any dough and she can't stay here for free."

"She signed on yesterday so she'll get Housing Benefit and dole money soon."

"And who's keeping her in the meantime?"

Reece blushed. "I am of course."

A catalogue of objections crashed Ben's mind: baby paraphernalia, nappies, broken sleep!

"You're a sucker for a sob story, aren't you Reece?"

He tried to sound indignant, although something more significant had occurred to him. He'd returned to Twickenham with the intention of warning Reece off Thea. He didn't really want to get heavy. He liked Reece and didn't want to lose his friendship. He knew the Canadian wouldn't take kindly to him meddling in his affairs. He wasn't sure how far the relationship between his friend and his sister had progressed, but he was determined to nip it in the bud. Here was a god-given opportunity. He'd make sure that Thea found out Megan had moved in at Reece's invitation.

"Okay, okay, but are the pair of you prepared to share your room with a baby?"

Reece looked startled. "It isn't like that," he protested. "I don't fancy her and she's not interested in me. I'm sorry for her, that's all. I'm just looking out for her until Connie comes back." He paused, then went on, "Look, Ben, it'll only be for a short while. They won't be any trouble. They don't seem to have much gear apart from a pushchair and a few clothes. Can't they stay here while Megan looks for something else?"

All at once Ben's face broke into a wide grin. "I've got a better idea. Why doesn't she take the attic room."

Reece took heart. Clearly, Ben wasn't going to turf Megan and Calum out. "Why don't I move up there?" he suggested impulsively. "The room she's in now would be much better for them. Those stairs to the attic are terribly steep."

"You're on," grinned Ben, giving Reece a slap on the shoulder. "I'm off to bed. Sleep tight."

"Ben, lots of people have been asking for you. Where have you been?"

"Birmingham." He paused at the door and, turning back, added with a hint of malice, "Thea sends her love."

On her return, Connie was astonished to find Megan installed with Reece and Ben. The arrangement pleased her. Perhaps now, Megan would stop badgering her about Christopher. When she called at the flat, the Welsh girl asked her where she'd been.

"Bahrain. I went to visit Mum and Dad," replied Connie.

"I didn't know they lived abroad," said Megan in surprise. "I thought you weren't close to them. You never talk about them."

Connie cut her short. Since Della's appearance earlier in the summer, she had been deeply troubled and, when Steve sent her the plane fare so that she could visit them during the holidays, she jumped at the chance to re-establish her relationship with the two people who had so lovingly brought her up. She had allowed Linda and Steve to believe her low spirits were due to pre-exam blues, and the happy reunion with her adopted parents quickly restored the self-esteem so brutally shattered by Della's cruel revelations.

Tactfully, she changed the subject for, despite her outgoing personality, Connie was a private person and she was in no mood to confide in Megan.

"Living here will be much better for you; once you can get Calum into a day nursery, you'll be able to look for a job," she told her.

"Yes, things are looking up," agreed Megan. Connie heaved an inward sigh -- her prodigy seemed happier, more positive -- but her next words dispelled her relief. "But I've still got to find out where Christopher's gone to. Perhaps you could ask his brother."

"Daniel's dropped out of college," replied Connie.

"Oh dear!" Megan looked crestfallen. She had been pinning her hopes on Daniel. "What about Robert, will he know?"

"I doubt it," replied Connie. "You'd better ask him, although I think he's got a steady girlfriend. They're always together. He won't be interested in playing cupid for you two any more."

"But he *must* help us. He's my only link to Christopher. Chris will be devastated if we lose touch. He wants to have a hand in Calum's upbringing."

Connie lost patience. "Grow up, Megan, forget all about Chris, can't you see it's over ..." She paused. "Can't you see he's given you the big heave-ho."

Megan's mouth trembled. Oh dear, thought Connie, now she's going to cry. Regretting her sharp outburst, she put an arm around Megan's shoulder and tried to comfort her. Megan shook her off.

"I'll sort this out on my own," she snapped defensively. "I can see you've had enough of me."

Connie tried to make amends. "Even if you can't forget Chris, get on with your life and maybe things will work out in the end." She paused. "Sorry, must dash."

Picking up her duffle bag, she gave a wave and left.

Reece took Ben's words at face value. He had no reason to doubt the black man's sincerity; it never occurred to him that, in her brother's eyes, Thea Jenson was out of bounds to a white man. His preoccupation with this mistaken go-ahead from Ben blinded him to the black man's real intention. It wasn't until months later, when things had gone beyond the point of return, that he understood why Ben had so readily agreed to Megan making herself at home in the flat.

On her part, Thea made up her mind to ignore her brother's advice. She had never dated a white man before and she was determined to carry on whether Ben liked the arrangement or not. They continued to correspond and to telephone one another regularly until one day Calum interrupted their conversation by throwing a tantrum at Reece's feet just as his mother was about to put him to bed. The more Megan tried to drag him away, the more the baby stood his ground, clinging to Reece's trouser leg and screaming at the top of his voice. This was largely due to the bond that had developed between the Canadian and the baby. Reece always found time to play with him, tossing in the air, tumbling with him on the floor. Calum never tired of such games, gurgling happily and begging for more each time Reece tried to put him down.

"What's going on?" asked Thea.

"I can't explain now," shouted Reece. "We'll speak later."

Thea was the first to phone back. Megan answered the call. Both women were taken aback since neither knew of the existence of the other. "I'll tell him you called," said Megan stiffly, and at the other end of the line, Thea was left wondering whose girlfriend she was.

September arrived and things settled down for the four friends. Connie began thinking seriously about her future. She was in her last year at college and was already attending auditions. Always a girl to aim high, she longed to secure a part in a West End musical. Her confidence soared and waned and it was always Ben who kept her spirits up when the dreaded rejection letter arrived.

Ben was involved in negotiations for Deceptions, Reece was working hard at Gardens Unlimited and Megan had found herself a job at Tesco's. Ben was the only one who noticed Megan's increasing dependence on Reece.

October became November, the Indian Summer broke and, one afternoon, Megan at last caught up with Robert. Heeding Connie's advice, she had waited, praying for news. She was on the check-out ringing up purchases for a harassed shopper when she caught a glimpse of Robert leaving the supermarket. Two troublesome toddlers were sitting in the woman's trolley, fighting over a packet of sweets; the moving belt was piled high with groceries.

"Robert!" shouted Megan impulsively.

He stopped and half turned a startled face in her direction. His eyes widened, then he fled.

"Wait!" she yelled and, without a second thought, she left her post and dashed out of the door after him.

"Hey, what about me?" shouted the abandoned customer, waving an angry fist. "You can't run off like that!"

But nothing was going to stop Megan. It was pouring with rain; the street was crowded. Elbowing people aside, she forged a path for herself, splashing through puddles, desperation urging her on.

"Robert, stop!" she cried, panting as her prey ran even faster. She caught up with him at a pedestrian crossing, snatching at his sleeve as a car hooted a warning. He looked her, an expression of panic on his face. "What's the matter with you?" she shrieked. "I'm not going to bite you, I just want to know if you've got any news of Christopher."

"I haven't," he snapped, shaking off her hand.

"I don't believe you; you're hiding something from me," frowned Megan.

"Course I'm not."

The lights changed and he started to cross the road. She was close on his heels. "Robert," she pleaded. "You've got to tell me."

Realising that he was cornered, he pulled her into the shelter of a doorway. They were both out of breath, both rigid with emotion. Looking into his eyes, she read despair and guessed what he was going to tell her. Her hand flew to her mouth. "He's not?"

Robert nodded. "Two days ago ..." he stuttered. "They found a donor kidney for him, but it was too late; he died on the operating table."

She would have collapsed had the boy not propped her up. "I'm so sorry, Megan," he croaked. "I had no idea it would end like this. I loved him too, you know. He's been my best pal since primary school." He let go of Megan's arm to rub a fist across his eyes, glancing around in embarrassment. Now that he'd been forced to tell her, his manner changed to concern. He no longer tried to get away.

"Did he ever talk about me? pleaded Megan, her voice a mere whisper.

Robert moistened his lips before replying. "He liked you heaps. He was going to look you up when he got out of hospital."

"Why did he disappear without telling me?" sobbed Megan.

"That was his mother's fault. She didn't want him to see me either, but Chris made such a song and dance about it that she gave way in the end."

The tears streamed down Megan's cheeks, mixing with the rain. Her hair was plastered to her head; her cheap shoes needed mending and were letting in water, but she didn't care.

"I'll walk you home, if you like," offered Robert.

"Thank you, there's no need," she gulped in reply and started to walk away, not looking where she was going, bumping into people, mechanically apologising.

Robert hurried after her and took her arm. "I'd better," he said. They covered the half-mile walk to the flat in silence.

Reece opened the door to them, recoiling in dismay at Megan's sad appearance. He helped her upstairs to where Calum was playing with his toys on the floor. The child toddled across to her, his arms outstretched. As if in a dream, she lifted him up. It was as if the terrible news Robert had given her had wrung the very life out of her.

"What's happened?" asked Reece, his amber eyes showing deep concern. Megan didn't answer.

Robert followed them up, although on seeing that responsibility had now passed over to another pair of shoulders, he started to run back downstairs.

"Hang on a minute!" called Reece.

The boy hesitated. He could easily make his get-away, but a sense of decency stopped him. He went back upstairs. Still clutching Calum, Megan collapsed onto one of the beanbags.

"It's Christopher," muttered the boy. "He died two days ago." He drew his hand down over his face, his cheeks reddening with shame and embarrassment. "I should have let Megan know; thought about it all night; couldn't bring myself to be the one to break the news."

"How come you brought her home?"

"She caught me in Tesco's. I didn't know she worked there."

Megan let out a howl of anguish drawing the attention of both young men back to her. She was rocking Calum back and forth so vigorously that he looked in danger of becoming completely disorientated. Reece went over to her and gently prised the bewildered child away. He turned to Robert. "You'd better go. I'll look after her, and thanks for bringing her home. What's your name?"

"Robert Parkes."

"How do you know Christopher?"

"We were at school together."

"Thanks for your help, Robert."

The boy started to go, then turned round. "Will it be all right if I call in tomorrow to see how she is?"

"Phone first; here's the number." Balancing Calum over his shoulder, Reece hastily wrote the telephone number down on the back of an old envelope and handed it to Robert.

"Cheers, see yer," called the boy as he lumbered down the stairs.

Megan's hysterical outburst had ebbed. Silent sobs now racked her slight frame. Occasionally, she would gulp for air as if in danger of suffocating. Reece gently drew her to her feet. "Go and have a lie down," he said. "I'll bring you a cup of tea and a couple of paracetamol."

Obediently she allowed him to lead her along the passage to her bedroom, only stopping briefly to glance back at Calum and mumble, "What about Calum's tea?"

"Don't worry, I'll see to that."

As he helped her onto the bed, she lifted her hand and stroked his face, whispering, "You're my guardian angel, Reece."

CHAPTER ELEVEN

Two days after leaving her post at the check-out, Megan received a letter from the Store Manager asking for an explanation. She ignored his letter and, the following week, the company dismissed her.

One of her workmates rang up and spoke to Reece -- Megan having refused to answer the call herself -- describing in glorious detail, amid outbursts of giggles, the mayhem the incident had caused. It appeared that the irate customer had made numerous enraged telephone calls to the manager, besides sending a letter of complaint to Head Office.

With each passing day, Megan slipped further and further into a catatonic state, isolating herself from the world. Occasionally, she would make an effort to pull herself out of depression, talking elatedly about her future plans.

By tacit agreement, Connie and Reece made certain she wasn't left on her own. She stubbornly refused to sign on at the dole, relying on Reece's generosity and Connie's handouts. Ben displayed a complete lack of interest in the matter. When Reece offered to pay Megan's share of the rent, he shrugged him off with, "See how things work out."

Ben's casual acceptance of a free-loader surprised Reece. He felt responsible for bringing the girl into the flat in the first place and now felt obliged to coughed up the shortfall when the rent fell due.

Two weeks after the incident, Thea turned up.

"Why didn't you tell me you were coming, Sis?" Ben asked.

She frowned and replied. "I did tell you I was coming. Bring my suitcase up." Pushing past him to go upstairs, she didn't see the smug expression on her brother's face.

She went into the living room where Calum was playing with his toys. Megan was curled up in the armchair staring blankly at 'Neighbours'. She barely lifted her head when Ben introduced his sister.

Reece appeared in the doorway, a smile on his face. "Hi Thea, what a surprise! Ben didn't mention you were coming."

Thea smiled back, but her expression was wary. There was a strange atmosphere, things didn't seem normal.

"Has Ben introduced you to our new lodger? Megan's a friend of Connie's and mother of this little chap," said Reece in a bid to normalise the situation. He picked up the baby. "Say hello to Thea, Calum."

Throughout these introductions, Megan remained silent. Reece beckoned Thea into the hallway. "Megan's had a nasty shock," he whispered. "Her boyfriend's just died."

Sympathy rushed to Thea's eyes. "How awful," she cried. "What happened to him?"

Reece briefly explained about Christopher. "Connie and I are taking care of her. I'm sure she'll pull through with our help."

This explanation satisfied Thea. "Can I hold him?" she said, putting out a hand and tickling the baby under his chin. He responded with a smile and raised no objections when Reece handed him over to her.

Ben joined them in the hallway. "I don't know where you're going to sleep, Sis," he grunted. "All the bedrooms are in use."

"Don't worry, Thea can have my room, I'll sleep on the floor down here," offered Reece. Turning to Thea, he went on, "I've moved the bed in the attic under the skylight so that, on a clear night, you can fall asleep looking at the stars."

"I don't want to put you out," said Thea.

"Don't worry, I'll kip down on Ben's floor. You don't mind, do you Ben?"

There was no way out. Ben knew he would have to let Reece sleep in his room for a couple of nights. He studied the pair, who were smiling at one another. Calum gurgled contentedly in Thea's arms. God! he thought angrily, they're playing happy families. This wasn't working out the way he'd planned. To break up the intimate moment, he barged past them with, "Do you have to take up the whole passageway?"

"Careful of the baby!" cautioned Thea.

Calum suddenly decided he was hungry and let out a yell. It was loud enough to startle Megan out of her semi-comatose state. She rushed out into the hall, shouting "What are you doing to my child?" Snatching Calum from Thea, she ran into her bedroom, slamming the door behind her.

Ben also disappeared into his room leaving Reece and Thea standing in the hall, looking at one another in bafflement.

Surprise had rendered Thea speechless. Suddenly, she regained her voice. "What's going on here? Why is Ben acting funny?"

"I've no idea," replied Reece. "You know what he's like, the peacemaker one minute, the stirrer the next." He pointed to the living room. "Go in there and make yourself at home while I make a cup of tea, or would you rather have coffee?"

"Tea would be fine, thanks."

When Reece joined Thea in the living room, she was sitting on one of the beanbags, watching the television. He placed her mug of tea on the floor by her feet and asked, "Do you want to watch this, or ..."

"Please turn if off," she said.

They sat side by side, cradling their mugs in their hands, both at a loss for conversation. They had spoken many times on the phone, yet now they were together under the same roof, an embarrassed silence had sprung up. Privately, Reece cursed the unfortunate welcome Thea had received and wondered what she thought about the situation.

For her part, Thea was torn by two conflicting emotions: seeing Reece again reaffirmed the feelings she had for him, but the strange scene she had walked into raised doubts in her mind. Was it true that Megan was a lodger, or was there more to it?

They both started to speak at once and stopped abruptly.

"Go on, Reece," she said. "Tell me all about your job and the course you're on. Is it going well?"

"Very well. Things are really looking up. What about you?" he asked. "How's your computer course going?"

"Mocks soon, then the real thing, but I think I'll get through."

"Then what?"

"I'd like to come down and work in London. It depends on Clelia, and Ben."

"Why Ben?"

"He doesn't want me to come down here. He doesn't want me hanging round his neck. He's got a lot going on in his life, I'd only be in the way." She laughed. "There'd be no room for me here."

Before he could stop himself, Reece said, "I could move out and with our joint salaries ..." He stopped short, realising that he was jumping the gun.

If Thea noticed she carefully covered up, saying, "Let's go out for a pizza tonight, I don't think I can stand another set-to with Ben."

Reece coloured and hesitated. "Umm," he started to say.

Thea stiffened. "If you don't want to, it's quite all right."

"Oh, I want to. It's Megan. I can't leave her alone. If Connie can come round and keep her company, it will be all right."

"What about Ben? Won't he be here?"

Reece shook his head. "You can't rely on him. Half way through the evening, he'd probably decide to go out."

"Who says you can't rely on me?" Ben stood in the doorway. He gave a deep rumbling laugh. "I'll do the babysitting, you two go off out and enjoy yourselves."

Thea and Reece exchanged a glance. Sudden mood changes on Ben's part were something they had both witnessed yet it never failed to surprise them.

"You're on," said Reece. "Come on, Thea, let's get going before he changes his mind."

Ben was lounging in the armchair watching Sky Sport when Megan emerged from her bedroom. She wandered into the living room, rubbing reddened eyes. Ben shot her a quick glance. "Sit yerself down and watch the football," he said.

"Can't we watch something else?"

"No, we can't."

"But I can't stand football," she protested.

"For Christ's sake!" snapped Ben. "It's my flat, my television and you're ..." He jabbed a finger at her. " ... you're only here under sufferance." To emphasize his outrage, he pressed the remote to raise the volume by several notches.

Megan's jaw dropped and she burst into tears. Ben frowned with irritation, then a flicker of conscience reminded him that he had promised Reece and his sister that he would look after the girl for the evening. Besides -- his mind raced -- he didn't want her breaking down completely. An institutionalized schizophrenic would do nothing to further his plans to split up Reece and Thea.

He reduced the TV volume and got up from the armchair. "Here," he said. "You take the comfy chair. I'll squat on the bean bag. There's only another half-hour of football, then you can choose what you'd like to watch."

Taken aback by his unexpected switch to geniality, Megan stopped snivelling and obediently went to sit in the proffered armchair. Forty minutes later, after extra time and the play-backs had been covered, Ben handed her the remote.

"Choose what you want," he said with a grin. "Fancy a beer?"

"Have you got any cider?"

"I think so."

The warmth of his smile had a reassuring effect on Megan. She had never had much to do with Ben. In fact, although she would never have admitted it, she was a little afraid of him. He was always dashing in and out of the flat, barely pausing to speak to anybody except to complain or swear. She had put him down as rude and uncouth. For the first time, she found herself the object of his rakish charm.

"Yes please," she replied.

He left her switching channels and went to sort out the drinks. Drawing up one of the bean bags, he squatted down beside her. Lighting up a joint, he caught her glance of disapproval. "Don't tell me you've never had a snort!" he said with an amused chuckle.

"Only once," she admitted. Her gaze misted. "Chris used to smoke once in a while and he ..." Her voice broke and she stopped mid-sentence.

"Here, have a try," offered Ben.

The tears swam in her eyes. Gulping back a sob, she took the joint from his hand, tilted her head back, closed her eyes and inhaled deeply.

"That's better," she sighed, returning the cigarette to Ben.

"It's good for you," he said. "Helps you unwind, eases away all those worries."

"Can I have another go?" she said.

"Sure thing."

He watched her relax, her head resting on the back of the armchair, her hands loosely dangling over its sides. Her voice was slurred when next she spoke. "It certainly helps. Where do you get it from?"

Ben let out a belly laugh. "That would be telling."

She lifted her head and smiled at him. "Go on, tell me."

"Certainly not, it wouldn't be right, a youngster like you ..."

"I'm eighteen," she said indignantly. "I'd like to try it again to see if I really like it."

"Okay."

Ben got up and left the room, returning with another joint in his hand. He lit up and handed it to her. Again, she took a long drag, giving it back to him and relaxing comfortably in the chair.

When Reece and Thea returned, Megan was fast asleep and Ben was watching a sci-fi film on Four. They stopped in the doorway in surprise. "Wow! You two look as if you've spent a cosy little evening together."

"We have," replied Ben.

Reece frowned. "Any trouble?"

"None at all. Megan got up shortly after you left. She's been quite calm under my pacifying influence."

"I don't believe it!" exclaimed Reece.

"We talked, we watched TV, we had a drink."

Thea gave a little giggle. "Ben the nursemaid. Well I never. I've seen everything now!"

"How did your evening go?" asked Ben, a needless enquiry because it was quite clear that Reece and his sister were both very happy.

Springing to his feet, he said, "I'll get you a beer."

Reece nodded; Thea refused. "No thanks," she said. "I've been drinking wine and I think I've had enough for one evening."

Ben disappeared into the kitchen, returning with a beer for himself and one for Reece. He was totally relaxed: all smiles and affability. Thea eyed him suspiciously, knowing her brother of old. When Ben was in this mood, it was a bad portent: the quiet before the storm. She wondered what scheme he'd got up his sleeve.

Megan's return to normality lasted into the next day. She seemed so much better that, after work, Reece and Thea went out leaving her on her own.

"Look Megan, this is Thea's mobile number," he said, handing her a slip of paper. "If you feel lonely or upset, just give us a ring and we'll come straight back."

"I'll be all right," she insisted. "You mustn't mollycoddle me, I've got over the shock now."

Reece looked at her with doubt in his eyes. "I mean it. We'll come straight back."

"Yes," echoed Thea. "We'll be in that pub just round the corner so it's no hassle to come back if you need us."

"Stop fussing, and clear off," said Megan with a smile of amusement. "There's a programme I want to watch on ITV, and it's just about to begin."

"Cheers then!" called Reece as he and Thea went down the stairs to the front door.

"I don't feel very happy about leaving her alone," he said. "Maybe I should call Connie and ask her to look in."

For the first time, Thea showed a hint of impatience. "Stop worrying, Reece, you heard what Megan said, she's over the shock."

"She relies on me."

Thea's heart gave a lurch. Were these the words of a man with a sense of responsibility or did he care more than he was letting on? Uncertainty made her defensive and she stiffened when he put an arm around her shoulders as they entered the pub.

A couple of drinks erased all thoughts of Megan and her problems from Reece's mind. He liked being with Thea; he liked her ready smile; the way she threw her head back and laughed with complete abandon when something struck her as funny; he liked the timbre of her voice with its nasal brummie accent and he liked the way she answered his questions almost before he had finished asking them.

Thea's emotions were in turmoil. She agreed with her brother's views that it was better to stick to your own kind. But the more time she spent with the flame-haired Canadian, the more she liked him.

Reece smiled at her across the oak table, chasing misgivings from her mind, but when he glanced at his watch and said, "Maybe we ought to get home to Megan," she couldn't hold back her annoyance.

"For heaven's sake, Reece, she's a big girl. It won't hurt her to be on her own for a few hours."

He looked surprised and grunted, "No, no, of course it won't."

After Reece and Thea had left, Megan switched on the TV. No sooner had the programme started than Calum let out a cry from the bedroom. She took his milk into him and he drank it eagerly, although when she put him back in the big bed they shared, his eyes opened wide and it was clear he wasn't sleepy. She tried to tuck him in, carefully rearranging the cushions by his side of the bed in case he fell out. The minute she left the room, he began to yell. She tried to ignore his cries, but they got louder and louder. Reluctantly, she went back to the bedroom and brought him with her to the living room.

He fell asleep on her lap. The programme finished and a documentary commenced: a medical study of terminally ill patients. Unwillingly she found her gaze trained on the screen, hypnotized into watching scenes of great sadness. Suddenly, the anguish of the suffering patients became too much. She snapped off the TV and took Calum back to bed, then went into the kitchen in search of a drink. Taking a can of lager out of the fridge, she went back to the living room and sank down on one of the bean bags, her mind filled with the heart-rending pictures she had just seen on screen. They brought about a wave of self-pity and, when Ben came home an hour later, he found her curled up in the foetus position, her hair awry and her face blotchy with weeping.

She looked up with a startled grunt as he walked in. "Where are the others?" he asked, slipping off his jacket and slinging it onto the back of a chair.

"I don't know."

He noticed the can of lager and said. "You need cheering up. Wanna share a joint?"

Megan straightened up. "Yes please," she replied.

"Where d'you get this stuff?" she asked him again as they sat next to one another on the step listening to the latest Robbie Williams' album and taking it in turns to take a draw at the joint he had produced.

"You *are* the inquisitive one," grinned Ben. "Just enjoy it while I've got it."

She rested her head back against the wall, closing her eyes and swaying gently to the music. "You know, you're lucky to have a sister," she observed. "I wish I had brothers and sisters."

"You wouldn't say that if you had four of them."

"Four?" Megan heaved a sigh. "I can't imagine what it must be like to be brought up in a large family. There was only Mum and Dad and me, and Dad's awfully stuffy." She turned to look at Ben. "He's a Methodist minister, you know." When Ben didn't speak, she went on, "Do you believe in religion and all that mumbo jumbo?"

Ben took another draw and handed the cigarette to Megan. "I dunno, though I do know that if all that heaven and hell stuff is true, there's no way I shall get through those pearly gates."

Megan burst into giggles. "God's supposed to be all forgiving, isn't he? And I'm sure you couldn't be all that bad."

Ben gave a chortle and stretched out his legs, crossing them at the ankles and lacing his hands behind his head. "I haven't been exactly law-abiding," he said.

Megan shrugged. "Sometimes I wonder what it's all about. Sometimes, I think I'd be better off giving up my independence and going home to Swansea, then Calum would at least have a secure future."

Ben drew back his legs and sat up straight. "You wouldn't be happy," he said quickly. "You'd be under your father's thumb, you'd have to rely on your ma for baby-sitting. Think of all those prying questions they'd ask each time you went out!" He had barely an inkling of what Megan's parents were like, but to suit his own purposes, he needed to paint as bleak a picture as possible. He searched his memory. "Why, aren't those Methodists the ones who sign the pledge?"

Megan giggled again. "Yes, but half of them don't keep to it."

"After living in London, you wouldn't be happy in a God-forsaken hole like Swansea."

"It's not a God-forsaken hole," protested Megan. "It's a very nice place as a matter of fact."

"Sorry, I thought it was a bit of a backwater." He took hold of her hand in his big fist and squeezed it gently. "Are you feeling better now?"

She smiled. "Yes thanks. It's amazing how a snort makes things look brighter." She wrinkled her brow and asked in a serious voice, "A puff now and again can't do you any real harm, can it?"

Ben threw back his head and laughed. "Cannabis is completely harmless and non-addictive. In my opinion, they should legalize it."

"Where do you get it?"

"You are persistent, aren't you?"

"I'm curious, that's all."

He leant towards her and said confidentially, "If I show you, promise you'll keep it to yourself."

She placed a hand on her heart and said, "I swear."

Taking her hand, he led her along the hall to his own bedroom. Megan hesitated nervously in the doorway. Ben gave a wide grin and, affecting a prim tone, said, "What's the matter, do you think I'm about to take advantage of you?"

"No, but what will Reece think if he finds me in here with you? He might think there's something going on between us and he wouldn't like that."

So she fancied Reece! Ben's eyes glinted with satisfaction. The innocent little Welsh girl was playing into his hands. He took his cue. "I never thought of that," he said. "Which means I won't be able to show you."

"It'll be all right, the others won't be home for hours," cried Megan.

He feigned indecision. "Maybe another time."

"No, please show me!"

He shrugged. "Okay," and led her into the room. Going to a built-in cupboard, he opened the door. Megan jumped back in surprise. An intense heat emanated from the confined area, which was thick with plants, reminding her of a jungle scene. The walls of the cupboard were lined with kitchen foil, metre upon metre of which had been carefully unrolled and fixed behind the hot water tank. Two neon lamps beamed down on the greenery, adding to the soaring temperature.

Megan pointed at the plants. "What are they? Oh, I see," she gasped, her eyes widening in comprehension. "You grow the stuff yourself."

Ben was still up when Reece and Thea arrived home. He greeted them airily, "Hi folks, enjoy yerselves?"

"Thought you'd be in bed, Ben. Haven't you got an early shift tomorrow?" replied Reece.

"I'm not tired." Ben gave a distracted wave. "Make yerselves comfortable."

Reece and Thea exchanged a glance -- neither of them wanting the other man's company -- and went into the kitchen, where they perched on bar stools and drank coffee.

"I've got to leave first thing tomorrow if I'm to catch the eight o'clock train," said Thea.

Reece reached for her hand. "Couldn't you stay another day, ring the college and plead sickness. I'll do the same."

She smiled, pleased by the way things were going. After her impulsive show of jealousy in the pub, they'd slipped into an uneasy silence, although her outburst had served its purpose since, as the evening wore on, Reece became more and more attentive.

"I can't do that," she said. "Much as I'd like to, it wouldn't be good for either of us."

"You will come back soon, won't you?"

"What's that?" Ben came into the tiny kitchen, went to the fridge and took out another can of lager. "You'd better think twice if you're planning on coming down again, Sis."

"Why?"

"You might not have anywhere to stay."

Thea sucked in her breath, her eyes glinting. "D'you mean I'm not welcome here?"

"'Course not, but I've got to think about the bread. I've got a few cash flow problems, letting another room would solve them."

"What?" cried Reece and Thea together.

Ben assumed a dejected expression. "Yes, I've been meaning to tell you, Reece, I'm going to move Megan and Calum into the living room so that I can let her room. I'd get at least sixty quid a week for it."

"But that's impossible," gasped Reece. "You can't expect the girl to sleep in there with me having to go through her room to get to mine. What about the TV? Besides, those stairs up to the attic room would be a death trap for Calum if he decided to explore." He shook his head. "It's just not practical."

Thea looked from one to the other, her mouth agape. Reece didn't comprehend, but she knew what her brother was doing. She'd seen for herself how fond Reece was of Megan and Calum: why, the warm-hearted Canadian treated Calum as if he were his own child! If the three of them were forced into even closer proximity anything could happen. In that moment, she hated her brother and, to hide her feelings, she stepped down from the breakfast bar stool and, turning her back on the other two, stood at the sink rinsing out her coffee mug. When the mug chinked against the tap, both men cast her a glance then continued with their altercation. Thea didn't turn round. Staring at her own reflection in the window pane, she drew in a deep breath and clenched her fists, cursing her brother's cunning, and raking her mind for an equally devious counterattack, finding none.

"Can't be helped," shrugged Ben. "Of course, if she paid her way it might be different."

"She does," insisted Reece.

"Does she?" Ben tugged at the ring-pull of the can in his hand and slurped down a mouthful of lager. "If I remember rightly, you paid her rent last month." His gloating gaze fastened on that of Thea's reflected in the window. She longed to retaliate, but knew a confrontation in front of Reece would do more harm than good. Her brother noticed this. Backing out of the room, he chirped, "Night Sis, have a good journey home."

CHAPTER TWELVE

In November Della telephoned Connie.

"Hi honey, it's me. Be a kind girlie, don't put the phone down on me."

Connie was taken aback. After their last encounter she hadn't expected to hear from Della again.

"Hello Della," she replied coolly.

Mixed emotions stirred in her breast. During her visit to Bahrain neither Linda nor Steve had mentioned Della and Connie had realised that Della had lied about being in touch with Linda. She had returned home determined not to allow anything to damage her relationship with her adopted parents. She told herself that, as far as she was concerned, Della was a distant relative, a black sheep, best forgotten. Consequently Della's phone call came as a complete surprise.

"I'd love to see you," lisped Della.

"I'm awfully busy, exams, auditions and all that stuff," replied Connie cautiously.

"Can't you spare just a little bit of time for me?" Della's tone was plaintiff.

"Where are you?"

"In London. Listen, honey, I've got a surprise for you."

"A surprise! What is it?"

Della's voice rose with excitement. "Pack your bags, sweetie, we're going to Rio de Janeiro for Christmas."

"What?"

Della giggled. "I've made enquiries about your father. Guess what? He owns a plush hotel in Rio. His football career took off in the 70's, he's become something of a celebrity."

Connie gave a gasp. "D'you mean, he's a famous footballer?"

"He used to be. He often played for Brazil."

Connie was impressed, although she made every effort not to let Della know. "What's that got to do with us?" she demanded.

"What's it got to do with us!" screeched Della. "He's your father, your own flesh and blood. He's rich and famous ..." She paused for effect. " ... and he wants to meet you."

"I don't believe it," cried Connie. "Do you really think he'll want to see me after all this time? No man in his right senses would welcome a grown-up illegitimate daughter he had no idea existed."

"Well, *he* does," retorted Della. "He's very friendly and remembers our time together with great affection."

"Just a minute." Connie's mind raced. "I thought you said it was a one-night stand."

"Hmm," sighed Della. "That wasn't quite true. As a matter of fact, we spent most of that week together while Lenny went off with some bird he'd picked up down by the pool. And we did write to one another for a few months afterwards."

"So he knew about me?"

"Yes," admitted Della. The tears welled up in Connie's eyes as Della went on, "You see, at that time, he was a budding left-winger in the second division; hadn't hit the big time yet. He was hard up and however much he cared, he couldn't be a father to you. Linda and Steve's offer was the only solution, surely you can see that?"

"I don't want to hear any more," croaked Connie.

"Listen to me, Conchita."

"Don't call me that!"

"It's your real name. Listen, honey, here's my number, ring me back when you've thought about it. I just know you'll say *yes.*"

Connie didn't ring back until the evening of the following day. Della was out. She swore under her breath and hung up. At mid-night, she was woken up by Della's return call. The infuriating lisp penetrated sleep-induced fuzziness.

"Have you had time to think about it, Connie? It will be the holiday of a lifetime. First class flight ..."

Connie roused herself. "Hang on a minute."

"As for the accommodation, it'll be the biz."

Connie sat up straight and clutched the receiver tightly to her ear. "Who's paying for all this?"

"He is, of course, your father."

"In your dreams!"

"No, really. Connie, he's dead keen to meet you."

Connie squeezed the receiver tightly. "No," she snapped. "No way." And slammed down the telephone.

The phone rang again. "Do you have to be so pig-headed, Connie?"

"It's madness, mother ..." The word slipped out by mistake, confirming her subconscious acceptance of her true parent.

"Aren't you curious? Don't you want to find out what he's like? It won't cost you a penny. Honestly, Connie, you'll never get this chance again. Think how sorry you're going to be if you miss out."

"Is he married, what will his wife think if we turn up?"

"She left him years ago, made off with the kids."

"How many children?"

"Two; hasn't seen them since. "He sends her a hefty cheque every month. Believe me, darling, he's got mega-bucks."

The more Connie listened to the story, the more unreal it seemed. "I've heard enough," she gasped.

"You'll come then?"

"No, I most certainly will not."

"But I've already paid a deposit on the tickets", wailed Della.

"That's your problem," shouted Connie and put the phone down.

With her mind clogged with her personal problems, Connie had little patience with Megan. She stopped agreeing to keep her company even though this annoyed Reece. At times, she felt tempted to take Della up on her offer. The departure was scheduled for the twentieth of December. Would there be any harm in meeting her father? She frowned in confusion. What was Della after? Did she see Javier de Oliveira Figueres as a future meal ticket? Connie shook her head vehemently. She wanted no part in that game.

But the unanswered questions plagued her. What was this famous footballer like? Was he as good-looking in real life as he appeared to be in photographs? After Della's revelations, she had surfed the net for back numbers of 70's newspapers, searching through the sports pages. There were several pictures of Javier de Oliveira Figueres in action, and also mention of his sideline in modelling and TV commercials. As a result of a little digging, she had unearthed some old magazines: there he was, resplendent in the scantiest of swimwear, globules of water running off his oiled black skin as he emerged from the rolling surf, his engaging smile advocating a brand of Brazilian toothpaste. No wonder Della had fallen for him! It was pride that held Connie back. Now was not the time to confront this icon. It would be far better to wait until she, herself, had achieved success in her chosen profession.

But by early December after more disappointing auditions, she felt so dispirited that she decided to swallow her pride and go with Della. When she phoned to break the news, the number was engaged. She put down the receiver and stood staring at the apparatus. It rang. She picked it up immediately and, with surprise, recognised an agent who had turned her down only days earlier.

"Connie, darling," he said. "Are you a fast learner?"

"What d'you mean?"

"Got you a part in Cinders at the Mayflower in Southampton. Fairy Godmother's broken her arm. Curtain up in five days time. Think you can make it?"

Connie gave a gasp. "Yes, yes," she cried. "Where are rehearsals being held?"

"Marvellous, darling, it's a super role. You get to sing and dance. Be there by eight o'clock tomorrow morning. Best if you travelled down today. You can have the other girl's digs; she's gone home."

"Yes," gulped Connie. "I'll be there this evening. What's the address."

"*Merci beaucoup*, darling, you're a life-saver," gushed the agent and proceeded to give her the details. "Ciao."

Connie could hardly read the directions she had excitedly scribbled down on a scrap of paper. Flinging her arms in the air, she did a mini-pirouette across the floor. Five minutes ago, she had been on the point of making a commitment that could have altered her life. This was better, this was the first step on the career ladder. Snatching down a suitcase from the top of the wardrobe, she began to throw clothes into it. There was no time to let anyone know, so she wrote a note asking Reece to be the messenger and posted it on her way to the station.

Connie's heart beat wildly as she went through the Stage Door the following morning. The doorman gave her a cursory wave. The place was empty. She walked across the boards and stopped centre-stage to look out at the rows of empty seats. Excitement coursed through her veins. This could be her big break.

"Well, I'm glad someone's decided to turn up," boomed a voice behind her.

Connie swivelled around and found herself face-to-face with a stout, mottled-complexioned man.

"I was told to come at eight," she replied.

"Do you always do what you're told?"

She realised he was teasing her and grinned back. "Only when it's in my own interest."

"What's your name?"

"Conchita Dixon, Connie for short," she replied.

A commotion from the wings prompted them to turn their heads. Several members of the cast ambled onto the stage. "Glad you've decided to join us," bellowed Stan.

He introduced Connie. "This is Fairy Godmother Number Four."

Connie's heart sank. So there had been three others before her!

"She's called Connie and she's our last hope so give her all the help you can. You've got to pull together, no more bad backs, no more 'grandmother's funerals'. I want you here sixteen hours a day if necessary. Okay, Scene Two. Take it from the top."

With Connie's departure for Southampton, Megan's dependence on Reece increased. Ben refused to change his mind about moving her and the baby into the living room so that he could let the second bedroom. In fact, he seemed bent on putting his plan into operation as quickly as possible and, when Reece returned from work the following day, he found Megan frantically trying to arrange her own and Calum's gear in a room without cupboard or shelf space.

"Why is Ben doing this, it's not as if we're being a nuisance. It's not as if Calum's a troublesome baby," she burst out on seeing him.

Anger drained the colour from Reece's face. "I don't know, but I'm going to find out," he retorted. "Where is he?"

"He's gone out," Megan informed him.

Reece stood in the doorway and looked around. Megan's three foot bed looked lost in the large room. It had been pushed up against the wall with cushions piled onto the sisal mat next to it -- a mother's attempt to protect her child should he roll over and fall out of bed in the night. The old-fashioned iron fireplace with its sharp edges and tiled hearth was a danger to an active toddler. He smothered a gulp as his gaze shifted to the far corner: the steep narrow staircase leading up to his own attic room, with nothing except a heavy curtain closing it off at the top, would be impossible to child-proof. His anger escalated. He didn't want Calum climbing up and meddling with his belongings. He thought of Thea and saw the situation through her eyes. Without a door dividing their sleeping quarters, he and Megan might as well be living together.

"You can't possibly stay in here, Megan," he began, then stopped short. "Where's the stereo?"

"Ben's taken it into his own room, but he's left the TV."

Megan ran over to him, crying hysterically and he found himself wrapping his arms around her for comfort. To calm her down, he said, "Don't worry, I'll make Ben see sense."

"He's threatened to throw me out. You must help me, Reece," begged Megan, looking up at him with a tear-streaked face.

"He can't do that." Reece's eyes blazed. "When's he due back?"

"I don't know. Help me, Reece, please, please," wept Megan.

"Stop crying," frowned Reece. "Maybe if I offered to give him a bit more rent he might reconsider, put you back in the other bedroom."

"You can't do that; you're already done enough for me."

Reece gave a cavalier shrug yet was alarmed. Megan was becoming dangerously clinging. His memory shot back a year or two, evoking the emotions of an immature youth. He had always shunned responsibility. His rejection of it had caused his break-up with Chantal. By the time he had come to his senses, his first true love had found herself another man. Now, with Thea, he had been given a second chance. He didn't want to lose her too. He looked down at Megan and saw that, by a twist of fate, he was being hedged into a corner, not by a headstrong girl like Chantal or a determined girl like Thea, but by a vulnerable teenager.

He recoiled as she whispered, "You're always there for me, Reece."

Several days later, Thea phoned Reece. "I'm coming down to London again," she told him.

His heart leapt. He longed to see her, but until the problem of Megan's sleeping arrangements had been resolved, he didn't want Thea visiting. "I'd love to see you but ..."

"Has Ben carried out his threat to let the second bedroom?" she asked.

"Sort of ... it's a bit awkward at the moment," stuttered Reece, realising with a surge of abashment that he was behaving like a naive adolescent. "Could you leave it for a couple of weeks and I'll work something out."

When she replied, Thea sounded suspicious. "Well, if you don't want me to come ..."

"Of course, I do, but I'm looking for new digs at the moment." He paused, uncertain as to how she would react to this news. After all, Ben was her big brother and despite the occasional sibling squabble, he knew that they cared deeply for one another.

The telephone conversation left Thea feeling hurt and confused. She resisted the impulse to rush down to Twickenham straightaway and find out for herself what was going on. She recalled Reece's kindness towards Megan and experienced a pang of jealousy. That pathetic little blond with her innocent blue eyes had inveigled Reece into protecting her.

Within a week, Ben had let the second bedroom. The new tenant was a young French student, who spoke little English and spent most of his time in the company of fellow foreign students. His name was Emil and he made no effort to fraternise with Reece or Megan.

Without telling Megan, Reece started looking for other accommodation, but with his college assessment coming up, he had little time to scour the 'Richmond & Twickenham Times' or visit letting agencies. The atmosphere in the flat was tense. Calum liked the TV sound turned up and the cacophony of voices and cartoon shrieks disturbed Reece's train of thought while he was studying upstairs in the attic. Even during the evening, after Calum had been put to bed, Megan made little attempt to adjust the volume.

Reece grew increasingly angry. One evening he lost his temper. "For God's sake, Megan, turn the bloody thing down," he shouted from the top of the stairs.

"What?"

He ran downstairs. "Turn the sound down, you selfish bitch, how can I be expected to concentrate ... ?" He stopped short.

Megan was curled up in the only chair in the room, her feet tucked under her, her head lolling against her arm. As he strode across the room, she raised her head and looked at him through half-closed eyes. He saw immediately what was wrong with her.

"You stupid little fool," he gasped, snatching up an ashtray from the floor and sniffing at its contents. "Where did you get this from?"

She smiled blearily up at him. "Ben can be quite kind sometimes. He understands how desperately lonely I am without Chris."

"What?"

"That's not being kind, you idiot, that's lunacy."

"He told me to help myself. That's being kind."

Reece grabbed her arm and pulled her to her feet. "Get your jacket," he said. "I'm taking you for a walk round the block and, when we get back, you'll drink some black coffee and tell me how you got started on this stuff."

"What about Calum?" she protested, limply waving an arm in the direction of the sleeping child.

Reece thought fast. Keeping his grip on Megan's arm, he dragged her along the corridor and knocked on the student's door.

"What do you want?" enquired Emil in his fractured English. His frown at being disturbed changed to amazement when Reece addressed him in French.

"*Regarde,* Emil, we have to go out for half an hour. Can you look after Calum? He's already asleep."

Without giving the student the chance to refuse, Reece propelled Megan down the stairs and out of the front door. By the time they had walked around the block twice, Megan was beginning to come round. In fact, on the last lap, she started to quicken her pace, saying with a hint of panic: "Must get back to Calum. Let's hurry."

"It's all right, Emil is looking after him."

"Who?"

"Emil, the student."

"No, not him! I don't trust him."

"Calm down," cautioned Reece, although her concern triggered his anxiety and he increased his pace.

The baby was still fast asleep; Emil's bedroom door was shut, his light out and, with a stab of guilt, Reece chastised himself for leaving the baby in such incompetent hands. He left Megan in her room while he made her a cup of strong black coffee.

"I'll be awake all night," she complained.

"It's for your own good," snapped Reece. His retort silenced her and she finished her drink.

"Promise you'll never smoke grass again," he said, and refusing to be satisfied by her almost imperceptible nod, he persisted, "I mean it, Megan, I need more assurance than that."

He placed a finger under her chin, tilting her face upwards. Her eyelashes glistened with tears as she whispered, "I promise." Then she took his breath away by asking, "I heard you talking to Ben's sister the other day. Is she coming down again?"

Reece stiffened. "No."

Reaching up, she gently caressed his cheek. "Thanks, Reece, I'll be okay now. You go off and do your studying. I'm going to bed."

By mid-December, Reece still hadn't found new lodgings. With Christmas approaching, he decided to leave the flat hunting until the New Year. He had spoken to Thea several times over the past weeks, hoping that she would perhaps invite him up to Birmingham for the festivities. So far, she hadn't.

"Why don't you and Calum take off for Swansea for Christmas?" he suggested to Megan. "I'll help you out with the fare. It would please your mother and father."

Megan pulled a face. "No way!" she retorted. "All those church services Dad would force me to go to, all those mothers' meeting Mum would expect me to help out at -- no *thank* you!" She widened her eyes. "Besides, I rather figured we'd be spending Christmas Day together, just you and me and Calum. I can cook the turkey, we can buy a tree. After all, Christmas is for children and Calum will be old enough to enjoy it this year." She rushed on. "I know he won't get many presents, neither of us can afford them, but there's always The Pound Shop and Kingston Market, and Connie's bound to send him something."

Reece looked at her in alarm. "I might be going away," he said.

Megan's face crumpled and she started to cry. Calum dropped the toy he was playing with and scurried across the floor to her.

"I might be going up to Birmingham," went on Reece.

The girl lowered her head into her hands and started crying, her thin body shaking. "What shall I do?" she wailed. "I can't stay here with Ben."

"Ben won't be around on Christmas Day, he'll be off somewhere with his mates."

She looked up at him. "All alone at Christmas; it will be awful."

"Go home to Swansea, I told you I'd pay your fare."

"No!" Clutching her arms across herself, Megan started rocking backwards and forwards. "I'll need something to keep me going." The telling words were almost inaudible.

The blade of emotional blackmail sliced through Reece's conscience. He stared at the small sob-racked figure, then lowered his gaze to the angelic baby pulling at Megan's skirt, and felt afraid. Was she genuinely scared of her own weakness? He wished Connie were around. She'd know what to do. But Connie had phoned to say that she would be spending Christmas in Southampton with the rest of the cast.

Reece didn't know what to do. His relationship with Thea had reached stalemate, yet he instinctively knew that she was as attracted to him as he was to her. "Sorry, Megan," he said at last. "But I really can't stay here over Christmas."

Megan bit her lip and murmured dolefully, "I understand."

The incident prodded Reece into making a decision. He telephoned Thea. Her response was warm and encouraging, but after a second or two, hesitancy crept into her voice. "We can't put you up, Mum's sister, Aunt Laila is coming to stay."

"That's all right, I can book into a B&B."

"I'm not sure whether Ben's coming up."

'What difference does that make?" Reece felt angry that Ben should once again get in the way of his plans to see the girl.

"It's just that he can be so disruptive. At Christmastime he comes over all sentimental and talks about retaining the family unit ..." She petered out. "It's not that I don't want to see you ...you know what Ben's like."

"He'll probably spend Christmas at Deceptions."

"I don't know ..."

He heard Imelda's voice from a distance, friendly and decisive. "Any friend of Ben's is welcome here. Hand me the phone, Thea." Her rich tones bellowed in his ear. "Reece, boy, come by all means. We'd love you to come, wouldn't we girls?" There was a chorus of assent from the background. "It's settled then, sweet. We'll see you Christmas Eve."

The line went dead. Reece stood looking at the receiver in his hand, realising that dating a white man was, indeed, a breakthrough for Thea. Clearly, she had not confided in her mother or Clelia. Her family knew nothing of their relationship. He was Ben's mate, not Thea's boyfriend. He felt hurt.

Megan took the news of Reece's arrangements to spend Christmas in Birmingham surprisingly well.

"Calum and I will have a nice quiet Christmas on our own," she said. "But I meant what I said, I shall buy him lots of little presents from the market. They won't cost too much. Will you come with me?"

Relieved at her apparent acceptance of the situation, Reece agreed and they spent the following Saturday buying gifts for Calum. They carried home a four foot tree, chose decorations and fairy lights while Calum gurgled happily in his pushchair. They took him to see Father Christmas and smiled proudly when he toddled happily up to collect his present.

Emil went back to France for the holidays and they saw very little of Ben, but two days before Christmas, he surprised them by turning up with a pile of gift-wrapped presents for Calum. Megan was overwhelmed.

"Must give the little chap a good time," grinned Ben. He was at his most engaging, playfully teasing Megan, throwing Calum up in the air and catching him. The child, wary at first, soon warmed to him.

Reece looked on with apprehension. He'd seen Ben like this before and he knew how the black man's mood could change without warning. The white teeth flashed as he said Reece. "I hear you're going up to see the folks. I can't manage it this year. Too much going on at the nightclub. Give them my love, especially Thea."

The words gave Reece a jolt. They seemed innocent enough, but you could never tell with Ben.

After he'd gone, Megan said brightly. "There, what did I tell you? Ben can be really generous." She knelt down on the floor and gestured at the pile of parcels in front of her. "Just look at all these presents. Gosh, there's even something for me! We're going to have a wonderful Christmas." Her eyes clouded. "There's only one thing spoiling it." Springing to her feet, she clutched Reece's hands. "Can't you change your mind and stay here with us?"

"You know I can't. We've been through all this before, Megan."

Spinning on his heel, he went upstairs to his room, firmly drawing the curtain across at the head of the stairs, but he could hear Megan weeping. Later, she called up to him. "I've made some Spaghetti Bolognese, do you want some?"

It would be unkind to refuse. Besides, he was hungry. "Yes please, I'll be down in five minutes."

They sat, side-by-side, eating off their laps. Seated in the high chair, which Reece had picked up from a charity shop, Calum tucked into his meal, banging his spoon on the tray.

"What time are you off tomorrow?" asked Megan, scooping up a forkful of spaghetti and twisting it into a neat bundle. A strand of pasta began to unwind itself, dripping sauce, as she waited for Reece's reply.

"Late afternoon," he answered. "I'll catch the crush, but it can't be helped. I've got a bit more shopping to do before I leave."

"Have you booked a B&B?"

"Yes."

"How long for?"

"Two nights." He wished she'd stop interrogating him. Each question jabbed his conscience. With increasing frequency, he was regretting having taken in the hapless waif. He should never have got himself involved with her. With a shudder, he recalled their chance meeting in McDonalds, recalled his impulsive offer of a bed for the night. If only he'd known!

As if reading his mind, she said from behind the shield of her long blond hair, "I'm such a nuisance, I expect you wish you'd never set eyes on me."

This comment was so close to the truth that it prompted a quick denial. " Of course not." He leant over and pushed Calum's plate more securely into position. "Why I would never have got to know this little fellow!"

Megan dimpled. "He called you Daddy the other day."

"What?" snapped Reece.

In an instant, the dimpled smile vanished. "Oh, I expect he did the same with Emil and Ben, but I never noticed."

Christmas Eve dawned overcast. Reece crept downstairs to find Megan and Calum still in bed. The girl raised herself onto one elbow as he went past. "You're not going yet, are you?" she asked, noticing he was wearing a coat.

"Not yet, I'm just going out to pick up a few more things."

"Have you bought them all presents?"

"Yes, just small things."

"What have you bought her?"

"Who?"

"You know, thingy, Ben's sister."

"I forget," said Reece.

He returned to find Megan still in her nightdress. She was sitting cross-legged on the floor, randomly flicking some playing cards across the room. Calum was pushing a matchbox car alongside the hearth, making engine noises. His nappy hung low between his legs, his face was covered with chocolate.

"My God, haven't you changed him yet?" gasped Reece. "What's the matter with you? Can't you be trusted to look after your own child?"

Megan tilted her small oval face up towards him and spoke in a desultory manner. "Didn't realise the time. I did give Calum his breakfast though."

"What did you give him?"

She giggled. "His favourite, a bar of chocolate."

"Is that all? What about his milk, his cereals?"

"It's all right, I gave him two bars."

"Megan, if this is the way you looked after the Goddard's baby no wonder you lost your job!"

"Losing my job had nothing to do with the way I looked after Jessica," protested Megan mildly. "I was a good nanny." She jutted her chin like a defiant child, then swivelled away to restart her game with the playing cards. "Do you know what? I got six cards to stand up against the wall just now. Isn't that amazing?"

Reece crossed the room in three long strides. Grabbing Megan's arm, he hoisted her to her feet, twisting her round to face him.

"Ouch! You're hurting me," she cried.

His grip tightened. "You've been smoking pot again, haven't you?"

She tried to wriggle free, took no heed of the fact that the strap of her nightdress had fallen off her shoulder revealing one breast. Holding up her free hand, she indicated with her forefinger and thumb the extent of her backward slip. "Only the teeniest little bit."

"Has Ben been back?"

She pouted and muttered, "He said it would cheer me up seeing as I'm going to be left all alone."

Reece lost his temper. "You had your chance. You could have gone home. What are you playing at Megan? This mooning around feeling sorry for yourself has got to stop. You can't mourn for Christopher forever. You've got to move on."

With an unexpected show of strength, Megan wrenched herself free from his grasp and, pointedly rubbing her wrist, complained, "It's all right for you. You don't know how it feels losing someone you love. I'll never get over it. Never!"

Reece kept his cool. His feelings of despondency, of desperation at losing Chantal rose in his mind as fresh as ever. He shoved the recollections aside and went into the kitchen to make Megan a black coffee and warm some milk for Calum. This done, he picked up the phone and rang Ben's club.

"What's going on, Ben?" he demanded.

"What d'you mean?"

"Megan's been smoking again. Did you give her the stuff?"

"Certainly not. She knows where it is, she must have helped herself."

"You've been encouraging her," accused Reece.

"Don't talk such fucking rubbish. Why would I do that?"

"Where's the key to your bedroom door?"

"I dunno." A pause. "In the lock, inside the room."

"Listen Ben, I'm going to lock the door and hide the key." He glanced round to see if Megan was within earshot. "It will be at the back of the bathroom cabinet, behind the mouthwash. She mustn't get her hands on any more. She'll crack up, you know, and if she does it will be your fault."

He put the phone down without waiting for Ben's reply and, after locking Ben's bedroom door and hiding the key, he returned to the other room to find Megan curled up in a ball on the floor with Calum grizzling beside her.

The girl needed to sleep off the narcotic effects and the child needed entertaining. With a sigh of resignation, Reece wrapped Calum up in his snowsuit and took him out in his pushchair. It felt strange and slightly embarrassing at first. He headed for the park without meeting anybody he knew. Calum chuckled happily until, finally, he dropped off to sleep, his thumb in his mouth. Reece glanced down at him fondly. Such a delightful child! Such an uncertain future! If only Megan could be persuaded to go home to Wales. He knew it wouldn't happen, not yet. He was convinced she'd go back one day, although he knew that the resentment she bore her father was still an open wound. He swivelled the pushchair round and wheeled the baby back to the flat.

Megan was lost to the world. He made a pot of tea and roused her. Startled out of a deep sleep, she took time to come to her senses. "Oh dear," she cried, suddenly alarmed. "Where's Calum?"

"Watching a DVD."

"It's dark, I must have been asleep for hours."

"You were. Are you feeling better?"

"Yes thanks." She smiled winsomely up at him. "You'd better hurry, or you'll miss your train." When he hesitated, she went on, "Don't worry about me, I'm going to be sensible from now on."

Encouraged by her apparent recovery, Reece grinned. "I'll just have a quick shower and throw a few things into a bag, then I'll be off."

Under the shower, he whistled a tune to himself. Things were looking up. His college assessment had been excellent and his manager had offered him a rise. Judging from Megan's response a few minutes ago, the girl had come to her senses; Ben was unlikely to put in appearance in Birmingham since he was tied up at the nightclub; Imelda and the girls were clearly pleased that he was joining them for Christmas. All that was left for him to do was to convince Thea that he really cared for her. He rubbed his limbs vigorously with the towel, resolving to persuade her to move down to London so that their relationship could really get off the ground.

He sped back to his room, barely giving Megan and Calum a glance. They were both engrossed in the television. Hastily running a comb through his hair, he gave his reflection a last-minute inspection in the mirror, snatched up his hold-all and ran back down the stairs.

"You're off then. Cheers, have a good time." Megan raised her arm in salute, spilling a small amount of liquid from the glass in her hand.

Reece waved back, then spotted a bottle tucked behind the chair. Fractionally, he hesitated, then dived out of the room and down the stairs, casting the significance of his observation from his mind.

CHAPTER THIRTEEN

While her mother and sisters talked excitedly about the Christmas festivities, Thea waited for Reece to arrive with a mixture of anticipation and nervousness. They didn't seem to notice her lack of interest. Imelda always threw herself into the preparations, with Hannah and Naomi squabbling about decorating the over-sized tree in the cramped living room. As always, Clelia was the peacemaker, calming frayed tempers, suggesting compromises.

Thea had spent a lot of time puzzling over the situation in Twickenham. Reece had promised to phone from the station when his train got in. Eleven o'clock came around, no call; then eleven thirty, still no call. The others went to bed. Thea started to watch an old movie, and at half past twelve, she too went to bed. Clelia heard her pass her bedroom door and whispered, "Don't worry, Thea, Reece must have missed the train. He'll come, you'll see."

"It doesn't matter," shrugged Thea, a little surprised at her sister's intuitive understanding. She had never hinted at her relationship with Reece to any member of her family.

Euston Station was heaving with commuters. Everyone, it seemed, was going somewhere for Christmas. Reece pushed his way through to the indicator board to check the platform for the eight forty to Birmingham. The station clock caught his attention. It said eight forty-one. He checked his watch. It said eight thirty-five. Shit! With a hiss of fury, he gave the watch a shake. He'd meant to get a new battery for it. Praying that the train was late, he raced towards Platform 6 arriving in time to see it disappearing from sight.

The ticket collector's good-natured face broke into a jovial grin. "You've missed it, mate."

Reece clenched his fists in irritation. "When's the next one?"

"Nine thirty, but there won't be any seats left. You'll have to stand."

He didn't mind standing so long as he got to see Thea by Christmas Day. He thanked the man and went in search of a cup of coffee. The self-service café was crowded. He sat down at a corner table, still feeling furious with himself. What would Thea think when he didn't turn up at the right time? Would she class him as unreliable, like her brother? Shit, shit, shit!

Why had he wasted so much time comforting Megan? The girl was a hopeless case, not worth bothering about.

A woman lugging a large suitcase and carrying a young child approached his table. She looked agitated. Reece sprang to his feet and pulled out a chair for her. She murmured her thanks, dumped the suitcase and sat down with a sigh of relief.

"Christmas Eve isn't the best time to travel," he commented.

"You're right," she agreed. "It's awful. I'm dying for a cuppa. I don't know how I'm going to get to the counter with the baby and the luggage."

Reece grinned. "I'll get it for you," he said impulsively.

The woman looked embarrassed. "Oh, I didn't mean. Really, I wasn't suggesting ..."

"It's all right," he said. "Can I get something for your baby as well?"

"No, thank you." She still looked embarrassed. "I've brought a bottle for him."

"Right, a cup of tea it is, and biscuits."

She smiled gratefully at him. "Thanks. You're very kind."

She was feeding the baby when he returned. Her dark head was bent over the child's blond curls. She looked up and thanked him as he sat down.

Reece took another glance at his watch. The hour hand hadn't moved. The woman noticed and said, "It's five past nine. What time's your train?"

"Nine thirty."

"You've still got a bit of time to spare."

"Yes," he agreed. The baby gave a burp, reminding him of Calum. Would Megan have kept her promise to keep off the booze and puff? Suppose she neglected the child and something dreadful happened to him! Ben might not get back to the flat. Sometimes he stayed out all night. He pushed the thought from his mind. Megan wasn't his problem.

The baby gave another burp, the woman produced a baby wipe and cleaned his chin. "I'm taking him home to see my mum and dad," she said proudly. "They've only seen him once."

Reece's thoughts flew to Megan's parents. *They* hadn't seen Calum for over a year. If only he'd managed to persuade her to go home for Christmas! His thoughts drifted back to when he'd left the flat earlier in the evening. Megan had looked so pitiful. Could she be trusted?

The woman with the baby was chatting to him, but Reece wasn't listening.

"Excuse me," he cried, springing to his feet. "I have to make a phone call."

Snatching up his hold-all, he pushed his way through the crowded café, through the station and out to the street. Finding a quiet corner, he took out his mobile and dialled the flat. There was no reply. What am I worrying about? he asked himself. Megan's probably gone to bed. He decided to phone Thea; the line was engaged. Again, he tried to reach Megan. There was still no reply. He stood rooted to the spot. Megan slept heavily, the phone wouldn't wake her. She must be all right, he told himself, after all, she'd promised to behave.

He went back into the station and almost bumped into the woman from the café. She smiled at him and hurried on. Suddenly, a knot of dread rose in Reece's throat. Pushing his way through the milling crowds, he rushed out of the station and hailed a taxi

Reece unlocked the front door and raced up the stairs. At the top, he stopped and listened. The flat was silent. Everything was perfectly normal. A rush of fury sent the blood rushing to his face. He'd let the nine thirty train go in response to an ill-founded premonition. There was nothing wrong. Megan and Calum were fast asleep. Just to make sure, he quietly opened the door to Megan's room and peered in.

At the far side, he could just make out the bulge of Calum's body tucked under the duvet. Of Megan there was no sign. The room was in darkness except for a yellow glow in one corner. It flickered and he saw that it came from a candle stuck in a jam jar. The draught from the ill-fitting window made the flame leap, prompting shadows to dance grotesquely on the opposite wall. He crept across the room, but his foot knocked against one of Calum's toys. It jangled noisily. A scream pierced the air. Megan leapt up from the floor and started kicking at some unseen adversary, her arms flailing in the air. Her eyes were wild and filled with terror.

Reece bounded across the room and wrapped his arms around her, trying to still the convulsions which had overtaken her.

"It's all right, Megan," he whispered and, as the shuddering eased, he slowly released her, stroking the top of her head and leading her to sink down onto one of the beanbags. "You'll be fine. There's nothing to worry about."

When he moved away to fetch her dressing gown, she called out in panic, "Please don't leave me."

He slipped the dressing gown over her hunched shoulders and handed her a tissue. She sniffed and gulped. "What made you come back?"

He decided to lie. "I forgot my debit card."

"Oh, I see, but what about your trip to Birmingham?"

"I'll have to go up there for the New Year instead."

"Won't Thea mind?"

Thea! He clenched his fists. What was he going to do about Thea? He'd lose her for sure now. She'd never trust him after this.

He gulped and said, "She'll understand."

With her face half hidden by a strand of blond hair, Megan looked up at him and, as the candlelight flickered, he was startled to see a sly expression glint in her eyes.

"You came back because of me, didn't you?" she muttered.

Involuntarily he stiffened; this was getting too close to the truth, a truth he didn't even want to admit to himself. "You'd better get some sleep," he said, and taking her by the hand, he led to the bed. Despite the furore, Calum was still asleep.

She climbed into bed, reaching up to give him a goodnight peck on the cheek. "Thanks, Reece, I'll make it up to you one day, I promise."

Reece went to snuff out the candle, mortified by his moment of panic at the station. The girl was somewhat neurotic, but clearly his concern for Calum's safety had been unfounded. The child had been fed and changed and put to bed properly. If his mother chose to spend half the night sitting in a candle-lit room practising yoga that was her prerogative. Who was he to take on the role of social worker?

Despite his angry state of mind, Reece sank into a deep sleep to dream about Thea. It took him several minutes to focus his befuddled brain as he felt a light touch on his chest and a whisper of breath on his neck. He began to respond, then sat bolt upright, thrusting aside the thin white arm encircling his body. Megan rolled away from him.

"What are you doing here?" His voice was hoarse with shock. He tried to stay calm, but in his somnambulant state, he was still not certain that the whole thing wasn't a dream.

Megan wriggled closer and smiled up at him. "I'm sorry, Reece, I didn't mean to startle you. You don't mind, do you, only I was lonely on my own?"

"Get out, get back to your own bed!" he bellowed.

Stunned by his anger, Megan cowered away.

"Get out," he shouted.

She scrambled out of bed and headed for the curtained doorway. Reece fell back on the bed. He couldn't think straight. His plans for a family

Christmas with the Jensons with perhaps a few romantic moments with Thea thrown in had gone totally awry. Now this! He'd underestimated Megan's condition. She must have been drinking. He hadn't smelt alcohol on her breath, but Vodka was odourless and he knew Ben kept a bottle in the kitchen cupboard. He remembered the half-concealed bottle he'd spied behind the chair as he'd left for the station. The puff! Surely she hadn't found the key to Ben's room.

He heard her sobbing and, when she started beating her fists on the floor, he knew he'd have to go and investigate. As soon as the holidays were over and things got back to normal, I'm out of here, he thought to himself. Enough was enough, Connie would have to re-take charge of her foundling.

Now fully awake, he got up, pulled on some shorts and a sweater and padded downstairs. As he turned into the room, Calum gave a small cry. Striding across the room, he grabbed Megan's wrist and pulled her to her feet and gave her a shake. But the more he tried to calm her, the more hysterical she became. The baby let out another cry. Reece spun Megan round and slapped her face. Her screaming stopped. She gave a gasp and a surprised look sprang to her eyes. But recovery was only momentary. Opening her mouth wide, she let out a prolonged howl. A glance towards the bed told Reece that Calum had reached the edge of wakefulness. Without a second's thought, he gathered the naked figure of Megan into his arms and took her back upstairs to the attic bedroom.

The shock of being lifted and jolted up the stairs silenced Megan. Reece dropped her onto the bed and stared down at her with undisguised disgust.

She bit her lip and stuttered, "I'm sorry, I'm so sorry." Conscious of her nudity, she folded her arms across her breasts and drew her knees up to her chest. Her gaze darted around in search of a means of preserving propriety.

"Here." Reece snatched up his bathrobe and tossed it to her. She gathered it around herself, tying the belt very tightly as if to ward off the evil spirits, which had led her to expose herself so shamelessly.

Lowering her head into her hands, she quietly wept. "Oh Reece, what have I done?" Her silent sobs made the scene all the more poignant. No longer hysterical, they racked her slight frame.

Reece looked on, not knowing what to do. A few moments ago, he had hated her, now his leonine heart pulsed with compassion. She was so young, so naive, so utterly vulnerable. He sat down beside her and held her close. At first, she resisted, edging away. Then, succumbing to weakness, she melted into his embrace.

Half an hour later, by tacit agreement, they climbed into bed to lay quietly, side-by-side yet separated, each concerned with coming to terms with their own demons. At last they both fell into an exhausted sleep.

Reece woke up first. He half turned and looked at Megan. No sense of shock this time, no jolt of repugnance. Despite her night of torment, she looked pretty although her eyelids were still puffy from so much weeping. He noticed that her eyelashes were surprisingly dark for someone with flaxen hair. On impulse, he leant across and gently kissed her slightly parted lips. She stirred, gave a little stretch and blinked open her eyes.

"Reece," she whispered, a tremor of apprehension emphasising her Welsh accent.

"It's all right," he replied, relieved that she seemed to have returned to normal.

She smiled and said, "Do that again."

She looked pale and inviting in the semi-darkness of the December morning, with her hair spread on the pillow.

"Happy Christmas," he said, kissing her again.

Reece wasn't sure what happened next; could never work out whether she drew him down to her or whether he simply responded to the sensuousness of the moment, but on that Christmas morning, with the baby still fast asleep downstairs, Reece and Megan made love.

Reece woke for a second time to find his hair being pulled. He tried to brush aside the annoyance, then realised that Calum was trying to climb up onto the bed. He sat up and picked him up. The child squealed with delight. For once, he wasn't going to be turfed out of the attic room. Megan was still asleep, snoring lightly. In the morning light, Reece's sympathy vanished. The night's incident had been a terrible mistake and it would never happen again. Reece prodded her.

"Megan, get up, Calum needs his breakfast."

She rolled onto her back and stretched lazily. Irritated by her lack of response, Reece dumped Calum on top of her and got out of bed.

She hugged him and said, "And how's my little boy this morning?" Calum gurgled happily. Megan looked up. "And how's my big boy?"

Reece stopped in his tracks. "What?" he snapped.

Megan shrank back under the duvet. "I'll come down and get some breakfast," she said.

"Don't bother, I'm going out."

"You can't go up to Birmingham today, there won't be any trains," she said smugly.

Anger robbed Reece of words. Had Megan been standing within reach, he would have slapped her. The heavy curtain he was shouldering back, the three paces it would take to reach the bed and, most of all, the sight of the baby bouncing up and down beside his mother, prevented an ugly incident. Swearing angrily, he ran downstairs, went into the bathroom and took a shower. He got dressed hurriedly and made his way out of the flat, passing the kitchen door on his way. Megan was in there, giving Calum his cereals. She cast him a timid glance as he passed the doorway, but said nothing.

He walked the streets for half an hour before gaining the courage to phone Thea. The call was a disaster. Thea was unforgiving, and who could blame her? His excuse of having to stay in Twickenham because of a sick friend was transparent. With his spirits at rock bottom, he went back to the flat.

Thea woke up on Christmas morning feeling miserable. Her younger sisters were disappointed too. At breakfast, their mother brought up the subject. "So Reece didn't come last night." She shrugged her plump shoulders. "He must have missed his train or got caught up in Twickenham. Never mind, your Aunts Lucilla and Laila will be here soon, and Cousin Jake will liven up the party. He's promised to be here by mid-day."

Thea nodded dully, picking at her plate of cereals. Her mother noticed. "What's the matter sweetness, lost your appetite?"

"I'm fine," protested her daughter while Clelia looked on sympathetically.

The younger girls chattered excitedly, trying to guess what presents they would have while Thea mused unhappily on how stupid she'd been to misread Reece's intentions. Ben had tried to warn her. She should have listened to him. It never occurred to her to pick up the telephone and find out whether Reece had left Twickenham until Clelia poked her gently in the ribs and quietly suggested it.

"I couldn't, he'd think I was chasing him."

"Don't be daft," retorted her sister. "You invited him up here, you've every right to find out where he's got to."

Before Thea could make the call, the phone rang and Imelda answered it. She stood half in, half outside the room, her frame filling the doorway, her friendly guffaws echoing round the kitchen. She nodded at the four expectant faces of her daughters and mouthed. "It's Reece. He's stuck in London, something about an emergency."

"An emergency? Let me speak to him." Thea ran across the room and snatched the receiver from her mother's hand. "Hello Reece," she said.

There was a pause before his voice reached her. "I'm so sorry I couldn't come. Will you forgive me?"

"Why?" she muttered. "Explain why."

He mumbled an excuse about helping out a sick colleague, apologised three times in a row until, unable any longer to hide her feeling, Thea said curtly, "Don't bother with any more lame excuses. Goodbye, Reece."

Imelda looked at her in surprise. "You cut him a bit short, didn't you? That was rude, my girl, that was no way to treat one of your brother's friends."

"He deserved it," retorted Thea, stomping out of the room.

CHAPTER FOURTEEN

Connie was enjoying herself. The Fairy Godmother part, although not a role she would have chosen for her debut, provided enough scope for her to be able to show off her prowess as a singer and a dancer, if not as an actress.

Some of the performers went home on Christmas Day, those remaining got together at the modest hotel where some of them were staying. They were an ill-assorted bunch of has-been's and would-be's.

Stan was his usual blustery self. He commanded centre stage as he knocked back whiskies at the bar. He amused the others with anecdotal bloomers from previous pantomimes. His deep crusty voice filled the tiny bar area. After his third drink, he looked around and rubbed his hands together. "Well, are we all present and correct?"

The meal was served in a private room with Stan seated at the head of the table. Connie watched as the leading lady and the choreographer vied with one another for attention. However, her interest in their play acting soon waned and she began to wonder how soon she could get away. Will, the young man sitting next to her was playing the part of Buttons in the pantomime. He had been very quiet during the meal, but while they were drinking coffee, he nudged her. "Let's get away from this lot as soon as we can, Connie. What d'you say?"

She snatched at the opportunity and, when the rest of the cast, made their way to the bar for more drinks, the pair made their escape.

"I don't know about you, but I've had enough of that crowd," said Will when they got outside.

"Me too."

"Your place or mine?" he asked.

"It will have to be yours, my land-lady's a dragon," replied Connie.

Will's room was small, but comfortable.

"This is far nicer than my digs," said Connie. "But I don't mind. After all, it's only for a couple of months."

"Where do you go from here?" he asked her.

"Back to Twickenham I suppose. What about you?"

"I don't know. I'll just have to wait and see what my agent has got lined up for me. Connie, I was watching you during the meal," went on Will. "You seemed distracted, but you seem more cheerful now. Were you feeling homesick?"

Connie was taken aback at his discernment. "I *was* feeling a bit low," she admitted.

"You miss your family?"

"It's not that.

"Boyfriend trouble?"

Connie shook her head. "No, it's just that I found out something recently which turned my world upside-down."

Will didn't press her, but before she could stop herself, Connie started telling him all about Della's devastating revelation and her invitation to accompany her to Rio de Janeiro to meet her real father.

Will didn't interrupt her. He listened quietly, leaning forward and rolling his empty tumbler between the palms of his hands, staring at the pattern on the carpet under his feet.

She stopped talking and studied his unruly fair hair, the quiff that wouldn't lay down, and wanted to stroke it. He got up to pour out more wine and as he sat down again, his grey-blue eyes were full of sympathy.

"That must have been an awful shock," he said. "Are you curious about your father? Do you think you'll ever make the trip over to Rio?"

Connie shook her head. "I don't know."

"Has your aunt..." He corrected himself. "...your mother flown out there on her own?"

"I've no idea, but I don't think she'd throw away the chance of a free holiday or, come to that, the possibility of a free meal ticket."

"She's that unscrupulous?"

"Huh! You don't know her." Her eyes filled with tears. "I wish she'd never come back to London, I wish she'd never told me the truth."

"Cheer up! I'm sure you won't feel that way once you've had a chance to get used to the idea." Will's words of consolation were old-fashioned to her ears. He was unlike the young men she usually mixed with. When he gave her a hug, it was comforting and unconditional. She felt like a child. All her life, she had been the strong one, the one to sort out problems, to confront adversity. She had been the protector, the rock. With a jolt of amusement she realised that she was in danger of becoming the proverbial agony aunt. This reversal of roles shocked her out of melancholy.

Gently easing away from him, she said, "I'm all right now, Will, really I am. It's late and ..."

He got up at once and said with a smile, "I'll see you home."

"What a cosy family scene," said Ben when he got back to the flat late Christmas afternoon and found Megan and Reece kneeling on the floor with Calum between them. "I see you've opened all your presents."

Megan jumped up and ran over to him. "Thanks ever so much, Ben, Calum loves his train set. It's the perfect model for his age."

"The sales assistant was very helpful," he replied with a grin.

He was in a friendly mood. Megan fussed over him, making tea and thanking him for his presents over and over again. Even Calum seemed to be warming to the arrogant brummie. Reece could barely bring himself to be civil.

Ben turned to him. "I thought you were spending Christmas with Ma and the girls, Reece."

"There was a change of plan," muttered Reece.

Ben stayed for a couple of hours, amusing Megan by telling her about unlikely incidents that he swore on his grandmother's grave had occurred at Deceptions. He romped with Calum and tossed friendly asides at Reece. Once again, the Canadian witnessed the Jamaican's ability to lay on the charm when he saw fit.

Megan gave Reece no opportunity to question Ben about the cannabis. When he'd checked, the key was still hidden in the bathroom cabinet and the airing cupboard hoard appeared undisturbed, although he was certain she'd been smoking puff or, heaven forbid, something more addictive.

The girl stayed within earshot, dogging their heels as Ben and Reece moved from living room to kitchen and back again. Her conduct reaffirmed Reece's conviction that her source of supply was linked to Ben. His impulse was to bring the whole thing out into the open, but it was Christmas Day and a glance at Calum playing happily with his new toys stopped him. Besides, he felt ashamed at the way he had handled Megan's breakdown during the night. Suppose she mentioned it to Ben?

After Ben had left and Calum had been put to bed, Reece and Megan watched television. His mind wasn't on the programme. All he wanted was for Christmas and the New Year celebrations to be over so that he could return to the normality of work. Megan seemed content, making him wonder whether he'd allowed his imagination to exaggerate her deluded state the evening before. He cast her a covert glance. He felt he ought to make an apology, but she was the first one to apologise.

"I'm ... I'm terribly sorry about what happened last night, Reece. I promise I won't disturb you tonight." Her voice croaked and a deep blush rose to her cheeks.

He felt his own colour rise and covered it by talking to her like an ageing uncle. "We'll forget all about it, Megan, but it must never happen again."

"I was out of my head," she whispered. "From now on, I'm really going to pull myself together. I've got to for Calum's sake and, besides, you're right, I can't grieve for Christopher forever. He wouldn't want me to. Next week I'm going to look for another job."

Her words rang with sincerity, prompting Reece to relax his guard a little. He smiled and said, "It's been hard for you, Megan, but you'll pull through. Goodnight, see you tomorrow."

As he turned to go upstairs, she jumped up and ran across the room. Standing on tiptoe, she gave him a peck on the cheek. "Are we friends again?"

"Of course," he replied.

Her positive attitude gave him renewed hope. If she really meant to find a job, she'd make new friends, go out a bit. He didn't mind babysitting occasionally and, by mid-January, Connie would be back to take over the responsibility. In the meantime, he'd go up to Birmingham and make his peace with Thea. He began to feel more optimistic. Soon, he would be able to put the whole unfortunate episode behind him.

The days between Christmas and the New Year passed without incident. True to her word, Megan made an effort to put the past behind her. She busied herself with domestic chores and made plans for the future. She spent a lot of time sitting cross-legged on the floor making notes and every day, she would read her catalogue of proposals out to him. Sometimes, it was two or three projects, sometimes, it was a list of possible employment outlets.

"I'm not qualified for anything other than working in a supermarket or a dress shop, but I suppose that's better than nothing. Of course the pay's terrible, but maybe when Calum goes to nursery school, I could go back to college. I must remember to ask Connie about that." She licked the tip of her pencil and added this reminder to her list.

On the day before New Year's Eve Reece rang the Birmingham number and spoke to Imelda

"Are you coming to see us soon?"

"I was thinking of coming tomorrow."

"Dearie me, not New Year's Eve! The big girls will be out, Ben's not coming and you wouldn't want to see the old year out with me and the little ones, would you? Why not leave it until the following weekend?"

Reece hid his disappointment. "That suits me," he agreed. "Thea and Clelia will be there, won't they?"

"Sure thing."

Spending New Year's Eve with Megan and Calum did not appeal to him. He had sacrificed Christmas, he wasn't going to sacrifice New Year. Then, he remembered an invitation one of the girls at work had given him.

"Come along to our party, bring a friend if you like. Any time after nine. Here's the address." She'd thrust a piece of paper at him and he'd put it in his pocket, although he hadn't intended to accept the invitation. Megan noticed him getting ready to go out the following evening and pulled a face.

"Where are you going? I was hoping you'd be keeping me and Calum company."

"Sorry, I can't. I'm going to a party and I've no idea what time I'll be back. I'll try not to disturb you."

It was a lively party. He left at four in the morning, sharing a minicab with a couple who were going in the same direction. For several hours he'd been able to forget his worries and enjoy himself. Even Thea's image had receded into the background.

Opening the door cautiously, he crept through Megan's room. He was about to climb the stairs to the attic when he heard her weeping. He hesitated, cursing softly under his breath, praying that she hadn't heard him.

"Is that you, Reece?" she called out, her voice muffled.

"Yes, I didn't mean to disturb you. Goodnight."

She let out a reverberating sob and called, "Come and talk to me for a minute."

"Can't it wait until the morning?"

Another sob, a desperate plea, "Please, Reece." Unwillingly, he crossed the room to her bed. "Look what he did to me?"

"What are you talking about?"

"He hit me."

"Who hit you?"

"Ben. Look!" She reached out a hand and switched on the nightlight.

Even in its dim glow, Reece could see that her left cheek was inflamed and her jaw swollen. He was lost for words.

"He called me a silly cow and pushed me out, and then he hit me."

"Pushed you out of where?"

"His room."

All at once, Reece began to suspect that she had been asking Ben for a smoke. "What were you doing in there?"

His assumption was wrong. She shook her head, wincing with pain. "It was midnight and I went in to wish him a happy New Year. I'd heard him come in you see."

Reece felt puzzled. It was unlike Ben to come back so early, especially on Old Year's Night.

"You'd better start at the beginning," he said.

Calum stirred, making them both start guiltily. "We can't talk here," she said, sitting up and swinging her legs out of bed. Snatching up her dressing gown, she ran to the attic staircase.

"Wait, Megan!" he called. "Don't go up there, we can talk in the kitchen." When she ignored him, he hurried after her, making a grab for her sleeve as she started to climb the stairs. She missed her footing and fell back into his arms.

Again Calum stirred.

"Shhh!" said Megan. Twisting round, she linked her arms behind Reece's neck and backed up the stairs, pulling him with her.

Brushing aside the curtain, she took two steps backwards and sat down on the bed, still refusing to release Reece, who landed on top of her. He jumped up immediately and moved away to switch on the light.

"What's been going on?" he asked, then gave a gasp when he saw the full extent of the damage to her face. "Ben would never hit a woman." A mixture of disbelief and anger brought a flush to Reece's face. He knuckled his fist. "If he did, I'll beat the shit out of him."

Megan hung her head. "You don't understand," she whispered. "I asked for it."

Reece's eyes narrowed. "What d'you mean?"

"I tried to get into bed with him."

"You did what?"

Her bottom lip started to tremble. "After you went out I was so lonely. I needed some comfort." She looked up accusingly. "You *hid* the Vodka. What was I to do?"

"For God's sake, Megan ..." He stopped mid-sentence. "That's beside the point, he shouldn't have hit you. I'm going down to sort him out."

She grabbed his arm. "You can't, he's got a girl with him."

Reece spun round to face her. "Are you saying you tried to make it a threesome?"

"A threesome?" For a moment, she didn't understand. "Of course not. What do you think I am?"

He snatched her wrist and shook her. "Tell me what happened, Megan."

"Like I said, I went to wish him a happy New Year. He seemed pleased, invited me in, poured me out a glass of wine. Said cheers and all that stuff, then he kissed me." She paused, as if to impress him. "Then he said: 'Got to get an hour's kip in. You can keep me company if you like. Stay and finish your drink.' He lay down on the bed and I sat down next to him. I still had half a glass of wine, you see. He took my hand and said he thought I was very pretty. He said, 'You know, Reece really likes you.'" She glanced up to see what reaction this statement would bring, but Reece didn't allow his feelings to show.

She went on. "I said, 'Of course he doesn't.' I finished my drink and he took the glass from me and pulled me down beside him. He said, 'He does, but he's shy with women.'" Her eyes widened. "Is that true, Reece?"

Reece ignored the question, asking instead, "Did he kiss you again?"

"Yes."

"Then what happened?"

"The doorbell rang. That's when he got nasty. I said, 'Who on earth can that be at this hour?' He leapt up and dragged me to the door saying, 'You've got to go.' I started to argue, then he pushed me out of the room." She began to cry, her shoulders shaking convulsively. "He led me on, then gave me the brush-off."

She looked pathetic, but Reece resisted the temptation to give her a reassuring hug.

"What happened next?"

"The bell rang again, wouldn't stop, whoever it was had their finger pressed on it. I was afraid it would wake Calum up and I started to run along the corridor, but I didn't move out of Ben's way quickly enough. 'Shift yourself, you silly cow,' he yelled and gave me a hard shove. His hand caught my cheekbone and I fell against the wall -- saw stars and everything. He didn't care; he ran off downstairs to answer the door."

"What did you do?"

"I staggered a bit, then ran into my room. I couldn't believe what he'd done."

"It sounds more like an accident to me," said Reece.

"He pushed me really hard," she hiccupped indignantly. Her brows drew together in a pained frown. "He didn't want me once the other girl arrived. Nobody wants me. First Chris, then Robert, now Ben's taking the piss out of me." The choice of words was alien to her and, even in her distress, sounded stilted.

Against his better judgement, Reece felt some sympathy for her. He sat down next to her and put a comforting arm around her shoulders. "Look, Megan, it's time you went back to Wales. This is no life for you. Go home to your parents and ..." He was going to add: 'grow up', but thought better of it.

She thrust his arm aside. "Now you're trying to get rid of me. Nobody cares. I wish I could die."

"Shhh!" he whispered. "You'll wake Calum up."

"I want to die," she wept. "Truly, I want to die. I could kill myself, you know. I know how to do it."

"Don't be silly," he said. "You're upset. Things will seem better in the morning."

Her sobs intensified until her whole body was shaking uncontrollably. Reece pulled back the duvet and lifted her into his bed. Laying down fully clothed beside her, he rocked her gently until she fell into an exhausted sleep.

CHAPTER FIFTEEN

With the Christmas and New Year festivities over, Reece wasn't sorry to return to work. The day-to-day routine pushed the melodramatic events of the past few days to the back of his mind. He did not, however, lose his determination to look for another bed-sit, although January wasn't a good time to move house. Agencies had very few lettings on their books and there weren't many in the 'Surrey Comet'.

He challenged Ben about Megan's injuries.

"I apologised," said Ben. "It was an accident. She took me by surprise, rushing at me like a wildcat. The kid's got guts, I'll say that for her."

In view of Megan's unpredictability and her slipped-in remark that she had asked for it, Reece accepted Ben's explanation and they shook hands on it. He was pleased to discover that Megan was looking for a job. She had rung up a few supermarkets and local shops, but with Calum crying or shouting in the background, her enquiries about employment were not taken seriously.

"Don't worry," said Reece. "Once Connie gets back, she'll help you out."

"I hope so," agreed Megan dejectedly.

He began to think that she was pulling herself out of depression, accepting without fuss his decision to go up to Birmingham the following weekend. After her earlier histrionics, this came as a pleasant surprise.

All the way up there on the train, he replayed his telephone conversations with Thea, wondering what kind of reception he would get from her. She was out when he arrived. Imelda greeted him effusively.

"Wonderful to see you, sweetness! Pity you couldn't make it at Christmas. Is your friend well?"

For a moment, he was startled and wondered whether Ben had been told his mother about Megan. Then he remembered his white lie. "Yes thanks."

Imelda fussed over him, demanding news of Ben, complaining that her favourite offspring did not keep in touch.

"He's been very busy with his new venture into the nightclub business," explained Reece. "He's very conscientious, you know."

Imelda clapped her hands together. "You no need tell me, son. My boy deserve de success. He work harder than anybody in der family."

Reece smiled and nodded, but doubted the truth of this, knowing that Thea was dedicated to her studies and Clelia to her nursing.

The door opened and Thea came in. Imelda let out a whoop. "Look who's here," she cried, giving her daughter a big hug. "I'll go make tea while you talk Reece." She disappeared into the kitchen, leaving the pair alone.

Thea's body language told Reece he was in for a lot of explaining if he wanted to win her round. She sat down at the table, half turned away, waiting for him to make the opening gambit.

"Sorry about Christmas."

She shrugged. "It doesn't matter. How's my brother?"

Reece wondered whether she'd already spoken to Ben. What story had he given her? He tried to keep the conversation general until they could talk in private. "He's fine, busy as usual."

Imelda bustled in with a tray of tea and cake. Her huge hips swung from side to side. Reece noticed, not for the first time, that her movements were graceful, her step light. He looked into her face and saw that, in middle age, she was still a handsome woman, her features a more mature version of Thea's. She poured the tea and, after handing round the biscuits, said "Tell us all your news, boy."

After a pleasant evening meal with all four daughters present, Reece began to realise that if he were to speak with Thea on her own, he would have to engineer the opportunity.

After the meal, Clelia's boyfriend dropped by to take her to see a film. Shortly afterwards, Imelda shooed Hannah and Naomi off to bed, leaving only the three of them.

When Thea got up to help her mother with the washing-up, he too picked up a tea towel, causing Imelda to chuckle and protest hotly. "Sit down, sweetness, this not men's work. Snatching away the tea towel, she pushed him away with soapy hands. He tried to resist but clearly, in her world, the male species didn't help with domestic chores.

Watching on, Thea momentarily relaxed her unbending manner and smiled in amusement. "Never argue with ma," she muttered.

When the washing up was done, Imelda settled her ample frame into her favourite chair and pressed the remote. 'Ghost' was just starting and she grinned in satisfaction. "Oh good, Whoopi Goldberg, I'll enjoy this."

Reece felt trapped. How was he going to get Thea alone? All evening she had been overly polite and, the more distantly she behaved towards him, the more desirable he found her. It was infuriating. They were behaving like a couple of strangers exchanging small talk. He longed to push aside the unseen barrier and tell her how he felt about her. While they were discussing the unusually mild weather and the latest film on circuit, he studied her, loving the way she tilted her head to one side when she talked, the way she used her hands to emphasise a point, and the way she looked down and wriggled her toes in order to avoid meeting his eye, when inadvertently, she dropped her guard.

At last, he plucked up courage and said, "I feel like a bit of fresh air, would you come out for a walk with me?" He made a joke of it. "I don't know the area and I might get lost out there on my own."

Realising that she couldn't avoid confrontation any longer, Thea agreed. They turned out of the flats and strolled towards the shopping precinct. Reece knew he couldn't afford to waste time.

He said: "You don't believe my excuse about a sick friend, do you?"

Thea hung onto her haughty manner. "Why, was it a lie?"

He touched her arm. "For goodness sake, Thea, let's get this out in the open. I was telling the truth, partly."

Under the yellow street light, he saw a spark of interest in her eyes. "Partly?"

"Yes, it was Megan. I couldn't leave her on her own. She's almost suicidal."

"How come she's your responsibility? Isn't she Connie's friend?"

He nodded. "Connie's in pantomime at Southampton."

"What about my brother, he's her landlord, shouldn't he take charge. Why do you have to take her under your wing?"

Briefly, Reece explained that Ben was out most of the time and that, for the sake of the child, he had been afraid to leave Megan alone. Although he gave an accurate description of the Welsh girl's hysteria, he knew his explanation sounded manufactured. There were clearly things he couldn't tell her: the fact that he'd slept with Megan; the injuries Ben had inadvertently inflicted on her.

Then Thea asked the million-dollar question. "Ben wasn't serious about moving the pair of them into the living room, was he?"

Reece averted his gaze as he felt his colour rising.

"He did, didn't he?" She pulled away from him, her shoulders hunched. "Why you're practically living together!"

"It's not like that. Honestly, Thea, you've got it all wrong. Since Christmas I've been looking for new digs, but I can't find any."

"Huh!"

Reece frowned angrily. "This is all Ben's fault. He's trying to break us up."

"That's what I thought at first, but I'm not so sure now. I think he was warning me." Spinning on her heel, Thea strode swiftly in the direction of home.

Reece hurried after her, but he soon realised that no amount of reasoning would soften Thea's attitude.

The next day, to avoid further embarrassment, he caught the mid-morning train back to London, apologising awkwardly to Imelda for his short stay. Her broad face broke into a grin. "Come again, boy, you know you're welcome any time. Get dat son of mine to come with you next time."

During the train journey, Reece sank into despair. Ben had sewn the seed of suspicion in Thea's mind and no amount of reassurance would drive it away. This realisation strengthened his determination to leave the flat and strike out on his own. Surely then Thea would believe that there was nothing going on with Megan.

By the time he got off the train at Twickenham Station, determination had replaced despondency and he walked briskly back to the flat. Turning the corner into the road, he stopped in alarm. There was an ambulance at the entrance to the flat. Slinging his overnight bag over his shoulder he bolted along the road, shouting: "What's going on?"

A paramedic was just about to close the vehicle door. He turned and asked curtly, "Do you live here?"

"Yes. Is it Megan?"

The paramedic's attitude softened when he recognised real concern in Reece's eyes. "I'm afraid the young woman's overdosed."

"Is she going to be all right."

The man nodded. "We've stabilized her. We're taking her in for observation. Are you a close friend?"

"Yes...no." Reece stumbled over his words, not knowing how to describe his relationship with Megan. We're flatmates. Who called you?"

"The landlord. Look, I've got to go. Call the hospital in an hour or two. With any luck, they'll discharge her later today."

"Can I go with her?"

The paramedic shook his head. "Better not. Don't worry, she's in good hands."

Reece watched the ambulance drive away. As soon as it was out of sight, he let himself into the flat and took the stairs two at a time. Ben was standing in the middle of Megan's room staring down at the chaos on the floor. The smell was appalling. Reece dropped his holdall and hurried over to the window, flinging it wide open. He spun round in dismay as realisation hit him. "Where's Calum?"

"Connie's got him."

"Thank God! What happened?"

"Let's get this place cleaned up, then I'll tell you," replied Ben, frowning grimly at the task ahead of them.

"Megan must have been out of her head," said Reece as the two men scrubbed vomit off the wooden floor, collected up broken glass and washed Calum's soiled toys that had been in the way when the mêlée began.

"She was. I came home and found Calum crawling around in this mess. She hadn't changed him or fed him all day. The poor little brat was yelling his head off."

"Was she unconscious?"

"Semi."

"What did she take?"

"Puff I suppose."

"She wouldn't have got into that state on puff alone. She must have got hold of something more potent. What was it?"

"How would I know?"

Reece started to get angry. "Come on Ben, I know I haven't given her anything; you're the only other person she sees."

"You don't know that. How do we know what she gets up to when we're at work?"

"She can't afford to buy the stuff, she's broke."

Ben looked surly. "Oh yeah! How d'you think she pays for the booze?"

"The booze? I thought it was yours."

"Think again."

Reece gasped in shock as the significance of this revelation dawned on him. "You mean she's been shoplifting?" He shook his head. "She wouldn't do that!"

"I told you, I don't know anything."

"What happened when you found her?"

"I walked her up and down to wake her up. When Connie got here she called the medics. Before they came, she whipped Calum into his pushchair and took him out. She said, they'd better not know about him."

Reece raised his eyebrows. Trust Connie to take charge. "But they must have seen there's a baby in residence. Did they ask questions?" he said.

Ben nodded. "Connie said, tell them he's with his grandparents for the weekend." Reece heaved a sigh of relief. Thank God for Connie! If things had been left to Ben, Calum would have been whisked away by the Social Services by now. Ben cut into his thoughts. "She thinks they'll send the Social round to investigate."

"She's probably right. How come she's home?"

"Got the weekend off, but she's got to go back tonight." The phone rang and Ben went to answer it. When he came back, he said offhandedly, "That was Connie wanting to know whether the coast was clear. She'll be bringing Calum back soon." He rubbed his hands together and glanced around. "Well, that's that. I'll be off now."

"Aren't you going to help me finish off?"

Ben flashed his arrogant smile. "I've done my bit. Ciao."

After he'd left, Reece continued cleaning up. The stench of vomit, soiled nappies and alcohol still permeated the room. He wondered what the outcome of Megan's breakdown would be. If the Social Services got involved, they might question the flat's suitability for a young child. The possibility strengthened his resolve. Tomorrow, he would start looking for other accommodation, take anything just to get out. But leaving Ben's flat didn't alter the fact that Megan could not be trusted on her own. For Calum's sake he had to force Megan to contact her parents and go home to Wales. His head reeled as he realised that there was a more pressing dilemma: who was going to look after Calum if the hospital decided to keep Megan in overnight?

When Connie and Calum arrived back, Reece greeted them both with a warm hug. Calum seemed unperturbed that his mother was missing. Gurgling happily, he pointed at Reece and said, "Dada."

Connie giggled.

Reece grinned. "This could be embarrassing," he said. He clapped a hand to his head. "There's nothing in the fridge for Calum's tea."

"Don't worry," said Connie, reaching under the pushchair and bringing out several tins of toddler food, disposable nappies and baby wipes. "I noticed that Megan had run out."

"I'll settle up with you," said Reece, but Connie waved off his offer.

"No need," she said. "I've just got my first pay packet and I feel rich."

Impulsively he gave her another hug and asked fondly, "How are you getting on, Connie?"

Her face lit up. "Well, really well," she exclaimed. "It's great fun, most people in the cast are nice and ..."

Reece raised an enquiring eyebrow. "And?"

"I've met a wonderful guy."

Reece looked at her in astonishment. For Connie to enthuse about a boyfriend was unheard of. "Tell me about him."

"His name's Will and he plays Buttons in the panto. I know that doesn't sound like much of a part, but believe me, he's really talented." All at once, she looked worried. "Have you phoned the hospital yet?"

"They said to leave it a couple of hours. I suppose we could phone now."

Connie picked up the receiver and dialled. Reece listened while she nodded and gave her best wishes. "They're keeping her in overnight," she said. "Will you be able to manage Calum all on your own? It will mean you'll be off work tomorrow."

"Don't worry, I'll manage. I'll phone in sick first thing."

"Thanks Reece." She hesitated, then said, "I feel awfully guilty for landing you with all this."

Reece experienced a surge of conscience. How many times had he mentally laid the blame on Connie, telling himself that Megan was her problem, not his!

"It's not your fault," he said.

But her next words brought a rush of panic. "I'm so glad you've taken her under your wing."

"It's only temporary, I'm moving out as soon as I can."

For a moment Connie looked alarmed. "But you'll still call in to see her, won't you?"

He felt ashamed of his overly defensive rejoinder, but knew that to rescind it would be asking for trouble. "I'll do what I can. I can't promise to be on hand all the time."

Connie smiled in relief and kissed him on the cheek. "I must go, my train leaves at eight."

"When do you finish at the Mayflower?"

"At the end of the month, unless something else comes along. Who knows, one thing leads to another."

"I hope it works out for you, Connie," he said. "I mean, with Will."

She smiled again and he noticed how her features softened when the boyfriend's name was mentioned. Clearly, Conchita Dixon had at last lost her heart.

CHAPTER SIXTEEN

Megan was discharged from hospital on Monday afternoon. She was driven home by a voluntary ambulance driver, who deposited her at the front door without speaking to Reece. Calum rushed into her arms and, as she picked him up, Reece noticed how pale and lethargic she seemed.

"I'll make you a cup of tea," he said. "And I've bought your favourite biscuits: custard creams."

She smiled wanly up at him from the bean bag she had sunk onto next to Calum's toy train set. "Thanks, Reece, you're really good to me. I'm so grateful. What would I do without you?"

"You should thank Connie. She took charge of Calum for you so the Social wouldn't ask questions."

"I didn't know she was back."

"It was only a fleeting visit. Hopefully, she'll be back for good by the end of the month."

Megan heaved a sigh. "I would love to see her pantomime. Couldn't we take Calum down to Southampton to see it?"

"He's too young. Besides, I can't get time off work." Wishing to put a stop to Megan's day dreams, Reece moved briskly to the door. "I'll make that tea now."

He returned with two mugs of tea and a plate of biscuits. He started to question her about her breakdown. "What made you do it? Was it a mistake?"

"Of course it was a mistake," she scoffed. "Why, I've everything to live for. There's you and Calum, the two people I love most in the world."

Reece stiffened. "What about your parents?" he said.

She shrugged. "Them too." Then she said something that took his breath away. "I'd really like you to meet them. Perhaps we could go down to Swansea for a visit one weekend."

"Weekends are difficult for me," replied Reece quickly. "I have to work most Saturdays, but you should go. It would be lovely for Calum to see his grandparents again."

Megan seemed to accept this and turned her attention to the baby. "Has Calum been all right without me?"

"Good as gold. Have the hospital prescribed any medication, anti-depressants maybe?"

"They gave me this." She delved into her pocket and drew out a prescription. "I was supposed to take it to the Hospital Pharmacy before I left, but I couldn't be bothered."

"You won't get better if you don't do as you're told," said Reece sternly.

Megan made a face. "I know, but I'm all right now, really I am."

"I've heard that before." He paused before asking the next question. "How did you come by all that booze?"

"Oh that." She flicked a wrist. "It was in the cupboard under the sink. Was Ben cross with me? I know I shouldn't have helped myself."

"He said it wasn't his, he said you brought it into the flat."

Megan straightened up, looking outraged. "That's a lie. Where would I get the money to buy alcohol?"

She was so indignant that Reece's suspicions were turned on their head. Weak people craving drugs and alcohol were notorious liars, but so were devious manipulators, like Ben. Suddenly the sequence of events leading up to Megan's breakdown didn't seem so clear-cut.

"Tell me what happened yesterday, right from the beginning," he said.

Megan swung her legs round to sit cross-legged, pulling Calum towards her as if for protection. The child wriggled free and went back to his toys.

"Well?" demanded Reece.

She pouted and hid behind her hair, fiddling with the frayed cuffs of her cardigan. "I want to put all that behind me, not dig it up and relive it."

Reece got angry. "I think in view of the sacrifices I've made for you, it's about time you became more cooperative," he snapped. "I've lied for you, phoned in sick at work. I still don't know whether they believed me or not."

Begrudgingly, she began to spill out what had happened after he had left for Birmingham. "It was all right at first," she said. "I watched TV and wrote letters of application." She pointed to a pile of papers in the corner. "Look for yourself. But by the evening I was feeling really lonely. You don't know what it's like. You're always so sure of yourself. I couldn't sleep because Calum kept waking up coughing and crying. It was awful, lying there in the dark, frightened to move in case I woke him up again. You don't know what it's like."

"Stop saying that and get on with the story."

"Sunday morning, the church-bells starting ringing. They were like a dirge for Christopher. I couldn't stand it. Ben had left his bedroom door unlocked so I helped myself to a joint. And I felt better. Then it wore off. There were some tablets in the bathroom cabinet so I tried a couple."

"Without knowing what they were? Are you mad, what about Calum, did you think about him?"

"He was quite happy, playing with his toys. I gave him biscuits and cereals so he wasn't hungry."

"You didn't bother to change him."

"Didn't I?" She was all innocence. "Was his nappy dirty?"

"What about the drink?"

She giggled guiltily. "I know I shouldn't have. Ben would never miss it. The bottle was already open you see."

Reece sprang to his feet. "You stupid little fool. Don't you see what's happening? Ben's encouraging you. You've got to get out of here."

"How?"

It was a loaded question. "We'll find a way," he replied.

"We could look for something together," said Megan hopefully. "Once I get a job, I'll be able to chip in with my share of the rent. It would work out perfectly."

Reece felt desperate. "No, Megan," he shouted. "You can't lean on me any more. I might go back to Canada. You must either learn to stand on your own two feet or go home to Wales."

With that, he spun on his heel and went upstairs to the attic room. Through the heavy curtain at the top of the stairs, he could hear her sobbing and frowned with self-loathing. What a heel he'd been! Pushing aside the curtain, he ran back downstairs and, taking her gently by the shoulders, lifted her to her feet. "Look Megan, you've got to go home. Give me the telephone number and I'll phone your parents and ask them to come and collect you."

"No!" screamed Megan. "I'll top myself, I will, I will."

Her hysterics increased and she seemed in danger of collapsing in his arms. He led her to the bed and sat down beside her, hugging her closely until the hysteria subsided while, Calum toddled over and plucked at his mother's jeans, his face screwed up ready to cry as her distress communicated itself to him.

Although he was nervous about leaving Megan on her own, Reece returned to work on Tuesday. Gardens Unlimited was a hive of industry. Stocktaking was in progress and any hope of taking time off to look for new accommodation was swiftly nipped in the bud.

He had checked on Megan before he left and she'd seemed calmer. "I'll start looking for a job when Connie comes home," she'd said phlegmatically.

Connie came back at the end of January. Reece was relieved to see her. Megan was less agitated, due to the Prozac she'd been prescribed, but he still felt under pressure. He cornered Connie at the first opportunity.

"I'm having awful trouble finding other accommodation. There's nothing out there at the moment; must be the time of year. Do you think I could move back into my old room?"

Her mouth dropped open. "Sorry, Reece, you're too late. Will's moving into your old room."

He smothered his disappointment and quickly realised the significance of her news: with Will in situ, Connie would have little time to help out with Megan. Panic rose and, for a fleeting moment, he considered chucking in his job at Gardens Unlimited and moving on. But he was now past his mid-twenties and it was time to settle into a career. The garden centre had offered him that opportunity; it would be foolish to let a slip of a Welsh girl snatch that chance from him. Resolutely he pushed aside the idea of quitting. There had to be another way out.

Then his luck changed. A bed-sit became available just up the road, in St Margaret's. "It won't be possible to move in until the beginning of March," the girl at the letting agency told him. "But we'll need your deposit by the end of this week if you want us to hold it for you."

Reece was relieved. All he had to do was break the news to Megan. He decided to wait until moving day.

Throughout January, Reece had seen very little of Ben. The Jamaican slept in late, leaving the flat mid-afternoon to take up his shift at McDonalds before continuing on to Deceptions for the evening, arriving home in the early hours. This arrangement suited Reece. Their friendship had been under considerable strain. He had heard nothing from Thea although he had written her several letters. He had made up his mind that once he had moved out of Ben's flat, he would pay her a surprise visit and beg her -- on bended knees if necessary -- to give him a second chance. He knew he had a difficult task ahead of him. Clearly, Thea believed he had been romantically involved with Megan. He had to convince her otherwise, and moving out was the first step.

Ben felt no antagonism towards Reece beyond his disapproval of the Canadian's interest in his sister. The eldest child of the Jenson family, he was the only one to have been born in Jamaica. Before emigrating, Imelda had suffered a series of miscarriages with one live birth: a brother born a year after Ben, who had survived for only a few weeks. Consequently, until he was nearly six Ben had been an only child. Those early years, during which he had been surrounded by aunts, uncles and cousins too numerous to count, had influenced him a great deal, their tribal beliefs and rituals remaining with him. Challenged, he would have hotly disagreed with this, priding himself on being totally open-minded and anglicized.

When, in 1975, Abe and Imelda decided to chance their luck in England, the entire Jenson tribe had risen in protest, accusing them of disloyalty and liberalism. He could still remember his mother's argument, repeated ad infinitum: "There's nothing for us here, honey sweets, and besides, ders plenty of our people over der - makin' good. We're headin' fer der sweet life." She would draw herself up regally - she was a lot slimmer in those days - to add, "We won't forget our own sort, no way, sweetness."

It was this indoctrinated memory, together with the high regard he cherished for his mother that drove him to manoeuvre the curtailment of the blossoming relationship between Reece and his sister. With his father's descent into drunkenness and violence, who else was there to watch over the womenfolk? It wasn't that he disliked the Canadian; on the contrary, for a white guy he was one of the best. It was just that he couldn't abide seeing him with his sister.

On the rare occasions that their paths crossed, he greeted Reece in a friendly manner and, now that Thea no longer seemed interested in Reece, his attitude to Megan changed. There was no longer any need to stir things up and when, out of Reece's hearing, the girl dropped hints that she fancied a joint now and again, he brushed her aside with avuncular admonishment.

Things had settled down so well in the household that, for the first time in weeks, Reece began to regret his decision to leave. Megan played at being housekeeper, making his dinner each night, and when he went up to his attic room later in the evening, she would hastily turn down the volume on the TV. This effort to humour him, together with Ben's cheerful and considerate attitude, made him realise how much he would miss their company. In addition to this, Calum had advanced by leaps and bounds. He was steady on his feet and beginning to talk and he greeted Reece with such affection that it was becoming increasingly difficult to point out to him that he was not his daddy.

"I've tried to explain," said Megan, looking worried. "Honestly, I've tried to make him call you Reece, but he doesn't take any notice."

Reece swung the child high in the air and caught him. "It doesn't matter," he said. "He'll forget me when I move out."

"Oh no!" cried Megan. "He'll never forget you. You're an important part of his childhood, he'll never forget you."

And certainly the little boy's adoration of him grew daily. It was flattering. As a result of this more settled atmosphere, Reece slept soundly and when Megan screamed in the middle of the night, his immediate fear was for Calum. Completely disorientated, he leapt out of bed, struggled into a pair of shorts and launched himself downstairs, shouting, "What's happened? Is Calum all right?"

Megan was standing at the door of the room in her nightdress, a hand clutched to her throat, her face sheet white. Unable to speak, she pointed a trembling finger at Ben who was lying in the hallway, blood gushing from a wound in his left arm.

Reece pushed her aside and ran to the West Indian. Ben was barely conscious.

"What happened?" he gasped. Then realising the seriousness of the situation, he turned to Megan and snapped, "Quick, phone for an ambulance."

The sharpness of his words jolted her into life and she squeezed past the two men and ran into the kitchen where the cordless was on re-charge. Reece snatched up a towel from the bathroom and swiftly made a tourniquet. Blood was seeping into the carpet and dripping through the banisters onto the stairs. A glance told Reece that somehow Ben had dragged himself up the staircase unaided. The front door was still open. A brisk wind whistled through the entrance, startling scattered leaves off the garden path onto the doormat.

"What happened, for God's sake?" asked Reece again as he pulled the makeshift tourniquet tighter in an effort to stem the flow of blood.

"No ambulance," gasped Ben, his eyes rolling back in his head in a frightening manner. "No ambulance, no Police."

"For Christ's sake, Ben, you're bleeding to death."

The Jamaican raised his head and muttered a telephone number. "Ring it, ring it," he managed to gasp.

Reece shook his head. "I didn't catch the number." He shouted to Megan. "Hang on for a moment, we may not need the ambulance."

Ben's urgency prompted Reece to take notice. With his ear pressed close to Ben's lips, he repeated the mobile number the injured man was mouthing so that Megan could dial it.

"She says she'll be round straightaway," said Megan.

"Straightaway? What does that mean? Is she far away? Did she say who she was?"

"No."

"We wait five minutes, then call the ambulance."

But barely three minutes had elapsed when they heard footsteps on the stairs.

"God Almighty, what's been happening?" came a husky voice, a voice that could have belonged to a member of either sex. Reece stood up and came face to face with the owner of the voice, a tall -- six feet at least -- North African woman in her mid-thirties. She wore a nursing sister's uniform and carried a medical bag. Her hair was cropped short and she had a wide friendly smile.

"Out of my way." She pushed Reece aside and set about inspecting the wound whilst firing a rally of questions at the victim, who was clearly in no condition to answer them. "Ben, what have you been up to now? Haven't I warned you about the types you've been letting in to Deceptions? Where's your commonsense? You won't live to see thirty at this rate."

"Is he going to be okay?" asked Reece.

Emil appeared at his bedroom door, looking bleary-eyed. "*Qu'est-ce qui lui est arrivé*?" he enquired.

The girl ignored him, answering Reece instead with, "He'll live. You did good, stemming the blood flow like that. Where did you learn to do that?"

"I picked it up along the way," said Reece casually, his thoughts winging back to his days with the travellers. Living with them had taught him basic first aid together with other useful tips on survival.

The French student looked at Megan for an explanation, but she was too shocked to respond, and since the nurse's body was shielding the victim from him, Emil did not see the seriousness of Ben's injury. Losing interest, he rubbed a sleepy fist over his eyes and returned to bed.

All at once, as if feeling left out, Megan spoke to the nurse, "Good thing it's not the other arm."

"You're wrong there, Ben's a south paw," came the scathing retort.

This response flawed Megan, who shrank back, frowning in puzzlement. She glanced at Reece for enlightenment, but he was too engrossed in watching Ben being patched up to pay her any attention.

Then, much to the surprise of her observers, the nurse stooped down and, seemingly without effort, swept the stocky Jamaican up in her arms. "Where's the bedroom?" she demanded.

Megan gulped and found her voice. "Through there, but you'll need the key." She darted into the bathroom ahead of the girl and returned with the key to Ben's room in her hand.

So much for my hiding place, thought Reece wryly. But he had to grant, that despite knowing where the key was hidden, over recent weeks the girl had not helped herself to Ben's cannabis. He flashed her a smile.

"He'll be okay. Ben's a tough cookie," said the nurse as she delved into her bag and brought out a bottle of pills. "Here's some painkillers. Be careful with them, they're extremely strong; too many could be fatal. I'll call in tomorrow after work." She turned to Megan. "You were lucky to catch me. Another fifteen minutes and I would have been asleep." She threw back her head and laughed heartily, unaware of Megan's anxious glance towards Calum's bedroom. "I sleep like the dead, nothing wakes me."

"What if he takes a turn for the worse?"

"Hospital, I've done all I can."

Reece spoke again. "I don't know how you managed to lift Ben up so easily."

Once more the hearty laugh. The girl rolled up her sleeve and flexed her arm. "I'm a member of a Ladies' Wrestling Club, darling."

Leaving both Reece and Megan dumbfounded, she picked up her bag and ran downstairs, slamming the front door behind her.

With the nurse's departure, Megan went back to bed, although Reece decided to spend the rest of the night slouched in an armchair at Ben's bedside. The West Indian slept through till morning, waking with a moan.

"What happened?" he asked, his voice slurred due to the heavy dose of painkiller the girl had given him.

Reece stretched his stiff limbs and said, "You tell me? That must have been some fight."

"Fight?" replied Ben, wincing as he attempted to shift his position. "There was no fight. Three of them sprang on me. One had a knife."

"So I see."

"Is it a deep wound?"

"You lost a lot of blood." Reece got to his feet and stood over Ben. "Who was that girl? Where on earth did you find her?"

"Jojo's an old mate of mine." Ben tried to move his arm and winced again. "She fixed me up good, didn't she?"

Reece looked doubtful. "I dunno. How qualified is she?"

"Well qualified," grinned Ben. "She's a sister at Kingston Hospital. Didn't she tell you?"

"She didn't tell us anything except that she'll call back to see you later today. You should have let me call an ambulance. It would have been better to go to A&E."

Ben shook his head. "I don't want the Police involved."

"Why not? Thugs like that ought to be taught a lesson. D'you know them? Let me report them."

"No way," protested Ben. "There's no harm done, so leave things be."

"No harm done! What about your arm?"

"It'll heal."

"You'll be off work for a week or two."

"I can still do my stint at Deceptions."

"Ben, see sense, you can't let them get away with it."

"I don't want to get the club a bad name."

"But they'll only come back again if you don't stop them."

"Shit! How many times do I have to say it: leave it alone, let sleeping dogs lie."

Reece's eyes narrowed. "This wasn't just a random fight was it?"

Ben gave a sneer. "'Course it was. Have a bit of respect for the wounded will you, and leave me alone."

"Not until I get the truth out of you."

Ben frowned angrily. "Bugger off!"

Reece persevered. "You can't expect Megan and me to be party to anything criminal."

Ben gave a raucous laugh. "You won't be involved."

"We will if the Police get wind of it."

"God, you sound like my ma!" He made a fist and punched the air with his good hand. "You don't know anything so you can't become involved."

Reece lost his temper. "By not reporting the incident, we've aided and abetted you and ..."

Ben pulled himself up to a sitting position, glaring and ready to spring at Reece. Even in his disadvantaged condition he looked formidable. "Don't give me that crap. Just get the hell out and leave me alone. But first, get me a drink." He sank back onto the bed exhausted.

Reece picked up a carafe from the bedside table and poured some water into a tumbler. Ben pulled a face. "I meant a beer."

"You'll be lucky," retorted Reece. "The strongest drink you'll get today is a cup of milky tea."

"We'll see about that," growled Ben.

Realising that there was little point in questioning the patient any further, Reece said, "You'd better behave yourself while I'm at work. I've given Megan strict instructions about booze and such-like."

He left the room feeling thoroughly disgruntled and twenty minutes later, left for work without speaking to Ben again.

By mid-day, the invalid was back on his feet, but his arm was giving Megan cause for concern. The wound had started seeping and even the iron-willed patient couldn't hide the pain it was causing him.

"I'll phone the doctor," said Megan, looking worried.

"Don't," snapped Ben. "Jojo's calling back this evening."

By the time Reece got home, the pain was clearly becoming unbearable. "Did you give him any of the painkillers?" Reece asked Megan.

"How could I, you took them with you," she said sulkily.

Reece clapped a hand to his head. Of course, he had slipped them into his jacket pocket the evening before, fearful of leaving such strong drugs within Megan's grasp. Given her history of indiscriminate tablet-taking it had seemed advisable.

"Take these." He thrust two of the tablets and a glass of water at Ben. "Jojo left them for you. She said they're very strong."

Ben gulped them down and, within minutes, his cheery grin returned. "They really work," he said, his voice almost sing-song. Reece and Megan exchanged a glance. Jojo hadn't exaggerated their potency.

She failed to call in person, telephoning instead and when Reece told her that, despite a slight seepage of blood through the dressing, Ben seemed all right, she told him she wouldn't call until the following day.

Reece felt uneasy about this and despite Ben's heated objections, he decided to sleep on a mattress on the floor in his room just to be on the safe side. It was as well he did. By the early hours, Ben was moaning and moving restlessly around the bed. His features looked drawn, his eyes glazed. One glance at his wounded arm was enough to send Reece racing to the telephone. He dialled for an ambulance, describing the patient's symptoms.

"The arm's swollen up," he said. "And the hand looks a strange grey colour. I'm very worried, come at once."

CHAPTER SEVENTEEN

Thea's anger at Reece slowly evaporated. Over the weeks, she regretted not having given him a fair hearing.

"You've blown it now," said her sister, Clelia. "Why are you always so impetuous?"

"I'm not," protested Thea. "You make it sound as if I'm in the wrong. I'm the one who's been let down. I stuck my neck out by asking him up here and he repays me by trying to sell me a garbled story about helping out a sick friend. Sick friend, my foot ..." She balled her fist. "I bet that pathetic little Welsh girl, what's her name -- Megan -- is a bit more than a friend."

"I thought the sick friend was someone from work."

"If you believe that you'll believe anything."

"You could go down there."

Thea looked outraged. "That would look as if I was chasing him."

"Why don't you phone him up and have it out with him?"

Furiously, Thea turned on her sister. "Stop telling me what to do."

Thea stormed out of the room. All she wanted was a bit of space so that she could sort out her emotions, but the flat was small, affording little privacy. Her sisters were always there and Clelia *would* insist on giving her knowing glances, hinting that she could see through her facade of nonchalance. In the end, Clelia's persistence wore her down.

"Okay, okay. You win, Clelia, I'll give Reece a ring tomorrow."

Clelia was never to know whether her sister spoke in earnest because, early the next day, Reece telephoned Imelda to tell her that Ben had been rushed to hospital.

The news sent the woman into panic. "Where's Thea?" she cried, flopping onto a chair, a hand clutched to her racing heart.

"What is it, Ma?" Thea dashed into the room at Clelia's bidding. It was always this way: the second eldest daughter was the one the family turned to in a crisis.

Her mother thrust the receiver into her hand. "It's Reece, he says Ben's been rushed to hospital, something about a knife wound. Oh sweet Jesus, oh sweet Jesus!" The chair creaked as she rocked back and forth.

"What's happened, Reece?" While he explained, Thea gasped and nodded, wrinkling her brows at Clelia who was standing next to their mother, a comforting hand on her shoulder. Still clad in pyjamas, the younger girls appeared in the doorway, their eyes wide with curiosity.

"I'll come straight down," said Thea. She glanced at the clock on the mantle shelf. "If I hurry I can catch the ten fifty; it gets in to Euston at one thirty."

"I'll meet you there," offered Reece.

Thea stiffened. "No need," she replied. "Get back to the hospital. Just give me directions and the name of the ward." Replacing the receiver, she turned to her mother and gave a watered-down account of Ben's misadventures. "He's been injured, but it's not life-threatening."

Imelda flapped a limp hand in front of her face. "Oh lordie, what a mess, first yer Pa locked up in jail, now yer brother in trouble. Reece said a knife wound..." Her voice rose hysterically.

"Calm down, Ma, and let Thea tell us what happened," said Clelia, as she chased her little sisters off to get ready for school. "Don't worry, you two, Ben will be all right. Thea will be able to tell us more after she's been to see Ben."

Reece was waiting for Thea in the hospital entrance. He hurried over to her.

"Thanks for phoning us," she said. "I bet Ben didn't want you to."

"How well you know him."

"How is he?"

"Okay now, but blood poisoning can be nasty. Besides, they discovered he had a fracture of the elbow. He should have come to A&E in the first place. I should never have listened to him."

Thea, frowned. "Who is this so-called nurse friend of his? We ought to report her."

"Ben won't hear anything against her."

As they got out of the lift, Reece took hold of Thea's elbow to lead her in the right direction. She didn't object.

"Hiya, Sis." Ben's greeting was cheerful. He was propped up in bed, his arm strapped up and in a sling.

"What on earth happened?" asked Thea.

"Had a scuffle at the nightclub," he replied casually. "All part of the job."

Reece and Thea stayed for an hour, leaving when Ben fell asleep. Neither spoke as they travelled down in the lift together. As they waited at the bus stop, Reece said, "It's really nice to see you again, Thea."

She coloured, knowing that the moment of confrontation could not be put off. Reece touched her hand and started to speak. The arrival of the bus stopped him. They climbed aboard, the dialogue put off for the moment. Thea stared out of the window for the entire journey and when they got off in Twickenham, the tenseness of her shoulders told him how nervous she was feeling. He prayed that Megan's reception would be welcoming. Since Ben's misadventure, the Welsh girl's behaviour had been surprisingly rational: no tantrums, no fits of depression. Reece could only put this down to the fright she had experienced, combined with her continued use of Prozac.

"Hello, Thea," she cried, as they entered and ran over to give the girl a peck on the cheek. Turning to Reece, she enquired after the patient.

"He's not too bad. They've managed to halt the blood poisoning and they've re-set his elbow. Whether he'll ever be able to box again remains to be seen."

"I must call home, Ma will be worried sick." said Thea.

Thea spent twenty minutes talking to her mother and sisters, obviously finding it difficult convincing her ma of Ben's improved condition. After she'd finished, she joined the other two in Megan's room, where she found Megan folding Calum's clean laundry and Reece romping on the floor with the baby. The domestic scene made her feel uneasy; clearly, the bond between the man and the child was very strong.

"Sorry I was so long," she said. "But Ma wanted to know every last detail."

Megan's next words surprised her. "I'm going to take Calum out for a walk in a minute, so you'll have the place to yourselves. By the way, Thea, there's a mug of tea over there for you."

Thea cupped the mug in her hands and smiled happily as she felt tension fall away. Covertly, she studied the inadequate living conditions Megan and her son were forced to put up with, experiencing a rush of pity for them. Ben could be a bastard sometimes! It would be just like him to use Megan and Calum as a wedge between her and Reece. With a flash of insight, she saw what an awkward situation Reece was in.

"Is the French student still here?" she asked.

Reece took this as concern for her own sleeping accommodation. "Yes, but don't worry, you'll be sleeping in Ben's room. I've tidied it up for you."

Thea stayed for two days, only leaving after Ben had been discharged from hospital. Both she and Reece were worried: less about his state of health, which seemed to be improving rapidly, more about the possibility of the Police questioning him about the stab wound.

"You will keep me informed, won't you?" she said as they sat sipping coffee in the station café half an hour before her train was due to leave.

During her visit, the discussion they had both anticipated hadn't arisen and, now, at the point of separation, they both privately hoped it would not be necessary.

Throughout Thea's stay, Megan hadn't once stepped out of line. She'd seemed subdued, if a little tearful sometimes, yet she never gave Thea the impression that she and Reece were anything other than flatmates. It was the affection between Reece and the baby that troubled the girl more than anything; it seemed to her that the child was being encouraged to see the Canadian as a male role model. She wondered whether Reece was aware of this.

Reece had been on edge throughout her entire visit. Being obliged to leave the two women alone together while he was at work had been the worst part. If Megan had intended to drop hints about the Christmas episode, she would surely have done so then. But as Thea smiled across at him, he knew the Welsh girl had been wise enough to keep her mouth shut on that subject.

"Ma's relieved that Ben's all right," said Thea. "She won't care if he can't box again, neither will I."

"Did I tell you I'm moving out of the flat soon?" asked Reece. Thea didn't reply, so he went on. "You do know that there's absolutely nothing going on between me and Megan, don't you?"

She gave a slight nod of her head and observed quietly. "You seem awfully fond of Calum."

His face reddened. "I am, but only as an uncle. Believe me, I can't wait to get out of there. All that baby stuff lying around the place gets on my nerves." He grinned. "I've even been forced to watch Teletubbies!"

Thea smiled. "Calum's going to miss you."

"Are you going to miss me?"

"A little," she teased.

Reece reached for her hand. "Are we friends again?"

"Of course we are. Would you like to come up for another visit?"

"Yes, I would and, now that I'm doing so well at Gardens Unlimited, they let me have the occasional week-end off."

The pair made their way to the platform. Smiling, Thea turned to face Reece, who took her in his arms and kissed her, a lingering kiss, which gave promise for the future.

The end of the month came and Will moved in with Connie. She felt as if she were walking on air. Throughout her entire adolescence and her early twenties she had had her share of fun. Never short of offers, she had been able to pick and choose boyfriends, encouraging them when the fancy took her, discarding them just as easily.

Will changed all that. She tried to analyse her feelings. After all, he was nothing special to look at, he was certainly no Casanova in bed, but his ready wit and quirky sense of humour kept her amused. She had fallen in love with him. It was as simple as that.

When he wasn't with her, she pondered suspiciously on what he was up to; when he was with her, she fretted about the times that he wasn't. She discovered a romantic nature deep within herself, a nature that led her to adore Will's good points, to excuse his weaker ones. Her rational self told her the affair would never endure, that eventually, his unpredictability, his outrageous sense of fun, would pall. In Will, Connie had met her match. She was in danger of spiralling into emotional dependence; a spiral that was spinning so fast she was unable to reverse its descent. Her self-absorption was not intentional. For three months, she literally forgot about her friends, shirked her studies and suppressed her ambition.

During this period, she felt no need for grass or booze. She was drunk on love. Nothing mattered except seeing Will. When Reece phoned her up one evening towards the end of February, she could barely curb her impatience. Will was due home any moment and she wanted to be ready for him.

"What's up?" she asked abruptly.
"It's Megan."
"Not again! Don't tell me she's overdosed."
"Nothing like that, but she is acting strangely."
"How?"
"She's gone terribly quiet and introvert, not hysterical like she was before."
"You should be relieved."
"It seems too good to be true."
"I thought you would have moved out by now."
"The let fell through, but I'm still looking."
Connie glanced at her watch. "I have to go now, Will's due home any minute."
"Wait, Connie."
"What is it?"

"I really am worried about Megan. She looks awfully peeky."

"It's because she doesn't eat properly."

"And I've heard her being sick; do you suppose she's bulimic?"

All at once, Connie's interest was aroused. "When is she sick?"

"In the mornings mostly ... oh my God! You don't think ... she can't be!"

"Pregnant?" Connie finished the sentence for him. "It sounds a bit like it, sweetie." There was silence. Connie spoke again. "Reece, are you still there?"

"Yes," he croaked, and his voice was enough to reveal the truth. His words came out in a jumble. "Things are going so well with Thea. This can't be true."

Connie interrupted him. "I take it, this could be down to you?"

"Oh no!" he groaned and put down the phone.

Reece was in a daze. Morning sickness! Why hadn't he realised? In panic, he cast his mind back to that fateful Christmas morning when a mixture of disappointment and compassion had coerced him into making love to Megan. The memory was more a blurred dream than reality, the details obscure, recalling it requiring concentration. He stood at the kitchen window staring at his own reflection, shaking his head in denial.

The door opened and Emil walked in. "*Pardon*," he said politely and his mouth gaped open when Reece brushed rudely past him. Without bothering to put on a jacket, the Canadian ran down the stairs and out of the front door. With his neck thrust forward and his hands rammed into his trouser pockets, he stalked along the road, staring at the pavement not noticing where he was going. After forty minutes, the chill air got to him and he turned into a pub he'd never been in before. There was just enough change in his pocket for a couple of pints. He stood at the bar and drank the first in one gulp. The barman watched him warily. Although less aggressive-looking since he had shaved off his beard, Reece's striking colouring and piercing amber eyes gave him a 'don't mess with me' demeanour. The barman continued to polish a tumbler with his tea towel, nodding a relieved "Goodnight, Sir," when, after the second pint, Reece slammed the empty glass down on the counter and left.

The beer did the trick. By the time he got back to the flat, he had convinced himself that his fears were unfounded. Megan had often made herself sick by drinking too much or by forgetting to look at the sell-by date on a jar left in the fridge. He wished he hadn't phoned Connie. Admitting having slept with Megan had been a terrible mistake. Suppose Thea got wind of it!

Megan was watching TV. With Calum asleep in bed, she had turned the sound down low and, as he entered, she pressed a warning finger to her lips and whispered, "He's only just dropped off. Do you want to watch some TV with me?"

Her concern for her son and her relaxed attitude dispelled the last remnants of doubts from Reece's mind. "No thanks, I'm off to bed."

"Goodnight, Reece."

The following weekend, he went to Birmingham. This was the second time he'd made the trip since he and Thea had put aside their differences. As on the previous occasion, they had a good time, talking a lot, laughing a lot, but Reece couldn't help feeling that their relationship was marking time. He longed to sweep Thea up in his arms and make love to her, not sneak a furtive kiss when her mother and sisters were out of the room. Things had to advance.

When the bed-sit had fallen through, he'd had a go at the girl in the agency, even though she was adamant that the landlord's change of heart was nothing to do with them. He'd stormed out, his refunded deposit back in his pocket, and trawled other letting agencies, viewing a dozen or more bed-sits, which were either too expensive, too small, too dingy or hampered by the 'no visitors' ban.

While he and Thea were having a meal in a pizzeria, he brought up the subject, suggesting that he booked into a guest house next time, but she wouldn't hear of it. "What would Ma say?" she gasped.

"Has she cottoned-on yet?" he enquired.

Thea shrugged. "You can't tell with Ma, although the other day she did say to me, "Thea, girl, you be seeing too much of that handsome young man lately."' Her mimicry of Imelda made Reece smile. Thea went on, "Ma wouldn't approve." Her eyes widened as she hastened to assure him. "It's not you, Reece. She really likes you, but she fancies I'll end up marrying a nice black boy. She'd never say as much, of course." Her face screwed into a disgruntled frown. "Ma's not like Ben; he revels in deliberately putting obstacles in our way."

"How do *you* feel, Thea?" asked Reece tentatively.

The girl looked bewildered. "I don't know, I honestly don't know." Reece was about to speak, but she went on, "I only know one thing: Ben's way would never stop me; Ma's way..." She tilted her head as she considered. "Well, discreet disapproval is more effective, and Ma knows it."

Despite Thea's semi-acceptance of her mother's traditional ways, Reece returned from Birmingham with a happier heart. One thing had come out of their conversation: Thea had real feelings for him. To win her round, all he had to do was to snatch her out from under her family's influence. And to do that, he had to step up his search for new accommodation.

Ben had gone back to work against doctor's orders. He'd responded to Police questioning with impassive neutrality, swearing that the incident had been a one-off and shaking his head in regret that he hadn't seen the faces of his attackers. And somehow he'd managed to avoid getting Jojo into trouble.

Once off painkillers, the numbing effect they were having on him, both physically and mentally, gradually diminished. The wound itself had healed, leaving him to cope with a bruised rib cage and a tender elbow. He had a high pain threshold, but the slow-healing elbow worried him more than he cared to admit. He could still hold things in his left hand, he could still write -- although to do so sent shooting pains up to his elbow -- but he couldn't fully straighten his arm or flex his fingers. The result of this worry was a constant display of bad-temper towards his flatmates. To add to his troubles, his mother telephoned to see how he was, innocently letting out the information that Reece had been up to Birmingham to see them.

"He never told me," growled Ben. "What's he up to? Hasn't he got anything better to do?"

"He enjoys seeing your sisters, sweetness," replied Imelda. "The little ones have fun with him and Thea loves showing him the city high lights."

This news blackened Ben's mood still further. He had misjudged the situation. Clearly, Reece and Thea were still keen on one another. He saw now that letting the second bedroom to Emil in order to push Reece and Megan closer had not worked. It had, instead, given the Canadian the boost he needed to move out. When roused, Reece was not as lackadaisical as he appeared to be. Ben's eyes narrowed. It was unlikely he'd ever find anything he could afford in the Twickenham area. But Gardens Unlimited was based in New Malden; what if Reece decided to leave the area, to move to where rents were lower, then he'd have no control over his sister's movements. Instinctively, he clenched his left hand, swearing as the pain shot up his arm. He wouldn't let it happen. Megan was putty in his hands; he'd use her.

Ben woke up with a stabbing pain in his arm. He rolled over onto his back, telling himself that it was just cramp, that it would pass. For the rest of the night he slept fitfully, but by morning, he knew that a visit to the doctor was inevitable.

His GP sent him to the hospital with a letter. "Looks like your arm needs re-setting," he said gloomily. "They'll X-ray it and tell you the worst."

"Thanks a lot," growled Ben.

He had to wait for over an hour in X-ray. The Australian nurse was attractive and sympathetic, but he was too concerned about his arm to flirt with her.

"It needs re-setting, I'm afraid," said the registrar, studying the scan. "You'd better go and wait in that cubicle over there."

Hours later, they let him out with his re-plastered arm in a sling. He hailed a taxi, thinking over the doctor's instructions to go home and rest. Instead, he directed the cabbie to take him to McDonalds in time for the afternoon shift and, in flagrant disregard to Company Rules, he carried out his duties. After hastily consuming a burger, he went on to do a stint at Deceptions although, by this time, he was beginning to feel light-headed.

His business partner tore him off a strip. "What the hell do you think you're doing? Fuck off home before you pass out."

"I'm okay," snapped Ben, brushing past him to go into the office and slamming the door shut behind him. Flopping into the swivel chair, he felt exhaustion wash over him. The hospital pharmacy had armed him with a further supply of painkillers, which he took out of his pocket and spilled onto the desk in front of him. There were still some at the back of the bathroom cabinet from the last time. Although he wasn't averse to sharing a joint or dropping the occasional E, the idea of relying on drugs as a medical necessity filled him with horror. He swept up the capsules and put them back in his pocket.

He let his head drop onto his chest, overwhelmed by a sense of weakness, a debility of spirit as well as of body. He had seldom been ill, never seriously. Two broken collar bones and a few cracked ribs didn't count. They'd healed quickly. And despite the threat of blood poisoning, the knife wound in his arm had presented no real problems. This was different. The pain was excruciating. He ground his teeth. Why had that moron at A&E been so cagey. In a day or two, he'd go and see his GP, demand that he give him a straight answer: 'Would his arm ever be of any real use to him?'

There was a tap on the door. He jerked upright as one of the staff walked in. "Sorry, Ben," she said. "Matt wants to know whether you'll be staying on this evening."

"'Course I will," he snarled.

April came, bringing a hint of spring. The Garden Centre was getting busy and Reece was finding it more and more difficult to find the time to look for digs. I'll take whatever comes up next, he thought in desperation, provided there are no restrictions on visitors.

May came and Megan continued to behave herself. Occasionally, when she could find a baby-minder, she took herself off for an interview, but as soon as her domestic situation came to light, she was firmly shown the door. Much to Reece's surprise, this lack of success didn't seem to bother her. She was now living on benefits and seemed to be able to manage. Reece often wondered what she did with herself all day long with only Calum for company. He refrained from enquiring for fear of evoking a tale of woe and discontent. He noticed that she looked less pinched than she had a few weeks earlier and he put this down to the better weather.

Calum's antics continued to delight him. Each evening when he got home from work, the baby would toddle towards him, his chubby arms outstretched. Reece would spend half an hour playing with him.

It was weeks since he'd seen Connie, but one evening, rather than face another of Megan's badly-cooked meals, he called in at McDonalds for a burger. Connie served him.

"Hi, Reece, what have you been doing with yourself?"

"Not a lot." He glanced around and saw that the place was almost empty. "Not many in here this evening."

"Boring, isn't it?" said Connie, wrinkling her nose. While she was fixing his order, she chatted. "I bumped into Megan the other day. Hasn't Calum grown?"

"Yes, he's a great kid."

"Megan looks very well." Connie glanced up enquiringly as she pressed the lid onto his milkshake. "I take it there's nothing further to worry about in that quarter?"

Deliberately misunderstanding the inference, he delved into his pocket for change and replied, "Megan's fine. I'm still looking for a bed-sit; you don't know of one, do you?"

Connie shook her head. "Sorry." She flashed him a grin. "Actually, Will and I are looking for somewhere."

"So it's still going strong between you two?"

He raised a quizzical eyebrow as the colour rose to her cheeks. He had never seen Connie looking coy before.

He carried his tray over to a table by the window and, much to his surprise, Ben joined him there. Reece eyed him with some circumspection since he seemed to be in an amiable mood. "How's the arm?" he asked.

Ben waved off his enquiry. "It's improving. Finish your burger, then we can go for a drink."

"Sure thing," said Reece, but he was still on his guard. Sudden friendliness on Ben's part was suspicious.

They spent a couple of hours in the pub before parting company without Reece learning the reason for Ben's affability. "I'm not going home yet, must show my face at Deceptions for an hour of so," said the West Indian. "See yer later."

As he mounted the stairs to the flat, Reece knew instinctively that something was wrong. Swivelling around the newel post at the head of the staircase, he could see Megan sitting on the carpet in her room. She was surrounded by several neat piles of Calum's baby clothes and soft toys.

"What are doing?" he asked.

"Sort ... sorting things out," she stammered.

He spotted the gin bottle on the floor beside her and, striding over, snatched it up, shouting "What the hell are you up to?"

She pressed a finger to her lips. "Shhh, you'll wake Calum." Folding her arms, she rocked back and forth singing to herself in a slurred voice, "Rock-a-bye baby on a tree top ..."

Reece grabbed her hand and hauled her to her feet. "Shut up, you little fool."

He dragged her to the kitchen, but as soon as he let her go, she almost toppled over. Dumping the half empty gin bottle on the work top, he said, "I'm going to make you a very strong black coffee." As he filled the kettle, he caught a glimpse of her tilting the gin bottle to her lips. "Give that to me," he yelled, yanking it from her hand and spilling most of its contents on the vinyl-tiled floor.

She swayed, grabbing the worktop for support and slumped towards him, giggling stupidly. He caught her under the armpits, hoisted her upright and demanded angrily, "What's brought this on?"

She pulled a face. "B ... bad news, Reece, b ... but never mind, gin g ... gets rid of unwanted babies, doesn't it?"

CHAPTER EIGHTEEN

Reece stood motionless facing Megan, all emotion wrenched out of him. Connie's suggestion that pregnancy could be the cause of the Welsh girl feeling unwell had long ago been banished due to the general improvement in her behaviour.

"You can't be!" he gulped at last.

Megan gave a coy smile. "I'm very fertile," she boasted as if this were a desirable accomplishment. "And you didn't b ... bother to take pre ... precautions, did you, Reece boyo?" In her drunken state, her accent had become very Welsh.

Unable to believe what was happening, he took her firmly by the arm and led her back into her room where he thrust her into the armchair and drew up a straight-backed chair to sit down opposite her.

"Are you certain, Megan?"

She flicked a wrist and tutted. "D'you take me for a f ... fool? Of course, I am. It's the same as last time."

Reece's brain went into top gear. Surely at her age and with another young child and no partner to help her, she'd easily be granted an abortion on the NHS.

She seemed to read his mind. "I'm five months gone, It's too late to get rid of it," she stuttered. "I've tried."

"Why didn't you tell me before, you little fool," he demanded.

She drew away, shielding her face with her hands. "Don't shout!. It's not my fault."

"Whose fault is it then? It's certainly not mine. You're the one who wormed your way into my bed."

Megan peeped from between her fingers like a child playing hide-and-seek. "Stop yelling," she croaked, tears trickling down her cheeks.

Reece sprang up from his chair and paced the floor. "For God's sake what are we going to do?"

Now that he was several feet away from her, Megan gained confidence. Dropping her hands to her lap, she tossed back her head and said, "I was trying to get rid of it by myself until you stopped me."

Reece halted in his tracks, an alarmed expression on his face. He glanced around the room, images of instruments of medieval midwifery and witchcraft springing to mind.

"You weren't going to ... no Megan!" Rushing over to her, he crouched down beside. "Promise me you won't try again."

She looked at him, all innocence. "You wouldn't care if I did."

"Of course I'd care," he protested. "We'd all care, all your friends. What about your parents, have you told them?"

She shook her head. "Dad would never forgive me a second time ..." Her eyes widened. " ... unless, of course, we got married."

Reece recoiled in alarm.

Megan blinked and went on with a half smile. "I know that's not possible. You're in love with Thea, aren't you?"

This blatant announcement of his innermost feelings shook Reece. Yes, he was in love with Thea. He had never admitted it to anybody.

"That's another matter," he said brusquely. "The question is, what are we going to do?" He scratched his head. "There's always adoption I suppose."

At this, Megan fairly shot up from her chair and launched herself at him. Balling her fists, she thumped his chest and stamped her feet, her head thrown back, her teeth bared. "No way!" she screamed. "No, no, no, no, no!"

The ferocity of her attack was totally unexpected. From behaving with the meekness of a kitten, she had changed into a wild cat. Reece couldn't understand her reasoning: one moment she was trying to abort her unborn baby, the next refusing to consider it being put up for adoption. Grasping her wrists, he held her at arms-length and shouted, "Hell, Megan, what *do* you want?"

A cry from the bed jolted them both. "Daddy!" Calum slid from under the duvet and ran across the room, his arms held out. Megan went limp and collapsed to the floor. Instinctively, Reece picked up the toddler, who poked his face and gabbled, "Dada play, Dada play." His mother let out a howl and curled herself into a ball, her hands clasped protectively above her head. Calum pointed at her. "Mummy play too."

Reece paced up and down with the baby while Megan sobbed, a foetal-coiled wreck, on the floor. Minutes passed, then she looked up, her cheeks blanched, her eyes blank. The hysterical desperation that had earlier torn her apart had drained away. Sober now, her speech clear, she implored softly, "I don't know what to do. Please help me, Reece."

Reece planned to wait up for Ben to come home. He was convinced the man already knew about Megan's condition. Once the girl had calmed down, he questioned her relentlessly, unable to believe that their one-off coupling on Christmas night could result in pregnancy.

"The baby's yours, there's been no-one else." She was unshakeable.

When she got upset again, he dropped the subject. One scene during the evening was enough. He made her a mug of Ovaltine, handed her a Nytol and, once Calum was asleep, insisted that she went to bed.

"Stay with me, Reece," she begged, and to keep the peace, he drew the armchair up beside the bed. "Hold my hand," she whispered sleepily. Obligingly, he took her hand and squeezed it lightly to give reassurance.

With only the quietly ticking clock and the hum of distant traffic for company, he was able to reflect on the girl's shattering news. An impulsive act of kindness had brought her into the flat. Why hadn't he listened to Ben. *He* had told him to send her packing the following morning? Instead, he'd given way to compassion and -- yes -- weakness. He thought of Thea and uttered a low moan. How was he ever going to extricate himself from this mess and win the girl he loved?

He was trapped. Between them, Megan and Ben had hoodwinked him. Reece closed his eyes and pictured Megan's naive smile, Ben's triumphant smirk. Why hadn't he cottoned on? First, there was Ben's willingness to let Megan stay at the flat, then his carelessness over the drugs. He saw now that the West Indian had intentionally manouevred Megan's dependence on him.

As for Megan, she'd played on his sympathy, displaying vulnerability. Was it genuine or feigned? Shaking his head, he acknowledged that he had always been too easy-going. He should have heeded Connie's warning and packed the girl off back to Wales instead of taking pity on her.

Connie also had her problems. Now that she was with Will, she'd been looking forward to moving out of her small bedsit, yet he always managed to put obstacles in the way. But when the landlord told them he was selling up, Will had no choice but to go along with Connie's suggestion that they find somewhere larger together.

She found the flat in mid-April, while Will was doing a week in Leicester. It was a large Victorian house converted into two flats. She fell in love with the place straightaway and impulsively agreed to take it even though the rent was far higher than she could afford on her own.

"Who does the garden belong to?" she asked.

"It's shared," explained the agent. "The downstairs flat has use of the patio area close to the house, the rest of the garden belongs to the tenants upstairs."

"That's perfect," she cried, imagining BBQ's on the patio on warm summer evenings.

She couldn't wait for Will to return at the end of the week. When he came in, she ran up to him, bursting with the news. His coolness took her aback. "Aren't you thrilled; is it too expensive; don't you like the area?"

"It's not that," he said.

She bit her lip waiting for his explanation. "What is it?"

"My agent got in touch while I was away and offered me a contract for the summer season, starting at the end of this month."

Relief flooded over her. He wasn't having second thoughts; he did still love her. She grasped his hands. "That's wonderful, Will! Is it in London?"

"No."

She squeezed his fingers. "If it's on the South Coast, you can commute."

He shook his head. "I'm afraid I won't be able to do that."

Her brow creased in irritation. "Why ever not? Don't tell me it's somewhere up North?"

When he didn't reply, she stepped away and shouted angrily. "For God's sake, tell me!"

"It's a world cruise," he said, his eyes shining. "Stand-up comedian, marvellous pay, fabulous opportunity."

Connie sank down onto the bed. "What about me?" she whispered, her eyes swimming with tears. Will sat down beside her, tensing when she rejected the arm he tried to put around her shoulders. "How could you?" she wept. "How could you do this just as things have started working out for us? A cruise! It's the last thing I would have thought of."

"It's a stroke of luck, Connie, four solid months of work."

She looked horrified. "Four months! That takes it to the end of August. The whole summer gone." Goodbye to BBQ's on the patio! She let out a howl. "What am I going to do about the flat?"

"You'll have to let it go, find something smaller."

"I can't."

"Why not?"

"Because I've already signed the Lease."

All that night, Reece thought about Megan's pregnancy, desperation driving him to look at the situation from all angles. She had fervently denied being with anyone else. But was she telling the truth? She'd been known to lie before. Hadn't she tried to get into bed with Ben on one occasion? Was she really as innocent as she claimed to be?

His sharp hearing picked up Ben's return. Swinging off the bed, he crept downstairs, tiptoed across Megan's room and went out onto the landing just as the West Indian reached the top stair.

"Why are you still up?" growled Ben.

"We have to talk."

"Not now, Reece."

Reece took hold of Ben's sleeve and spun him round to face him. "Yes, now!"

"Bloody hell! Mind what you're doing, you moron."

It was only then that Reece saw Ben's arm had been re-plastered. "Sorry, mate," he said, dropping his hand to his side. "But we've got to talk."

"Can't it wait?"

"No, it fucking can't. Let's go into your room." He ushered the other man ahead of him down the corridor, past the French boy's room and they both sat down on Ben's bed. For the first time, Reece gave his friend something more than a cursory glance and realised that he did, indeed, look as if he were in pain. "What happened to your arm?"

"Had to have it reset. They buggered it up the first time."

"Sorry to hear that."

"Not half as sorry as me."

"Look, it's about Megan. You know she's pregnant, don't you?"

"I kinda guessed."

"Is it yours?"

Ben's eyebrows rose comically. "Mine!" Tossing back his head, he rocked with laughter. "Mine? You must be joking."

Reece began to feel irritated. "I'm serious," he said, realising with a little shock that he had been pinning his hopes on a secret liaison between his flatmates, however unlikely this might be.

Ben stopped laughing. "What the hell would I want with a silly little kid like Megan?" He gave a snigger. "It could be Emil's."

"Don't take the piss!"

Ben was still grinning. "S'no good, you can't wriggle out of this one, Reece. It's yours."

"It can't be." As he uttered the words, Reece knew that Ben would see through his denial.

"I guessed you'd slept with her and it didn't take long to work out that she was in the club."

"Why didn't you say something?"

Ben shrugged his right shoulder. "S'none of my business." An amused smirk crept across his face. "Could be she's seeing someone secretly. What about that mate of her boyfriend, Robert something-or-other? You know, the one that brought her home when she jumped ship at Tesco's?"

"Robert Parkes! He's just a kid like her. Has he called round lately?"

"How would I know? I'm out most of the time."

"You're here during the day."

Ben glowered. "For fuck's sake, I'm not her keeper. Vamoose, I gotta get some shut-eye."

Reece could see there was nothing to be gained from continuing the discussion. He got up and went to the door. "You're not lying to me, are you Ben, not about this?"

"Bloody hell, stop making such a song and dance about it. Get her to do away with it. I've got a telephone number you can have. It'll cost you but ..."

Reece heaved a sigh. "It's too late," he said. "She's too far gone for that."

"You idiot!" shrieked Connie when Reece told her the news. "You prime-time idiot! What are you going to do?"

"Shhh!" warned Reece, glancing around the café.

"Well?" insisted Connie. "What next?"

"I haven't a clue."

"You're not going to walk out on her?"

"Why does everyone assume it's mine?" snapped Reece angrily.

Connie raised a sardonic eyebrow, but said nothing. Draining her cup of coffee, she put it back on the saucer with a rattle. Reece stared down at the surface of the table between them. He had deliberately arranged to meet Connie in a trendy Richmond coffee shop rather than McDonalds where they might have run into people they knew. He didn't want his problems getting an airing over the grapevine.

"If it is mine," Reece raised his head and stared into Connie's eyes. "And, bear in mind I said, *if*, then of course I'll provide for it." He thumped the table with his fist. "But that's as far as it goes."

Connie gave him a knowing smile. "I don't think that solution will sit well on Megan," she said.

"It's a case of like it or lump it, because I've got my sights set on someone else."

"Thea Jenson? You'll be lucky! Do you really imagine she's going to take kindly to this bombshell?"

"She doesn't have to know," he muttered hopefully.

"You must be joking. It's my guess, Ben's already told her. Have you heard from her lately?"

"No, but ..."

Connie leant back in her seat and said, with a snort, 'You've messed up big time, Reece. Thea won't want you now." He looked so forlorn, she couldn't help taking pity on him. "Maybe if you get things sorted out, you can still talk her round. From now on, you must get your priorities straight."

Reece sighed. "I know you're right."

After a moment's silence, she ventured. "You're not the only one with problems I've got bad news too." She went on to explain that her landlord had decided to sell the house and that she'd put down a deposit on a flat to move into with Will.

"That sounds great, Connie," said Reece.

"Trouble is, Will's been offered a four-month contract and he can't move in with me at the moment. The rent's too high for me on my own. I don't know what to do." Her brow puckered thoughtfully. "Of course, we could solve the problem between us." Reece didn't look up, but Connie noticed his shoulders stiffen. "Megan and Calum could move in with me."

"Yes," he gasped. "That would be perfect for Megan. She's eligible for Housing Benefit and, of course, I'll pay maintenance if it turns out the child's mine, but what happens when Will's contract ends?"

"They can stay. There's plenty of room and the more people who share, the lower the rent. What about you?" asked Connie. "Would you move in too?"

Reece threw up his hands. "Christ no! I've got to free myself from Megan's clutches."

Connie shook her head. "You'll never be able to do that now, Reece," she said quietly.

CHAPTER NINETEEN

It was several days before Reece summoned up the courage to telephone Thea. Clelia answered the phone.

"Thea's gone out," she replied bluntly.

"When will she be back?"

"Can't say."

It was clear from the girl's tones that Thea had given instructions that she didn't want to speak to him. His only recourse was to write to her, but setting pen to paper took even more soul searching. He sat in his room scribbling on sheet after sheet of notepaper, then tearing them up whilst, from downstairs, baby-talk exchanges between Megan and Calum reached him, a constant reminder of his predicament. The child may not be mine, he kept telling himself, but until the birth he had to accept the blanket of uncertainty, which hung over him. The thirtieth of September was the date she had been given. He glanced at the calendar: it was weeks away. If the baby was black, he would have the last laugh except, of course, the mere fact that there was any question of him fathering the child was reason enough for Thea to give him the elbow. Whatever the outcome, he would insist on a blood test. In the end, he wrote a brief letter to Thea, setting out the facts as they were: that his night with Megan had been a one-off and that he had no feelings for the girl.

Megan was excited about moving into Connie's flat and assumed that Reece would be moving in as well. He resisted the idea for over a week, but Ben's sour mood and his own lack of success in finding alternative accommodation drove him to change his mind. His job was going well. He passed his college exams with flying colours and, as promised, was given more responsibility and a pay rise, although this additional income was soon swallowed up by Megan's dependence on him.

Megan put on weight and seemed more cheerful. Connie, on the other hand, missed Will and moped about the place, looking bad-tempered. Despite the pleasure of having more space, plus a large patio area outside, there was a heavy atmosphere in the flat.

In August, everything changed. Connie got a part in a production at Richmond's Theatre-on-the-Green. Her spirits soared. Once Calum was in bed, the three flat-mates gathered together in the large airy sitting room to celebrate with Champagne. It was a warm evening with a gentle breeze blowing the pale green curtains which shielded the open French windows. They had moved indoors because Megan complained about the midges that buzzed around the pond three steps down from the patio.

When Megan held out her glass for a refill, Connie said, half-joking, "You mustn't overdo it in your condition."

"You sound just like my mother," giggled the Welsh girl.

Connie looked horrified, then dissolved into fits of laughter. "Heaven forbid! I never want to have kids. You won't catch me up to my eyes in disposable nappies and baby wipes."

"Will might have something to say about that," rejoined Megan.

Connie tossed back her head. "He can take a running jump if that's what he wants from me."

Reece listened to this exchange with idle curiosity. Since the audition, he'd noticed a change in Connie. Will still called her regularly, but she no longer dashed to the phone to answer his calls. Out of sight, out of mind, he mused. Quite the opposite in his case, the less he saw of Thea, the more he missed her.

As the evening wore on, Connie gave them a preview of a couple of her song and dance numbers, stumbling a little as the alcohol took effect.

"Look, it's finished!" cried Megan, holding the Champagne bottle upside down. "Have we got any more?"

"No worries, I've still got this." Connie dived into the cupboard and brought out a bottle of Glenfiddich.

Reece held up restraining hands. "Megan mustn't drink spirits," he said earnestly.

"Don't be such a fuddy-duddy," pouted Megan.

Undaunted, Connie produced a bottle of red wine. "This won't hurt her," she said.

"No!" cried Reece in alarm. "Not for Megan. She's had enough."

Despite Reece's objections, it was well into the small hours before they got to bed.

The next day was Saturday. Reece struggled out of bed and sloped into the kitchen. Connie was already there, bowed over the table, staring at a beaker containing a thick yellow concoction.

"What the hell's that?" asked Reece.

She brushed a fly away from her hair with a desultory hand and said, "It's Ben's recipe. He says it's foolproof, and I must say, I've never seen him with a hangover. Want to try some?"

"No thanks," replied Reece emphatically. With a groan, he lowered his head into his hands. "Why did I let you lead me astray last night?"

Connie smothered a chuckle and said, "Do you think you could you manage a coffee?"

"Er, no, later perhaps." He frowned and added, "I hope Megan's all right."

"Sleeping like a baby. I looked in on her."

"I think we ought to talk about what's going to happen when Will comes home," said Reece. "Have you told him we've all moved in? "

Connie gave a shrug. "No worries. "Will and I have split up."

"Since when?"

"Since yesterday, but he doesn't know yet."

"That's a sudden decision."

She shrugged again. "Not really, he virtually signed his own discharge papers when he took the job on board the liner. Conchita Dixon won't wait around for anybody."

Reece raised an enquiring eyebrow. "Is there someone else."

She laughed. "My career."

He grinned back. "You're incorrigible!"

All at once, she looked excited and, turning eagerly towards him, said, "It's taking off, Reece, I can feel it in my bones."

He patted her hand. "I'm sure you're right."

"Right about what?" Megan stood in the doorway, a voluminous figure in a cream nightshirt. Her blond hair was tousled, her eyes bleary. Suddenly, she shuffled round and headed for the loo.

"Hadn't you better go after her?" cried Reece.

Connie took time getting to her feet. "She'll be all right." Nonetheless, she followed the other girl into the bathroom.

Megan felt ill for the rest of the day. She alternated between resting on the bed and lying, full-length on the sofa idly flicking from channel to channel on the TV. Reece took charge of Calum, playing with him on the patio, taking him to the swings when he got bored, stopping off to buy disposables and other necessities the young mother had forgotten to purchase.

Connie went off to a rehearsal, returning late in the evening, looking even more exhilarated than earlier in the day.

"What are you doing tomorrow?" asked Reece, hoping that Connie would be around so that he could get out at lunch-time for a pint and a sandwich with a couple of pals.

She wrinkled her nose, though not with displeasure. "More rehearsals."

Sunday dawned warm and sunny. Megan got up late, again leaving Calum in Reece's charge. Claiming backache, she spent the morning sprawled on the sun lounger on the patio.

"I'll take Calum to the swings," called out Reece as she was dozing off.

"Thanks," replied Megan, twisting around in her chair and blowing Calum a kiss. "Be a good boy for Da ..." She started to say, stopping just in time and hoping he hadn't noticed.

"See you later," he called back as he left the house.

Megan enjoyed being pregnant. People made a fuss of her; they made excuses when she didn't do her share of the chores. Reece was wonderful with Calum; a natural father. There was nobody else in the whole house. She could, she thought to herself, go down into the main part of the garden. There was no one to stop her. It was a long garden, tapering at the end. She squinted at it through narrowed eyes, reminded of her home in Wales. The landlord had hired a regular gardener to come in once a week so it was always immaculate. A flash of sunlight caught something shiny in the pond, fish swam in and out of the water lilies, dragonflies darted between the irises, out of bloom now, but still standing upright like soldiers on sentry duty.

She felt content. The future no longer frightened her. The new flat was much pleasanter and more convenient than Ben's place. Calum loved it. They had their own room, plus the use of the living room when Connie wasn't practising her dance routines or going over her lines. Besides, Calum could play outside in the fresh air although of course, you had to keep an eye on him because of the drop to the pond. She wondered whether the landlord could be persuaded to erect a fence along the edge of the patio.

The shiny object in the pond again caught her attention. She shielded her eyes against the blinding sunlight, yet couldn't make out what it was. Curiosity got the better of her. Struggling out of the chair, she slipped her bare feet into her flip flops and shuffled to the edge of the patio, one hand supporting her aching back. A Koi Carp swam above the shiny object, sending ripples outwards in a perfect circle. She crouched down awkwardly, leaning forward over the pond. All at once, the toe of her flip flop caught in the crazy paving and she started to lose her balance. Instinctively, she flung out her arms to steady herself, but the only thing within reach was a clump of dying irises. With a scream of fright, she toppled over and landed head first in the water.

"Hi, Megan, we're home," called Reece as he manoeuvred the pushchair over the threshold. Releasing Calum, he let the little boy run ahead of him through the sitting room out onto the patio.

As he folded up the buggy, he could hear the two-year-old gabbling incomprehensibly, and smiled to himself. He strolled outside, then leapt forward in alarm. Calum was balanced precariously at the top of the steps leading down to the garden, pointing at the pond. "Look! Mummy swim."

Snatching up the child, he thrust him inside the house, closing the patio door.

Turning back, he saw that Megan lay stretched out in the pond; her head, turned sideways, rested on one of the edging stones, her hair was spread out in tendrils, entwined in the pond's floating greenery. The loose pink chiffon top she was wearing had filled with water and was floating out around her oversized belly, revealing a glimpse of her breasts, heavy now in readiness for the birth. Her legs, in their cut-away jeans had a whale-like appearance as they dangled uselessly just below the surface. With relief, he saw that she was breathing.

He jumped down into the water, which reached to the middle of his thighs. Megan was unconscious. Clearly, she had been knocked out when her head hit a sharp edging rock. She had a nasty gash on the head, but the rock had saved her life, since although her body was completely submerged, her head rested on a flat stone just above water level. Thanks to Reece's ungainly leap into the pond, agitated waves lapped at Megan's slightly parted lips. She gave a moan and her eyes flickered open. The wound on her forehead widened, sending out a fresh gush of blood to tinge the surrounding water.

Reece was frightened to move her. Suppose she had broken some bones, or damaged the unborn child! All at once the tiny life the girl carried inside her became important to him. If, as she maintained, the baby was his, then it bore his genes; one day, it would become a separate entity, grow into a man or a woman to reproduce in its turn. With a sharp intake of breath, he acknowledged that he had become an active part in life's cycle. Under the influence of the travellers, the continuity of life had fascinated him. He recalled studying the throbbing humanity co-existing, sometimes harmoniously, sometimes with feudal aggression, in the Commune on the outskirts of Montreal, where birth and death had been an everyday occurrence, the former dealt with joyously, the latter phlegmatically.

Megan's eyes flickered open again.

"Are you hurt?" he asked anxiously.

"My head."

"Anywhere else?"

"I...I don't think so," she stammered.

Tentatively, he lifted her up, climbed out of the pond and laid her gently on the sun lounger. Her face was chalk white, contrasting with the bright blood dripping onto the paving from the wound on her head.

"My God, what's happened?" Connie stood at the French window, Calum's small hand clutched tightly in hers. The child was howling.

"Call an ambulance, Megan's had an accident," he called out.

Connie stayed behind with Calum, while Reece went in the ambulance with Megan.

"Is she going to be all right?" he asked the paramedic.

"I should think so, the head wound's not too deep"

"What about the baby?"

"We'll soon know," came the prompt reply. "She's gone into labour. Are you the father?"

Reece nodded. At that moment, it seemed expedient not to argue the point.

"When's it due?"

"She's got another four weeks to go."

The man gave an encouraging smile. "Don't worry, eight-month babies are usually all right."

By the time they reached the hospital, Megan was having regular contractions. They rushed her straight through to the Labour Ward, giving Reece instructions to wait outside.

He bombarded each passing orderly with questions. No one seemed to know what was happening. At last, a nurse approached him. He leapt up, his feet squelching in his ruined Reeboks. Before the ambulance had arrived, he had just had time to change out of his wet trousers, but panic had induced him to thrust his feet back into the wet trainers. "Are you the father?"

He evaded the question. "What's happening?"

The nurse led him to a seat and sat down beside him. "Don't worry," she said. "Megan's fine at the moment, but it's a breach birth. If she'd gone full-term no doubt the baby would have turned. I'm afraid, the early labour was induced by her accident. It's most unfortunate."

"Will she be all right?"

"We've every reason to believe so. I'm sure she'd like to see you before we take her into theatre?

Reece gulped. How could he refuse?

Megan smiled as he walked in. "The outfit suits you," she murmured, referring to the unflattering scrubs they had given him to wear.

She looked like a child. If it hadn't been for the huge bump beneath the starched white sheet, she could have been taken for a girl of no more than sixteen. A plaster covered the wound on her forehead. It crinkled as she frowned against another contraction, obediently doing her breathing exercises until the pain had eased. She reached for his hand and gave it a gentle squeeze. "It'll be all right, Reece."

It should be me reassuring her, he thought with a rush of shame. Why is she so brave while I'm so scared?

Another contraction brought a moan from her lips. Her grasp tightened, her nails digging into his palm.

The nurse touched his shoulder. "Time to go; we'll call you in the minute the child is born."

"No, Reece, stay!"

He gave a hard swallow and gave the nurse a pleading glance. She took the hint, saying kindly to Megan. "Better not."

Reece paced the corridor for half an hour, then remembered that he'd promised to telephone Connie.

"How is she?" she demanded.

"She's in the operating theatre."

He heard Connie gasp.

"They're having to do a Caesarean." His voice broke. "She looked pretty rough before they took her down."

"Poor Megan," whispered Connie.

"Is Calum all right?"

"Yes, he's fine. I think he misses his mummy." She paused, then said, "Look, Reece, we've got to sort out what we're going to do once Megan brings the baby home; I mean, about helping her look after it during the first week or two, especially now she's had to have a Caesarean."

"I know," he said quietly. "But let's take one step at a time."

"Ring me as soon as you get some news."

"Of course."

Reece went back to his pacing, his mind filled with misgivings. The actual father of the baby was of little importance at this stage. Megan's welfare took precedence over that and whatever the outcome, he knew that he was now too deeply involved to disentangle himself for the first few months at least. His thoughts flew to Thea and he prayed that time would not make her forget him.

"Mr Cassidy?"

"Yes." He leapt up and dashed towards the voice.

The nurse he'd seen earlier came over. She looked at him oddly. "Your partner has had a little girl," she said. Taking his arm, she led him to a row of chairs and they sat down side by side. "It was a complicated birth; the child's small, only five and quarter pounds and, I'm afraid, Megan lost a great deal of blood."

Reece held his breath as he waited for her to go on. Was she going to say that the child was black?

"And with the shock of her accident, I'm afraid we'll have to keep mother and baby in for a few days." He heaved a silent sigh. Was that all? To tell the truth, it was expedient. The breather would give Connie and himself time to sort out their priorities.

The nurse smiled at him kindly. "Would you like to see them now?" His heart gave a jolt as he followed the nurse to the crèche.

Left at home with Calum, Connie spent time tidying up the flat. She took a scrubbing brush and a bowl of hot soapy water out to the patio and washed away the bloodstains on the crazy paving.

The pond looked slightly the worse for wear: a couple of crushed irises, a damaged water lily, a straggle of weed spilling onto the grass. Thankfully, there were no dead fish floating on the surface, or was there? She ran down the steps and poked her hand into the water only to retrieve one of Megan's green flip flops; the other was still on the edge of the patio. The blood on the rock onto which Megan had fallen had been washed away by the gently lapping water. Calum watched her from the safety of his highchair as he chomped on a rice cake. When the phone rang, she raced indoors to answer it.

"A girl! So small! How's Megan? Never mind, Reece, we'll manage somehow."

As she replaced the receiver, she didn't feel so confident. There were five days left to Opening Night, five days of arduous rehearsals, five days in which to sort out baby minding for Calum, the purchase of a cot and all the other extras a new baby needed.

All at once, the weight of responsibility seemed insurmountable. "Why now?" she cried aloud. "Why now?"

The doorbell rang. Frowning with displeasure, she went to answer it. Will stood on the doorstep, his holdall at his feet.

CHAPTER TWENTY

Reece followed the nurse along the corridor. She stopped at the very end and said, "In there," indicating a swing door through the window of which he could see rows of cots lined up, each with a label hanging from it.

"Which one?" he gasped. "They all look the same."

The nurse gave an amused smile. "I think you'll be able to pick out which it is."

As she spoke, his gaze came to rest on cot with a wailing baby in it. Tiny fists pummelled the air. Their owner's face was flushed bright red, the eyes screwed up, the mouth wide open. He knew at once she was his. A shock of auburn hair grew into a widow's peak above fiery eyebrows.

With his remaining doubts dashed away, he leant over the cot to get a closer look.

"You can touch her if you like," said the nurse.

He looked up startled. "Can I?"

"As a matter of a fact, she needs feeding. I'm afraid her mother is in no fit state to breast feed yet. Perhaps you'd like to feed her."

Reece raised his hands in alarm. "I don't think I'm ready for that," he gulped.

The nurse laughed. "Don't worry, you'll soon learn. I'll leave you here for a few minutes while I prepare the feed."

Reece turned his attention back to his daughter and, as if to oblige him, she momentarily stopped yelling and opened her eyes. They were deep blue, like Megan's. The nurse came back armed with a bottle and a packet of baby wipes.

"Hold these for a minute," she said.

Lifting the baby out of the cot, she folded a blanket around her and carefully taking back the feeding bottle, handed the small bundle to Reece.

He panicked and protested, "I might drop her."

"No you won't," replied the nurse with an amused smile. "Well, are you going to have a shot at feeding her? It might be useful when you get home because Megan is going to need a lot of help."

Reece's first lesson in fatherhood lasted twenty minutes, after which he was surprised to discover that he was reluctant to hand back his charge. He thought about Calum, reminding himself that in next to no time, the tiny creature swaddled in his arms would be running around noisily just like her brother.

When he got home from the hospital he couldn't stop himself from raving about the child's beauty. "She started off looking like all the others," he proclaimed proudly to Connie. "But now that I've held her and fed her, I can see she's quite unique."

"I should think she would be if she's got flaming red hair," observed Connie. She gave him a quizzical look, clearly puzzled by his change of attitude. Pointing to the little boy playing with his toys on the floor, she said, "We mustn't forget to pay this little fellow some attention."

"I would never do that," exclaimed Reece, sweeping Calum up, throwing him in the air and catching him again, a pastime the child loved. Putting the toddler down, Reece became serious.

"What are we going to do while Megan's in hospital?"

Connie raised protesting hands. "Don't look at me. I've got rehearsals all the week."

"I can't have much time off."

"Maybe I can help."

Reece looked round in surprise. Will was standing in the doorway, a wide grin on his face. "I take it Connie didn't tell you I'd got back?"

Reece went over to shake hands with the other man. "No, she didn't," he replied, giving Connie a questioning glance. Hadn't she said she was ditching Will?

"I'm offering my services," said Will. "I've nothing to do this week: no auditions, no rehearsals. And I think Calum's taken quite a fancy to me."

Reece didn't reply at once. He had to concede that this was true since the child had looked up and given the other man a welcoming beam. Yet coupled with relief that their problem may well be solved, there sprang a feeling of resentment. He had always been the little boy's role model, his surrogate daddy. He didn't want Will muscling in.

Connie, however, had no such scruples. "Oh Will, would you? It would solve all our problems." She glanced across at the Canadian. "Wouldn't it, Reece?"

With three pairs of eyes turned in his direction, Reece had no choice, but to concur. "Great," he said rubbing his hands together with over-zealous enthusiasm. "Great! Thanks Will."

Reece visited the hospital every day. The baby made progress, the mother didn't. He spent hours sitting beside Megan, holding her hand, trying to assure her that everything was going to be all right. The nurse persuaded him to take her for a walk. "Her wound is healing well, she should keep moving. We don't want those stitches tightening up, do we?"

Bent almost double, Megan leant on his arm for support as he walked her up and down the corridor.

"Don't you think you ought to phone your parents, Megan?" he suggested.

She turned on him furiously. "What for? Another lecture from Dad? He already thinks I'm condemned to end up in hell, I don't want him rubbing it in."

Reece looked astonished. "You don't really believe in all that rubbish, do you?"

"I don't know what I believe," she mumbled.

To change the subject, he delivered his daily record of Calum's antics, explained how Will was coping and raved about the beauty of their baby daughter. Megan wasn't interested. He tried to amuse her by describing the pitfalls and successes of Connie's opening night. "I'll take you to see the show," he said.

"If you like," she replied dully.

After ten days, he sought out the Sister in charge. "What's up with Megan?" he asked. "Why are you keeping her in?"

"It's a precautionary measure," replied the woman. "In her state of mind, with two young children to care for, we're afraid she won't be able to cope if we let her go home."

"It's only a fit of baby blues, a normal environment will be helpful," protested Reece.

"It's more complicated than post-natal depression," the Sister went on to explain. "There's something medically wrong with her. She won't even feed the baby herself. We're making tests. Believe me, we'd love to send her home -- we're very short of beds -- but it would be imprudent at the moment." She smiled at him. "Your regular visits with news from home are the best possible medicine for Megan. You're doing great, she badly needs a rock to lean on."

A rock to lean on! The implication of the nurse's words sent a shiver of dread down Reece's spine. All along, he'd told himself that once the baby was born, Megan would be too busy to feel depressed, that any yearning for booze or grass would be banished from her mind, that things would get back to normal. What a fool he'd been, imagining that his burden would be little more than financial, that he and Thea would be able to take up where they had left off.

And there was a further complication, one that he had not anticipated: when he held his daughter in his arms and looked into her eyes he knew there was no way he would be able to relinquish contact with his child. Her thick auburn hair was the exact match of his own crowning glory, the tiny cleft in her chin a replica of his own; even her little hands seemed familiar. He remembered reading somewhere that all newborn babies resembled their fathers, nature's way of verifying paternity.

Megan ignored her baby. When the nurse wheeled the cot in, she barely gave it a glance; when Reece sat beside her, cradling the child, she turned her head the other way.

On the second Sunday after the birth, he found her sitting on the balcony, fully dressed. It was a warm September day and, for once, she greeted him with a smile, offering her cheek for a kiss.

"You look better, today," he said. "How are the stitches."

"Fine, look, I can stand up straight now." She stood up and demonstrated. Sitting down again, she said, "I can go home whenever I like."

"That's great news, Megan." He paused warily. "You'll have to start looking after the baby yourself. By the way, have you thought of a name for her?"

"She doesn't need one."

"What d'you mean?"

"She doesn't need to be called anything."

He began to get angry. "Of course, she does." In his mind, he had already chosen a name: Mary, after the beloved sister who had been so sadly taken from him.

Megan shook her head. "There's no point in giving her a name, I've decided to go for adoption."

"Adoption?" gasped Reece. "You said you wouldn't hear of it!"

"That's what you wanted, isn't it?"

He could barely speak. "That was before I saw her," he breathed.

She gave a snort of derision. "Before you were certain she was yours, you mean."

He found himself hotly denying this. "It wouldn't have made any difference whose child she was."

"Liar!"

"I meant it," he protested. "You can't be serious, Megan. You can't let her go. She's beautiful, she's ours. I'm going to stick by you, provide for her."

She cast him a scornful look. "Provide for us! Oh yes, but who's going to have the responsibility of changing her nappies, taking care of her when she's sick, teaching her good manners, telling her not to make the terrible mistakes I've made ..." Running out of steam, she buried her head in her hands and burst into tears.

Reece crouched down beside her chair. "Megan, you don't mean this. You're upset, not thinking straight. She can take my name, she's our child for goodness sake."

"I can't cope," she wept, her shoulders convulsing. "This is the only way."

"Don't give up, I promise you we'll manage."

Gradually, she stopped sobbing and peeping out from between her fingers, whispered. "You'll stand by me, you'll ... you'll marry me."

"Marry you?" He stood up and looked down at her. Her face was pale except for the still livid scar on her forehead. He gave a gulp, reminded of the fright he'd suffered only days before when he'd found her in the pond.

Under his scrutiny, she let out a howl. "You see, you don't really care. You'll let me down. In a few months you'll be off after some other girl, Thea or someone. I'm going for adoption and that's final."

"No!" he shouted, drawing the attention of a passing nurse, who stopped in her tracks.

"Is everything all right?" she asked.

They both nodded and, looking slightly puzzled, the nurse continued on her way.

"I've already seen the Social Worker and someone's coming to see me tomorrow about signing the papers."

"You can't," he retorted. "She's my daughter too. I'll do anything, adopt her myself ..."

"I won't let you. If anyone's going to have her, it has to be a stranger."

"You can't let her go to a stranger. She's mine and I've got every right to claim her."

"You've changed your tune."

"Maybe I have. But I won't give way on this."

"You don't have to," muttered Megan looking down at the floor and twisting her hands nervously. "It could all be resolved very easily. No fights, no unpleasantness; just do what you know you ought to do."

Reece threw up his hands. "All right, Megan, we'll get married. I'll set the wheels in motion first thing tomorrow. How long does it take?"

She pushed back a strand of hair and gave a half smile. "Three weeks I think." Suddenly, she started crying again. "You won't let me down, will you Reece? I mean, I really love you, I'm not just doing this for the baby's sake. Do you love me?"

Hunched in the chair in front of him, she seemed a forlorn and defenceless creature. Moved to pity, he took her hand and squeezed it. "I care for you a lot," he said.

She sniffed into a tissue. "I was thinking of Katherine for the baby's name. What do you think?"

He looked startled, then said decisively, "Mary Katherine."

"Yes," she agreed. "I like that."

"I'd like to hold my baby," said Megan the next morning when the nurse woke her up.

"Is that a good idea?" she asked tentatively. "I believe you're seeing someone about adoption this morning."

Megan waved a casual arm. "I'm not going ahead with it. Please cancel the visit."

The nurse's face lit up. "I'm glad to hear it," she said. "What changed your mind?"

Megan smiled back at her triumphantly. "Reece and I are getting married," she said. "Now, we'll be a proper family."

The nurse was so moved, she gave Megan a spontaneous hug. "I'll go and fetch the little one right away."

Megan took the small bundle from her and, for the first time, studied her baby. Yes, she did resemble Reece, so much so that he hadn't once questioned her paternity. "We're calling her Mary Katherine," she told the nurse.

"That's a lovely name. After you've fed her, the doctor will be round. You will probably be able to go home later today. Will your partner be coming in?"

"After work," replied Megan. "I'll phone my friend at the flat and get her to give him the baby clothes I need."

When Reece arrived, Megan was pacing the floor impatiently, Mary Katherine sleeping peacefully in the cot next to her bed.

"Have you got everything?" she asked excitedly. The apathy of a few days ago had vanished, replaced by a gleam of anticipation.

Reece produced the items that Connie had selected and watched while Megan changed and dressed their daughter in baby clothes that had once been Calum's. She looked up at him as she expertly finished fastening up the Babygro. "It a good thing I had nearly all white things for Calum," she said.

Once they were in the minicab on their way home, she cleared her throat and said, "Did you get it?"

"Get what?"

"The Licence."

"Oh that! No, I haven't had time yet."

Momentarily, Megan's face lost its happy glow. "You won't let me down, will you, Reece?"

Glancing down at the tiny bundle in her arms, he heaved a silent sigh and murmured, "Of course not."

The front door was open when they arrived home. Calum wriggled free from Connie's grasp and ran to his mother. Swiftly, Reece took the baby from Megan, fearful that she would be crushed by her brother's impetuous affection.

"How my little boy has grown!" she exclaimed.

Connie laughed. "But you only saw him the day before yesterday when I brought him up to the hospital."

"I know, but it was different in there. Unreal, somehow."

Connie drew Will forward. "This is my friend, Will," she told Megan. "He's been awfully good with Calum. I don't know how we would have managed without him."

Megan was brimming over with gratitude.

"Thanks Will," she cried. "Thank you so much."

Calum wouldn't let go of his mother. He dragged her into the flat and showed her around as if she had never lived there. Taking her out to the patio, he pointed at the pond. "Mummy not swim."

She laughed, impulsively stooping to sweep him up in her arms, but remembering in time that her stitches had still not completely healed.

"I think it's time for tea," said Connie, ushering them all inside.

His mother's nagging telephone calls finally persuaded Ben to pay her an overdue visit. She greeted him with hugs and kisses, then stepped back and delivered a tirade of recriminations: "What kind of a son are you, neglecting your poor ole ma, forgettin' all about your darling sisters! What if yer pa showed up again!" She wagged a finger in his face. "You don't care 'bout yer own family, son. You got your plum good life down dare in London, them pretty gals ..." Imelda rolled her eyes expressively and waggled her huge hips.

"Give over, Ma, them gals ain't that pretty," protested Ben, aping his mother's accent, while behind her back, his little sisters clamped their hands over their mouths to stifle their giggles.

All at once, Imelda's mood changed. "We got good news, son," she said. "Our sweet Clelia's got herself engaged to dat honey-boy, Nathan." She waited for Ben's reaction.

"Good for her," he said.

Imelda turned on him. "Why you not married yet? Why I de only mama round here with no gran kids?"

Ben gave an exasperated shrug. "Let's not go into that, Ma."

The door opened and Thea walked in. On seeing Ben, a disgruntled frown glanced across her face.

"Hi, Sis," he said.

"What are you doing here?" she snapped back.

"Thea sweetness, dat's no way to greet your brother," crooned their mother.

Thea continued to glare at Ben, who met her gaze with his customary insolence. The younger girls, intimidated by their elder siblings' mutual animosity, giggled nervously and turned their attention to 'Hollyoaks'. Imelda heaved a sigh and hurried off to fix supper.

"Let's go somewhere quiet, I've got something to tell you," said Ben.

"I'm not interested in anything you've got to say."

"You might be interested in this."

Thea frowned. "I doubt it. Clear off and leave me alone."

Ben persisted. "Reece has moved into Connie's new place with Megan and Calum."

Thea remained impassive. "So what?"

Ben paused before dropping his bombshell. "Megan gave birth last Sunday." He paused for effect. "...to a baby girl with a thatch of red hair, just like her pa."

Thea gave a gasp. "Good for them," she snapped, but she couldn't hide the tears that rushed to her eyes.

Ben returned from Birmingham feeling even more disgruntled. He lounged in a corner seat of the train nursing his throbbing arm, knowing that he would never again set foot in the boxing ring.

Also, he felt uneasy about the way things had been left between Thea and himself. He had expected defiance or denial of affection for Reece from her. What he hadn't foreseen was a display of bitter disappointment. He loved his sister and the last thing he had wanted to do was to hurt her. But she couldn't seriously consider marrying a white man - a honky! Or could she? He had no doubts that Reece was a decent guy, rated him as one of the best. The Canadian was impetuous and gullible, but well meaning. He thought back over the past year, admitting to himself that he had as good as driven Megan into Reece's arms. But I couldn't have foreseen the outcome, he thought smugly, wincing as a commuter dragging a suitcase along the aisle knocked against his arm. "Watch it mate!"

"Sorry."

He settled further back into the seat and closed his eyes, dozing fitfully until the train pulled into Euston.

The next few weeks passed uneventfully. With so many helping hands, Megan coped well. Calum loved the attention bestowed on him and his baby sister, who was turning out to be a good natured infant, sleeping through any amount of noise and confusion.

Reece put off getting the marriage licence, claiming forgetfulness or lack of time whenever Megan challenged him. September slipped into October and the four flatmates' routine seemed set. Connie and Will shared the largest room, but Reece couldn't help noticing that they were cool with one another and he began to wonder how much longer the situation would continue. After all, it was weeks since Connie had told him she was splitting up with Will. He could only imagine she had deferred telling him for her own convenience.

He and Megan were not sleeping together. On her return home from hospital, much to Reece's relief, Megan made it clear that her scar was still too tender to consider cohabitation. Megan and the two children slept in the second bedroom while he slept in the small, claustrophobic box room. Despite its inconvenience, this suited Reece. It gave him a bolt hole, a place where he could forget his troubles, imagine that things were different. Sometimes, he forced himself to be practical, to consider the future. He would lie on his bed making plans, yet his obstinate mind would veer away from reality, coercing him instead to come up with impossible schemes until, in the end, he would fall asleep, waking in the morning with no better idea of what to do next.

Things came to a head in November with Connie's show going on tour and Will being offered a leading role in a play up North. This coincided with a marked improvement in Megan's health and energy.

"We must get married before they go," she said to Reece. "Get down to the Registry Office tomorrow and fix it up." She turned excitedly to the others. "When do you leave?"

"The second week in December," they said in chorus.

Connie cast Reece a concerned glance. "Will you be able to organise it in time?"

He met her gaze bravely, sensing that her real cause for concern was not the time factor. It was his reluctance to tie the knot.

"No problem. You two will be witnesses of course?"

They nodded, responding warmly to Megan's display of affection as she hugged them both and chatted on about buying a new dress for the occasion.

He delayed his visit to the Registry Office until the end of the following week.

"Well?" said Megan on the Friday. "You did go today, didn't you?"

"Of course, but unfortunately they were closed."

"Closed?"

"Yes, I hadn't realised they're only open between certain hours."

"Oh Reece," cried Megan, bursting into tears. "We'll never fix it up in time if you don't get a move on."

He tried again, taking time off work to get there during opening hours, but the date Megan had asked for was already booked up. Relief swept over him. Reprieved again! Connie and Will's departure dates came and went without the wedding being arranged. Megan was getting more and more upset.

"I knew you'd let me down," she accused him. "You've got no intention of marrying me. You just said that so I wouldn't go ahead with the adoption."

"What nonsense!" he protested, although he knew she was right. "I know, I'll organise it for Christmas. A Christmas wedding, how about that?" He held out his arms and, after a show of unwillingness, she ran into them.

"Promise?" she whispered, sniffing back tears.

"I'll take time off on Wednesday and fix it up."

He was on his way to the Registry Office when he bumped into Thea outside McDonalds in King Street. For a moment, he thought she was going to walk straight past him. But she didn't. They stood staring at one another for several seconds without speaking.

"Hello Thea, how lovely to see you. How are you?" he said at last.

"Fine, how are you?" Her reply was tight-lipped.

"Very well. Fancy a coffee?"

"No thank you."

"Please," he implored.

She looked at her watch. "I'm meeting Ben in half an hour."

Unwilling to take no for an answer, he took her arm and guided her to a small help-yourself café. Whilst in the queue at the counter, he kept a close eye on her, afraid she might get cold feet and run off.

"Would you like anything to eat?" he enquired.

Thea shook her head. "Just a cappuccino please."

He carried the tray with their coffees to a table and they sat down opposite one another. The café was crowded, the tables pushed close together and people kept brushing past. It wasn't easy to talk privately.

"I've missed you," he said, reaching for her hand as she went to put sugar in her coffee.

She quickly withdrew her hand and, looking down intently at her cup, murmured, "Have you?"

He began to feel irritated by her apathy. "Of course I have. None of this is my fault."

She looked up and raised a disbelieving eyebrow. "Isn't it?"

"You know how much I care for you."

"Enough to marry someone else. When was the wedding? Ben said Connie told him it was planned for early December so that she and Will could be witnesses."

"It never happened, and they've both moved on now."

"So, when is it to be?"

He thrust out his chin and said, "It isn't going to happen." Again he reached for her hand and, this time, she didn't draw away. "We had such a good thing going between us. Let's not spoil it. Give me time, I'll clear up this mess I'm in with Megan. Just give me time," he pleaded.

"How much time?" she asked with a touch of bitterness. "A month, a year? I can't wait that long. I'm going to get on with my life without you, Reece Cassidy." Pushing back her chair, she got up abruptly, her coffee untouched. "Got to go. I don't want to be late for Ben. He's got an appointment to see a consultant."

"Why? What's wrong?"

She stood looking down at him with a haughty expression on her face. "If you're interested, he seems to be losing the use of his left hand."

"What? How?"

"It's to do with that stabbing; it may have damaged the nerves."

Before he could question her further, she swivelled on her heel and walked out of the café. Reece jumped up, nearly knocking over the table. The untouched coffee cup slid to the floor, smashing to pieces at his feet, its contents splashing the jacket of a woman sitting close by.

"I'm terribly sorry," he said, trying to ease past her to follow Thea.

"I should think so too," she retorted, dabbing her sleeve with a paper napkin. "This jacket is dry clean only, you ought to pay for it."

Reece didn't wait to argue. Weaving his way in and out of the tables, he rushed out of the café.

Outside, he glanced both ways, but Thea had vanished. Hurrying along the road towards McDonalds he jostled passers-by and dived into the restaurant ahead of a woman struggling with a shopping trolley. Neither Thea nor Ben were there.

CHAPTER TWENTY-ONE

Thea watched Reece hurry out of the café, but she dodged into a shop doorway in order to avoid him. She watched him dash in and out of McDonalds, then rush off in the opposite direction. Once the coast was clear, she made her way to the meeting place arranged with her brother and waited anxiously for him.

Ben turned the corner into York Street, head bowed, gaze scanning the pavement. When he looked up, she waved. His stance altered. Straightening his shoulders, he cocked his head impudently and ambled across the road, whistling through his teeth.

"Hi Sis."

"Hi Ben, how are you?"

"Great," he replied. "Don't know why we're going really, the arm feels better today."

"None of that," she replied firmly, tucking her hand through his right arm. "I've not come all this way for nothing. Let's get going, or we'll be late for your appointment."

The clinic was within walking distance and Ben was shown in almost straightaway.

"Do you want me to come in with you?" asked Thea.

"No," Ben started to say, but the young woman doctor cut in, "It might be as well. Are you Mrs Jenson?"

Thea grinned, exposing her slightly protruding teeth. The smile lit up her whole face, revealing the friendliness of her nature. "No, I'm Ben's sister," she said.

After examining the patient, the consultant sat down at her desk and made notes. Thea's heart beat fast. Why was it taking so long? She'd noticed with alarm, the grimace of pain on Ben's face when he lifted his arm to shoulder level. She'd noticed, too, the delay he demonstrated in picking up small objects. It was almost as if he were psyching himself up to make the effort.

"Well," said the doctor, putting her pen down and swivelling her chair round to face them. "You've obviously suffered some damage to the nerves in your arm."

"Is it permanent?" asked Thea.

The woman looked serious. "I'm afraid so. However, the good news is, it's unlikely to get any worse."

Thea edged to the front of her chair. "What about physiotherapy, exercise?" she asked.

"It won't do much good, I'm afraid."

Throughout the exchange, Ben sat studying the floor, a glowering frown on his face.

"Was this due to an accident?" asked the doctor.

Thea and Ben spoke together.

"No," said Thea.

"Yes," said Ben.

"My brother was involved in a fight," Thea hastened to explain. "It wasn't his fault."

"It was an accident," insisted Ben.

The doctor looked from one to the other, clearly more inclined towards Thea's explanation. She pressed the tips of her fingers together and said, "It's just that you might have a case for compensation if you went to the Courts."

This time, Thea glanced at her brother for his reaction. It was firmly negative.

"Can't do that," he said. "It happened too long ago."

"It's not too late, some claims go back years," said the woman. "If I were you, I'd certainly look into it, whatever the circumstances."

Ben uttered a disbelieving snort and got to his feet. "You've told me the worst and that's all I need to know. Come on Thea."

Thea stood up, looking embarrassed. "Thank you for your advice," she stuttered.

Ben plucked at her sleeve. "Come on Sis, let's get out of here."

Reece walked home in a state of bewilderment. Seeing Thea again had placed a whole new perspective on things. He couldn't marry Megan; he couldn't tie himself to a woman he didn't love even for the sake of his daughter. How was he going to break the news to her?

When he reached the flat, he couldn't bring himself to turn into the gate. Thea's image was still too fresh in his mind. Frustration and anger brought a rush of blood to his cheeks. He remembered those dark days in Paris, when Chantal had rejected him. He carried on beyond the house, punching a garden wall as he walked past, grazing his knuckles, the need to express his fury by some physical means becoming intolerable. At the corner of the road, he turned and ran back. Dashing indoors, he ignored Megan's pleas for help with the children, slammed into his bedroom and changed into a pair of sports shorts and vest. Shoving a towel and some jogging trousers into a sports bag, he slung it over his shoulder and ran out of the house to head for the Sports Centre.

It was only afterwards, that he realised how differently he had handled Thea's rejection of him. In Chantal's case, he had made for the nearest bar, got smashed and picked a fight with a gang of skinheads, coming off worst of course. This time, he spent a couple of hours in the gym, sweating out his anger. By the time he got home, he was perfectly calm.

Megan was curled up on the sofa in front of the TV, the remote in her hand. She barely looked up as he entered.

"What are you watching?" he asked.

She flicked a wrist. "Some shitty talk show programme. The stuff they churn out these days pisses me off." It was so unlike her to use such language, that he knew her underlying grouse was with him, not the directors of television. "Where've you been?" she asked.

"Down to the gym, I needed a workout."

"Did you get the licence?"

Reece gave a swallow and, stalling for time, placed his sports bag on the floor with studied deliberation. "Got there too late," he said. "Missed them by a hair's breath."

"Liar!" she screamed, flinging the remote across the room and leaping to her feet.

He was forced to take a step backwards as she launched herself at him, stopping less than a foot away. Poking a finger in his face, she shrieked a barrage of obscenities at him. Her limited knowledge of such vocabulary combined with the harmony of her Welsh accent rendered the onslaught extremely repetitive, making the hard consonants rattle like bullets from a softly whirring airgun. If the situation hadn't been so serious, the scene would have been comical.

"Shut up, Megan!" he bellowed, grabbing her wrists and giving her a shake.

She stopped her verbal onslaught and demanded, "Well, what have you got to say for yourself?"

"We need to talk."

"I thought that's what we *were* doing."

"Stop being silly, and listen."

Freeing herself from his clasp, she sat down on the sofa and, with her hands folded on her lap, looked up at him expectantly.

He braced himself and began. "I can't do it, Megan, I can't go through with it."

"It doesn't have to be Christmas, it can be any time," she replied.

"You're not listening to me. I can't marry you, not at Christmas, not ever."

"It's that Thea, isn't it?"

When he didn't reply, she started to tremble and, in an effort to regain control, clenched and unclenched her fingers, making the knuckles crack. "You can't let me down, Reece, you promised. Why, I gave up the chance of adoption because of you."

He crouched down in front of her and took her hands in his. "No you didn't. You had no intention of seeking adoption. It was only a ploy to get me to marry you."

"It wasn't," she protested. "You'll see, I can still arrange it. I'll phone up the people tomorrow."

"No you won't, Megan. You love Mary as much as I do, you'll never give her up." He pulled her gently to sit down on the sofa, his large paws still covering her small hands. "I'm really fond of you, and Calum's like a son to me, but I can't tie myself down, not now, not yet. Don't worry, I'll provide for you. It won't be easy, but somehow I'll find a way."

"How?" she said. "It won't last. You'll be off with Thea or someone else, leaving us to fend for ourselves."

"No, I won't, I promise I won't. And now that Connie and Will have moved out and I've taken over the lease of this place, the first thing we've got to do is find a lodger for the big room."

Megan lowered her gaze in disappointment. "I ... I rather thought you and I would move in there." With a spurt of animation, she said, "We could still live together; the children could have the second bedroom and, if necessary, we could let the box room."

Reece raised a sceptical eyebrow. "That wouldn't work, it's too small. We'll have to leave things as they are at the moment and let the big room. Might even get a couple, which would mean more rent."

Realising that she wasn't going to get anywhere with further argument, Megan nodded. "All right, but you won't walk out on us, will you?"

"Of course I won't," he replied, giving her hands a gentle squeeze.

"I'm tired." She got up and walked to the door, where she turned to look at him. "Who knows, you might change your mind in a month or two."

The first applicants took the room. Their names were Aubrey and Aidan. "They call us the Double A's," explained Aidan, the more loquacious of the two. He twittered a lot, frequently breaking into peals of laughter. "Oh he is a one!" he chortled when Aubrey suggested that perhaps the rent was a bit high.

"You're the first people to view the room," stated Reece. "So there's no way I'd reduce the rent at this stage."

"It's loverly, Aub," cooed Aidan enthusiastically. "Just look at the view." He turned earnest eyes on Reece. "Can we use the garden?"

"Only the patio, but it's quite big and gets a lot of sun."

"Ooh, I like that," Aidan gasped. "We're great sun-worshippers, aren't we Aub?"

The other man nodded. "We'll take it," he said, rubbing his chin reflectively.

They paid a deposit and shook hands after arranging a mutually convenient moving-in date. "Thank you both so much," gushed Aidan as they parted on the doorstep.

Megan was delighted with their new lodgers. "Why, they're such gentlemen!" she trilled. "So polite and thoughtful. You don't see much of that these days."

"We'll see," replied Reece guardedly, secretly amused by her naivety. But he too was hopeful that this pair, with their fastidiousness and nest-building inclinations, would fit in well with the current domestic scene. Besides, he thought to himself, gays love children and they might come in handy for baby-sitting.

The Double A's settled in very quickly. Eager to be of help Aidan took over most of the housework. It transpired that he had a part-time job in a bookshop while Aubrey, the main, although not very successful, breadwinner was a ghost writer and free-lance journalist working from home. Hence, Aidan freely explained, they were obliged to rent instead of getting themselves locked into a heavy mortgage. "We did it once," he went on. "But ended up with negative equity, a fatal mistake, still ..." He flicked the feather duster over a pile of videos. "Who knows what's round the corner. Aub's next book might be a bestseller."

"So he's writing a novel?" interjected Megan.

Aidan threw up his hands in a gesture of approbation. "He's a gifted writer, the next Sebastian Faulks."

"Who's he?" asked Megan, whose range of reading only went as far as the latest Danielle Steele. Mostly, she flicked through 'Marie Claire' and 'Hello' while sitting in front of the television.

"Darling, I'll get Aubrey to let you read a chapter if you like."

Megan restrained him. "No, please don't bother him. I don't have much time for reading, what with looking after the children."

Christmas came and the Double A's went off to Torquay for the Christmas break, leaving Megan and Reece alone. The Canadian was obliged to resign himself to spending Christmas in Twickenham. There was nowhere else to go and, besides, to leave Megan on her own with two young children would have been unkind in the extreme. Earlier in the month, he had tentatively suggested that she might like to take Calum and Mary down to Wales to see their grandparents. Once again, she vehemently rejected the idea. "They don't even know about Mary," she protested. "I don't want to give them a shock at Christmastime."

Reece looked surprised. "D'you mean you haven't told them yet? Aren't you being rather hard-hearted? After all, they are the child's grandparents."

Megan shrugged this off. "It's better that way."

Although they both made an effort, Christmas Day was quiet and boring. Calum was excited, but Mary was fretful. Reece showed concern, pacing the floor with her and muttering about phoning the doctor.

"No need," said Megan. "She's got a bit of a cold, stop fussing."

Much to their surprise, Ben turned up on Boxing Day. "Hiya, happy Christmas!" he said, adding mischievously, "Don't look so amazed. I am allowed to call on my friends if I want to."

After the usual greetings, Ben glanced around and said, with an appreciative smirk, "Nice place! You sure as hell have fallen on your feet this time, man!" Placing a bottle wrapped in tissue paper on the table, he rubbed his hands together gleefully and asked expectantly, "Well, how did it go?"

"How did what go?" said Megan.

He grinned, showing his perfect white teeth and said, "The wedding of course."

Reece and Megan exchanged a glance. "It never took place," snapped the girl. Picking up the baby, she took Calum by the hand and, despite his protests, led him out of the room. "Come on you two, time for bed."

"I seem to have put my big foot in it," said Ben after Megan had closed the door. "What happened?"

"Like she said, it never took place. We decided against it."

Ben jabbed a finger in Reece's chest. "*You* decided against it," he said.

"Whatever."

"Pity Thea didn't know."

"What d'you mean?"

"She got herself engaged to Troy."

"Troy?"

"An old flame, been keen on her for years."

"He's black of course?"

"It's better," sniffed Ben. "Each to his own, eh?"

"You talk a load of shit. Thea and I really care for one another."

"You'll get over it."

"Have they set a date for the wedding?"

"End of January."

"That soon?"

Reece couldn't hide the hurt in his eyes. It had never occurred to him that Thea had anybody else waiting in the wings. What a fool he was! An attractive girl like her wouldn't stay unattached for long.

"I'd better be going." Ben pointed at the bottle. "I brought some bubbly. Keep it until you've got something to celebrate."

The ache in Reece's heart turned to anger. "Wait a minute." Picking up the bottle he brandished it in front of the other man. "Is that why you came? To gloat?" Ben drew back in alarm as the bottle brushed across his face. "Well, you can piss off and take your fucking bubbly with you. Get out, get the hell out of here!"

Ben snatched up the bottle with his right hand and it was then that Reece realised how limp and useless his friend's left arm was. With a shock he saw that much of Ben's arrogance had dissipated. He seemed almost defenceless as he stood, clutching the bottled wrapped in its bright red tissue paper.

"What's up with your arm?" The words came out in the form of a growl as anger and pity wrangled for supremacy.

Ben shrugged. "S'nothing."

"I thought Thea said something about going to see a consultant."

The belligerence returned. "When did you see Thea?"

"Never mind. Is it true?"

"Yeah, there's nothing they can do." The life seemed to drain out of the Jamaican. He placed the bottle back on the table and sat down. "Look mate, about you and Thea, I've got nothing against you. Honest to God, I haven't."

He hunched his shoulders and rested his head in his hand. "It's a family thing, yer see. Ma would be devastated. It's just not right, the girls marrying ..." He stopped short. "Sorry!"

"Go," said Reece quietly. "Just go."

The West Indian got to his feet and left the flat, leaving the bottle of Champagne on the table.

Ben's spirits sank lower and lower as he walked away from the house. He'd lost Reece's friendship. He'd outraged his sister, but blood was blood and, at the end of the day, she would always be there for him, as he would for her. Friendship was different. You had to work at friendship. He'd never understood that before now.

Entering York Street, he kicked an empty beer can into the gutter before going into a pub, swearing under his breath as he automatically put out his left hand to push open the door. It wasn't the pain that bothered him, it was simply that it wouldn't do what he told it to do.

He ordered a pint of lager and took it into the darkest corner, away from the bar. Tonight was not a night for bumping into old mates, or chatting up the birds. Tonight was a night for introspection, for drowning his sorrows in isolation.

The more he reflected on what he'd deliberately manipulated, the more he hated himself. Would Ma be *that* upset if Thea ended up with a white guy? After all, although they lived in a black community, they had come from Jamaica to a white man's country with little more than the clothes on their backs. And, undoubtedly, the family was far better off here than they had been back home. All four of his sisters had been born in Birmingham, all had Brummie accents, all shared the Midlands sense of humour.

His thoughts turned to the younger ones: Naomi, the ten-year-old was very pretty, Hannah, the twelve-year-old was rebellious. It wouldn't be easy telling them what to do. He thumped the table with his fist, drawing a nervous glance from a couple of gossiping teenagers on the next table. God, he'd really messed up! The only good thing in his life was Deceptions. He glared at the arm with loathing. But now he was a virtual invalid, it was going to be harder to keep on top of things. He couldn't land a decent punch any more, he couldn't even write out the accounts without regularly resting his wrist. Those yobs from the competition who'd beaten him up had a lot to answer for, but if he were truthful, they'd done to him no less than he would have done to them given half a chance.

After ordering another pint, he returned to his table only to find it occupied by two couples.

"I was sitting there," he said, his stance shrieking aggression.

Both young men eyed him warily, for despite his lack of inches, his massive shoulders and thick neck picked him out as a formidable opponent. Then, one of them, afraid of losing face in front of the girls, said, "Sorry, mate, it's ours now."

Before the stabbing incident, a fight would have ensued. Now, he backed down, grunting, "Okay."

Going back to the bar, he went to perch on a stool, taking a thirsty gulp of his pint. More laughing youngsters pushed their way to the bar. Suddenly, he felt out of place. He was no longer a kid. What the hell was he doing on his own in a downbeat pub on Boxing night? Draining his glass, he left the pub and went home to his empty flat. The phone was ringing when he got in.

"Where the hell have you been?" It was Jojo.

"It's none of your fucking business."

"Well, this is!" she retorted. "Someone's squealed, the fuzz are onto you."

"What for?" he snorted, mentally ticking off his latest catalogue of shady deals, convinced he'd covered his tracks.

"Don't worry, it's nothing to do with Deceptions. The local fuzz are cracking down on grass, you'd better empty out your airing cupboard if you don't want a heavy fine. You got caught once before, didn't you?"

"Thanks Jojo," he cried and, moving with the agility gained from his boxing days, he raced into the bedroom and began emptying the cupboard. It took several trips downstairs to rid the flat of the evidence. In the small garden in front of the building he hurriedly glanced around for a hiding place, his ears alert for the sound of approaching police vehicles. Picking up the heavy pots one by one, he tossed them over the high fence into his neighbour's garden. Spinning on his heel, he took the stairs two at a time, ran into the bedroom and tore down the giveaway aluminium foil from the airing cupboard walls. Going to the bed, he managed to lift the mattress high enough to slide the foil under it.

At the sound of hammering at the door, he dropped the mattress into position and lifted the rug to toe a tell-tale heap of earth out of sight beneath it.

His left arm throbbed so painfully that he found himself gritting his teeth as he went downstairs to answer the door.

Two uniformed officers thrust their credentials in his face, demanding entry. He knew one of them by sight, an officious character, unpopular with local pub and restaurant owners. He waved them inside and followed them upstairs, noticing when he entered the room that the top part of the bed was slightly askew. As they began their search, he edged towards the bed and kneed the mattress into place.

"There's nothing here, Gov," said the more junior of the policemen.

The senior man turned a furious face in Ben's direction. "What have you done with it, lad?"

Ben's broad features split into an arrogant grin. "Done with what?"

The officer pursed his lips, then addressed his subordinate. "Take a look outside, Sergeant." Turning back to Ben, he snarled, "Someone must have tipped you off."

"What for?" replied Ben, adopting a pained expression, which wasn't difficult in view of the agony his arm was giving him. His heartbeat had almost returned to normal as his confidence grew. They wouldn't find anything now.

"Sir, could you come down here," called the sergeant from the garden.

Ben's heart started galloping again.

"You needn't come down with us, Sir," said the officer in charge, placing emphasis on the word 'Sir'. His face bore a smirk of grim satisfaction.

From the top of the stairs, Ben could hear mumbling voices. He went into the living room and opened the window. The officers were huddled together talking. Then, he saw one of them kick an empty flowerpot against the wall. After that, they drove off.

Once the coast was clear, he went out into the garden and inspected the offending flower pot, realising that it was nothing more than an abandoned pot blown onto his property by high winds the night before. With a chuckle, he got a step ladder and climbed into his neighbour's garden to retrieve the precious plants, handling them more gently this time and working quietly in order not to disturb the occupants of the surrounding houses. A couple of the plants were beyond salvation, but he could see that most of them would recover with a little t.l.c. The night was cold and his arm throbbed unbearably. He swore under his breath as he carried the last of the plants upstairs. Who was the moron who'd grassed on him?

At last, totally exhausted, he slumped onto the bed and fell asleep.

CHAPTER TWENTY-TWO

The following day, Megan and Reece deliberately avoided one another as much as possible. Neither of them mentioned Ben's visit. Sensing Megan's black mood, Reece prayed that it would pass without more angry words and, in order to defer a confrontation, he stayed out of her way for most of the day. Once the children were in bed, she cornered him.

"I'll never forgive you for humiliating me yesterday."

"What do you mean?" he asked, knowing full well what she was referring to.

"Not letting Ben know the wedding was off."

"Sorry, it slipped my mind."

"Slipped your mind! How could a thing like that slip your mind?"

"It just did, I'm sorry."

"He must think I'm a real idiot. Now, I suppose, he'll go telling that sister of his that the coast is clear for her."

Reece gave Megan a searching look, remembering that she had left the room before Ben broke the news of Thea's engagement. He wondered whether that would change her attitude.

"It wasn't intentional," he muttered contritely.

He couldn't appease her and, for the rest of the week, she pointedly ignored him, calling Calum to her whenever the little boy begged the Canadian to play with him. When Reece went to pick up his daughter, Megan rushed to the cot and barred his way, saying, "Leave her to sleep, you know she's got croup."

In consequence, they were both relieved when the Double A's came back from Torquay. Aidan and Aubrey arrived laden with presents for everyone, uniting Reece and Megan in embarrassment.

"What are we going to do?" whispered Megan. "I only bought something very small for them."

"I didn't buy them anything," said Reece.

"Shall I rush out and get something else, the shops will still be open?"

Reece shook his head. "That would be too obvious. We'll just have to brazen it out. After all, most of the stuff was for the children."

"I suppose so," agreed Megan.

This conspiratorial whispering brought the cold war to an end and, in fact, during the following week, Megan became quite cheerful. The Double

A's, with their helpfulness around the house and their general optimistic outlook, had a therapeutic effect upon her.

"I love having them here," she confided to Reece. "Especially Aidan. He makes me laugh, he's so funny."

Reece spent the next couple of weeks trying to make up his mind whether to go up to Birmingham to see Thea. Finally, he decided that a telephone call would be safer. Landing on her doorstep unannounced might embarrass her. Thea answered the phone.

The preliminaries dispensed with, he brought up the subject of Ben's arm. "Is there any hope of improvement?" he asked.

"I don't think so," she replied, adding reflectively. "He's changed a lot recently. The injury seems to have sobered him."

"I've noticed," agreed Reece. "He called in the other day with news of you. I understand congratulations are in order."

"Yes," she said quietly. "Troy and I are getting married on Saturday the 31st." She paused. "So that's both of us spliced."

Reece gave a start. So Ben hadn't passed on the news that the Christmas nuptials never took place! "Er, Megan and I didn't make it to the altar."

"Oh," she said. "Well, these things happen."

After that, there seemed little more for either of them to say so they said goodbye and ended the call.

Early in February, he bumped into Ben. Their initial greeting over, he cleared his throat and asked, "Did the wedding go off all right?"

Ben flashed him a grin. "Sure did. We don't mess about postponing things like some people."

"As a matter of a fact, ours is fixed for early March," retorted Reece. "And you're invited."

This was a total lie, but he couldn't stand Ben's gloating and, besides, there seemed little point in putting it off now that Thea was no longer available.

After leaving Ben, he went straight round to the Registry Office, bought the Licence and booked the date.

"Oh darling, I knew you'd come round to it in the end," cried Megan, when Reece broke the news to her.

Mechanically, he returned her embrace while Calum, delighted that his two favourite people seemed so happy, raced across the room and hurled himself into the fray. Megan stooped to pick him up, tears streaming down her cheeks.

"You're going to have a proper daddy, now, my precious," she whispered. Calum chuckled and waved an arm towards Reece. In his eyes, he already had a proper daddy.

"I've booked it for Friday, 27 March," said Reece. "And I've asked Ben to come. Is that all right?"

"Of course it is. And we'll have to get in touch with Connie and Will."

"How? We don't know where they'll be."

"Connie's sure to phone up this weekend, we can tell her then. Oh, Reece, I'm so excited. Let's tell the Double A's!"

Lowering Calum to the floor, Megan sped from the room. He could hear her tapping on their lodgers' door and he hoped she'd have the sense not to burst in on them. He still wasn't sure whether she knew about their sexual proclivity. They followed her along to the living room.

"Brilliant news, my darlings!" cooed Aidan, taking Reece's hand and shaking it vigorously. Then, overcome with enthusiasm, he threw in a hug as well with a peck on each cheek. Aubrey was hardly less exuberant although he did hold back on the continental kissing.

"This calls for a celebration," said Aidan. "Let's open a bottle of plonk."

"We can do better than that, we haven't opened Ben's Champagne yet," exclaimed Megan.

Reece remained distant throughout this discourse. He felt as if he were acting a part in a play. Only Calum, playing happily on the floor with his train set and Mary Katherine, gurgling in her baby seat, seemed real. "I think we should save the Champagne for another occasion," he started to say.

Aidan butted in. "No way, we'll buy another one for the Big Day."

"Let me get Calum and Mary to bed and we can have a party," suggested Megan. "That will give us time to put the Champagne on ice."

While Megan was sorting out the children, the Double A's rushed off to the supermarket, bringing back a bagful of snacks to go with the drink. Once the children were settled for the night, the four flat-mates gathered in the living room. Reece opened the Champagne, the pop of its cork brought a sobering thought: there was no going back now. He had committed himself to a lifetime with Megan, the third girl in his life: the third and most unlikely choice. It's funny, he thought, you never know what fate holds in store for you.

After a couple of glasses of bubbly, however, he found himself being swept along by the excitement. Despite protestations from both Reece and Megan Aubrey pledged to take on the cost of a limousine to get them to the Registry Office. "You've got to get married in style," he insisted.

For his part, Aidan couldn't be restrained from organising the catering. "Leave it to me, I'll see that you get a splendid spread," he promised. "How many will there be?"

Megan did an intoxicated count on her fingers. "There's us four and the children, there's Connie and Will ... hic ... and there's Ben." She turned to Reece and asked guilelessly, "What about Ben's sister ... hic ... and her new husband?"

Reece was so taken aback that for a moment, he couldn't speak. "No!" he retorted once he'd regained his voice. "We can't possibly ask them."

Realising that she had committed a terrible *faux pas*, Megan quickly changed the subject. "It really doesn't matter how many come ... hic ... we'll fit them all in somehow."

"What a pity it isn't summer," said Aubrey. "It would be lovely to hold a party on the patio."

In an effort to recover her composure, Megan said, "I suppose we ought to ask the people upstairs."

"And your parents of course," said Aidan.

She shook her head, a horrified expression on her face. "They're too old to travel."

Aidan and Aubrey hotly protested at this excuse, and Reece looked askance. "What nonsense!" he said. "We must ask them."

"No, we can't. Honestly, it would be awful, they're such prudes, they wouldn't allow drink and loud music."

The last comment put a stop to any further argument from the Double A's. Reece, however, still looked worried. "It's a pity," he said with a shrug.

During the next few days, Megan brought up the subject of Reece moving into her room.

"There's no rush," he said. "Let's wait until nearer the wedding."

Megan accepted this with mixed feelings. He wants it to be romantic, she told herself, since we can't afford a honeymoon. In her head she made plans, rearranging the box room to accommodate a child's bed and a cot, shifting her king-size bed to the other side of the room to give more privacy when the door was opened.

As predicted, Connie telephoned. She couldn't hide her surprise at the news of the much postponed wedding.

"Will you be my bridesmaid?" asked Megan.

"I will, provided you don't expect me to wear a frilly pink dress."

Megan giggled. "Of course not. What about Will, do you think he'll be able to make it?"

"Not a chance, I'm afraid, he's up in Newcastle that week."

"I'm banking on you to help me choose my outfit."

"Next weekend I'll be in Wimbledon. We could meet and go shopping," suggested Connie.

"Thanks, Connie, that will be great."

When Reece arrived home, she told him about the call. "Will you be able to baby-sit all day Saturday?"

"Of course, I can. You and Connie can go off and enjoy yourselves." Taking out his wallet, he drew out a handful of notes. "Get yourself something really pretty to wear."

His unexpected generosity brought a flush to her cheeks. "Thanks darling," she cried, throwing her arms round his neck and kissing him.

The girls spent a happy day together. For the first time in ages, Megan had money to spend on herself. She felt like a duchess.

"See you on the Big Day," said Connie as they parted company at Twickenham Station.

The 27th arrived and, promptly at 11 o'clock, a white limousine pulled up outside the flat to pick Megan up. At her insistence, Reece had kipped down with Ben the night before. "It's unlucky for us to meet again until the ceremony," she'd said.

Megan was so excited that at first she didn't notice how quiet Reece was. But while they were waiting to be called in, she whispered, "Are you all right, darling, only you look so serious."

He managed a smile and whispered back, "Wedding nerves."

Ben had made an effort for the occasion. He was wearing a mid-blue silk and woollen suit with a self-striped white shirt and a yellow tie. Dressed formally in a tailored jacket, his shoulders look massive.

"Bloody hell, you've pulled out all the stops," Connie murmured in his ear.

"Had to get kitted out for Thea's wedding, didn't I?" he replied with a chuckle. "Gave my sister away, now I'm Reece's fucking Best Man, hope that's not a portent for the future. How about it, shall we tie the knot, Connie?"

"Not even if you were the last man on earth," she retorted.

"Why not? I think I'm a good catch."

"Because I know that even if we were marooned on a desert island, you'd find someone else to shag."

Their banter was cut short by a steward appearing at the door and calling out, "Cassidy and Hughes please."

They all filed into a small room where they took their seats in front of a table decorated by a lavish flower arrangement.

"Are we ready to begin?" asked the Registrar.

Megan and Reece stepped forward, closely followed by Calum until Aidan pulled him back and sat him on his knee.

Connie studied the bride and groom as the Registrar's voice droned on. Megan looked very pretty in a cream knee-length dress with a matching jacket embroidered with imitation pearls. Connie had curled her hair for her and it was held back from her face by an Alice band of spring flowers.

Reece was wearing a sober grey suit. He'd had a hair cut and looked tidier than Connie had ever seen him. Connie had chosen a dark red satin number, which complimented her smooth dark skin. Held up by shoestring straps, it was shorter and tighter than Megan's. To combat the chilly March wind, she wore a fake fur stole she'd found in a charity shop. She had drawn the line at wearing a flowery headdress, but at Megan's insistence, had agreed to carry a small bouquet.

Back at the house afterwards, the Double A's took charge. Aidan busied himself serving canapés while Aubrey poured the wine. Their neighbours joined them and soon the party was in full swing. The wedding cake was a surprise. Two-tiered, it was elaborately decorated with flowers and butterflies made of icing and marzipan, the top tier supported on gothic-style pillars. Megan hadn't expected anything so grand.

"Oh, isn't it wonderful!" she cried. "But we won't cut into even a third of it."

"You can save the rest for Mary's christening," said Aidan.

Megan's face fell. "Oh, I don't think we'll be having her christened," she said.

"Yes we will," said Reece firmly. "Calum as well."

"He's already been christened. Dad made me," said Megan sulkily. "Now you're trying to tell me what to do!"

The popping of the Champagne cork broke the tension between the newly-weds.

"Here's to a long and happy marriage," said Aubrey. "And now I think it's time for a few words from the Best Man."

Ben took his cue, describing some of Reece's embarrassing moments, including the fight outside McDonalds, which had resulted in their friendship.

After a few rather more serious words from Reece, someone started up the stereo and the real celebrating began. Connie was the first to leave.

"So soon, it's only half six," protested Megan.

"Sorry, but I must make tracks, I've got an early rehearsal tomorrow morning," explained Connie. "By the way, I've got something for you two." She delved into her bag and handed Reece an envelope. "You must open it at precisely seven thirty."

"What is it?"

"Never mind. Just promise me you'll do what I ask." Megan and Reece both nodded. "Don't forget," insisted Connie.

They looked puzzled and nodded again.

"Don't worry, I won't let them forget," said Aidan, who was obviously party to the secret.

Megan looked sad after Connie had gone. "She's the best friend I've ever had," she confided to her new husband. "Better than that Isobel I used to go around with at school." She took his hand. "Let me show you something."

Sneaking out of the room, Megan led Reece to the box room, which the evening before she had rearranged for the children while he was at Ben's.

"What do you think?" she asked.

"It's fine."

She led him on to her bedroom, flinging open the door in triumph. He was impressed. It had been transformed: the usual jumble of discarded clothing put away, the floor hoovered, the net curtains washed, the bed moved to give more space in front of the dressing table.

"You've been working hard, Megan," he said.

She looked so happy, colour in her cheeks for the first time for months, that he took her in his arms and kissed her.

"I do love you," she whispered. "I always thought Chris was the only one for me, but you changed all that."

"Hey you two," called Aidan from the hall.

They drew apart and Reece said, "We'd better go back to the party."

"Come on you love-birds," cooed Aidan as they joined him. "It's nearly half seven, time to open your envelope."

The remaining guests gathered around as Reece slit open the envelope.

"What is it?" cried Megan excitedly as Reece stared at the contents.

"It's a hotel voucher," he said. "For a two-night stay in the Madeira Hotel in Brighton."

"We all chipped in," explained Aubrey. "Couldn't let you get spliced without a honeymoon."

Megan and Reece were speechless. She reached for his hand, tears of happiness streaming down her cheeks. Then she gave a gasp. "What about the children?"

"All taken care of," said Aidan. "Me and Aub will play at mummies and daddies for the weekend."

For a moment, Megan looked worried, but excitement soon swept away her misgivings. A weekend away from the disturbance of children was a gift from heaven.

"Thank you both so much," she croaked, tears streaming down her cheeks.

As they drove towards the station in the minicab, Megan snuggled up to Reece. They'd changed out of their Wedding finery; Reece wore a smart pair of chinos and a dark green sweater and Megan wore a flared blue shirt with a pale lemon top.

"It's a good thing Connie insisted on me buying this outfit as well when I went shopping with her. I suppose she knew about this trip."

After their evening meal, they took the lift up to the next floor, but on going into their room, both felt embarrassed. They had only slept together once and that was more than a year ago, besides which, the circumstances of that coupling had been unusual to say the least: Megan had been under the influence of drink and drugs; Reece had been emotionally involved with another girl.

He let her get into bed first. When he came out of the bathroom, she was lying on her back, her blond hair spread over the pillow. She looked incredibly young and vulnerable. Suddenly, he felt enormously distanced from her, both by age and experience. She lifted her hand and beckoned him over and he saw her shiny new wedding ring flash in the light of the bedside lamp.

My God, he thought in shock, I've done it, I've actually married her!

"Shall I switch off the light?" she asked.

He nodded and got into bed beside her. She rolled over to face him and he took her in his arms, obligingly performing his marital duties.

Long after she'd fallen asleep, he lay awake. He could hear her gentle snoring -- she'd jokingly warned him about this -- but it wasn't the snoring which kept him awake. His thoughts strayed far from the girl beside him in the hotel bed to another girl who was 200 miles away. A surge of bitterness crashed his mind, scattering the 'what if's' and the 'if only's'. He visualised Thea in the arms of an unknown man. It was all he could do to restrain himself from shouting out.

Pulling back the duvet, he went into the bathroom and took a cold shower.

CHAPTER TWENTY-THREE

Connie's landlady handed her the small package as soon as she entered the house. It had been re-directed from Tennyson Avenue to Woodstock Road and then forwarded to her present digs.

"Hello dear, this came just after you left this morning."

"Thank you," replied Connie, looking slightly mystified. She didn't recognise the handwriting and there was no return address on the back of the packet. She tore it open and spilled out the contents: a batch of photographs and a letter. It was from Della. She stiffened, unwilling to acknowledge Della's existence. It was well over a year since she'd heard from her.

She started looking through the photographs. The first one was of a man standing by the side of a swimming pool, dressed in Bermudas and a vest t-shirt. Although well into middle-age, he appeared to be in very good shape. Caught waving at someone, his smile was wide and friendly. She turned the photo over. Della had written: *I told you your father was handsome, didn't I?*

She flipped through the rest until, driven by curiosity, she dug an old magnifying glass out of a drawer and studied the pictures more closely. What she saw pleased her: Javier de Oliveira Figueres was, indeed, a good-looking man.

It was a while before she could bring herself to read Della's letter. Dated two weeks earlier, it opened with the usual greetings, but as she read on, Connie felt there was a sadness underlying the jauntiness of the words. Della claimed to have had a wonderful time in Rio. Javier had received her warmly, welcomed news of his daughter, expressing regret that she -- Connie -- hadn't gone out there with her mother. *He wanted me to stay, but I decided not to, Connie*, Della concluded, *I'll explain why when I see you. Please let me know when I can come and see you. I know you're on the road, but I'll travel anywhere to catch up with you. Call my mobile. Make it soon.* The last sentence had a ring of desperation to it.

Connie held the letter in her hand for some time. The last thing she wanted was to get involved with Della again, yet the letter's contents puzzled her. She couldn't get the words out of her head. Why wouldn't Della take the opportunity to stay in Brazil with a rich hotel-owner? Commonsense took over. The story was a pack of lies of course. But sleep wouldn't come and she woke in the morning feeling tired and irritable.

The morning's rehearsals were tough. The director had decided that, every week, the song and dance sequences needed fresh life breathed into them. He was unremittingly critical and the dancers had to commit a lot to memory. Unless she put her heart and soul into it, Connie knew she could easily make a mistake and she didn't want to get on the wrong side of the much-feared dance instructor.

After a gruelling eight hours of practise, she returned to her digs completely exhausted. Della's letter and the photographs lay on the bedside table. She could 'accidentally' leave them in a drawer and move to the next port of call. She spread the snapshots out on the bed and knew that she couldn't do that. Taking her mobile out of her pocket, she dialled Della's number.

"Darling, I just knew you'd call! How are you?" came Della's girlish voice. Without waiting for a reply, she rushed on, "I'm so proud of you. A star! My daughter's a star!"

"Not yet!" protested Connie. "I've only got a part in the chorus. The show's doing well. We're getting good reviews. By the way, thanks for sending the photos."

"What do you think of your handsome old man?"

The phraseology angered Connie. Your handsome old man, implied fond familiarity, not an estranged parent. She didn't reply.

"I must come and see you, darling."

"Here in Manchester? Can't you wait until we come down south again?"

"This can't wait." Connie had never heard Della sound so serious.

"All right then, I'll get you a complimentary ticket for Saturday's show."

"Thank you darling. And on Sunday, can we spend some time together?"

"Of course." The frown on Connie's brow belied the enthusiasm in her voice.

Della waited at the Stage Door. Connie had promised to take her back stage, but now that the time had come, she wished she'd called off the visit. How would Connie introduce her? Was she suitably dressed? Would she be able to curb her nonsensical chattering? Connie didn't understand that it was brought on by nervousness.

When the time came, Connie introduced her as her long-lost aunt. The dancers were friendly. My type of people, thought Della. Afterwards, she exclaimed, "What a nice crowd! They're all so kind; it's just like one big happy family."

"It's not always like that," countered Connie. "Some of the girls are terribly bitchy."

"It's to be expected, I suppose, living at such close quarters."

"That's why I opted to find my own digs," explained Connie. "They're a bit further from the theatre, but at least I get away from the rest of them once the performance is over."

After a visit to Pizza Express, Della said she wanted to go straight back to her hotel. "I'm a bit tired, after all, I've been doing a lot of travelling lately." She checked off on her fingers: "Rome, Paris, London."

Connie cast her a quizzical glance, wondering how she managed to afford such trips. "All right, I'll pick you up tomorrow morning about eleven."

"Goodnight dear, sweet dreams," replied Della.

After seeing her daughter safely into a cab, she went into the hotel and made straight for the bar. The barman greeted her jovially. "What can I get you, Madam?"

She ordered a Scotch and bought a packet of Dunhills, lighting up with trembling fingers.

"Not in here, Madam," said the barman. "I'm afraid you'll have to step out into the courtyard to smoke."

She went outside, shivering in the chill night air. The first draw helped to calm her nerves. It had been a tremendous strain to behave herself in front of Connie. She had seen the relief in the girl's eyes when she'd turned up suitably dressed. The longing for a drink and a smoke had made her fidgety and she was aware that she had been playing with the collar of her jacket as if trying to pluck off a loose snag of thread. She hoped that no one else had noticed. However, experience told her that the young singers and dancers chatting in the dressing room were too involved with themselves to care about the agitated behaviour of Connie's long-lost relative.

Stubbing out the cigarette, she went back into the warmth of the hotel and took another gulp of her drink, savouring the reassuring burn in her throat. Hopefully, she hadn't let Connie down. The second whisky brought the return of confidence. What did she care what people thought! The barman caught her eye, and winked. She was still sober enough to have the grace to blush -- not from shyness, but from shame. At her age, she ought to be here with a husband visiting grandchildren, not planning to drop a bombshell in her abandoned daughter's lap.

The third scotch dispatched shame. The barman wasn't bad looking; fiftyish, balding, a little over-weight perhaps. She wondered what time he got off work. She needed a shoulder to cry on and, if the price for comfort was a one-night stand, then so be it! She stumbled across to the bar, ordered a double Scotch and tried to start a conversation. Somehow, the words became incoherent. She looked at him. He was very handsome.

"I think Madam's had enough," he said, not attempting to serve her.

She wagged her finger in his face. "I know when I've had enough. Give me another one."

He shook his head, looking concerned. "That would be unwise."

"Just one?"

Afraid of trouble, he beckoned the manager, who came over and tried to persuade her to leave the bar. Holding out her room key, he asked formally, "Would you like help to go upstairs, Madam?"

"Help? I should say not!" She let go of the bar counter and tottered towards the lift, her ankle twisting under her as she tried to balance on her stiletto heels.

The barman and the manager exchanged a glance, the latter following behind at a discreet distance. Somehow, she managed to reach her room, where the manager hurried to lend her a hand with the key.

"Thank you," she lisped coyly.

He gave a little bow and walked back down the corridor.

Della gave a little shudder. So much for the comforting arms of the barman! Her mouth twisted in a grimace. She'd had a narrow escape. Closer examination had shown him to be an ugly bastard. She collapsed onto the bed and slipped into semi-consciousness. A gut-wrenching pain searing through her stomach brought her back to the world. With her arms clutched across her middle, she staggered to the bathroom and threw up in the loo.

The heaving went on and on. After what seemed like hours, she collapsed, exhausted, into a crumpled heap on the bathroom floor, staying there until the first soft grey rays of dawn filtered through the blinds. This was the hour when reality faced her. Stiff of limb and dry of mouth, she struggled to her feet and studied herself in the mirror: dyed blond hair in disarray, eyes puffed and bloodshot, cheeks blotched, jaw slack. She stuck out her tongue. It was coated. God, what a sight! She gripped the sides of the washbasin to stop herself from slipping to the floor. What had the consultant said? "It's malignant, Mrs Wilberforce. However, if you submit to surgery, there is a slim chance, and of course, you would need to change your lifestyle. I'm sure your husband will give you the support you need." Her husband! Hank Wilberforce was long gone! She stared back at her reflection and considered the dismal forecast: hair loss, continuing nausea, pain. All that without the compensation of booze and fags! I can't do it alone, she wailed.

Things were going well for Ben. He was proud of what he'd achieved at Deceptions. The nightclub was doing well. He was pleased that he'd managed to drive a wedge between Reece and his sister. Reece was safely married to Megan in Twickenham and Thea and Troy had set up home on the outskirts of Coventry. As for Abe, since getting out of Winson Green he had gone off to Glasgow on some hair-brained scam cooked up with another loser he'd met during his time inside.

The only cloud on the horizon was the trouble with his arm, but Ben told himself this would improve with time. The Consultant had been overly pessimistic. She hadn't taken into account that he was very fit. Yes, he told himself, the nerve-ends would eventually heal and his arm would be as good as new.

All that remained was for Ben to take advantage of his current affluence to re-house his mother and sisters somewhere out of Abe Jenson's reach. Without telling them, he found a pleasant semi on a new housing estate not too far from where they now lived, and made an offer on it.

When he took Clelia and his mother along to view the place, Imelda trembled with emotion and choked back a sob, exclaiming, "Son, this is far too classy for the likes of us! We not live here. What I gonna do without Bessie and Sissy? They's the best neighbours I's got. How I get do my shopping down de market? And de girls, what about der school?"

"Ma, Hannah and Naomi are old enough to take the bus to school and, as for the market, Clelia would drive you there now that she's passed her test. If she's not around, you can take a taxi."

"Me, take a taxi!" Imelda rolled her eyes and gave a loud chuckle, her generous frame wobbling with mirth. All at once, she stopped laughing. "You'm serious, Son?"

"'Course I am. I know it's different from what you've been used to, Ma, but think how easy it will be to keep clean and tidy. Everything's new: washing machine, dishwasher."

"Dish-washer, huh?"

Clelia butted in, "All the latest labour-saving devices, Ma."

Imelda shook her head. "It's beautiful, sweetness, but I don't understand such things." She shook her head, the tears streaming down her plump cheeks. "This house not right for us, boy."

Ben began to look annoyed, especially when Clelia nudged him and whispered, "What did I tell you, you'll never get Ma to move out of that flat."

But he wasn't beaten yet. "Listen up, Ma, Pa's out of the slammer and as soon as he's short of bread, he'll come looking for you."

"Your Pa don't scare me none," retorted Imelda with a toss of the head.

"You know that's not true, Ma, and I can't protect you. I've got a business to run. Can't keep running backwards and forwards from London."

Still his mother wouldn't yield. Ben kept trying. "Bring the girls down to Twickenham then. I'll find you a nice house down there."

"No," said Imelda. "I not come all de way across de sea from Jamaica to keep moving round like a gypsy-woman."

"Ma," cried Ben in exasperation. "The new house is only three miles away from the flat. It's still in Birmingham. Besides ..." He played his ace. "... just suppose Pa does catch up with you! He might start knocking Hannah and Naomi about."

Imelda threw up her hands in dismay. "What you keep frightening your poor ole ma for?"

Tact wasn't Ben's strong point, but he kept his cool. "It's the only way to make you listen. Honest, Ma, I'm only thinking of you and the girls. It's not far from the centre; you could invite your friends out here for tea."

"And how they gonna get here, Son, tell me dat?"

"I'll set up a standing order with a minicab firm."

Imelda didn't reply, although Ben could see he was winning her over. "There's a nice little garden, and you know how you love pottering around growing herbs and flowers."

He could almost hear the thoughts wending their way across his mother's mind. He knew her so well. In her heart, the cons would outweigh the pros, yet at the end of the day, her concern for her young daughters would drive her personal preferences away.

The tears began to stream down her face again. "Yes, go ahead, sweetness." She patted his arm affectionately. "You'm a good boy, Ben."

Three days later, Ben drove back to Twickenham in his new Golf. Following the traffic onto the busy motorway, he gave a wince as he changed gear, reminded of the limited mobility in his left arm. Thrusting aside the fear it posed him, he put down his foot and surged into a gap, narrowly missing a more cautious motorist. The Golf was an interim measure; next year it would be a BMW. He'd ignored the advice of his GP to go for an automatic.

He felt satisfied with what he had achieved: Contracts had been exchanged, Completion was awaited. Now Imelda and the girls could move in. After having overcome her initial disinclination to be uprooted, Imelda had thrown herself whole-heartedly into the project, as he had known she would. Clelia was overwhelmingly grateful to him for his generosity, relieved that her mother would be settled before she and Nathan got married. And the two younger girls were excited at the prospect of living in a proper house in a posh area, instead of a cramped high-rise in a run down neighbourhood.

Since her wedding, he had had little contact with Thea. Despite giving her away in lieu of their father, the relationship between sister and brother had remained cool. It was as if the split with Reece had crushed her emotions. From being a feisty, outspoken young woman, she had withdrawn into herself. If such an admission had been within the realms of his comprehension, Ben would have been forced to admit that this coolness towards him hurt a great deal.

Usually when troubled, he went to the gym and exercised off his depression, now the continuing difficulty in using his arm denied him this outlet. In consequence, his mood was black by the time he arrived back in Twickenham.

"I loved your performance so much, Connie darling," lisped Della, when they met up the following morning in the hotel bar. They sat side-by-side on a cream leather couch, two cappuccinos and a plate of muffins on the table in front of them. They had the place to themselves, the only other occupant being the barman, who was busy polishing glasses.

Connie's eyes lit up with pleasure. "Did you really enjoy it? You know, moth ..." She nearly slipped up again. " ... Della, I've been promised a bigger part in the next production."

"Have you, dear? How nice!"

Connie felt rebuffed by the sudden inexplicable fading of Della's interest and almost snapped a retaliatory riposte, but a smothered gasp from her mother curbed it. Without warning, the older woman doubled over, clasping her stomach. Alarmed, Connie put an arm around her shoulders. "What's the matter? You look awful," she cried.

"Don't worry, it'll pass," whispered Della.

"What is it? Are you ill?"

"Give me a minute, there's a good girl."

But her mother's agony seemed to go on and on. In desperation, Connie waved at the barman, but he wasn't looking in their direction. "Let's get you upstairs to your room," she cried.

As the two women struggled across to the lift, the barman noticed and summoned the manager's help. Somehow, between them, Connie and the manager managed to get Della up to her room.

"I'll call a doctor," he said, looking concerned.

"There's no need," gasped Della. "I know what's wrong." She took a deep breath. "The pain will pass, believe me."

Connie exchanged a worried glance with the manager. Clearly, the latter envisaged the arrival of a siren-squealing ambulance at the hotel entrance with paramedics and stretchers causing a disturbance in the lobby.

"I'll look after her," Connie assured him. "If this doesn't pass in five minutes, I'll call a doctor. Can you recommend one?"

The manager scribbled a name and number on a scrap of paper and handed it to her. "Don't let this go on for too long," he advised. "It may be a heart attack or a stroke."

This drew a weak smile from Della. "It's not," she said.

After the manager had left the room, Connie helped her mother undress and get into bed. The pain seemed to be easing and the colour began to return to Della's blanched cheeks. Connie eyed her suspiciously. "Was this due to over-indulgence?"

"Probably," murmured Della, closing her eyes.

Connie wondered what to do. She knew she ought to stay, but she had promised to attend an extra rehearsal in an hour's time. The choreographer wanted to rearrange one of the dance routines.

When Della fell asleep, she was afraid to switch on the television in case she woke her, so to pass the time, she wandered into the bathroom. The stack of packets and jars on the glass shelf above the wash-hand basin made her jump back with shock. She picked up one or two, but couldn't decipher the chemical ingredients. Clearly, Della was a very sick woman and Connie knew she had to find out more. Hurrying back into the bedroom, she checked to see if Della was still asleep then started going through the wardrobe and drawers for clues as to her mother's illness.

The search revealed nothing. The only option was to wait until Della woke up and question her. Connie glanced at her watch. She was already late for the rehearsal and there was no way of getting in touch with the choreographer as she didn't know her mobile number and the Box Office would certainly be switched to answer phone on a Sunday.

Swearing under her breath, she decided to dash over to the theatre and blurt out her apologies. As she crossed the room, she remembered that she hadn't searched Della's handbag. She picked the Gucci bag up from the floor, wondering how her mother had come by it. Had it been a gift? It seemed Della had had her share of admirers, or had her well-heeled father, Javier de Oliveira Figueres, been persuaded by guilt to lavish presents on the mother of his illegitimate daughter?

Despising herself for this intrusion into her mother's domain, Connie opened the bag and tipped the contents on to the dressing table. The usual paraphernalia spilled across its surface: Italian leather purse stuffed with credit cards, glasses case -- she had never seen Della wearing spectacles -- make-up bag containing compressed powder, eye liner and lipstick, an A4 envelope postmarked London on the back of which was scribbled her own contact address. She hesitated before opening the envelope. Searching through her mother's clothes and her medicine cabinet was one thing, reading her mail was another.

Della turned onto her back and started to snore. She had drifted into a deep sleep. It was now or never. With a trembling hand, Connie withdrew the letter from its envelope and saw that it was typed. Intuition told her it contained the information she was seeking. She walked to the window and looked out at the busy road below before unfolding the sheet of paper. Still, she couldn't bring herself to read it. Surely her mother had the right to privacy!

She reflected on her own life, knowing that only once had she allowed her independence to be threatened. It had taught her a lesson. During her brief fling with Will she had permitted emotion to direct her actions. For a few mad weeks she'd lost her way. When Will had left to take up his post aboard the luxury liner, she had suffered agonies imagining him chatting up single young girls or dancing with frustrated middle-aged divorcees. In letters and telephone calls, she had opened her heart to him, sharing her innermost feelings, revealing her weaknesses, belittling herself by begging him to return before the four months were up. But gradually, time had lessened her jealousy and she had realised that the spark between them had become nothing more than a flickering flame, extinguished by the slipstream of his departure. She had come out of the affair firmly determined never to let such a thing happen again. She felt violated despite the fact that, to her knowledge, Will had never betrayed her trust. By delving into her mother's affairs, would she be encroaching on Della's independence?

When another reverberating snore came from the bed, Connie shoved the letter back into its envelope without reading it. Creeping across the room, she replaced the items in the handbag and dropped the bag back on the floor. Then, she sat down in the armchair and waited for Della to wake up. She had to make her tell the truth. She'd missed the rehearsal. That didn't matter any more.

Della opened her eyes and blinked, not recognising where she was. Slowly, agonisingly, memory returned. The room was in semi-darkness. She must have been asleep for hours, but the pain had gone and, except for a heavy weariness, she felt quite well. In her mind, she replayed the morning's episode, her cheeks burning at the memory of being helped upstairs, at the embarrassment of Connie getting her undressed and into bed. What revulsion her daughter must have felt as her body's many blemishes were uncovered: the spare tyre; the cellulite; the wrinkles. Connie must have shuddered with disgust and made off as quickly as possible.

A deep reverberating sigh from beside the bed made her start. Turning her head, she saw that Connie was slumped in the armchair not two feet away. She was fast asleep. She looked so beautiful, so perfect. Tears rushed to Della's eyes. Her beloved daughter had kept a bedside vigil. An explosion of emotion prompted her to lift herself up so that she could study her more closely.

She recalled the jibes Connie had flung at her when she had revealed her true parentage to her. Most of those accusations were unfair. For years Della had followed her daughter's progress, lurking near the school to watch her come out of the gate, chattering and laughing with her friends. Over the years, she had managed to learn the dates of Sports Days and, keeping her distance, had watched Connie win the 400 metres and the long jump. With secret envy she'd seen her daughter hug Linda and Steve as they applauded her achievements. On one occasion, she had risked discovery by sneaking into the School Hall to watch her take the lead in the Sixth Form production of West Side Story.

Again, Connie stirred. Della held her breath, gripping the duvet cover with clenched fists. All she wanted was to hug her daughter, to tell her how much she loved her. She reflected on the Christmas visit to Rio. On her arrival Javier had greeted her with genuine warmth, but his enthusiasm had soon waned. He had his pick of women; tourists from all over the world flocked to his hotel. What did he want with a middle-aged divorcee who was fast approaching her sell-by date? He'd been generous, setting up a bank account for her. This had enabled her to visit the capital cities she loved so much. But recently, the bank had informed her that the account had been closed and, once again, she was left with the unreliable alimony cheques, which always arrived late and were never enough.

Connie opened her eyes. "Oh," she exclaimed. "You're awake. How do you feel?"

Della wiped the tears from her cheeks. "Much better." She relaxed her grip on the cover and flapped a hand. "You see, I told you there was nothing to worry about."

Wistfully, Della realised she was defeating her own ends. She had come to Manchester to tell her daughter everything, to beg for her help. Face to face, she knew she couldn't do that. It would be too cruel.

She said cheerfully, "What time is it, honey?"

With a burst of energy, she threw back the duvet and put her feet to the floor. But the sudden movement sent the blood rushing to her head; she swayed, put out her hand to steady herself and would have fallen if Connie hadn't caught her.

"I'm all right," she gasped. "It's only hunger. Let me get out of this old nightie and we can go and eat. Be a dear, get that blue skirt and jumper out of the wardrobe for me while I have a quick shower."

Connie frowned angrily. Pushing Della back onto the bed, she pulled the chair round to face her and sat down. "We're not going anywhere until you tell me what's wrong with you."

They argued for several minutes, although Della knew that, in the end, Connie would win. There was no way the girl was going to be fobbed off. She sighed, folded her hands on her lap and, like a dejected pupil kept in after school, submitted to the inevitable and told Connie about her illness.

"Cancer!" gasped Connie. "Six months? But there must be some treatment you can have!"

Della shook her head. "They can only extend my life by ..." She shrugged. " ... a further five or six months, possibly."

Connie grasped her hands and squeezed them. "There must be a way. Whatever happens, mother, you've got to accept treatment. Twelve months is better than six." She gave a sob. "I can't bear to lose you when I've only just found you." The tears flowed as she leant towards Della. "Have you told Linda?"

"Of course not. What could she do? I don't want her rushing back to the UK in a panic. Her place is with Steve." She wrenched a hand free and clapped it to her forehead, agitation forcing a torrent of undisciplined words from her lips. "God knows, I've given Linda enough problems over the years. Those two have bailed me out time and time again. I'm not going to give them any more hassle." She thumped her fist down on the coverlet. "I'm not, I tell you."

"But you must undergo treatment," insisted Connie. "Do it for me."

Della shook her head. "Lose my hair, feel nauseous. It's bad enough enduring bouts of pain, with chemotherapy I'd be sick *all* the time. I can't take it Connie."

"But Mother, I'll be there for you, we'll beat this thing together."

"You've got your career to think of. Everything is working out for you. Forget about me, I'm a no-hoper." She hesitated. "I only came back to say 'goodbye'"

"No!" shouted Connie. "I won't let you give up, please, don't talk like that; I can't bear it."

She threw her arms around her mother, hugging her tightly. Della's heart convulsed. How many times had she imagined this moment: a reunion with her estranged daughter! Too late! Why did everything happen too late?

She gave a weak smile and, pushing Connie aside, she got up and went into the bathroom. At the door she paused and looked back. Connie was curled up in a crumpled heap on the bed, her shoulders heaving under the weight of her grief. In that moment, Della knew that there was no way she would attempt to extend her life. Connie was better off without her. She would resign herself to the inevitable and let nature take its course.

CHAPTER TWENTY-FOUR

Reece spent the rest of their honeymoon weekend in a trance-like state. Megan appeared not to notice his distraction, chattering non-stop, eagerly pointing out the sights, although from time to time, she did look wistful and plaintively beg Reece to phone home to check on the children. He firmly refused, saying that the Double A's had everything under control, and that in the unlikely event of a problem, they would get in touch.

The weather was clement and it was the first time that either of them had been to Brighton. To keep his bubbly teenage bride happy, Reece followed her lead. They browsed in The Lanes, meandered to the end of the pier and visited the Royal Pavilion. He tried to keep their conversation superficial, dreading moments of intimacy. He deliberately kept her out late so that, by the time they got to bed, she was tired. He avoided pillow talk by turning away from her to feign sleep as soon as it was decently possible to do so.

In her innocence, Megan was unaware of any shortfall in their lovemaking. Despite being the mother of two children, her knowledge of sex was limited to the fumbling of teenage urgency and the alcohol-induced seduction of a man who was simply being kind to her. She couldn't recall either event in detail, only that each encounter had resulted in pregnancy. For this reason, she had listened to Connie's advice to go on the pill, advice her new husband had wholeheartedly endorsed.

On their return to Twickenham, the Double A's greeted them warmly. There were vases of flowers everywhere. Calum ran into Reece's arms, shouting, "Daddy, Daddy," and the Canadian swept him up above his head, jostling him playfully from side to side.

Reece handed him over to Megan and went to look at Mary Katherine, who was asleep in her cot. The others followed him into the little box room, crowding the doorway. Calum scrambled down from his mother's arms and pushed his way through to peer through the bars of the cot at his little sister.

"How have they been?" asked Megan anxiously. "Reece wouldn't let me phone home."

"Quite right too," said Aidan, nodding his head approvingly.

"Did Mary keep you awake at night?"

"The poor little mite had a bit of colic, but nothing too dreadful," said Aubrey. He smiled proudly. "Aidan's a natural with babies, you know."

Reece caught Megan's eye and they exchanged an amused smile.

"You've done a great job, lads," said Reece. "Thank you so much."

"Our pleasure," replied Aidan, adding with a wicked giggle. "So how did the honeymoon go?"

Megan blushed, but Reece's reaction took the others by surprise. "It's none of your business," he said curtly, pushing past to leave the room.

Aidan, always ready to take offence, called out sarcastically, "Pardon me for asking."

"Leave it out, Aid," said Aubrey.

April, May and June were the busiest months at the garden centre and consequently Reece had little time to dwell on his new status of family man. Five days a week, he went out early and came home late. At first, Megan made a big effort to please her new husband, having his dinner ready for him the minute he walked through the door, making sure his shirts were washed and ironed.

During this period, the Double A's made themselves scarce. As Aubrey put it, 'you lovebirds need time to get used to married life'. Megan welcomed their discretion; Reece would have preferred their company. In the months since the wedding he had tried to resign himself to married life, although sometimes the enormity of the step he had taken made him tremble with fear. Once or twice, he came close to leaving. It would be easy to cut loose and take off. After all, he told himself, if he flew back to Canada and rejoined the travellers, nobody would be able to trace him.

But when he came home each evening and saw Calum running towards him calling, "Daddy, Daddy," and Mary reaching out her chubby little arms, he knew there was no way he could abandon the children.

Gradually, things began to change. It was Aidan who drew his attention to Megan's increasingly depressed state of mind. "Are you keeping something from us, Reece?" he asked one evening.

Reece looked up sharply from his Motoring Magazine. "Keeping what from you?"

"We're not expecting another pair of tiny feet, are we?"

"Good God, I hope not," retorted Reece in panic. "What makes you think that?"

Taken aback by Reece's strong reaction, Aidan tried to wave off his tactlessness, but Reece wouldn't let it go. "What the devil d'you mean? Come on, out with it!"

Knowing he'd allowed himself to be pushed into a corner, Aidan replied defensively, "It's just that Megan seems a bit under the weather lately. She barely talks, she can hardly bring herself to bother with the children."

"Are you saying she's a bad mother?" snapped Reece.

"Of course not, dearie, but she does seem preoccupied. Come to that ..." Having been coerced into giving a direct answer, Aidan now felt obliged to speak his mind. " ... you're not looking too happy these days. What's up with you?"

Aubrey walked into the room and, sensing tension, asked, "What's going on?"

"That's what I'm asking Reece," replied Aidan. "But he doesn't seem to think there's anything wrong with Megan."

Aubrey clicked his tongue. "Why don't you keep your prying nose out of their business, Aid?"

Aidan looked hurt. "I wasn't prying," he protested. "How dare you accuse me of prying! I thought Megan might be pregnant again."

Hoping to assuage Reece's anger, Aubrey said, "Sorry about that, he gets carried away sometimes."

Aidan's jaw dropped. "What are you on about? I never get carried away. I was trying to help, that's all." Spinning on his heel, he minced across the room, still declaring his good intentions.

Aubrey started to follow him, but the altercation between the flatmates had given Reece time to think. "Wait a minute," he said. "Tell me exactly what you mean about Megan."

The Double A's came back into the room and stood side by side in the doorway. Aubrey looked serious, Aidan triumphant.

"She's thoroughly miserable, can't cope, doesn't want to chat like she used to, haven't you noticed?" said Aidan.

He cast a glance at his partner, who took the cue. "We could be wrong." He hesitated. "We think she might be on something."

"You mean drugs?"

In two seconds, dismay and shame transformed Reece's features. Swathed in self-pity, he had failed to notice the tell-tale signs: his dinner dished up sloppily, the soiled laundry left on the bathroom floor, the dirty dishes piled on the draining board, Megan's mood swings. As far as he knew, the Double A's had no knowledge of her chequered history. This observation from a third party could mean only one thing: she had slipped back into her old ways.

Instinctively, he jumped to her defence, saying hotly, "It can't be anything like that. I expect she's just over-tired." Forcing himself to remain calm, he went on, "Thanks for drawing my attention to it. I'm grateful to you."

He went back to his magazine, needing to left alone. He wanted time to fathom out where and how Megan was getting the stuff. There was one person who would know: Ben Jenson.

Ben was outraged when Reece challenged him about Megan. "What the fuck do you think I am? I'd never do a thing like that."

"Well, you did before," butted in Reece.

"That was different. I knew what I was doing. She was living under my roof and I was able to keep an eye on her. Besides ..." He gave Reece a withering look. " ... she was the one that spilt the beans, the little idiot!"

"What are you talking about?"

"I got raided by the fuzz. It was Megan's fault; she must have blabbed in the pub."

"You can't blame Megan," protested Reece. "It must have been a mistake, she wouldn't deliberately grass on you."

"Maybe not," conceded Ben with a scowl. "But she yaps a bit too loudly sometimes."

"Did they find anything?"

"The fuzz? No, Jojo gave me the tip-off.

Reece refrained from asking how Jojo had come to be in the know about a police raid.

"No harm done then," he said. "Are you still growing the stuff? Could Megan have got it from you?"

Uneasy at being pressurized, the black man gave a reluctant nod. "Yeah, but I swear on my grandmother's grave I'd never ..." He slapped Reece on the shoulder and gave a wide grin. "Listen up, you moron, you're my mate. I'd never let Megan near the stuff now, out of respect for you. No way! I admit I've done some shit awful things in the past, but I'm not that much of a slime-ball." Laughing heartily, he gave Reece another slap on the back.

"If not from you, where did she get it from?" persisted Reece.

Ben gave a shrug. "It's easy. Just hang around outside the college for a day or two. You can always get hold of it if you want it badly enough."

Reece mumbled under his breath, "Where would she find the cash?" Ben lifted a knowing eyebrow, but kept his counsel. The Canadian gave a gulp. "Not shoplifting, Megan's far too naive for that!"

"Naive! I'd call her devious," muttered Ben.

Reece opened his mouth to speak. Before the words of protest were formed, he realised that Ben was probably right. Nonetheless, Ben's gloating expression irritated him, fanning his rejection of such an explanation

He shook his head and said, "She must be squeezing it out of the housekeeping."

But the seed of doubt had been sewn. Only last week, Megan had declared she was on an economy drive, and certainly the meals she served up were far from wholesome: beans on toast, spaghetti hoops, tinned stewing beef. Reece's doubts redoubled. These were items that could easily be slipped into a shopping bag hanging on the back of a pushchair.

"You'd better find out what she's up to before it's too late," said Ben with a snort. "If she gets hooked, she won't be any fucking use to anybody."

With this unsolicited advice ringing in his ears, Reece hurried home, determined to have it out with Megan.

Ben dropped his couldn't-care-less attitude the minute Reece left the flat. He was angry at the world, angry at himself. After two years of constant pain in his arm, he was being forced to accept that being disabled was a fact of life. In the early days, he'd tried working out -- even risked a sparring session in the gym -- only to be in agony the following day. He knew his days in the boxing ring and on the karate mat were at an end. He was pushing thirty-one and he felt like a has-been. He reminded himself how far he'd come: from the poverty of an obscure village on a Caribbean island, through the State-Assisted hand-outs of a Birmingham Council Estate, to the affluence of owning his own flat and running his own business.

Yet in the area of personal relationships, he had failed dismally. At a time when two of his sisters were settled, when most of his friends had paired up, even got into the parenting game, he was still on his own. He had dozens of acquaintances, an endless list of casual girlfriends, but few real friends and no soul mate.

With a rush of self-pity, he realised that he envied Reece and Thea. Despite the obstacles put in their way, despite his own devious interference, despite enforced separation, they still loved one another. He heaved a troubled sigh. If only he could turn back the clock!

Megan tried to concentrate on what she had to do. Putting the children to bed used to be routine: tea, a little time for play, bath, a bed time story, then lights out. Somehow, these days, this seemed more difficult to achieve. She forgot things: to warm the milk, to clean the children's teeth, even to change nappies. Once, she struggled to force ten-month-old Mary's Babygro onto her screaming three-year-old brother until Aidan, alerted by the furore, came to her rescue.

"Silly me!" she giggled, not noticing Aidan's frown of concern.

He lost his temper and, not one to pull his punches when roused, said acidly, "For God's sake, Megan, pull yourself together. If you and Reece have lost the spark of love, at least have the grace to think of the children."

"Funny boy," squealed Megan, flapping a hand at him. "I adore Reece, you know that." She widened her eyes. "And he worships the ground I walk on."

"You could have fooled me."

At that moment, Reece walked in. "What's going on?" he asked, taking in the general disarray and his wife's uncoordinated behaviour.

"I'm helping Megan put the kiddies to bed," explained Aidan with a quick glance back over his shoulder. "Do you want to say goodnight to them?"

Reece gave both children a cuddle, then pulled Megan into the living room and pushed her down into the armchair.

"What the hell's going on, Megan? Why was Aidan putting the children to bed?"

She pulled a face and, adopting a little-girl voice, replied, "I got in a bit of a muddle that's all."

With his discussion with Ben still fresh in his mind, Reece knew he had to find out what Megan was up to. She looked pathetic, slumped in the chair, her blond hair uncombed, her T-shirt stained with baby food. She noticed his gaze focused on her grubby jeans and said, "I've been so busy, haven't even had time to shower today."

"Where are you getting it from, Megan?"

She feigned incomprehension. "Where am I getting what from?"

"The puff, the marijuana."

She burst out laughing. "Don't be silly, darling. I'm not on that stuff any more. You weaned me off it, remember!"

Reece got angry. Grasping her by the wrists, he yanked her to her feet. "This is no joking matter. Answer me, where does it come from?"

Still, she refused to take him seriously. "Now let me see, I think I read somewhere ..." She jerked away from him, squinting, and held up a knowledgeable forefinger. "I know, it comes from Indian hemp."

Before he could stop himself, Reece gave Megan's face a resounding slap. In her state of blissful euphoria, the force of the blow sent her off balance. She let out a yell.

Aidan and Aubrey rushed into the room. "What's happening?" demanded Aubrey.

"He hit me," shrieked Megan pointing an accusing finger at her husband.

Reece was in shock. He could scarcely believe what had happened. His volatile nature had landed him in many a fist-fight, but he had never struck a woman. He was mortified.

"Megan, I'm so sorry," he gasped, stepping towards her, his arms outstretched.

She drew back, a hand clasped to her burning cheek, while the Double A's stared at him with a look of disgust.

He tried again. "I didn't mean it, Megan, please believe me, I've never struck a woman before."

Spinning on her heel, she fled from the room. The Double A's continued to stare at him. For the first time, he noticed how piercing Aubrey's eyes were.

Aidan gave a shudder and said in a high-pitched voice, "I can't stand violence in any shape or form."

Reece was overwhelmed with shame. "I don't know what came over me," he said.

"The girl needs help," said Aubrey. "What are you going to do about it?"

"Don't worry, I'll look after her. I'll make it up to her." Their continued silence pressed him into further resolutions. "I'll put a stop to her habit, right now, before she's really hooked." Still they said nothing. "I must, for the children's sake."

Persuaded by his sincerity, Aidan's glacial attitude thawed. He clasped the Canadian's arm. "We'll help you, we'll stand by you, won't we, Aub?"

Aubrey didn't seem so keen. "It's not up to us," he stated. "Reece is her husband, let him sort it out. It's his fault she's in this mess."

Aidan drew himself up to his full five foot five and puffed out his cheeks. "Huh, aren't you the righteous one. I suppose you've never done anything to be ashamed of."

Swinging from one side of the fence to the other was characteristic of Aidan. Reece had seen it before. Aubrey's influence on his impressionable partner was powerful. Aidan was full of hot air, incapable of making a decision for himself, yet his kind heartedness and friendly disposition helped to camouflage the lack of social graces which would, otherwise, have stamped the more forceful partner as one of life's loners. Relationships depended on Aidan, commonsense on Aubrey.

"I must go to her," said Reece.

Brushing them aside, he left the room and went to tap on the bedroom door. He expected her to tell him to go away. Instead, he heard her whisper, "Come in, Reece." She was lying on the bed, her eyes puffed from weeping. "I'm so sorry, darling, I've let you down, haven't I?" He went to sit on the edge of the bed and took her hand. She dropped the sodden tissue she was clutching and squeezed his fingers. "I'll never touch the stuff again, darling, I promise."

"How did you get hold of it?"

She looked shamefaced. "I promised not to tell anybody."

Reece's anger flared. "For God's sake, you can tell me."

She drew away nervously. After a moment's thought, she apparently decided it would be more sensible to come clean. "There's this guy who waits outside the college; I don't know his name."

"Yes you do. Tell me!"

"I don't, honestly I don't," protested Megan hotly.

Reece didn't pursue his questioning, knowing that if she did give him the name, he wouldn't shop the guy for fear of involving Megan herself. "How did you pay for it?" he asked.

"I told you, I'm on an economy drive."

"Don't give me that. You've been shoplifting, haven't you?"

Her attempt to look indignant failed. Pulling at her bottom lip with her finger and thumb, she admitted, "It wasn't much, wouldn't amount to more than fifty pounds. I'll never do it again, I promise."

"You were lucky not to get caught."

"I know," she gulped.

Overwhelmed by a surge of compassion, he reached out to touch her flushed face, and said, "I'm so sorry I hit you. Does it still hurt?"

To his relief, she didn't cringe away. Instead, she lifted her head and smiled wanly at him. "It was the shock more than anything, but it made me realise what a fool I've been. I will never, never steal anything or take pot again."

"What made you do it?"

All at once, she sprang forward and flung her arms around his neck. "Oh Reece, I've been so lonely. You've been ignoring me lately."

With a shudder of shame, Reece raked his mind for excuses. "I've been terribly busy at work. You know, late spring, early summer, the busiest months of the year. I realise that's no excuse of course, and I'll spend more time with you from now on."

She unwound herself from around his neck and knelt back on the bed, her hands resting on his shoulders. "And I promise faithfully to be a better wife. Things will be fine from now on, you'll see."

As if needing to lend weight to her pledge, Megan leapt off the bed and starting picking up the discarded clothes covering the floor. Reece started to help her, but she pushed him away. "Go and watch TV. I'll fix us something to eat in a minute."

"No," said Reece decisively. "I'm taking you out for a meal. I'm sure the Double A's won't mind baby-sitting."

Throughout July and August things looked up, with both Reece and Megan making a determined effort to keep their promises. However, as the nights began to close in, gloom descended on Reece. The long summer evenings had been easier to cope with: a glass of wine on the patio after their meal or a stroll by the river -- the Double A's were always willing to baby-sit -- had helped to lift his spirits.

One day, he bumped into Ben in York Street and the two friends went to the pub for a drink.

"How's your ma and the girls?" asked Reece.

"Fine."

"No trouble from your pa?"

"No, he's still up in Glasgow. They're safe now I've got them to move house. By the way, Clelia's getting married."

"To Nathan?"

"Yeah. It's been a bit of an on-off affair. Now the idiots have at last decided to tie the knot. Ma keeps nagging me to get spliced." He mimicked Imelda. "What's a pretty boy like you doing all on yer ownsome? Dem girls down south must be short-sighted. Move back up here, son, and you'm find yerself a nice West Indian girl to marry. Look at your sisters, sweetness, they got no darn trouble finding husbands."

Reece burst out laughing. "What did you say to that?"

"I told her: next year, I'll think about it next year. She don't know half the truth."

Reece looked startled. "What d'you mean?"

"Thea and Troy: it's not working out."

"Have they split up?"

"Not yet, but it looks as if it's going that way."

After leaving Ben, Reece went home with the knot of resentment grinding in his gullet. Thea was unhappy, he was unhappy. What were they doing living apart in misery when they could be so happy living together?

He snapped at Megan when she asked him to help her put the children to bed. The next day, the weather took a turn for the worse and the atmosphere in the flat deteriorated even further. In the evenings, the Double A's kept out of the way and Reece often went out. He became crafty at making up excuses: he needed to discuss projects with colleagues from work; Ben wanted advice about the nightclub; he was out of shape and needed an hour or two down at the gym. Megan didn't believe him, but he didn't care.

Calum was growing up quickly. Now that he was three and a half, he went to Nursery School each morning, with either Megan or Aidan collecting him at mid-day. It was a unusual arrangement and raised a few eyebrows amongst the teachers at the school.

Megan relied heavily on Aidan, both for practical help and emotional stability. Treating him as a confidante, she opened her heart about how much she loved Reece and about how mistaken she had been in believing that Christopher would be her only love. "Chris was just a passing fancy," she said airily. "Puppy love. I admit I was devastated when he died, but our relationship would never have lasted."

Aidan, although nearly twice her age, was just as emotionally immature and perfectly able to relate to her way of thinking. He enjoyed sharing her secrets, although unable to keep anything to himself, he relayed most of what she told him to his partner who, being both older and wiser advised him not to become too involved in the affairs of their ill-matched landlords.

Having gained confidence in herself and her marriage throughout the summer, it came as shock to Megan when Reece again became distant. She wanted to question him, but lacked the courage, the memory of his slap across her face still fresh in her mind. He had mentioned that he'd bumped into Ben and she wondered whether his change was down to something the black man had told him.

In November, the Double A's announced that they were taking a holiday.

"Oh," said Megan. "Where are you going?"

"India," replied Aidan. "We've always wanted to go there and Aub's just made a tidy little sum on a series of articles so we've decided to push the boat out."

"Brilliant!" cried Megan. "I've always wanted to travel. Do you know, the nearest I've ever got to going abroad is Barry Island!"

The Double A's chuckled and Aubrey said, "Never mind, dear, your chance will come. Who knows, Reece might take you to Canada one day."

But within a couple of days of their departure, Megan was at her wit's end. Without Aidan to cheer her up, the gloom of the approaching winter closed in on her. Reece was so wrapped up in his own unhappiness that he failed to notice her despair. She rang Connie in Manchester, only to find that she had moved on. Quickly jotting down the new location, she resolved to telephone the theatre that evening to find out where her friend was staying.

When Reece arrived home late she was sitting on the sofa sipping coffee. "How was your day?" she asked.

"So, so."

"I tried phoning Connie this evening, but she's changed her mobile number and I ended up phoning her digs."

"Did you manage to speak to her?"

"No, the show's moved on to Blackpool, but Connie's left."

"What do you mean, left?"

"She's left the show, baled out."

"Why would she do that?"

"I'm not sure. I hope she gets in touch soon."

"She's probably found something better," said Reece, picking up his newspaper.

"I think it's because her mother's ill. She's going to look after her."

This sounded so unlike Connie, that Reece put his newspaper down and looked directly at Megan. "Are you sure? I thought her parents were still in Bahrain."

"So did I, but that's what one of the girls in the chorus told me."

"She must have got it wrong." He frowned. "What made you phone her?"

"I was feeling a bit fed-up, cooped up here with only the kids for company. Mary winges most of the time and Calum won't stop asking questions."

"What d'you expect, he's coming up for four; he's bound to ask questions."

"You should be forced to put up with baby talk all day long!"

"Calum's at nursery school every morning so why are you complaining?"

The conversation fizzled out after that. Megan turned her attention to the TV screen and Reece to his newspaper.

Things went downhill. Unable to bear the tension, Reece went out every evening. He felt ashamed of himself, but the more time he spent with Megan, the more terrified he was of losing his temper with her. Everything she did irritated him. If she was feeling bad-tempered, her droning voice drove into his head like drill; if she was in a loving mood, her excessive show of affection would force him back into his shell; if she was quiet and contemplative, he became panic-stricken that she might be smoking marijuana again.

From time to time, he questioned her about it and she vehemently denied using drugs. Sometimes, when she went out shopping, he would search the flat, poking his fingers into all the hiding places he could think of. But he found no sign of cannabis.

When a postcard, picturing the Taj Mahal, arrived from India, Megan brightened up. She stuck it up on the mantle piece and gazed at it longingly. "I wish I could have gone with them," she sighed. "When can we afford to take a holiday abroad, darling?"

"We haven't got two pennies to rub together, we can't afford a holiday in the UK, let alone take a trip abroad?" snarled Reece.

Sometimes, he sought out Ben on the pretext of sharing a jar together. In reality, he was after news of Thea.

"Is she still with Troy?"

"Yeah, they're trying to work things out. By the way, did you know Megan called round here the other day?"

"What did she want?"

"To chat I suppose."

"Did she bring the children?"

"Only Mary, Calum was at nursery school."

"She didn't stay long then?"

"No."

Reece went home feeling more miserable than ever. Thea was trying to patch things up. That was typical of Thea. He admired her so much; she had far more grit than he had.

It was early evening. He opened the door to find Calum and Mary Katherine still up and dressed. Calum ran up to him. "I want some juice, Daddy."

"Dada." Mary toddled up behind her brother. She looked a mess, with food stains down her dress and her nappy, clearly soaked, hanging down between her legs.

"Calum, where's Mummy?" asked Reece, picking up his daughter and carrying her at arms-length to the bathroom. Calum followed him.

Laying the baby on the changing mat, he started to strip off her soiled nappy. "Where's Mummy?" he said again.

"Mummy's got tummy ache."

"Tummy ache?" This didn't sound like Megan. "Are you sure?" asked Reece, still busy cleaning up his daughter.

"She's got a nasty pain here." Calum pointed to his head.

"You mean she's got a headache? Has she gone to bed?"

"Yes, bed."

Having sorted out Mary, Reece turned his attention to the little boy and when both children were changed and ready for bed, he took them along to the master bedroom.

"Mummy would never forgive me if I put you to bed without your giving her a goodnight kiss."

He opened the door quietly and walked in. Megan was slumped across the bedspread, her hair lank, her cheeks blanched. On the bedside table was a collection of empty glass jars and torn open packets. A collection of pills was scattered around her. Pushing the children away, Reece rushed to her side and felt for her pulse. As he lifted her more securely onto the bed, something fluttered to the floor. Calum ran across the room to pick it up, whereupon his little sister toddled over and snatched it from him. They began to fight for right of possession, shrieking at one another.

"Shut up you two!" he shouted.

Both children froze. Scooping up one child under each arm, he dashed down the hall and practically threw them into their bedroom, slamming the door on them. Then, he rang for an ambulance.

CHAPTER TWENTY-FIVE

Reece managed to get in touch with Connie through her former landlady at the Manchester B&B.

Shocked by the news, Connie gasped, "I always knew Megan was a walking disaster, but this …!"

"I'm so glad I've been able to contact you," said Reece. "I was afraid you'd disappeared forever. I thought you'd want to come to the funeral."

"Of course, I do. When is it?"

"Next Friday in Swansea."

"Swansea?"

"Yes, her father insisted that we took her home, and under the circumstances, I couldn't refuse. Oh Connie, it's been terrible."

"I'll have to arrange for someone to look after my mother."

"Your mother? Why, what's happened?"

Briefly, Connie explained about Della's illness and the revelation that she was, in fact, her mother, not her aunt. The conversation left Reece baffled. Why on earth hadn't Connie confided in her friends earlier?

Ben drove Connie, Reece and the two children down to Swansea. It was, of course, the first time that the Reverend and Mrs Hughes had met their son-in-law and their grand-daughter.

Reece hoped that seeing her grandchildren would help Brenda Hughes cope with her grief. He had inferred from Megan that her mother was a frustrated, inhibited woman, completely dominated by her over-bearing husband and, in some ways, he had been more in dread of meeting her than the Reverend Hughes himself. However, he found her sympathetic although one look at her haggard features and ill-fitting clothes told him that she was a very unhappy woman who, over the years, had let herself go. The children brought a smile to her face. She fussed over them, exclaiming on how tall Calum had grown, and delighted in Mary Katherine, whose bright auburn hair and amber eyes were accentuated by her translucent complexion.

A few hours in the company of Megan's father was enough to give Reece an insight as why his young wife had run away from home. Cold and judgemental, the loss of his only daughter had done nothing to soften Charles Hughes' sanctimonious manner.

For the funeral, Brenda Hughes wore deepest black, sporting an out-of-date felt hat which, throughout the service, she kept adjusting. Back at the rectory afterwards, she darted from one group of mourners to another, barely stopping to exchange more than two words with anybody. She frequently went into the kitchen to check on the hired help; two young girls in black dresses with white aprons. They ran back and forth with trays of salmon and cucumber sandwiches and cups of tea.

Connie and Ben helpfully took charge of the children while Reece mingled dutifully, shaking hands with the mourners -- distant relatives and neighbours of the Hughes -- whom he had, of course, never met before and was never likely to meet again.

After the visitors had departed, Connie and Ben went off to spent the night in a B&B, but Brenda insisted that Reece and the children should stay with them in the parsonage. He spent a restless night, sleeping in Megan's bed with Mary in Calum's old cot and Calum on a mattress on the floor. The light of dawn showed it to be a bright, sunny room, fresh and sweet-smelling due to the bowl of pot-pourri Brenda had placed on the chest of drawers.

After their eventful day, the children slept late, giving Reece time to survey the room. It was a teenage room, straight out of a fifties movie: pink bedcover, kidney-shaped dressing table with a flower-etched mirror, a corner wash-hand basin. Soft toys crowded the top of the wardrobe and a cabbage patch doll straddled a rocking horse in the alcove. Megan's personality beckoned to him from every corner.

He was plagued by unanswerable questions. What had induced the simple young Welsh girl to take her own life? The Coroner had called it an accidental overdose, but he hadn't known about the ripped-up postcard. Closing his eyes, Reece could recall Megan's message quite distinctly. The seven telling words: 'Sorry darling, I can't take any more' were written in red biro on the back of the picture of the Taj Mahal, which the Double A's had sent from India a few weeks earlier. Her large childish scrawl almost obliterated Aidan's careful handwriting.

While tidying up a few days after the terrible event, Reece had come across the postcard under the bed. The squabbling children had ripped it up on the afternoon of his gruesome discovery. He had tossed it into the waste paper bin, until the red writing caught his eye. Retrieving it from the bin, he had put the pieces together, sitting alone for an hour afterwards staring at Megan's last words and deliberating on what to do about it. Finally, he'd opted to get rid of the postcard. In future years, the children might ask about their mother. It would be far kinder to let them believe she had died by accident.

And the pills! The Coroner had wanted to know how she'd got hold of such strong painkillers. Reece had pleaded ignorance. But he knew. He knew she'd stolen them from Ben's flat because the lazy slob had been careless enough to leave them lying around.

Until now he hadn't allowed himself to grieve for Megan. Now he did. Lying on the bed she had slept in for seventeen years, he felt overwhelmed by her presence. During the three years of their relationship, she had wrenched pity, affection, duty and loathing out of him. He had seen her as an irritating kid sister, a hanger-on. He pictured her as she had been when he first knew her: her joyful relief at being offered a bed for the night; the love shining in her eyes when she gazed at her sleeping baby son. She had been too fragile for the environment into which fate had thrust her. Letting out a tortured howl he gave in to wretchedness and remorse, sobbing into the pillow in order not to disturb the children.

Calum poking him in the ribs brought him to his senses. "Why are you crying, Daddy?"

Lifting the child up onto the bed, he ruffled his blond hair and hugged him. "I was feeling a little bit sad," he said.

"Don't feel sad, Daddy, Nana's taking us to the sea-side today.

"That's right, I almost forgot. You do know that it will be too cold to go in the water?"

The little boy nodded. "But we can build a sandcastle, can't we?"

"Please can we stay with Nana, Daddy, please, please?" begged Calum.

Reece looked at Brenda. "Are you sure you can manage?" he said. "They're quite a handful. I'd stay on, but I have to get back to work."

"They'll be fine," Brenda assured him.

"I'll be back to collect them next weekend." He rubbed his hands together, looking concerned. "What about your husband, are you sure he doesn't mind?"

Brenda stiffened. "They're his grandchildren too."

On the way home, Reece travelled in the back seat. Connie soon dropped off to sleep so he killed time studying the back of Ben's thick neck as the black man raced the Golf, dodging from lane to lane, cutting up other drivers.

Glancing back over his shoulder, Ben signalled towards the girl and grunted, "I'm not surprised she's tired, you should have seen her last night, the randy little scrubber."

A surge of fury coursed through Reece. The arrogant son-of-a-bitch showed no respect. Here he was, slagging off Connie the day after Megan's funeral just as if the three of them had come down to Swansea on a joy ride. Anger re-surfaced. Ben was directly responsible for the girl's death. If he hadn't left his bloody painkillers in the kitchen when Megan went to visit him, she would never have died. Why hadn't he kept them somewhere safe? He knew how strong they were, and he knew Megan's record.

Connie woke up, yawned, stretched and started talking to Ben. Reece half listened, not joining in. All at once, he heard her mention her mother.

"We can't stay in that B&B up in Manchester much longer. Della mustn't spend her last few months in a dump like that. I don't know what to do."

"Put her in an old people's home," suggested Ben.

"An old people's home! Why, she's not even turned fifty!" Connie sounded outraged.

"Can't you find one of those hospices where they take terminally ill people?"

An intake of breath. "I couldn't do that."

"She can't live with you, she'd be a millstone round your neck."

Reece gave a start as Connie shrieked back, "She's my mother. What d'you want me to do, leave her to die all alone?"

"She wasn't there for you when you were young and what about your career? Surely you're not going to sling in the towel just as you're getting started?" argued Ben.

"I can put it on hold for a while."

"You can't do that. You've barely had time to show what you can do. It would mean starting again from scratch."

"No it wouldn't, I've got my Equity Card," protested Connie.

For a couple of minutes, they were silent, then Ben said, "Why don't you and your ma move in with me?"

"What?" gasped Connie.

"I've got room, Emil's moved out. Your ma could have his room and you could take the attic."

"I couldn't afford it -- two rooms! Oh no, that would cost too much. My savings won't last forever."

Ben took his hand off the steering wheel and patted her knee. "You can stay for nothing."

Connie cast him a suspicious glance. "What d'you mean?"

"Like I said: move in whenever you like. It won't cost you a penny."

Reece was astounded. What's he up to? he thought, willing himself not to intervene.

Connie turned her head to stare at Ben. "D'you really mean that?"

My God, she's going to fall for it! thought Reece.

She spoke again. "No strings?"

"No strings," Ben assured her with a wide grin.

"I won't be an unpaid housekeeper, I won't sleep with you just when you feel like it. Last night was a one-off, we're not going to drift into anything more permanent."

"What d'you think I am?" retorted Ben indignantly.

"It's just until ... Della may not have long," stammered Connie. "Three months at most."

"Stay for as long as you like."

"Thank you so much, Ben," whispered Connie, leaning over and planting a kiss on the black man's cheek.

Reece sank back in his seat. He could hardly believe what he'd just heard. Connie was prepared to risk her career for the sake of her maverick mother and Ben was prepared to help her out. The animosity he had harboured against Ben during the journey slipped away. There were always two sides to people, even Ben.

Connie went straight to the station when she got back to Twickenham and caught the first train back to Manchester, arriving at the B&B mid-evening. Della was already in bed.

"How was it, darling?" she asked.

"Oh you know, terribly sad. Megan's mother was in an awful state when we got there. Seeing her grandchildren cheered her up."

"Ah, grandchildren!" sighed Della. "I'm afraid that's something I shall not live to see."

"Cut it out!" retorted Connie, her hackles rising. "You wouldn't see any even if you live until you're ninety. I have no intention of tying myself down to a brood of screaming kids."

Della fell back on the bed, deflated. "You know, Connie," she whispered. "I was half expecting you not to come back."

"What on earth made you think that?"

"I watched a programme on TV; you know, one of those documentaries about young hopefuls at stage school. I can't believe you'd give up so much for me. How will you get back into the circuit?"

"Don't worry about me," replied her daughter airily. "I'll make it one day, just you see."

"That's the trouble," said Della sadly. "I won't."

"Oh, Mother, if only you'd let the medics treat you!" She brightened up. "I've got some good news; we're moving down to London."

"Are we? How come?"

"Ben's invited us to move in with him, rent free."

"That's very generous of him. Does that mean I shall see something of Megan's poor dear husband?" mewed Della.

Connie pulled a face and said in exasperation, "You never give up, do you?"

"I fancied him the first time I set eyes on him," sighed Della.

Connie studied her, a line from 'Anthony and Cleopatra' flashing across her mind: *'Age cannot wither her, nor custom stale, her infinite variety;'*

The once pretty features were pale and drawn, the bleached hair in need of a touch-up, yet Della had managed to retain her flirtatious sparkle. Connie took her mother's hand and squeezed it. "You'll like it down in Twickenham. We'll be able to window-shop in Richmond and visit the Theatre."

"That'll be lovely, dear."

"We'll leave tomorrow first thing, if you're up to it," continued Connie.

The older woman nodded, closed her eyes and drifted off to sleep, her lips half-parted in a smile. Connie found it impossible to look away from her. How frail and vulnerable she looked, this feisty lady who, until recently, had never been short of men friends, had taken it as her right to be pampered and indulged! Where are these suitors now? she wondered. Even the celebrated Javier de Oliveira Figueres had turned his back on the naive woman-child who had borne him a daughter.

With a flash of insight, she saw her own future: a West End star, Paris, Broadway! But what was the price of success: a following of fans, a horde of hangers-on? How could you distinguish the loyal from the disloyal? How could you find true love with suspicion in your eyes?

For an instant, she felt a pang of yearning for Will. She'd been in love with him, but their combined career expectations had got in the way. They were too alike; too opinionated, too ambitious to allow the other to take the lead. Will would have tried to upstage her and she would have retaliated in like manner. It would have been a hapless partnership. Nonetheless, the memory of it brought tears to her eyes. Angry at herself, she forced her thoughts away from Will and made a resolution: whatever it took, one day, she would be famous and then, and only then, she would go to Brazil to seek out her father.

The Double A's looked shocked when Reece arrived home without the children.
"Do you think it's wise to leave them with their grandparents? asked Aubrey.
"Why ever not?"
"The Hughes might try to get custody."
"Don't be ridiculous," retorted Reece. "I'm their legal guardian, they can't take them away from me. Besides, having a couple of lively youngsters around is the last thing the Reverend Hughes wants."
"What about Megan's mother?"
"Brenda? She doesn't have much say in anything."
Despite this initial irritation, Reece was relieved to have Aidan and Aubrey around. He missed the children more than he would have imagined. His thoughts kept straying to Thea. During the trip to Wales, he hadn't liked to question Ben. To touch on the subject at such a sad time would have been insensitive, but he intended to find out whether Thea was still with Troy at the first opportunity.

The following weekend, he took the train to Swansea to pick up Calum and Mary. They were happy to see him, but the parting from Brenda was distressing. Charles Hughes was as cool and unapproachable as ever, although his wife was in tears as they got into the taxi to go to the station. He promised to bring them back to see her again.

Life settled into a routine with Calum at play school and Mary Katherine in nursery. Calum, in particular, fretted for his mother and although he accepted that she had gone to heaven, he couldn't understand that he would never see her again. The Double A's were helpful, especially Aidan, who took great pride in settling the children in bed at night by telling them bed-time stories.

Reece called at Ben's flat more frequently now. This was partly to lend Connie support as her mother's health deteriorated and partly to talk about his own problems. However, mainly, it was in the hope of gleaning information about Thea.

"Have you heard from your sister lately?" he asked Ben one day.

"Yeah, she keeps in touch," came the reply.

"How is she?"

"Fine."

In his inimitable way, Ben held back the all-important information, forcing Reece to ask a direct question "Is she still with Troy?"

The black man pretended to be engrossed in the snooker on TV. "Eh, what did yer say?"

"Is she still with Troy?"

"Yeah, they seem to be making a go of it."

This was not what Reece had wanted to hear, but he told himself it was better to know than not to know. With summer coming, his despondency grew. He was still busy at work, yet his enthusiasm for the job had waned. Sometimes, he talked to the Double A's about his fears for the future, using them as a sounding board.

"Why don't you pack up and go back to Canada?" said Aidan one evening.

This suggestion surprised him because it coincided with his own thoughts. He could just about afford the fare for himself and Calum -- Mary Katherine could still travel free of charge -- but what would he do once he got there? To find accommodation and a job with two young children in tow would be well nigh impossible.

Aubrey made a suggestion. "Why don't you contact your brother-in-law? He might be able to help you find work."

"Howard? I've no idea where he is."

"You could try tracing him.

"How?"

All at once, the Double A's became animated. "Through the Internet of course."

"I wouldn't know where to start."

"Aubrey would," exclaimed Aidan, clasping his hands together in a frisson of excitement. "You can find out anything on the web, can't you, Aub?"

Aubrey nodded, his broad face lighting up with enthusiasm.

"You might waste hours trying and then come up with nothing," protested Reece, although he knew this wouldn't bother Aubrey, who prided himself on being a surfing whiz kid.

"Don't be negative."

Still Reece was resistant. "I don't think it would work."

His thoughts scanned the miles to his homeland. He loved Canada: the vast expanse of unspoilt countryside, the bear-hunting, the canoeing, the fishing -- Calum would love it - the small towns with their pioneering history, the lack of pollution -- Mary Katherine's asthma would almost certainly disappear. It was a far healthier place in which to bring up his children. Then his thoughts flew back. To leave the UK would bring down the final curtain on his hopes for a reunion with Thea. Maybe Ben was right; maybe different races and cultures didn't mix.

He realised the Double A's were staring at him. "Do you really think surfing the net would work?" he asked hesitantly.

"It might," argued Aubrey. "I'll start tonight. What Howard's full name and last-known address?"

Connie's devotion to her mother astounded Ben and Reece. The Canadian couldn't help commenting on it.

"I would never have put you down as a carer, Connie," he remarked one Saturday evening when he called round to keep her company.

She gave a sheepish grin. "To be honest, it wasn't in the blueprint."

"You're doing a wonderful job. Are you sure you can cope? I mean, you could move Della into a hospice if things get too bad."

"No, I can't bear the thought of her passing her remaining days surrounded by strangers. God knows, she's had her share of ups and downs, never really had a stable relationship or a permanent home. This way, she will at least know that I'm on hand for her."

"How bad is she?"

"It varies; some days she gets up and comes in here to watch TV for a couple of hours; sometimes, she stays in bed all day, sleeping." Anguish spread across Connie's face. "It's terrible, she's drugged up to the eyeballs with all the medication they've given her." Reece leant over and patted her hand, a gesture that brought her close to tears. "I feel so awful about not telling Linda and Steve," she said.

"What d'you mean?"

"Della doesn't want me to tell them. She says she's caused them enough trouble over the years."

"Bollocks!" exploded Reece. "Linda and Della are sisters, you must tell Linda."

"And go against Della's wishes? Linda doesn't know Della has spilt the beans on our true relationship."

"I'm sure she'll understand. Talk to Della."

"I've tried, believe me!"

Looking serious, Reece said quietly. "I think you have to tell Linda; she'll never forgive you if you don't."

Connie bit her lip. "Then it will all come out."

"Does it really matter? Some things are more important than secrets, you know."

"Linda believes I still think of her as my mum." She gave a self-conscious laugh. "And in a way, I do. It's funny, isn't it? I've got two mothers. Most people are content with one."

"You're not making sense, Connie. Didn't you go over to Bahrain to visit your parents soon after Della appeared on the scene? When you came back, I thought you said you'd sorted everything out."

Connie flicked a wrist. "Oh I did sort it out -- in my head, but I didn't tell Linda and Steve what Della had told me. I simply said Della had turned up unexpectedly. You should have seen their faces! I could tell they were worried. I couldn't tell them the truth after that. It would have been too cruel. They've been so wonderful to me. How could I confess that I knew the Adoption Society story had been a sham?"

Reece's serious expression didn't waver. "It doesn't change anything. You've still got to let them know. I'm sure Linda will fly over straightaway."

Connie buried her head in her hands. "I can't," she wept. "Not yet, maybe towards the end. If they come back now, Della will be so angry with me. Later, when..." Her voice trembled. "Later, perhaps, not now."

Reece got up and paced the floor. How could he lay down the law when, only months earlier he had been guilty of destroying the postcard on which Megan had stated she wanted to die! Commonsense came to his rescue: the big difference was that Linda and Steve were adults, not tiny children needing protection.

"You're shelving the issue, Connie," he said. "Linda won't thank you for it. She'll want to see her only sister while she's still able to communicate, not be confronted with a semi-conscious ..." He stopped short, unable to find the words to carry on.

Connie leapt up and launched herself into his arms. "Oh Reece," she cried. "I know what I should do; I haven't the courage."

He hugged her close, stroking her curly hair with his large freckled hand. Her tears dampened his shirt collar. When she began to calm down, he held her gently at arms-length and said, "Ring them up now; I'll stay with you while you do it."

For the umpteenth time, Reece inspected the tickets and the passports. He'd checked-in their luggage and now there was an hour to kill before the Air Canada Flight took off. Four-year-old Calum stood obediently beside Mary Katherine's buggy. The little girl kicked her feet and squealed, trying to gain her father's attention.

The farewells had been heartrending, especially Connie's. He had rarely seen her cry, but on their departure, she had sobbed unashamedly, begging him to keep in touch, to send photos of the children, to call her once they arrived in Vancouver. "I can't bear the thought of never seeing you again," she burst out.

He'd tried to keep his emotions under control, but failed and croaked, "We're only a flight away. You can come and visit us."

Ben had been gruff and non-committal. "Best of luck, mate, you deserve it." Then, as Reece had left the flat, he'd raised his damaged left arm to wave, and winced. "Shit! See yer!"

The Double A's had been sentimental. But they had lent practical help too. Aubrey had spent hours on his computer, surfing the net, finally coming up with the information about Howard Keighley. It seemed Reece's brother-in-law had pulled himself together, put the tragedy of his wife's death behind him and started up a new business on the outskirts of Vancouver. He now ran a successful market garden company with a dozen employees. He'd e-mailed back that he would be pleased to see Reece and his young family. Furthermore, there was a vacancy in the work-force which, given the credentials he had now acquired, Reece would be able to fill.

In view of the success of Aubrey's latest venture, the Double A's decided to take over the lease of the flat when Reece left. On the eve of his departure, they came out with shattering news.

"Guess what?" said Aidan, excitement rendering him almost incoherent. "We're going to adopt."

"Adopt what?" asked Reece, seeing in his mind's eye, a pampered Chihuahua or a Burmese Blue. What the Double A's got up to had, long ago, ceased to surprise him.

"A baby of course!"

This *did* take his breath away. "You can't be serious?" he gasped.

To stop his over-enthusiastic partner from indulging in a long-winded explanation, Aubrey spoke up. "We've started making arrangements. Of course, we'll have to go to the States, they won't let us adopt here, but it's all in hand. The whole process should be complete in three months."

"Ah," sighed Aidan. "It will be lovely to hear the sound of a child's voice in this flat again."

Reece was so shocked by the news that he didn't even try to talk them out of it. All he managed to come out with was a tentative, "I hope you know what you're taking on."

To keep the children amused during the wait at the airport, he bought Calum the latest Power Rangers action figure and Mary Katherine a soft toy from the Disney Shop. Then he walked around and around the Terminal building, his head filled with thoughts of Thea. He could almost hear Connie chastising him: "Reece, it's no good dwelling on 'if only's' and 'what if's'."

At last it was nearly time for their flight. He wheeled the pushchair towards the Departure Gate and was just about to go through when he heard his name being called over the tannoy. He stopped in surprise.

"Are we getting on the plane now?" asked Calum

"Shhh!" cautioned Reece, bending down and pressing a finger to the little boy's lips.

Suddenly, he heard his name called again, this time from close quarters. "Reece, wait!"

He stood up and spun round, recognising the Birmingham accent.

"Thea!"

She was running towards them, her jacket flying open, her bag slipping off her shoulder. He stared at her open-mouthed as she stopped abruptly two feet away from him. He stepped forward and clasped her hands.

"I couldn't let you go without saying goodbye," she gasped. "Oh Reece, will I ever see you again?"

He could hardly believe his eyes. Here she was, the girl of his dreams and he was about to board a plane to the other side of the world.

"There isn't even time for a coffee," he said.

She laughed. "I didn't come here for a coffee."

"How did you know we were flying out today?"

"Ben rang me."

Reece frowned. It was just like Ben to rub salt in the wound.

"It's not what you think, Reece." Thea's next words dispelled his irritation. "He wanted me to get here in time." She smiled and went on huskily, "Yes, believe it or not, Ben's had a change of heart about us. You see, I've left Troy, my marriage is over. I'm filing for divorce."

Another announcement echoed around the Terminal Building, prompting Thea to slip her fingers from Reece's clasp. "That was your last call," she whispered. "Write to me. I'm staying with Ma."

Reece crouched down and took his daughter out of the buggy in readiness to board. He stood up, the baby cuddled in his arms, two bright auburn heads pressed together, two pairs of amber eyes reflected in Thea's sunglasses. He stood the child down beside him, holding onto her reins.

"Thea," he croaked. "Will you fly out once we're settled?"

"Yes." She nodded and removed the glasses to reveal tears streaming down her cheeks. Impulsively, she flung herself into his arms. He hugged her still holding the reins, almost pulling Mary Katherine off her feet. Thea gently withdrew from the embrace and began to back away, her gaze never wavering from his face.

Calum grew impatient. "Come on, Dad!" he shouted.

"I meant it," Thea called out. "As soon as I've got everything sorted: the formal separation, the sale of the house ..." she trailed off.

"I love you, Thea," Reece called back as his son tugged at the hem of his jacket and dragged him through the gate.

Lightning Source UK Ltd.
Milton Keynes UK
UKOW051913181111

182313UK00001B/40/P